HUNTING HOUR

ALSO BY MARGARET MIZUSHIMA:

Stalking Ground

Killing Trail

HUNTING HOUR

A Timber Creek K-9 Mystery

Margaret Mizushima

CROOKED
LANE

NEW YORK

Copyright © 2017 by Margaret Mizushima.

Published in the United States by Crooked Lane Books, an imprint of The Quick Brown Fox & Company LLC.

Crooked Lane Books and its logo are trademarks of The Quick Brown Fox & Company LLC.

Library of Congress Catalog-in-Publication data available upon request.

ISBN (hardcover): 978-1-68331-277-2
ISBN (ePub): 978-1-68331-278-9
ISBN (ePDF): 978-1-68331-280-2

Cover design by Melanie Sun
Book design by Jennifer Canzone

Printed in the United States.

www.crookedlanebooks.com

Crooked Lane Books
34 West 27th St., 10th Floor
New York, NY 10001

First edition: August 2017

10 9 8 7 6 5 4 3 2 1

For my sister and brother-in-law,
Nancy and Greg Coleman,
and their family

Chapter 1

Tuesday, Mid-April

"Whom do you trust, Mattie?"

Mattie drew her knees up, hugging them to her chest. The question her therapist posed made her pause to think. Finally, she answered. "Robo."

From across the living room, where he was lying on his dog bed, her German shepherd cocked his head, ears pricked.

Although the Skype image on Mattie's laptop wavered occasionally, it was still clear enough to see the change in her therapist's expression. The kindness in Dr. Lisa Callahan's smile radiated warmth that could melt even Mattie's reserve.

When her brother, Willie, contacted her last fall after years of silence, he'd opened a Pandora's box of repressed memories centering on her abusive father that had sent her reeling. She'd been unable to process them by herself, so she'd sought counseling with Lisa, a therapist who specialized in trauma and often worked with cops and soldiers.

"Robo has evidently proven himself trustworthy," Lisa said. "What does it feel like inside your body when you think about trusting Robo?"

Every week for the past two months, they'd talked about feelings, and Mattie knew the drill—eyes closed to search inside before opening them to share what she'd found. "It feels safe. With Robo, I can let down my guard. Relax."

Mattie sat on her living room floor, her back to the couch, her laptop on the coffee table in front of her. While Lisa waited for her to expand on her response, she squirmed inside, but she couldn't think of anything else to say.

Lisa let her off the hook. "Safety is a basic human need. I imagine it's a relief to let down your guard."

"Yeah." A spiral notebook that Mattie used for assignments and journaling sat on the table beside her computer, and she flipped open the cover, picked up a pen, and wrote the word "Trust" on a blank page, underlining it twice. "Trust is a hard one for me."

"It's hard for a lot of people. Let's focus on that feeling you get when you're relaxing with Robo. Reestablish that feeling."

Exhausted from months of poor sleep, Mattie tried, but a niggling twinge of anxiety had crept in and tightened her chest.

"Think of one of your friends," Lisa said, "and how you feel about the concept of trust with that person."

Mattie thought of Cole Walker, the local veterinarian, but her feelings for him were so balled up, she didn't want to untangle them in front of her therapist. "I don't have many friends."

"Colleagues, then. You've talked about some of the people at work before."

Mattie shook her head. The first person that came to mind was Chief Deputy Ken Brody.

"What?" Lisa asked, apparently in response to the expression on Mattie's face.

"I was thinking about Brody. I would trust him with my life, but I'd never trust him with my feelings."

"That's a good observation."

"There's no one I'd rather have at my back, but I wouldn't share anything personal with him."

"Pay attention to that part for a moment . . . that feeling of guarding yourself. Then tell me about it."

Mattie needed only a second. She was well aware of this feeling—this wariness of others. It seemed like her approach with the entire world. "There's a sort of tightness in my muscles through my whole body. Like I'm going to need to protect myself."

"Fight or flight."

"Yeah."

"That's good work, Mattie. You're much more aware of your body's reactions to your feelings than you were before. And I especially like how you can isolate how you feel about your colleague Brody. Let's move on to another person you work with."

Instantly, Mattie thought of the departmental dispatcher, with her flowing, hippie-like garments and wide-open approach to life. "Rainbow. I guess I would call her a friend. Yeah, she's a friend even though we don't have much in common."

Lisa nodded. "How about your level of trust with her?"

"She's easy to be around, but I don't share my feelings with her. Not anything important anyway."

Lisa used that look, the expression that meant *I'm listening; keep talking.*

So Mattie did. "Rainbow is a kind person. She wouldn't do anything to hurt me on purpose. I don't think she'd try to hurt anyone. I guess I don't tell her much because she's the one who does the talking when we're together."

"These are probably all reasons why you would call her a friend. Do you think you could share something about yourself with her?"

Mattie rolled her shoulders. "Right now, I'm having trouble staying relaxed, and my muscles are pretty tight. But I think Rainbow is the type of person I could trust."

"There are times when the brain tells you that you're okay even when your body is guarding or holding itself ready to protect you, either emotionally or physically. Pay attention to that. That's part of emotional self-reliance."

Mattie picked up her pen and wrote "Emotional self-reliance" in her notebook.

"Let's do this exercise with one other person . . . the woman who recently moved to Timber Creek, the detective you've mentioned whom you seem to like."

When Mattie closed her eyes, she discovered a feeling of lightness and warmth associated with the brassy detective that surprised her. She grinned. "Stella LoSasso. She's like a cross between a mother hen and Godzilla."

Lisa smiled back. "And trust?"

"I guess I would trust her with almost anything. She'd have my back in a shootout, and she looks out for my best interests. She already knows my deepest secrets, but she doesn't judge me. Well, I guess I could say she judges me all the time, but not in a bad way. More like she wants what's best for me. That's the mother hen part."

"Sounds like qualities you appreciate."

Mattie's phone vibrated against the coffee table. She'd turned off the ringer during her therapy session but left the phone where she could see it. An emergency text told her to call the sheriff's department.

"I'm getting a call from the station, Lisa. I need to check in."

Lisa frowned. "All right, but I hate for you to miss your session. You look like you need it. How are you sleeping, Mattie?"

"Not very well." Flashes of memory had been haunting her for months, and sleepless nights stacked up one after another. Only when total exhaustion took over could she fall asleep.

"It's time to address this issue," Lisa said. "Is there a place in your town where you can get some bodywork, like massage or craniosacral therapy?"

Anya Yamamoto at the Valley Vista hot springs did massage, but . . . no way. "I'm not sure."

"That's your assignment this week. Take a look at what's available in the area. The other thing you might consider is breath training and stretching. A yoga class could combine both."

"I don't think we have yoga classes in Timber Creek."

"While you're looking for a massage therapist, ask around about yoga too. I think the running that you started as a teen has helped you with your emotions all these years. But I think you should add in more stretching, even if you do it on your own."

Urgency built inside her. She needed to call the department and didn't have time for this. "I can do that. But, Lisa, I really need to sign off now."

Lisa gave her a look. "Okay. But think about trust and emotional self-reliance and what they mean to you, and we'll discuss it at your next session."

By the time Lisa confirmed their next appointment and signed off, Mattie's shoulders had tightened into knots. She made eye contact with Robo, and he lifted his head eagerly.

"Come here." After scrambling up from his cushion, he came to her and sat, and she hugged him close while she dialed into the office.

Sam Corns, the night dispatcher, answered. "Mattie, we need you to go to the junior high. We got a girl missing from there. Brody will meet you out front."

Her thoughts leapt to Sophie and Angela Walker, Cole's daughters. She loved those kids as if they were her own, but her feelings for their father had grown complicated. Despite her yearning to be a part of their family, she'd had to take a step back a few months ago.

"Who is the girl?"

"Last name—Banks."

Her relief turned to guilt. *Someone's* daughter was missing. "Tell Brody I'll be right there."

She slipped on a khaki coverall with the Timber Creek County Sheriff's Department emblem on the sleeve and hurried to retrieve her service weapon from the gun safe mounted on the wall inside her bedroom closet. Robo dogged her tracks and then broke out into his happy dance when she went to the door. He loped to their vehicle, full of energy.

It took only a few minutes to get to Timber Creek Junior High. She parked curbside on the street that ran directly in front of the decades-old redbrick building that dominated the campus. A subsidiary mobile building that housed classrooms sat next to it.

The sun had traveled to linger above the western mountains; shadows were long and the springtime air cool. Mattie rolled down her windows.

"You're going to stay here," she told Robo, watching his ears fall. "I'll be right back."

Giving Robo one last glance, she saw that he'd resigned himself to stay, watching her from the back window, and she walked up the sidewalk toward the school's entrance. Brody and the school principal, along with a man and a woman she didn't recognize, stood at the base of the steps that led to an ornate portico that ran along the middle of the building, its white columns freshly painted.

"I think you already know Deputy Cobb, Mrs. Ketler," Brody said when Mattie joined the group.

"Yes." The principal offered a handshake.

"And these are Candace's parents, Burt and Juanita Banks."

Mattie scanned their faces while they shook hands. Burt's bloodshot brown eyes dominated his rather square face, and Mattie caught a whiff of alcohol when he said hello. He had a bushy beard and wore his dark hair slicked back from his forehead.

Juanita Banks appeared small as she stood beside her husband. She'd wrapped a saggy black sweater around herself, clutching it in place with crossed arms. Dark circles underlined her rather narrow-set green eyes. Her straggly brunette hair appeared to have escaped the anchor at the nape of her neck hours ago, and her grip felt limp and clammy when she shook hands.

"What's the concern, Mr. and Mrs. Banks?" Mattie could have asked Brody, but she wanted to hear it directly from the parents. It also gave Brody a chance to hear them state the problem twice, a method commonly used with missing children.

"Candace hasn't come home, and she was supposed to be there three hours ago." Despite the smell of alcohol, Burt seemed sober enough when he spoke. "We came to see if she stayed at school."

"We didn't have any after-school activities today," Mrs. Ketler said. "As far as I know, Candace left with the other children at the end of the day."

"At what time?" Mattie asked.

"Three o'clock."

"Did you see her leave?"

Mrs. Ketler shook her head. "I didn't. I've contacted one of the teachers that supervised the children's departure, but she didn't notice Candace leave specifically. As you can imagine, we have a great deal of foot traffic out front here when the final bell rings."

Mattie remembered it. She'd gone to this very school herself, and she'd driven past or sat out front in her cruiser at the end of the school day many a time since hiring on with the sheriff. It was a zoo out here that time of day. But she still wasn't sure why this girl's failure to return home on time would warrant calling out two off-duty police officers. She looked at Brody.

"Candace has asthma, and Mr. and Mrs. Banks are concerned that she's gone someplace alone and had an attack," Brody said.

Now it came clear. Mattie looked at Juanita. "How severe is her condition?"

"Bad." Juanita started to say more, but her husband interrupted.

"She takes medicine after school but didn't get home to take it today."

Mattie looked at Burt. "And you were home then?"

"He wasn't." Juanita looked down at the ground and muttered under her breath, "Even though he was supposed to be."

"The boys were at home," Burt said. "They said they never saw her."

"Are you sure she didn't go home, take her medicine, and go out again?" Mattie asked.

"The boys were watching TV," Juanita said, giving Burt a sidelong glance. "They would have noticed their sister come in. She wasn't there to fix them a snack, and that made an impression."

"Does Candace carry a rescue inhaler or something like that?"

"She does," Juanita said, "when she remembers it. It's in her bedroom on her dresser today."

Brody nodded toward Mattie's SUV. "I thought we'd try to follow her with Robo."

Mattie scanned the premises, imagining all those footsteps and different scent trails coming out the large double doors of the school, crossing over the portico in a human herd, passing down the steps and spilling out into the schoolyard. Even as she stood there eyeing the area, several boys that looked to be in their early teens came onto the property and headed toward them, laughing and jostling each other. "Hi, Mrs. Ketler," one of them called.

"Hi, Jimmy," she called back. "Excuse me a minute. Those boys share some of Candace's classes. I'm going to ask if they've seen her."

As the principal walked away, Mattie could almost see the woman's scent trail mingling with all the others on the sidewalk. What Brody had in mind would be a Herculean task for Robo.

Mattie turned to the parents. "Do you have an article of Candace's clothing with you?"

"What do you mean?"

"If I ask my dog to search for her, I'll need something that Candace wore recently, not something that's been freshly laundered. A T-shirt or something."

"There might be a sweat shirt in the back seat of the car," Juanita said.

"Wait a minute and I'll go with you. I should be the one to handle it."

Juanita's brow furrowed. "Why's that?"

"It keeps your scent from mingling with Candace's. Which way is your house?" Mattie thought she'd start Robo working in the direction toward the girl's home, out about forty or fifty feet to avoid the scent congestion at the front door.

Burt pointed to the west, into the older part of town, and gave her their address, a location a few blocks from her own house.

Mrs. Ketler came back, the teenage boys drifting along in her wake. Mattie noticed an older couple who looked like they might be out for an evening stroll walking past on the sidewalk. Scent trails everywhere.

"The boys haven't seen Candace, and they don't recall seeing her leave the school," the principal said as she rejoined the group.

"I'll go see if we have a scent article," Mattie said to Brody before turning to Juanita. "Let's go to your car."

Juanita led her to an older sedan with faded blue paint parked near where Robo was waiting. She opened the rear door and exposed the interior. Both the seat and floor were filled with clutter: fast-food bags and wrappers, papers and receipts, jackets and sweat shirts. Juanita pointed to a turquoise hoodie lying on the floor. "That one belongs to Candace."

"I'll pick it up after I get a bag from my vehicle to put it in. Do you have a picture of Candace with you?"

Juanita opened the front door on the passenger side and pulled out a handbag. She rifled through its contents and extracted a wallet, which she opened, then searched through the plastic sleeves holding photos. "Here's one, but it's old," she said, handing it to Mattie.

It must have been taken several years ago. Candace looked maybe seven or eight years old. "How old is she now?"

"Thirteen. I think this was her third-grade picture."

Mattie stored the image in her memory—curly brown hair, the same brown eyes of her father and narrow features of her mother, although not as extreme. Very cute. The girl reminded her of Sophie Walker.

She used her cell phone to take a snapshot of the photo and passed the picture back to Juanita. "Wait here. I'll be right back."

After retrieving a bag from her SUV, Mattie placed the hoodie inside and zipped it shut. She could feel Robo's eyes drilling into her and figured he knew exactly what was going on. She told Juanita to rejoin the others and then returned to him. He began to jump around inside his compartment, making the car bounce, his energy level shooting through the roof.

Wishing she'd had time to give him the evening exercise she knew he so desperately needed, Mattie opened up the back hatch, and Robo rushed the door. "Wait," she told him using a stern voice. "Sit."

Robo eased into a hovering sit, watching her eagerly while she took out his equipment. She exchanged his leather collar for the working one made of blue nylon and put on the tracking harness they used when searching for people. He charged toward the door again.

"Wait!" She felt responsible for setting up this energy bomb inside her partner. "Settle down. You need to listen."

She poured a splash of water into his collapsible bowl to moisten his mucus membranes and enhance his scenting ability. Despite his distraction, he lapped a few times.

After strapping on her utility belt, she placed the bagged sweat shirt into one of its pockets and clipped a short leash onto Robo's collar. "Okay, you can unload."

Robo leapt down and circled at her feet, barely able to contain his excitement. Avoiding getting entangled in the leash, Mattie told him to heel and led him to a tree. "Take a break."

She stayed with routine, although Robo barely lifted his leg before beginning to circle again. Frustrated by her dog's lack of focus, she commanded him to heel and led him westward on the sidewalk.

Fatigue made her body feel sluggish and heavy, but she tried to stride out and project the role of leader. Although Robo pushed the boundary between heel position and surging out front, he seemed to make an effort to do as he was told. Mattie headed to a place about fifty feet from the school, in a direction she assumed Candace would take to go home. She planned to quarter that area to see if Robo could pick up a scent trail.

Once there, Mattie told Robo to sit while she exchanged the short leash for a longer one, clipping it onto his harness. Typically she would let him search off leash, but today it didn't seem like a good idea.

She opened the bag that held the scent article and let him poke his head inside. He gave it a thorough sniffing before she took it away. "Search."

Robo put his nose to the ground, sniffed a couple times, then raised his head to trot toward the west. Mattie let the leash play out about ten feet, keeping it slack to give Robo the freedom to go where his nose might take him. Instead, he trotted up to a tree on the edge of the schoolyard, lifted his leg, and marked the tree as his territory.

Astonished, Mattie tugged the leash tight in a harsh correction. He'd never reacted to a search command like *that* before. Taking a moment to redirect his attention, she lowered the scent article for him again, but he didn't seem interested. Mattie gave him another search command.

He milled around the bushes and trees, sniffing and pawing, and then moved to another clump of foliage. Mattie checked each time to see what was holding his attention, but he didn't stay long enough in an area to indicate he was finding anything. He seemed to be flitting from one interesting scent to another and not focusing on his job. Testing her authority.

Growing impatient, Mattie snatched the leash in both hands and yanked Robo's collar, pulling him back beside her at heel position. "Robo, sit. You know better. Listen to me!"

Brody sauntered over to join them, thumbs hooked at the top of his utility belt. "What's up, Cobb?"

Mattie gave him an exasperated look. "He's not finding anything. This is asking too much, trying to find one scent trail in a schoolyard."

Brody nodded as he studied her. "Looks like he's not even trying."

The truth in his observation did nothing to dampen her temper. "Give us some time," she snapped.

"Take all the time you want," he said, lengthening his words in the oh-so-patient tone he sometimes used. "But let me make an observation."

Mattie met his gaze, narrowing her eyes at him. He was treading on her territory.

"You're not working together like you usually do. He's got all the energy, and you've got nothin'."

She struggled to control her temper. Brody might actually be onto something. Her exhaustion and Robo's lack of exercise were a bad mix.

"Start over," Brody said. "Chat him up like you usually do. Get yourself excited too."

"Is that all?"

Brody shrugged one shoulder. "Just sayin'."

"We'll try again." She turned away before glancing back and nodding toward the people who were gathering at the front of the school. "Can you do something about this crowd?"

"I'll take care of it." Brody strode back toward the school.

"Heel," she told Robo and began jogging toward the vehicle. While headed in that direction, she decided to swing wide and jog around the perimeter of the schoolyard to give her dog the exercise he craved. Robo trotted at her side, his mouth opening in a happy grin.

I should have done this in the first place.

Mattie completed two laps around the block, went back to her SUV, and offered Robo some water. He drank it eagerly. Then she began the patter that revved up his prey drive.

"You wanna go to work now, Robo? Do ya?" She continued to use a high-pitched voice as she led him toward the southwest corner of the property, avoiding the west side, where he'd failed to work previously. He pranced beside her in heel position and waved his tail, his eyes fixed on her as if awaiting instruction; he appeared much more like himself—intent and on the job.

Brody had dispersed the crowd, although a few people lingered around the school boundary, as if hoping to watch the show. Mattie decided to ignore them. Once she'd reached the point where she wanted to start, she asked Robo to sniff the scent article. This time he gave it his full attention and went right to work, quartering the area she directed, nose to the ground, and moving his head back and forth as he searched. She unsnapped his leash and trusted him to do his job, hurrying behind to keep up, occasionally directing him to sweep around the school perimeter in a large circle.

When they reached the east side, Robo hesitated at the sidewalk, giving it a thorough sniffing. Then he trotted away from the school, keeping his nose to the ground. Surprised, Mattie followed.

She glanced behind to see Brody following at a distance, alone. Before she turned her attention back to Robo, she heard Brody shout at a group of boys to stay put, and she knew he'd keep the bystanders in line so that she and her dog could focus on the track.

Robo led her eastward for several blocks and then across the street, heading for the high school. He kept his nose down and didn't hesitate; Mattie felt certain Candace had come this way instead of going west toward her home. Robo continued along the sidewalk toward Timber Creek High and then turned onto school property.

He skirted the edge of the school, moving along the rough stone-and-metal siding of the walls toward the side doorway. His ears pricked forward, and he paused to sniff the sidewalk, circling the area outside the door, nose down. Mattie imagined the trail he'd been on mingling with all those scents left by other kids, and she feared he'd lose the track.

But Robo kept searching, and he stayed with it until he moved off again toward the far corner of the building. From there, he picked up speed, heading up a well-trodden pathway that led to the hill at the backside of the building, which students had dubbed Smoker's Hill even before her own tenure.

The steep incline challenged Mattie's tired muscles. She'd walked this trail countless times as a teen—and yes, once she'd been one of the teenage smokers the hill was named for—but it had been years since she'd been back here. Even so, nothing had changed. Same elevation rising at a diagonal toward the top, same vegetation made up of dry grasses, rabbit brush, sharp yucca and cactus, everything just beginning to green. Same boulders and outcroppings dotting the hillside, providing plenty of places to hide.

Ambush. Something she thought of every time she followed Robo into this type of terrain. She scanned the hillside, telling herself she was silly to worry.

This is the hill behind the school, right here in town, for Pete's sake. Still, she kept a watchful eye on the boulders as she climbed.

Would she find Candace up here, casually sharing a cigarette or a joint with a friend? Surely a kid with asthma would know better than to smoke.

Robo continued up the trail, his ears darting forward and back. About halfway to the top, he breached a rise that led into a depression surrounded by scattered boulders and rocks of all sizes. After following him down into the bowl, she scanned the area, realizing no one could see her from the bottom of the hill. Isolated.

There were changes on the ground, torn sod and footprints, as if there'd been a scuffle. They spoke to her.

Something's wrong.

The hair on her neck rose about the same time it did on Robo's. Something bad had happened here; Robo could feel it, and so could she. She glanced behind her to see if Brody was near, but the rise blocked her view.

She hurried to keep up with Robo, who was trotting off-trail now and heading around a rocky outcropping farther up the hillside. He disappeared behind it, and Mattie ran to keep him in sight. Sprinting uphill, she rounded the rocky area and found him sitting beside a clump of rabbit brush, staring at her.

"What is it? What did you find?"

She spotted something under the brush. Denim . . . jeans. The setting sun provided dim light. Shadows gradually took shape. Jean-clad legs.

Mattie squatted beside Robo, gently pushing the brush aside so she could see what lay beneath. She heard and felt Brody come up beside her, but she couldn't divert her gaze to look at him.

The girl lay on her back, hands folded on her chest, eyes closed. Only the broken fingernails, blue-tinted lips, and red abrasions on her face belied her peaceful repose. Curly brown hair—no doubt it was Candace. Dead.

Mattie sucked in a breath and slipped an arm around Robo, hugging him close while her eyes rose to meet Brody's shocked expression.

"Shit, Cobb," he muttered. "What the hell's going on in this town?"

Chapter 2

Cole Walker glanced around the dinner table and smiled with satisfaction. Both his daughters sat in their seats wearing pleasant expressions and looking happy. When his kids were happy, he was happy. Things were good.

Angela, who'd been through a rough patch and appeared to be coming out on the other side, sat across from him and met his gaze with her blue eyes—so like her mother's. She wore her blond hair pulled back in a ponytail, and a few strands had fallen loose to curve around her face.

Sophie, her brunette curls tied back with one of the gauzy scarfs she'd taken to lately—this one a brilliant turquoise and one of her many favorite colors—sat in her place on Cole's left. Her brown eyes twinkling, she leaned over to kiss Belle, who was sitting beside the girl, watching her every move. Their Bernese mountain dog was an avid Sophie fan during mealtime. Bruno, their Doberman pinscher, sat on the floor between Cole and Sophie, waiting his turn for her attention.

Cole absently stroked the top of Bruno's head, where the black hair grew straight and silky between his ears, while he thought of how things had improved since last fall, when he'd made the decision to seek counseling for his daughters. After their mother left them a year ago and then refused to see them, and then one of Angela's friends had been killed last summer, the girls had been overwhelmed with grief and confusion. Mattie had encouraged him to seek professional help, and thank goodness he'd followed her advice.

The high school counselor had recommended a therapist in Willow Springs who specialized in child and family counseling, and while at first the weekly visits had been difficult, the sessions had proven to be a worthwhile investment. Now they made the trip only as needed, and although life could still be a bit bumpy—when was life with two kids not?—things had smoothed out considerably.

"*Platz*," Cole murmured to Bruno as Mrs. Gibbs approached the table bearing a platter with roasted chicken, potatoes, and carrots accompanied by their delicious aroma. The big dog went into down position, and Cole gave him a final pat on the head. Bruno had been trained in Germany, and although he was now fully bilingual, having quickly picked up English commands, the entire family enjoyed reinforcing his German vocabulary.

"This looks mighty fine," Cole said, counting his lucky stars once again for their resident housekeeper. Molly Gibbs had joined them last fall, creating some rebellious turf protection from Angela, but the woman's unflagging support and genuine concern for his children's well-being had eventually won over even the recalcitrant teenager. Along with a little help from their therapist.

Mrs. Gibbs flashed him a quick smile to acknowledge his appreciation, making the crow's feet at her green eyes crinkle. After placing the platter in the middle of the table, she took her seat to his right, unfolded her cloth napkin, and placed it in her lap, smoothing it over her black trousers. The rest of them followed suit while Cole recalled pizza boxes, hamburger wrappers, and paper napkins from takeout during the months he'd spent trying to do everything on his own after Olivia left.

"Angela has a fantastic plan for the school yearbook," Mrs. Gibbs said in her lilting Irish brogue. She nudged the platter Cole's way for him to serve. "Do you want to tell your dad about it?"

Angie began talking about her work on the yearbook committee, mentioning photo layouts and page spreads, her face and voice animated, her enjoyment of the project apparent.

As soon as he filled Sophie's plate, she slipped Belle a small piece of chicken. Placing a hand on her arm to get her attention, he shook his head no. She grinned, showing the small gap between her large front incisors.

He shifted his focus back on Angela, who hadn't paused in her monologue. Her being this chatty was a rare thing, and he was grateful for her involvement in something wholesome at school.

Lord knows there are plenty of other things she could be involved with that could get her into trouble.

His cell phone jingled inside his pocket. Angie narrowed her eyes when he reached for it.

"I'll just check to see who's calling," he said, knowing how much she hated for his work to interfere with their family time. He'd grown to respect that.

He didn't recognize the number, so he pushed the call through to voice mail. He'd hoped it might be Mattie. Although she'd shared meals with them often during the winter months, she seemed preoccupied lately and had turned down his invitations. He missed her.

"Go on," he said to Angela, putting the phone back in his pocket.

Apparently mollified, she continued to describe the yearbook cover. After listening and commenting for a few more minutes, Cole decided it was time to include Sophie in the conversation. It might keep her from slipping tidbits to Belle.

"That all sounds great, Angel," he said. "What about you, Sophie? What's going on at your school?"

She shrugged, giving him that vacant look children get when asked to sum up their day. "Nothing."

"You know what? I looked at the calendar this morning and realized your birthday is next week."

"You shall be nine years old, dear Sophie," Mrs. Gibbs said with a grin. She wore her gray hair short and permed tightly against her head like a cap, looking every bit the role of grandma that she seemed to be fitting into, a role that Cole's own mother didn't seem to want. "What shall we do to celebrate, young miss?"

Sophie's face lit up. "Can we have cake?"

"Why, certainly. You can choose what kind. Shall we have a party?" Mrs. Gibbs shot him a look, asking his opinion.

"We might do that," Cole said, although he didn't want to have to deal with a large gaggle of giggling girls. "It depends on what you have in mind."

"You should have a sleepover," Angie advised.

Sophie's face took on a look of wonder. "I've never had a sleepover before."

Cole realized that neither of the girls invited their friends over like they used to before Olivia left. Were sleepovers a rite of passage for girls Sophie's age? He turned to his housekeeper. She had two daughters who appeared to be self-supporting adults; she apparently knew what she was doing when it came to raising girls. "What do you think, Mrs. Gibbs?"

"I think it's a fine idea." She drew both Sophie and Angela in with her gaze. "We should keep it small, only three guests at most. We could have your favorite dinner."

"Hamburgers," Sophie said.

"Yes, and cake and ice cream. Angela and I could plan some games, and we could tell stories. So many delightful things we could do."

With Mrs. Gibbs taking charge, Cole was growing to like the idea more and more. "Maybe we could play charades or Pictionary."

Mrs. Gibbs nodded at him, and he felt a glow at being included in their camaraderie. These instances when his family clicked were rare and something he treasured.

His cell phone jingled again. When he checked caller ID, he realized it was the same number from earlier. "This is the same caller. Someone might have an emergency. I'll be right back." As he excused himself from the table, he checked in on Angie, glad to see that she seemed too excited and involved with planning Sophie's party to be miffed with him.

He connected the call. "This is Dr. Walker."

A male voice boomed in his ear, making him pull the phone away. "Hello. Dr. Walker?"

"Yes, this is Dr. Walker."

"Gus Tilley," the man fairly shouted.

Cole had done work for Gus before, although it had been quite some time since he'd last seen him. "Hi, Gus."

"I got a problem."

There was a long pause. When the man didn't go on, Cole filled the gap. "What's wrong?"

"It's Dodger. You remember Dodger?"

"Your dog, right?" Tan and white, mixed breed, neutered male, medium size, friendly with strangers. He could conjure the dog better than an image of Gus. But then, that wasn't unusual.

"Yep. He's got somethin' in his ear."

"Can you see it?"

"His ear?"

"No, I mean the thing inside his ear. Have you taken a look?"

"I can't see anything, but he's holding his ear funny, and he keeps scratching at it."

Cole thought of a grass awn, a wiry seeded-out stem that worked its way into a dog's fur or crevices and could cause an infection after it burrowed in. The dog probably needed his attention, but it didn't classify as an emergency.

"It could be a grass awn, Gus. I could take a look at him in the morning."

"I . . . uh . . . I don't know. Can you look in there tonight?"

"The office is closed. Emergencies only. Do you feel like this is an emergency?"

He answered quickly. "Yes, it is. He needs us to help him tonight."

Gus was a bachelor who lived up Soldier Canyon Road in a log cabin that sat on a small acreage near the national forest. He kept a few head of cows and a horse, which he'd called Cole out to work on for routine things like inoculations. Though an odd man, he seemed quite fond of his dog and the posse of feral cats that lived in the barn.

The distress Cole heard in Gus's voice tugged at him. "I'll see him tonight if you think it can't wait. How soon can you get here?"

"I'm at the edge of town at the gas station. A few minutes."

So Gus had already driven the half hour into town from his home. No wonder he insisted on being seen. "I'll meet you at the clinic."

Cole disconnected the call and went back into the kitchen, where the three women in his life were involved in a lively discussion. Mrs. Gibbs had picked up pad and pen while he'd been gone and was taking notes. Perhaps this simple party had become an extravaganza while he'd turned his back, and he hoped things hadn't gotten out of hand.

"Sorry, but I have an emergency at the clinic. Should only take twenty or thirty minutes, and then I'll be back." He scanned the three faces tilted his way and decided they all appeared okay with the news. He was in the clear. "You girls want to come with me?"

"I've got homework, Dad," Angie said. "Better not."

"I'll go." Sophie jumped up from the table and carried her dishes to the sink.

Cole cleared his own dishes, thanking Mrs. Gibbs for dinner. He heard Angie offer to help load the dishwasher, but Mrs. Gibbs declined and told her to go ahead and do her schoolwork.

"Grab a jacket, Sophie," he said. "Real quick. Gus will be here any minute." In fact, he heard the sound of a vehicle rattling past as he stepped into the garage and opened the door. Sophie trotted through the kitchen, dragging her jacket with one arm through a sleeve and Belle dogging her tracks.

"Belle, you stay here," Cole told the dog, making her stop in stride. The big dog sat and gazed longingly at the door with her ears low.

"We'll be back soon, Belle," Sophie reassured her in a lilting voice as she followed Cole, shutting the door firmly so that Belle wouldn't be tempted to challenge their decision.

"Load up into the truck," Cole said. "Gus just went by."

The clinic was only about two hundred yards farther up the lane, so Cole and the girls usually walked the short distance, but he didn't want to keep Gus waiting. He opened the near door of his truck, which carried a mobile vet unit in the bed, and hoisted Sophie up into the driver's seat, where she scrambled over to the passenger side.

At the clinic, Cole recognized Gus and Dodger standing out front, waiting. One of Dodger's perky ears was lopped over and rolled back, and even while Cole helped Sophie down from the truck, the dog sat and carefully dug at the inside of the ear with his hind paw.

Gus had changed since Cole last saw him. The tall, lanky man had grown even thinner, and his pale-blue eyes were sunken in his gaunt face. He'd let his sandy hair and beard grow long, both streaked with gray. Cole might not have recognized him if he'd met him on the street.

As they approached, Cole introduced his daughter. "This is Mr. Tilley, Sophie. Gus, my youngest, Sophie."

Gus cast his eyes toward the ground and took off his battered and stained felt hat. Fingering the brim, he murmured a how-do-you-do, while Sophie chimed in with her friendly hello. Then the man slouched into an anxious-looking heap as he examined the area in front of the clinic, keeping his gaze on anything but Sophie.

As Cole took in the man's sagging clothes, shaggy beard, and sunken eyes, he wondered if he'd been sick. He turned to unlock the clinic door. "How have you been, Gus?"

"I'm fine, Dr. Walker. You?"

"Can't complain. Let's bring Dodger in here to the exam room." Cole held the door open for the man to enter and then went to swing the exam room door wide as well. Sophie skipped across the lobby, following Gus and his dog and looking pleased with her evening adventure. She went to the far side of the room, grabbed a pair of latex gloves, and pulled them on, getting ready to work. Cole suppressed a smile.

"Let me take a look at you, Dodger," he said, holding out his hand for the dog to sniff. They'd met before at his place, and the dog seemed as friendly as he'd been on his own turf. "Can we lift him up to the exam table, Gus?"

"I can do it." Gus easily lifted the dog onto the table and held him steady in a light grasp. Dodger opened his mouth and panted. Nervous.

"So it's this ear, right? Can you hold his head for me, like this?" Cole demonstrated how he wanted Gus to secure the dog's head, and then picking up his otoscope, he held the ear firmly so he could take a thorough look. The ear was reddened where the dog had been scratching, but he couldn't see any foreign objects lodged in it. No grass seed or stem, no ticks, no mites. Nothing but the irritation.

He reached for some antiseptic ear cleanser. "His ear looks irritated, but there's nothing in there that I can see. I'll clean his ears out for him. Maybe he once had something in it, and he's gotten it out on his own. Or he reacted to some grass or something."

Cole squirted a small amount of cleanser into Dodger's ear, set down the bottle, and rubbed the liquid into the ear canal. As soon as Cole set down the ear wash, Sophie moved forward to pick it up. She stood beside him, holding the bottle ready so she could hand it to him for the next ear. "I don't think there's anything in there now, Gus, but I'll send this home with you so you can clean his ears out daily for a few days. If it doesn't get any better, call me and I'll take another look."

Gus watched Cole demonstrate how to clean and then wipe out Dodger's ears. Using a low, conspiratorial tone, he asked, "Do you think somebody put something in his ear and then took it out?"

The question surprised Cole. "Why would someone do that?"

"Maybe they wanted to make him sick." Gus shifted his eyes away from Cole, giving him a sidelong glance.

"I don't know why anyone would want to do that. Do you?"

"To get at me."

"Why, Gus? Are you having trouble with someone?" Cole was thinking of a neighbor dispute. They weren't unheard of out in the woods. People squabbled over boundaries, water rights, fences, you name it. "A neighbor?"

Gus shook his head, his gaze darting away from Cole's each time he tried to hold onto it.

"Do you think someone did something to Dodger's ear?" Cole asked.

"I'm not sure," Gus said, and he appeared to be backpedaling. "Probably not."

"Because if you do, we could have someone from the county humane society investigate. There are laws about injuring an animal on purpose. You don't have to put up with it."

Gus shifted his feet. "I don't know. Don't want that."

Cole had finished washing Dodger's other ear. "Let me take one more look in that ear and make sure we didn't dislodge something when we cleaned it." Both ears were bright pink after the cleaning, and Cole still found nothing.

Gus lifted his dog down to the floor, both of them looking relieved to end the procedure. Following the two into the lobby, Cole went to the backside of the reception desk to enter the visit into the computer and settle up the charges. He could hear Sophie begin spritzing the exam table with antiseptic spray, cleanup being her favorite part of working at the clinic. He knew she would wipe the table until the stainless-steel top shined.

After paying his bill, Gus turned to leave, leading Dodger across the lobby to the front door.

"Let me know how he's doing tomorrow, Gus. Give me a call sometime in the morning." Cole followed him outside.

"I will, Doc. I'll keep an eye on him tonight."

It looked like Gus needed rest more than Dodger needed someone to worry over him. "Just get some sleep. Dodger will be okay."

After following Gus outside, Cole watched him load the dog into his truck cab and drive away. The lop-eared Dodger took his seat on the passenger side, his silhouette in the back window.

Gus seemed stressed or nervous or . . . something, Cole thought. Something seemed off, but he couldn't quite put his finger on it.

Chapter 3

Her arm still around Robo, Mattie knelt beside the girl's body, taking in the details. She let herself slump forward, sharp pebbles digging into her knees. This was the third dead body Robo had found in less than a year. If their mission was to reduce crime here in Timber Creek, they weren't doing a very good job.

Brody's knees popped as he squatted beside the girl's head. Neither of them touched the body. "Blue lips. Suffocation?"

"Asthma attack? Or something worse." Mattie gestured toward Candace's face and then her hands. "Several scrapes on her face. Something abrasive against it. And look at these fingernails. Broken. Scrapes on her hands too. She fought."

A pit opened in Mattie's stomach. *Someone killed this kid.*

"Yep. Better treat this one as a homicide," Brody said, his voice pitched so low, it was a growl.

"What about this posing?" Mattie said, nodding toward the girl's hands crossed upon her chest.

"Someone who knew her."

She wondered if it could be more than that. "Someone who might have cared about her?"

"Maybe."

Mattie roused herself and scanned the area. The rocky outcropping surrounded them, blocking sight from all directions but skyward. It gave her a hinky feeling. Someone could be hidden, watching. "Do you think the killer is still around?"

Brody stood and scanned the area. "Doubt it."

"Robo could probably find his trail, see where he went."

Brody nodded. "Do it."

Mattie stood and gestured away from the girl's body, encouraging Robo to sniff the perimeter around the site. "Can you find the bad guy, Robo? Find the bad guy. Search."

Patrol dogs didn't always need a scent article to track someone, especially if the target was fleeing the scene of a crime. The guilty often emitted a sweat that left an odor dogs could pick up readily, and Mattie hoped that would be the case here.

"Do you need backup?" Brody called to her as she followed her dog downhill.

"You'll have to stay here until the others come." Mattie threw the words over her shoulder. "Follow me when you can."

Robo showed no hesitation, putting his nose to the ground and trotting away from the gravesite, telling Mattie that whoever left Candace under the brush must have also left a strong scent trail. Maybe this wasn't a stone-cold killing. Maybe Candace's death had horrified the person responsible. Someone who knew the child and cared about her enough to pose her in that peaceful way. The thought made her nauseous, and she focused her full attention back on Robo.

Smoker's Hill was a bare hogback, with its sloping side nestled up to the high school and a ridge running along the top. Robo headed down but away from the school, farther south beyond the area where she'd observed signs of a struggle. Skirting around cactus, yucca, and sagebrush, he continued downhill while Mattie jogged behind, keeping an eye on the terrain at her feet while glancing ahead to spot a possible ambush. Chances of someone lying in wait seemed slim; she supposed the fugitive she was tracking would have tried to put as much distance as possible between him and the girl's body.

It didn't take long for Robo to reach the bottom of the hill, and he came to a stop at a rusty barbed wire fence that ran along the barrow ditch beside Highway 12, the major highway in and out of Timber Creek. When Mattie joined him at the fence, he crouched and began to crawl under the bottom strand. She pulled it up to give him more space below the sharp barbs. Once he was clear, she pushed the strand downward so she could squeeze between it and the middle one. A barb poked her in the back and caught her khaki coverall as she scooted through. She pulled away from it, hearing the fabric rip. No matter. She was used to getting tears in her uniforms while following Robo, and Mama T, her foster mother, helped her mend them.

Robo went along the road with his nose to the ground, stopping ten yards away and sniffing in all directions. Then he came back and sat at the edge of the highway. Dead end.

The guy must've parked his vehicle here. If he'd parked right, he'd have entered the driver's side. But who knew? Speculation wouldn't get them very far.

But the tire tracks left at the side of the road might.

"Good boy." Mattie patted Robo firmly on his side while he leaned against her legs. He raised his head and bumped his nose on the pocket of her utility belt, the one that held his treat for completing a mission—a yellow tennis ball.

She heard a car coming toward them on the highway, so she pulled Robo into the barrow ditch to watch it cruise past. White four-door sedan, Buick, two passengers—a man and a woman. She made a note of the license plate number in her pocket notebook, despite knowing there would probably be no need to follow up. They were most likely just travelers on the road, not killers. Though traffic on this road was typically sparse, the body up on Smoker's Hill made her more cautious about people passing through town. She would keep an eye out.

"What's up?" Brody asked as he made his way down the slope to the fence.

"Dead end. But I'm certain the person we want got into a vehicle right here. Maybe on the driver's side, which could mean he'd left it here during the time of Candace's death. We found some tire tracks."

"Let's secure this area. Detective LoSasso is calling in the crime scene unit from Byers County, and they can take a mold of this track."

Robo nudged her utility belt again. Having learned how much his routine meant to him and how important it was to give him what he expected, Mattie leaned forward to pat him on his side. "I need to throw the ball for Robo."

"I'll put up the tape. Check back when you're done."

Mattie led Robo a safe distance from the highway to a grassy area near an abandoned adobe building, him dancing at her feet while she pulled out his tennis ball. With her heart breaking for Candace, Mattie began to play with her dog.

Robo wore a silly grin as he loped back toward her with the ball locked between his sharp white teeth. He'd finished growing since they'd become partners and had fleshed out, now tipping the scales at about one hundred pounds. He was the most handsome German shepherd she'd ever seen, his glossy black coat lush and thick, high-lighted with tan markings.

Her stomach churned as she thought about the posed corpse, suggesting that whoever did it had cared about the dead child. Someone like a parent.

Burt Banks smelled of booze. And he wasn't home with the kids like he was supposed to be. So where was he? It made her sick to think a father might kill his own child, but this guy had to be their number-one suspect, at least at this moment.

She threw the ball until Robo's interest flagged and then stored it back in its pocket. After leaning over him, ruffling his fur, and giving him a long hug, she told him it was time to go back to work. He trotted beside her at heel, tail waving, and looking for all intents and purposes ready to go. It seemed that his boundary testing, some-thing common with these intelligent dogs, had ended—at least for now.

Brody had stretched crime scene tape from the fence posts to a spike he'd placed near the asphalt, creating a boundary to protect the tire tracks. While she'd been playing with Robo, she'd noticed several locals stopping to talk to him, and he'd waved them all away. She'd also noticed he'd written down license plate numbers as they drove off, telling her his radar was operating on full alert like hers.

Reminding Robo to heel as they crossed the road, Mattie joined Brody on the other side. "I want to take Robo back along the scent trail and flag any footprints we can find," she told him.

"Sounds good." Brody extracted his cell phone from his shirt pocket. "I'll inform Sheriff McCoy. He and LoSasso are at the gravesite, and I've told them about the tracks here. When the CSU gets here, they'll work the gravesite first. Garcia's on his way to stand guard down here, and I'll come up as soon as he arrives."

Mattie nodded and led Robo back to the wire fence. After crossing through, she began the patter to rev him up and then asked him to search for the bad guy so he would lead her back along the scent trail. She'd never tried this kind of challenge before, asking Robo to go over a scent trail twice, but it was similar enough to one of his other skills—backtracking a thief's trail while searching for evidence—that she hoped he'd know what to do.

Robo took the command in stride, putting his nose to the ground and taking her back uphill. In the dimming light, she found several prints and partial prints that she marked with orange flagging tape on short metal spikes. Large size, flat sole, rounded toe, and square heel. Maybe a work boot, probably too large for a woman. But again, assumptions could be misleading.

Halfway up the hill, Robo darted off to the left and sniffed under a dense clump of rabbit brush. He stretched forward, his neck lengthening in the pose he used to touch something with his mouth. Then he turned to sit and stare at her.

"What did you find?" Mattie squatted beside him, putting one arm around him to brace her tired body, and peered beneath the plant. A black thermal cap rested against the base of the brush. It looked clean, like it hadn't been there very long.

Did the killer drop this on his way down the hill?

"Good find, Robo. Good boy!" After patting her dog, she marked the item with an evidence spike and photographed it with her cell phone, leaving it in place for the crime scene techs to process. "Let's see if we can find something else."

As she neared the gravesite, she spotted Detective Stella LoSasso and Sheriff McCoy. She also recognized a third figure as Dr. McGinnis, Timber Creek's sole physician and the Timber Creek County coroner. Sixty-something, the doctor had a mop of silver hair, which he wore longish in a 1960s style reminiscent of The Beatles. It drifted around his head in the light breeze that flowed uphill, making him easy to identify even in the dim light. Stella was snapping photographs of the body while McGinnis hovered next to it. When Stella finished, he squatted down to get a closer look.

"So she was found at six thirty-seven, and school let out at three o'clock," McGinnis said. "That's our window."

"That's right," Stella said, looking up at Mattie and acknowledging her with a nod before turning her attention back to the doctor. Dressed casually in jeans and a brown jacket with a Timber Creek County Sheriff's Department emblem on the sleeve, the detective looked like she'd left home immediately when called after hours. She'd scraped her long chestnut hair back and secured it at the nape of her neck, and the twilight touched on natural highlights that ran through it.

"Did you find footprints?" Sheriff McCoy asked Mattie quietly as she drew near. McCoy was a large African American man, easily six foot three, and he presented himself in an unflappable manner that made Mattie glad to have him in charge. No surprise to her that she also felt a small amount of comfort in his presence, since he'd been the young deputy who'd rescued her when she was six years old, the night her family fell apart.

"Yes," she said. "I marked them. We've got several good ones. Robo also found a cap on the same route."

McCoy raised his brows and nodded before looking back at the body, drawing Mattie's attention toward it as well.

Dr. McGinnis was probing the victim's face with gloved fingers while Stella held a flashlight. "We've got some rigor setting into her jaw and facial muscles, but . . ." He looked up at Stella. "May I move her slightly?"

"Yes, but let's move her as little as possible for you to get the information you need. I'd like to preserve this scene for our CSU."

Apparently Stella believed they were dealing with a homicide too, though accidental death would have to be ruled out. Someone had been up here with Candace, and that someone would know exactly what happened.

Dr. McGinnis lifted one of Candace's arms and then replaced it, pushed gently against a leg. "Rigor is starting in her extremities. I'm thinking she's been dead right around three hours, maybe a little less."

Stella glanced at her watch. "It's five after seven right now. So you're estimating around four o'clock, maybe shortly after."

"Rough estimate."

"I understand." Stella passed a gloved hand near Candace's face without touching it. "Petechiae here."

Dr. McGinnis touched the tiny purplish-red spots that dotted the area around her nose and mouth. "Yes, most likely from suffocation. But no bruising on her neck." While Stella continued to train the light on the girl's face, he raised one of her eyelids and revealed bloodshot whites around the staring, opaque eyes.

Stella swept the light to Candace's hands. "She has some broken fingernails. Let's go ahead and bag her hands before we do anything else."

While the two worked with the body, Mattie tried to come to grips with what this meant. A thirteen-year-old girl's life had ended—a life that didn't have a chance to even get properly started. Although the father had come to mind as her first suspect, she tried to think of other possible motives for the teen's death. *Drugs.* Every recent death in Timber Creek had been drug related. They had to at least consider it.

But there were other options too. What about teen rivalry or jealousy? Timber Creek didn't have a gang faction, but infighting among the different groups—the jocks, goths, cowboys, nerds—wasn't uncommon. Even so, it was hard to imagine one of them killing another.

A random killing by someone passing through town? Another long shot. Whoever killed Candace appeared to have known her.

And the people who came up this hill were typically kids or some-one else associated with the school.

Stella's conversation with the doctor brought her attention back to them.

"I'm glad you could identify Candace," Stella was saying. "Saves us from having to make her parents do it."

McGinnis wore a somber expression. "I've been this child's doc-tor since she was a little girl."

Mattie hadn't thought of that. But of course, this man was the only doctor in town.

Sheriff McCoy spoke, his voice deep and solemn with sympathy. "I know how hard this must be for you, Dr. McGinnis. Can you share any thoughts about her and what might have gone wrong up here?"

The doctor nodded, but he looked back at Stella. "I need to get a body temperature. Under the arm will do. We can disturb her clothing as little as possible."

"All right." Stella assisted, both of them moving the girl's body with care. "This is a skimpy top she has on under her jacket for this time of year. And pretty fancy underwear."

Mattie caught a glimpse of a black spaghetti-strap-and-lace con-coction covering a chest not yet fully developed. The girl was barely past the training bra stage.

After placing the thermometer, McGinnis shifted from kneeling to settle back on his heels to wait, obviously uncomfortable hold-ing the position on the rocky ground. He looked up at the sheriff. "Candace had a respiratory condition, asthma, and several allergies that would set off her episodes. Her condition has been relatively under control with medications during the past few years. I haven't seen her in my office as much as I used to. But it concerns me that it looks like she's died of asphyxia."

"Any thoughts on that?" Stella asked.

"There are some plants up here that might have set her off," McGinnis said, glancing around the area. "You should search her pockets for her inhaler."

Mattie spoke up. "Her mother said she found Candace's inhaler on her dresser at home."

McGinnis looked at Stella. "Another thought . . . she could have choked on something like a piece of hard candy."

"Shall we look in her mouth?" Stella asked.

"We should," McGinnis said, carefully removing the thermometer, reading it, and then making a notation on a pad. "But if it's lodged between her vocal cords, I won't be able to see it."

"Let's have you take a look anyway."

McGinnis took a scope from his kit, and while Stella helped him open the girl's jaw as much as possible considering the rigor, he peered inside. "I can't see anything. If there's anything there, it'll stay put for the medical examiner to find."

Each time Stella and the doctor moved the girl, they returned her to the position in which she'd been found, arms bent and hands crossed carefully on her chest. Stella gestured toward the corpse. "Do you have an opinion about the posing?" she asked McGinnis.

Pausing to think, the doctor stared at Candace and spoke slowly. "It looks like someone who cared about her put her in that position."

"I agree. Or someone with remorse," Stella said.

McGinnis shrugged. "I suppose so."

"Most kids carry a backpack or something to and from school," Mattie said. "I haven't found anything like that up here."

Stella acknowledged Mattie with a nod. "Let's turn her slightly, Doc. Doesn't look like there's anything under her, but I'd like to take a peek."

The two rolled Candace to one side. "She's a tiny thing," Stella murmured. "That's enough. There's nothing here. Let's put her back the way she was."

After doing so, McGinnis rose from where he'd been squatting, joints creaking. "I have enough information to call the death and complete the paperwork. The body will go to the Byers County medical examiner as usual, right?"

Stella nodded. "I'll make sure you get a report."

Although the initial meeting between detective and coroner had been somewhat contentious, Mattie noticed that Stella seemed to be making more of an effort now that she was a formal member of the team. Perhaps Sheriff McCoy's impeccable manners were rubbing off on her.

"Can you tell us anything about her family?" Mattie asked McGinnis while he was putting his equipment and notes back into his bag.

"She has two younger brothers. Mom's a hardworking lady— often looks tired when she brings in the children."

"And the father?"

McGinnis frowned as he stripped off his gloves. "I've never met him. Seems strange after all these years. Works at the mine in Rigby if I remember right."

"Thank you for the information, Dr. McGinnis," McCoy said. "Is there anything else you might be able to tell us?"

"Not off the top of my head. Other than the asthma, there's nothing different about this child than any other that comes to my office. We can provide medical records if you want. Just bring us a warrant."

McCoy nodded as he said good-bye.

After McGinnis left and was winding his way downhill, avoiding the areas that were marked with orange tape, Brody came uphill from farther south to join them. His eyes swept the scene, apparently taking in the stage of investigation they were at, and then stopped on Sheriff McCoy. "Has anyone told the parents yet?"

McCoy shook his head, looking grim. "Not yet. I'll do it. Detective, do you want to join me?"

Stella's face also showed distaste for the task. "I'd better. We'll need to talk to them first. See if they have any ideas about how or why this happened to their daughter."

Mattie stood very still beside Robo. She'd already thought about what her role should be, although she wasn't too excited about it. "I'd better go with you too. I think we should get permission to go through Candace's room, and I'd like to see if Robo finds any drugs. Or if he hits on something anywhere else in the house for that matter."

Everyone's attention turned toward Mattie, but Stella responded first. "I suppose you're right. We'd better look into it, considering the drug problems we've had in town. And the sooner the better, before anyone has a chance to clean things out. Sheriff?"

"I agree. Deputy Brody, stand guard here until the CSU arrives and then work on a warrant for the girl's house. Let's call Deputy Johnson back on duty to stand by at the high school and show them the way up here. Tell him to stop anyone else from coming up the trail. We need to keep people away from this scene."

"I'll take care of it," Brody said, his ice-blue eyes fierce. The last body they'd found was that of his sweetheart, and Mattie could tell that finding this one had reawakened his pain.

Stella fell in beside Mattie as they followed Sheriff McCoy downhill. "What are you thinking?" Stella asked.

"Nothing solid, but homicide. Drugs, teen infighting at school, random killing from someone passing through town, maybe someone either from school or her neighborhood that she was at odds with. But my primary suspect . . . her father."

Stella looked at her sharply. "Why her father?"

Mattie shared her reasons—his absence at the house, his drinking.

"I'll keep that in mind," Stella said.

They'd reached the area of torn-up terrain, now surrounded by tape. Sheriff McCoy had stopped beside it. "This could be where she was killed," he said. "Or if her death was accidental, as Dr. McGinnis suggested, maybe someone was trying to help her with an asthma attack."

"Seems like more of a scuffle than that," Stella said, scanning the area and then looking back uphill. "Odd that the killer carried her uphill to leave her body."

Mattie shared her observation that the gravesite was hidden from both the school and highway. "Maybe that's why she was taken uphill. To avoid detection from down below."

McCoy nodded his agreement. "Must have been someone with muscle."

"True," Mattie said. "Although she's not very big." And with a sense of outrage, it struck her again that their victim was only thirteen years old.

As a group, they turned and continued downhill toward their grim mission, delivering the news to Candace's parents. And if Mattie's suspicions about Burt Banks were true, they'd be delivering the news to her killer.

Chapter 4

At the high school parking lot, they loaded into McCoy's silver Grand Cherokee, Stella riding shotgun and Mattie and Robo in the back seat, and drove to the junior high. There, Mrs. Ketler was waiting on the front steps with Burt and Juanita Banks, their expressions etched with concern.

Juanita Banks stared at them as they approached, her eyes moving from one face to another. She must have read something in them, because she blanched, and her body seemed to shrink as they drew near.

Sheriff McCoy led the way. "Please, let's go inside," he said, gesturing toward the school doorway.

Burt crossed his arms. "Tell us what you know."

Juanita sagged, and McCoy stepped up to grasp her elbow, easing her down to sit on the steps. Mrs. Ketler hovered beside her.

McCoy straightened. "I'm sorry, but I do have bad news." He cleared his throat and tugged lightly at his collar, his face showing his distress. "We've found Candace. And I'm sorry . . . she's deceased."

Juanita groaned, folding forward and hugging her belly.

"Oh, dear God," Mrs. Ketler murmured. She sat down beside Juanita on the step and put her arm around her. "What happened?"

Burt's nostrils flared as he sucked in a breath. "Are you sure it's her?"

"Dr. McGinnis has identified her body for us," McCoy said.

"That quack? What does he know?"

"Shut up, Burt. You don't know anything." Juanita's voice wavered. With grief or with rage? Mattie couldn't tell.

Stella moved closer to Burt, observing him, perhaps noticing the odor of liquor on his breath that Mattie could smell from a distance.

Burt glared at his wife and then shifted his gaze to McCoy. "Take me to her. I wanna see for myself."

"I'm sorry, but I can't do that now. We don't know your daughter's cause of death yet, so we're not letting anyone into the area where we found her."

Juanita was moaning, holding herself and rocking, but McCoy's words must have caught her attention. "Where? Where is she?"

"She's near the high school, Mrs. Banks. We'll let you see her as soon as we can."

"We'll go now," Burt said, turning to head for his vehicle, a battered gray truck.

"Wait, Mr. Banks," McCoy said. "I need you to stay clear of the area. We're bringing in professionals to take care of Candace, and we need to give them space to do their work."

Burt caught a toe on an uneven place in the sidewalk and stumbled while Stella stepped around to block his way, grasping his arm as if to assist him. He straightened, striking away her hand. Mattie and Robo moved closer, Robo's hackles raised.

"Just trying to keep you from falling, Mr. Banks," Stella said in a soothing way. "You can help by talking to us, and we'll take you to Candace as soon as we can."

"Is Candace alone?" Juanita asked the sheriff.

"There's a deputy watching over her."

Juanita covered her face and sobbed into her hands.

"How did she die?" Burt demanded.

"We don't know her cause of death yet," McCoy said. "But it will be investigated."

"Small-town cops," Burt muttered. "Like *that's* going to do any good."

"Mr. and Mrs. Banks, could we take you to your home while we wait?" McCoy said. "It's getting cold out here."

Streetlights had switched on, and the temperature dropped after sundown.

"I'll drive you home in your car, Mrs. Banks," Stella said. "Mr. Banks, perhaps you could ride with Sheriff McCoy."

Mattie appreciated that the detective had decided to isolate the parents from each other. She must be intending to interview them separately.

"I'll drive my own car," Burt said.

"Mr. Banks, I can't allow you to drive right now, so I'll take you home," Sheriff McCoy said. And then he turned to Mrs. Ketler. "Thank you for your kindness, Mrs. Ketler. I'm sure Mr. and Mrs. Banks will need your help in the days to come, but for now, please feel free to return to your home. We'll more than likely want to speak to you tomorrow. Will you be here at school?"

"Yes," Mrs. Ketler said, her eyes searching McCoy's face and then moving beyond to stare into the schoolyard. "I'm not sure what to say to the students in the morning."

McCoy removed a business card and pen from his pocket and scribbled on the card's back. "This is my cell phone number. Please call me later this evening and we'll decide on a plan."

The principal took the card, and McCoy turned his attention to Burt. "Let's go to your home, Mr. Banks."

Burt had lost some of his steam, and he allowed the sheriff to lead him to his Jeep.

Mattie took Robo to their SUV and loaded him in back, wishing she could be a fly on the windshield inside one of the two other cars. She'd like to be privy to whatever conversations were taking place with the parents, but she had to be satisfied with getting information pertinent to Candace's death secondhand.

With Stella leading the way, they crossed Highway 12 and traveled in a three-vehicle caravan to the Banks' house on the west side of town. Mattie parked on the street behind McCoy's Jeep in front of a single-story ranch-style home built with weathered logs. Considering the age of many of the houses on this side of town, it might have been close to one hundred years old. Five towering spruce trees filled the front yard, their dropped needles preventing the growth of grass but giving the house a cozy-cabin appearance. There were no curbs or sidewalks on this street, but the area looked well kept—free of clutter, weeds, and debris. A large black kettle filled with dirt sat by the front door, and Mattie imagined Juanita planting pansies or geraniums in it once the threat of springtime frost had ended.

By now, it had turned dark, and a chilly breeze gained strength from the west. She thought of the crime scene techs doing their duties by the powerful, portable lights she knew they would bring with them. They all had a rough night ahead.

She hoped that Stella had gained permission for them to search Candace's room. As she exited her vehicle, she caught Stella's eye, and the detective gave her a nod that told her everything was a go. She went to the back of her SUV and opened Robo's compartment.

"You're going back to work, buddy," she said in a quiet tone. She didn't want to rub a drug search in either parent's face, and she especially didn't want to set off Burt. Best to change Robo's collar to the one he wore specifically for narcotics detection here in her patrol vehicle and rev him up quietly before entering the Banks' home.

Robo's excitement settled as soon as she fastened his special collar around his neck, and he adopted his familiar businesslike attitude. Mattie invited him out of the back of the SUV and then told him to heel as she led him toward the front door. Stella and Juanita were waiting for her there, while Sheriff McCoy and Burt appeared to be deep in conversation inside the sheriff's Jeep. Evidently, Burt was opening up to him about something. Mattie slipped past, hoping not to interrupt them.

"We'll let Deputy Cobb take a look in Candace's room while we talk to your sons," Stella was saying to Juanita as Mattie approached. "Deputy, Mrs. Banks has approved a narcotics sweep of her daughter's room. She believes you won't find anything, but if something's there, she'd like to know about it."

Mattie nodded and followed the two inside the house, straight into the kitchen. Juanita's sobbing had ceased, but she walked stooped forward, her arms clutching her middle. Television noise came from the room beyond.

"The boys are in the living room," Juanita said, looking toward Stella as if for guidance.

"Where is Candace's room?" Mattie asked.

"Through the living room and down the hall, first door on the right."

"Deputy Cobb will go on through while we stay with your sons." Stella guided Juanita through the kitchen, her hand on the mother's elbow.

A quick visual sweep told Mattie that the kitchen furniture and appliances were old, though not quite as old as her own. The tan, brown-flecked linoleum on the floor appeared clean, and the beige laminate countertops, for the most part, tidy. Though there were breadcrumbs and jars of peanut butter and jelly out as well as a few dishes in the sink, the small mess was most likely from the kids making a snack.

The living room was dark, lit only by light from the television. Juanita moved as if automated to an end table beside the sofa and turned on a lamp. Two young boys, both elementary school age, sat on the sofa, and their eyes widened as they looked away from the television and saw the strangers behind their mother. Both of them ended up staring at Robo.

Mattie proceeded through the room without pause, flipping on a light switch as she entered the hallway. The stubby shag carpeting looked like it dated back at least twenty years, but the groomed surface showed that someone had vacuumed it recently. Apparently Juanita Banks prioritized housekeeping, despite working outside of her home. Mattie realized that once again she was making assumptions, but even though she knew little about Burt Banks, she couldn't imagine him trying to make sure the house stayed tidy.

Mattie opened the first door on the right and went inside, turning on the overhead light. At first, she thought the place had been tossed, but closer inspection revealed the normal mess and clutter of a teenager's bedroom: books, papers, and clothing scattered about;

bed unmade, with comforter and blankets draped to the floor; soda cans and dirty dishes stacked in various places. Across from the bed sat a chest of drawers and a dresser with a large mirror. A bulletin board hung over the bed's headboard with photographs, drawings, and greeting cards pinned to it.

Looking past the general mess and homing in on specifics, a few things stood out. Many of Candace's shirts looked like they'd be more appropriate for summer than for early spring—tube tops, crop tops, and tanks with spaghetti straps. More revealing than Mattie expected for a girl her age, but consistent with what she'd been wearing at the crime scene.

She crossed over to the bed and scanned the photos pinned to the bulletin board. Here was a shot of Candace sandwiched between two high school boys that Mattie recognized, both boys with their arms around her. She made a mental note of their names. And here, another shot of Candace with one of the school jocks, whom she recognized as the team quarterback. They were posed together, the much larger boy bending over Candace so the two could stand cheek to cheek, both of them puckered up with a big kiss for the camera.

Mattie's alarm bells were ringing. What was Candace, a thirteen-year-old junior high student, doing with these high school boys? She feared she knew the answer.

She decided to start the narcotics sweep at the bedroom doorway, move around the room to search the furniture, and then end with the closet. After patting Robo on the side and ruffling the fur at his neck, she unclipped his leash from the active ring on his collar and snapped it onto the dead ring so she wouldn't distract him with inadvertent obedience signals. She withdrew a pair of latex gloves from her utility belt and slipped them on. "Okay, Robo, find some dope."

Robo pinned his ears and turned into a sniffing machine. While holding his leash lightly in her left hand, Mattie used her right to guide him around the room, indicating under the bed, and giving him plenty of time to search the clothing and bedding that lay scattered about. His delicate black lips fluttered as he whiffed each item.

She opened each drawer and carefully moved the clothing for Robo to check. A flash of red from the bottom of the pile caught her eye, and though Robo didn't alert, Mattie certainly did.

Oh, for Pete's sake! Closer inspection had revealed a set of peekaboo lace underwear in firehouse red.

With a sinking feeling, Mattie closed the drawers, leaving the clothing where she'd found it.

She opened the closet door and saw nothing unusual; clothes seemed sparse with plenty of bare hangers, but then most of Candace's things were apparently on the floor. Robo sniffed shoes thrown every which way and items of clothing that Mattie indicated. She was reaching above to inspect the upper shelf when a bellow came from the living room. Burt. And he was heading her way.

Mattie turned to face the doorway while Robo jumped in front of her, his eyes pinned on the door. Burt Banks hurtled into the room, his face filled with rage.

With hackles raised, Robo charged to the end of his leash, barking fiercely and showing his teeth. Mattie was ready and stopped him short of reaching the man.

Burt halted in his tracks, no less enraged. "Get the hell out of here!"

Relieved that she'd put Robo on a leash, Mattie tried to stay calm. Any wrong move from her would escalate Robo's protective response. "Robo, out," she said firmly, using the command to signal release of a captive or the end of a bite-and-hold maneuver. She wanted to make sure Robo knew that was not where his mind should be. "Down."

She could tell he didn't want to do it, but Robo exchanged his bark for a low growl and went into down position, his chest rumbling his displeasure. Hoping it would keep Burt at bay, Mattie decided to let him grumble. By now, Sheriff McCoy and Stella were right behind the man, and McCoy stepped around to block him from Mattie.

"Hold on there, Mr. Banks," McCoy said, palms raised in a stay-back gesture. "My deputy has your wife's permission to be in here."

"I don't care what she said. I say get out!" Burt raised a fist, causing a fresh wave of growls from Robo.

McCoy stepped closer, looming over the man. "You don't want to fight us, Mr. Banks. Calm down and we'll talk."

Juanita appeared at the bedroom doorway, and the small room was feeling way too crowded. "Robo, quiet," Mattie murmured, wanting to reduce the tension, and Robo's growling ceased.

Lowering his hand, still fisted, to his side, Burt eyed the sheriff.

Juanita slipped past her husband and went to the bed. Bending to pick up the bedclothes, she murmured, "I don't clean the children's rooms."

Stella moved to intervene. "Don't worry about straightening things now, Mrs. Banks. We need to leave the room as it is."

Juanita looked at Mattie. "Did your dog find any drugs?"

Mattie knew the woman would face her husband's wrath later for letting her search. She'd earned the right to know. "No, ma'am." And then she added for Sheriff McCoy's information, "I've completed the search except for the upper shelf in the closet."

"Get out of my baby's room," Burt said with a catch in his voice.

The tinge of grief, combined with the man's rage, made Mattie's gut tighten. Her mind leapt to her own parents, bringing back her childish observations of their interactions, but she pushed them away, studying Juanita's face instead, trying to get a read on her emotions. The mother had sunk down on the bed, perching on the edge as if her legs could no longer hold her, and she was glaring at Burt. Mattie read sorrow and fury there—a fury so intense, she wondered if it could be called hatred.

Flashes of what she'd found here in Candace's room came to mind: revealing shirts, trashy lingerie, suggestive pictures of Candace with boys older than she. Knowing that girls with a history of childhood sexual abuse often became promiscuous teenagers, hard questions formed inside Mattie's brain.

Had Burt Banks ever molested his daughter? And did he have anything to do with her death?

Chapter 5

Sheriff McCoy eventually talked Burt down, but Robo didn't relax his guard and neither did Mattie. She watched his hands, her body tense and poised, ready for a strike. But something had drained the fight out of Candace's father. He sagged back against the doorjamb and put his hands to his face. She wondered what thoughts he might be hiding, and a cold finger trailed down her spine.

"Juanita," Stella said quietly. "Is there a neighbor or someone in town who could look after your sons?"

Staring at the floor with a blank expression, the mother dipped her head in a slight nod.

"Let me help you call someone," Stella said. "We're going to need to have some time alone with you and your husband. And I don't think the boys should be with us when we go see Candace."

The two left together. The quiet vibration of Sheriff McCoy's cell phone in his pocket seemed to shatter the room's stillness. Burt dropped his hands from his face, and Mattie's alert system kicked up another notch. She watched him carefully while McCoy removed his phone from his pocket and answered it. Robo also stood guard.

"Yes, Deputy."

Must be Brody calling.

"Good. Bring it to the Banks' home now." He gave the address and disconnected the call.

McCoy looked at Burt. "Chief Deputy Brody is on his way with a warrant to search Candace's room." When Burt Banks stiffened and drew himself up into a fighting stance, McCoy added, "It's common procedure at any unattended death where there's a suspicion of homicide, Mr. Banks. And like I explained to you earlier, that's what we suspect. It appears that someone was with your daughter when she died, and if that person killed Candace, we'll waste precious time and leads if we don't search for them right now. Does that make sense?"

Burt glared at the sheriff, still unable to back down.

"The best thing you can do for Candace is to let us do our job. We can wait a few minutes for the warrant to get here, or with your permission, Deputy Cobb can complete her search."

Burt waved a hand in dismissal before turning his back and moving down the hall. "Go ahead and do what you have to do. You will anyway."

"Finish up in here, Deputy," McCoy murmured before leaving Mattie alone with Robo and her suspicions.

She went to the closet and stood on tiptoe, peering up into the shelf. At first glance, it seemed to be filled with mementos from the girl's past: stacks of board games, puzzles, and picture books. Deciding to remove the first layer, Mattie took out the stack of board games first. Placing the boxes on the floor, she opened the lid on the top one—Candyland. She didn't find what she'd expected. No playing board, no pieces, cards, or dice.

Instead, the box contained porn magazines and a cell phone.

Mattie sat back on her heels, taking it in before replacing the lid and setting the box aside. The other boxes from the shelf held no surprises—she simply found the games and puzzles that the labels declared. A thorough search of the books and other items on the shelf revealed nothing else unusual.

Stella reentered the room, pulling on a pair of gloves she'd taken out of her jacket pocket. "A neighbor came over to sit with Juanita. The sheriff made coffee, and he has Banks in the kitchen drinking it. Brody arrived with the warrant."

These succinct statements summed up the situation outside Candace's bedroom. To sum up the situation inside, Mattie opened the lid on the Candyland box, and Stella nodded as she took in the contents. Then Mattie went to the dresser, opened the drawer, and removed the peekaboo underwear.

When she held it up, Stella's eyes widened. "Good Lord," the detective muttered. "Candace seems a little young for stuff like that, but maybe not these days. I could be showing my age."

"Surprised me too." Mattie led her to the bulletin board, and this time she shared her thoughts. "These boys are in high school, much older than Candace."

"We need their names."

Mattie pointed to each one, stating the boy's name in turn.

"You already know them?"

"Remember, I run the drug intervention program at the high school. I know a lot of the kids there."

"Are these kids considered high risk for drugs?"

"Not that I'm aware of. Part of the jock crowd. All athletes."

"Fits the profile of someone with muscle carrying her uphill," Stella said.

"I suppose so."

"We'll need to interview them." Stella continued to examine the photos, pursing her lips, a sign that told Mattie she was deep in thought.

Mattie decided to give her something else to think about. "The family dynamic is off."

Stella nodded, saying, "Yeah," as she looked away from the photos and met Mattie's gaze.

"I suspect the father of molesting Candace."

Stella squinted. "What makes you say that?"

Mattie waved a hand around the room. "This evidence. Girls who've been molested often grow into promiscuous teens."

"We don't know if she's promiscuous yet."

"That's what it looks like."

"You might be overly sensitized to this subject," Stella said.

"Maybe that's not a bad thing."

Stella studied Mattie's face, and Mattie wondered what the detective was reading there. She arranged her features into a neutral mask.

"I'll take your suspicion into consideration," Stella said after a long moment. "I've already talked to Juanita. She's pissed at him for being drunk and for not being home with the kids. He works at the mine in Rigby and stops at a bar in Hightower on his way home. He's been drinking away a lot of his paycheck, and she's sick of raising the kids by herself and doing all the work to keep up the house. She didn't say one thing about suspecting him of abusing her children."

"She might be in denial. Or afraid to report."

Stella shrugged. "Could be. I'll think about it. For now, let's bag these things as evidence. I'll go through that cell phone back at the station. Juanita confirmed that Candace does carry a backpack. Have you found it yet?"

"No, but the only area I've searched thoroughly is the closet. Robo cleared the entire room for narcotics, but we still need to go through the rest of this stuff piece by piece to see what else we've got."

"Okay, let's get started."

★

The backpack didn't turn up during the rest of their search. Leaving the room with Robo at her side, Mattie followed Stella into the living room, where Juanita sat with the neighbor, a Hispanic woman with a round face and kind eyes. A few strands of silver highlighted her black hair at her temples, and Mattie guessed her to be around Juanita's age, early forties. Stella introduced her as Rosie Gonzales, and the lady acknowledged the introduction with a shy nod.

"We're finished in Candace's room for tonight, Juanita," Stella said, "but I'm going to tape it off and not let you in there to clean until I've had a chance to look at it again during daylight."

Juanita nodded slowly, as if she was barely able to move. Rosie reached toward her, and the two of them clasped hands. One tear trickled down Rosie's cheek, making a fluid track on her smooth skin. Mattie made a mental note to add this woman to their list of people to interview, thinking she would be a valuable source for providing insight into the family dynamics.

"We're going into the kitchen now to talk with the sheriff," Stella said. "Is there anything I can get for you?"

"No. Just tell me when I can see my baby." Juanita's breath caught.

"I'll see where we're at and then check back with you. It'll take a while, but we won't forget you."

Giving Mattie a glance, Stella walked through the living room and went into the kitchen. Mattie and Robo followed.

McCoy sat at the Formica-topped table with Burt, half-filled teal coffee mugs sitting in front of them. Burt had lost his belligerence, and without it, he appeared shrunken and bleary eyed. When Sheriff McCoy looked up at Stella, he gave her a nod, and a signal seemed to pass between them. Stella took a seat at the table.

Mattie didn't know if she should stay or go. She decided one of her colleagues would direct her to leave if they wanted to reassign her current duty, and since neither of them did, she stayed in the background, leaning against the kitchen wall. With a hand gesture, she directed Robo to sit beside her and he did, his pink tongue showing as he opened his mouth in a gentle pant. He shifted his gaze back and forth, keeping an eye on Burt while watching Mattie for a signal.

"Mr. Banks, we've finished searching Candace's room for tonight," Stella said. "I think you'll want to know that no drugs were found."

"I didn't think there would be any." Burt gave Stella a hard look.

"I'm glad that we can confirm that. You might already be familiar with the contents of Candace's room. Would you say so?"

He rolled his eyes. "God, no. The room's a pigsty. Juanita makes her keep the door shut. But I know my daughter, and she wouldn't be involved with drugs."

Stella nodded. "Do you venture in there to visit with her about her day and such?"

"Haven't been in that room for a long time."

Mattie didn't believe him.

"Tell me about Candace," Stella said.

Banks stretched his legs out under the table and eased back in his chair, putting one hand up to his chin. His lips turned downward and his eyes reddened. "She's a good girl. Helps her mother. Loves her dad."

"She helps around the house?" Stella asked.

"Watches her brothers, helps Juanita with the cooking."

"I know you work in Rigby, Mr. Banks. When do you get time to spend with your family?"

"Mostly time off between shifts."

"Do you drive back to Timber Creek every night?"

"I stay at the boarding house part of the time during the week. Come home when I have days off."

Shifts at the mine were long, often lasting up to ten days, and commuters came home during extended time off, which could be for four days or even more. Several old-fashioned boarding houses had sprung up in Rigby to accommodate the crew.

"So you have a day off tomorrow and can be here with your family," Stella said. "That's good."

Banks nodded, noncommittal, looking down at the mug that he fiddled with in his hands.

"That's a long drive to Rigby. How long does it take?"

"Varies. Depends on if you get behind a string of looky-loos on the pass. I figure an hour and a half."

"And today?"

He looked up and met Stella's gaze, a touch of belligerence returning to his posture and tone. "About that long. I stopped in Hightower. Told the sheriff about that already." He glanced at McCoy as if to confirm.

McCoy nodded at him, an expression of what might be construed as encouragement on his face, the look he used to keep a person talking.

"I stopped at a bar and probably had too much to drink." Burt's nose reddened and his eyes welled. He swiped at his nose with the back of his hand. "I shoulda been here instead."

At least that's something you and your wife could agree on, Mattie thought.

She didn't feel one bit sorry for him. People who shirked their parental responsibilities for the sake of alcohol would get little sympathy from her. Family should mean everything in the world to a person. It was a thing to be treasured.

"Which bar did you stop at?"

Burt's eyes narrowed. "The Hornet's Nest."

Stella used a sympathetic tone to keep him going. "And what time did you get home?"

"Don't know." Burt paused, scratching his chin lightly and looking thoughtful. "I got here about the same time as the wife. Didn't look at a clock. She was bent out of shape about Candace being gone and her inhaler being on the dresser. Upset way out of proportion."

Mattie squirmed in place against the wall, trying to contain her anger. *How can he belittle his wife's concern, considering the fact that his daughter was found dead?*

Looking up at her, Robo panted. Realizing that she was setting off his distress, she tried to relax. Her problem with claustrophobia kicked in, and she felt like the walls were closing in on her. She needed to get out of this room.

McCoy's cell phone vibrated. "Excuse me," he said, getting up from the table. He went to the door and stepped outside onto the porch, closing the door softly behind him. Mattie wished she could follow, but she wouldn't leave Stella alone with Banks and no one as backup.

"Tell me what you think might have happened to Candace, Mr. Banks," Stella said.

He stared at her for a long moment. "I have no freakin' idea. That's what I hope *you* can tell *me*."

"I can assure you, we'll do our best to find out."

The sheriff came back inside, drawing everyone's attention. "Do you need more time, Detective?"

"We're done with what we need to do here tonight."

"They've got Candace secure in the ambulance. We can take you and your wife to see her now."

"I'll tell Mrs. Banks," Stella said, rising from her chair.

Relieved that she could go outdoors, where she could breathe, Mattie straightened, Robo rising to stand beside her. Making eye contact, McCoy moved his head toward the door, indicating he wanted to talk to her outside.

"Wait here for Detective LoSasso, Mr. Banks. We'll leave momentarily," McCoy said and then stepped outside, leading the way. With Robo beside her at heel, Mattie followed him a short distance from the house toward where they'd parked their vehicles.

"What have you found?" McCoy asked quietly.

Mattie summed up the evidence they'd gathered.

"Good work. Go ahead and clock out now. We'll meet at the office at the regular time tomorrow."

"I thought I'd take Robo back on the hill to search for Candace's backpack."

McCoy paused, thinking it over. "It makes more sense to do that during daylight. It won't go anywhere tonight with the crime scene unit up there. I'll post Deputy Garcia there to keep an eye on things so we can go over the scene one more time in the morning before we release it. Detective LoSasso will go to the autopsy early. Once we know exactly what we're dealing with here, we'll form a plan."

Mattie hated to go home now. She felt an urgent need to be working, but McCoy was the boss. "All right. Call me back if you need me."

"You've already put in extra time, Deputy. Get some rest tonight. If we're dealing with a homicide, things will heat up during the next few days."

Stella stepped out onto the porch, followed by Candace's parents and Rosie Gonzales.

"Let's all go in my vehicle," McCoy said, hurrying to open the Grand Cherokee's back door.

Juanita, still huddled over, leaned on her friend as Rosie ushered her to the Jeep and helped her get inside. Stella moved to the other side to get into the back seat, leaving the front passenger seat for Burt.

As Mattie loaded Robo into his compartment, she realized she'd dodged a bullet by being released to go home. The absolute last thing she wanted to see tonight was Juanita's grief when she saw her dead child. She swallowed against the tightness in her throat and leaned forward to bury her face in Robo's fur.

Chapter 6

Wearing cozy sweats and woolen slippers, Cole turned off the television and padded toward the kitchen. The kids and Mrs. Gibbs had gone to their rooms hours ago. When he'd last checked, Sophie was sound asleep with Belle on the bed beside her, and Angie was finishing up her homework. He assumed that by now, she would be asleep too.

Mrs. Gibbs had brought her own television from her daughter's house in Denver, and she'd made it a habit to retire early to her room each evening. Cole suspected it was as much to allow him time to be alone with his kids as it was for her to have a break and some private time for herself.

The oak floor and spotless granite countertops gleamed when he flipped on the light. He hated to sully Mrs. Gibbs's territory, but he needed a snack before he turned in for the night, and besides, he'd learned that she didn't bat an eye at dishes left in the sink or footprints left on the floor. Though she kept the space clean, she never scolded him or the girls for living in it. In turn, he'd noticed they all pitched in and did their part to help out. Once again, he felt grateful for the gem he'd found as a housekeeper.

He opened the refrigerator door, leaning against it while he examined the leftovers. Before he could decide, his mind drifted to Mattie, and he stood staring at the food while cool air from inside the fridge washed over him.

He missed her. Last October, she'd rescued him from a killer who'd stalked him through the forest, and then she'd rescued him again when he had to tell the kids about it. She seemed to know the right way to explain the seriousness of his situation without terrifying them. Afterward, she'd visited his household often for dinner, and they'd all enjoyed it, even Mrs. Gibbs. But then, Mattie seemed to withdraw. Though she returned his phone calls, she made one excuse after another to decline his invitations. He'd given up after a while.

Maybe it was time to try again. He closed the refrigerator door, pulled his cell phone from his pocket, and texted: "If you're still awake, give me a call."

His cell phone rang just as he'd gone back to trying to decide what to eat. He checked caller ID.

"Hi, Mattie."

"You're up late."

It was good to hear her voice. "I was about to have a snack before bed and decided to call you. It's been a while since we checked in with each other."

"A snack sounds good. I think I missed dinner."

"Come over. We have a refrigerator full of food."

There was a long pause before she spoke. "I was just heading home from work. I've got Robo with me."

"Bring him along. You're working late."

Her breath released in a soft sigh, and when she spoke, she sounded tired. Or sad. Maybe both. "I need to talk to you anyway. It would be better in person."

"Sounds ominous."

"It's not good. I'm headed your way. Be there in a couple minutes."

"I'll meet you out front."

Cole went through the living room with the intention of turning on the porch light, but as he passed through, Bruno caught his eye. The Doberman had been stretched out on a dog cushion, sound asleep until Cole entered the room. Then he rolled to his chest and raised his beautifully sculpted head, with its long thin nose and mahogany markings. He pricked his black ears and stared at Cole, fully alert and waiting to see what his next move should be. Cole liked that about him—he didn't miss much and was always on guard, yet he'd fit into the family seamlessly.

"Let's go outside, Bruno." Cole flipped on the porch light and opened the front door.

Bruno scrambled to his feet and followed him onto the porch, going down the steps and ranging around the yard's perimeter at a trot. Cole figured he'd better let Bruno and Robo greet each other out here instead of inside, where their exuberant play would awaken the entire household. It interested him how the three big dogs—Belle, Bruno, and Robo—had instantly formed a pack; possibly because they were all young and had been well socialized as pups. Belle played the alpha role, while Bruno and Robo acted like two buffoons, racing each other and wrestling around in the grass as Belle looked on in disdain or, even more likely, completely ignored them.

Headlights pierced the darkness at the end of the lane and headed his way. Bruno alerted and stood like a statue at the edge of the yard, chuffing out a low bark and growling deep in his chest.

"It's okay." Cole moved down the steps and stood beside him. "That's just Mattie and Robo coming."

Maybe it was the magic word, "Robo," that made the difference, because Bruno stopped growling, though he remained at attention at the edge of the yard. As Mattie's SUV drew up and parked, he trotted in circles around it, obviously pleased by the arrival of these night visitors.

While Mattie set the brake on the car and turned off the engine, the porch light illuminated her vehicle enough to see Robo's dark silhouette moving back and forth in his compartment as he tried to keep track of his friend. Cole couldn't help but smile, both at the dogs and at his own eagerness to see Mattie. He felt like trotting out to her vehicle and circling around it in glee with Bruno.

But as soon as she got out of her SUV, he could see that something was wrong. Though the light from the porch was dim here at the edge of the yard, it lit the expression on her face enough to see that it was set in a tight, grim frown.

She's come here with bad news. Again.

As predicted, Robo and Bruno raced around the yard while Mattie walked toward him, her manner subdued. "Hi," she said.

"It's good to see you, Mattie." He found himself moving toward her with open arms, and she walked into his hug like it was the most natural thing in the world. But something had changed in the past few months. She felt slight in his arms, fragile. Nothing of the solid strength he was used to.

When she pulled away, he took a step back to examine her face, and alarm rattled him deep inside. Mattie looked beyond tired. Fatigue etched lines around her eyes, and they sent him back to the day Olivia had left him. She'd worn the same soul-weary expression.

"You've had a bad day," Cole said, taking her arm and leading her toward the porch. "Let's go inside and get you some food."

"I'm not sure I can eat yet." Mattie allowed him to guide her up onto the porch before stopping. "Let's let the dogs play for a few minutes while I tell you what's happened. You need to know."

Robo and Bruno growled in play as they chased each other around the yard.

"What is it?"

"Do you know the Banks family?"

Cole thought for a few moments. "No, can't say as I do."

Mattie breathed a sigh; it sounded like one of relief. "We found their daughter this evening, Candace Banks, dead up on Smoker's Hill."

"Good grief, Mattie!"

"It's going to be announced at school tomorrow. I wanted you and the kids to hear it from me, because I think one of her brothers might be Sophie's age or close to it. She probably knows him. Might even know Candace."

Cole felt a blow to his midsection. His girls were just beginning to recover from their losses this past year, and now this. "Do you know yet how she died?"

"We don't. Autopsy in the morning."

Cole could tell she was torn up about it. He slipped an arm around her, pulling her against his side to offer comfort. She was shorter than he, and she tipped her head to rest it against his chest as she stood in the shelter of his arm.

"I'll ask Sophie in the morning if she knows Candace or her brother and then take it from there. I appreciate you giving me a heads-up."

He felt her nod before she moved away.

"Maybe I'd better take Robo home now," she said. "He missed his dinner."

"And you said you did too. Are you still feeding him the same food as the last time he ate here?"

"Yeah, haven't changed it."

"I've got food for both of you then. Come inside." Cole moved toward the door.

Mattie hesitated, but then she followed. "All right." She turned and spoke to Robo in a quiet but firm tone. "Robo, come."

Robo trotted her way with Bruno galumphing along behind.

"These guys turn into clowns when they're together," Cole observed, trying to lighten Mattie's mood and knowing that a reference to the dogs was probably his best bet.

And he was right. She smiled. His heart felt instantly lighter too.

"They do. They're like a couple of boys let out of school," she said.

"Okay, boys. Settle down," Cole said to the dogs. "Everyone's asleep inside," he said to Mattie.

"Robo, heel," she said, and Robo fell into line, making Bruno settle down too.

They all filed into the house in an orderly fashion, with Cole leading them into the kitchen. He headed to the pantry, where the dog food was kept, and began to fill an extra dog bowl with food. "Go ahead and look in the fridge, Mattie. Anything is fair game."

After Cole set out food for Robo, Bruno went to his own dish to clean up what he'd left there earlier. Mattie had taken out leftover chicken from dinner, some potato salad, and a green Jell-O concoction that had pineapple and little marshmallows in it. Cole went to the cabinet to get dishes.

"Bruno and I already ate, but it looks like we're both going to eat again to keep you two company."

Mattie smiled at him, and he could see that the smile didn't quite reach her eyes. He also noticed the gray shadows that circled them.

"Better than eating alone," she said. "Mama T always said that little piggies eat better when there are more at the trough."

After filling their plates and sitting down at the table, they both dug in, eating in silence for a few moments. She seemed to have an appetite, and he was glad to see it.

After she'd had a chance to eat most of her food, he spoke. "We've missed you."

She looked down at her plate instead of at him. "Same here. How are the girls doing?"

"Better. I was just thinking tonight how well things seem to be going for both of them. We're at an only-as-needed stage with our counseling."

This time the smile reached her eyes. "That's wonderful. Good news to hear tonight."

"How about you, Mattie? How are you doing?"

The smile faltered, although he could see she was putting on a brave face. "I'm doing fine—that is, until this evening."

Her left hand was lying loosely on the table, and he covered it with one of his. "Are you really doing okay?"

She glanced at him sharply before looking at her empty plate. "I've been working on things," she said with hesitation, "but I'm all right . . . really."

She withdrew her hand to reach for her water glass. He noticed a slight tremble in her fingers.

Angie's voice came from behind him. "I thought I'd find Dad in here raiding the fridge, but I didn't know you'd be here too, Mattie."

Joy filled Mattie's face as she rose from her seat. Cole turned in his chair to watch her cross the room to give his daughter a hug. A part of him acknowledged that he wished she'd greeted him with that amount of pleasure.

"It's good to see you, Angie," Mattie said.

"You too. Why haven't you been at school lately?"

The two parted, and Angie moved to the cabinet to get a small bowl, placing it on the countertop. Robo trotted over to greet her, and she bent to pet him.

"I've been there," Mattie said. "We're doing a freshman rotation with the program, so our paths haven't crossed."

Angie filled the bowl with Jell-O. "I've been working on the yearbook. We need to get some shots of you and Robo at school."

Mattie grinned. "Oh, wow. Are you sure?"

"Of course. We'll put it in the section with the rest of the school programs."

Mattie looked at Cole. "I never thought I'd be in the yearbook again."

"Maybe we could mention that you're an alumni," Angie said.

Alumna, Cole thought, but he didn't correct her. "What a great idea."

After Angie joined him at the table and Mattie took her seat, they chatted a little bit more about the yearbook, and then he decided to break the news about Candace Banks's death. He wanted to see how much impact it had on Angela and what he was going to have to deal with.

"Angel, do you know Candace Banks?" he asked.

"I know who she is."

"Is she one of your friends?"

Angie gave him one of those looks of hers. "Uh . . . no, Dad. Candace is in junior high."

Of course . . . how could I even think that someone in high school might be friends with someone from the junior high? "How well do you know her?"

"I know of her. She's got quite the reputation."

"What do you mean?" Cole asked.

Angie gave him a sideways look before glancing at Mattie, who sat quietly, looking down at the table, fiddling with a spoon. "I don't think I should say. You'll freak out."

"Oh, come on, Angel. You should know me better than that."

Angie gave him a skeptical look before explaining. "She's got a reputation with the guys. They talk about her a lot, brag about making a 'Banks deposit.'"

Cole jolted upright when her meaning hit him. "Good God!"

Angie slid a look toward Mattie. "Told you he'd freak out."

Mattie lifted her face from where she'd been examining her plate, giving Angie a slight nod before looking at Cole with sadness.

Angie must have caught Mattie's expression, because hers became wary. "Why are you asking about Candace, Dad?"

"Candace was found dead this evening. Behind the high school."

"Oh, my gosh! Did someone kill her?"

Mattie shook her head. "We don't know yet. I don't want you to jump to that conclusion."

Why wouldn't she? There'd already been others killed in Timber Creek, others with even closer ties to his daughter. "Her death will be announced at school tomorrow, so I wanted you to have advance warning. And Sophie might know Candace's brothers. Mattie says they're closer to her age."

Angie met his gaze. "Poor Soph. We have to tell her in the morning, Dad. She'll just have to deal with it."

Cole realized that Angie's teenage wisdom best described what they all were going to have to do. Deal with it. It seemed like that's what his life was all about of late.

Mattie sighed, rose from the table, and carried her dishes over to load in the dishwasher. "Thanks for dinner. I hate to eat and run, but I'm beat, and I have to be at work early in the morning."

After saying good night to Angie, Cole walked Mattie to the door, opening it for her and following her onto the front porch. He was worried about her. She looked thin, haunted, and worn out. Whatever was bothering her had to go back further than this afternoon's terrible experience of finding the body of a dead child. He'd ignored these signs with Olivia; he didn't want to make that mistake again with someone else important to him.

He touched her forearm. "Mattie, wait."

She paused and turned to look up at him, the porch light illuminating her features. Robo trotted into the yard and started sniffing the flower beds.

"I feel like something's wrong. I mean something other than Candace. Are you all right?"

She broke eye contact and turned to watch Robo. "I'm just tired."

"It looks like more than that. Like something's been eating away at you."

"I'll be all right. I just need a good night's sleep." She stepped off the porch, leaving him to drift behind in her wake. "Don't worry."

He grasped her arm to stop her. "It looks like something's bothering you. I don't know. I don't have a very good track record with this kind of thing, but I feel like it's more than just needing a good night's sleep."

She turned to him again with a half smile on her lips. "I look that bad, huh?"

"Of course not. You look as good as ever. It's just that . . . Well, if you need to talk, I'm here for you." He realized that although he wanted to express his feelings, he wasn't quite sure what they were. "The kids and I really care about you, Mattie. I don't want you to be unhappy, and if there's anything I can do to make things better for you, I want to try."

"It's something I need to deal with on my own. Things will get better eventually. Right now though, I've got to go home. Robo, come on!"

After she put Robo in the back, Cole opened the car door for her. It felt like she was drawing away, and he didn't know how to stop it. She scooted into her seat, and he clasped her hand as it lay on the steering wheel. "I hope you'll come over to see us again soon."

She tried to release his grip, but he wouldn't let her put him off. A frown crossed her brow as if she'd grown irritated. "I'll be tied up with this investigation."

That felt like a dismissal, and he let go and stepped back. "Stop by whenever you can. You're always welcome."

She started her engine as she spoke. "Thanks. Say hi to Sophie and Mrs. Gibbs for me."

He nodded and closed the car door, stepping back while keeping his eyes on her. He raised his hand to wave, but she didn't look up as she reversed her car and drove away. It left him unsettled. Lonely.

Strange how seeing her again stirred up these feelings. It was easy to go his own way, focused on family and work, and let the days go by without seeing someone who meant so much. He knew he missed her, but he didn't realize how long it had been until she was standing there in the flesh, looking so different.

How do I feel about Mattie?

He respected her. She'd had a rough childhood, but she valued family and justice like he did. And she seemed to love his kids. That was important. And they had other things in common, like the way they loved animals, valued safety in their home and community, and had respect for others.

Quit the analysis and figure out how you feel.

Sheesh, counseling could come back and bite you in the butt. Okay, he liked her a lot, and he thought she cared for him too.

He wouldn't let her pull away. Not unless he knew for a fact that she didn't want to have anything to do with him anymore.

★

Mattie drove home with her mind in a whirl. While it had been good—wonderful, in fact—to see the two Walkers again, being near Cole, getting to be close enough to feel his warmth and receive his generous hugs, made her chest ache. Last fall, she'd realized that she loved him, but being around him and his kids through the Christmas season had taught her something very important.

Cole still loved his ex-wife.

Although that wasn't the sole reason she'd pulled away, it was a large part of it. The other part was the fact that she needed some time and space to work through the shitstorm that her father had left inside her. She longed to be with Cole and his children in the worst way but didn't see how it was possible under the circumstances.

Poor Candace. Had her father caused the same turbulence and distorted worldview inside her? Mattie felt certain that he had. And if so, had it somehow contributed to her death?

She parked outside in the darkness in front of her home, wishing she'd left the porch light on for herself. Feeling hollow, she turned to Robo, and he moved forward so that she could pet him. An all-consuming sadness descended upon her as she thought of Juanita Banks, who grieved the loss of her only daughter, and she wondered about her own mother, who'd willingly left *her* only daughter behind.

She swiped at her eyes and fought back tears as she popped open Robo's cage to let him exit out the front with her. She wouldn't let herself be distracted by her own garbage; she and the others had a case to solve.

Chapter 7

Wednesday

Cole's assistant entered the clinic with her usual greeting. "Hi, hi."

Sitting at the computer, Cole glanced up and then settled back in his chair to take in her new hairdo. Typically, Tess had unnaturally red hair, which she wore cut short and gelled up into small spikes, but today she had something new going on. Blue tips. A base of red with blue spikes. She looked like a walking ad for Independence Day.

"Hey," Cole said with hesitation. He didn't know if he should mention her hair or not.

"Do you like my new 'do?"

"It's colorful."

Tess gave him a patronizing smile, sort of like the one Angie had perfected. "Tom doesn't like it either."

Tom being her husband. "I didn't say I didn't like it."

"Hmm . . . Didn't need to." She took off her jacket and hung it up on one of the wall hooks. "Do we have a big morning scheduled?"

Cole got up from the computer so that she could have her seat. "Not too bad. Just routine office stuff. No surgeries today, but we need to get some instrument packs set up and sterilized if you can get to it."

"I'm on it."

The first clients of the day entered, and Cole escorted the couple and their dog through the swinging door into the treatment room. The phone was ringing as he left the lobby.

When he finished giving the dog its vaccinations and called his next client in, Tess signaled that she wanted to talk to him at the pass-through. He excused himself and met her there.

"Gus Tilley just called and scheduled an appointment to have you preg check his mare. He was already in town, so I worked him in next. I juggled your schedule a bit to do it."

Cole frowned. "I saw his dog last night. He called me after he'd arrived in town then too. I'll have to talk to him about calling first before he makes the drive for routine appointments."

"I'll take care of it."

"Explain to him that we might have been out of the office, and he would have wasted his time trailering his horse into town."

"Okay. I never would have thought of that," she said, giving him one of her sassy grins before turning away.

Cole realized he'd been micromanaging again. Tess would break him of that habit someday, although it was a bad one and she hadn't yet succeeded, even after all these years.

He finished up with his cat client, went through the kennel room to the back door, and let himself into the horse treatment area. He heaved the rolling door open to the outside and found Gus Tilley waiting with a short, stout, Quarter Horse mare. Cole remembered her. Sorrel in color, white star on the forehead, went by the name Lucy.

Gus glanced up at him before hanging his head and slapping the end of the mare's lead rope gently against his thigh, looking like a man who'd been well chastised.

Cole hoped Tess hadn't been too harsh. "Hi, Gus. Bring her on in."

"Sorry, Doc. Didn't know you were so busy today."

"No problem. I just don't want you to make that drive sometime when we can't work you in."

"My phone's out. I've been using the phone at the gas station at the edge of town."

"Oh, no! Will they get out there to fix it for you soon?"

Gus hung his head, looking embarrassed. "I must've forgot to pay the bill."

Cole wondered if he was having money trouble and decided to drop the whole thing. He unlatched the endbar of the stocks and swung both it and the sidebar wide open. "Go ahead and lead her in here."

Gus led the mare slowly into the metal stanchion, and Cole closed it so that she was standing inside the sturdy rectangle that would hold her still while he worked on her. He took the lead rope from Gus and tied the mare's head to the front for extra security.

Gus was still looking ill at ease, so Cole opted for levity in an attempt to make him feel better. "I have a rule here at the clinic. No one should get hurt while we work on the animals," he said, going on with a grin, "especially not me."

Gus nodded while alarm touched his face.

Attempt failed. "Just kidding, Gus. Lucy's never given us any problems before."

Cole took his portable ultrasound machine out of the storage cabinet against the wall and began to set it up on a stainless-steel table beside the stocks. "How's Dodger's ear this morning?"

"Better, Doc. Thanks for seeing him last night."

"He must've had something in his ear and then scratched it out. Sounds like we're on the right course with him."

The machine set up, Cole put on a long plastic glove called a sleeve that covered his entire left arm. After squirting lubricant on it, he began the procedure to clear the mare's lower bowel of fecal matter. Once the bowel was clear, he flipped on the machine and gently inserted the transmitter, guiding it up to a place that was directly above the mare's uterus. He watched his progress on the ultrasound screen and paused when he reached the right place.

The uterus looked perfectly normal for an open mare. No pregnancy.

"I'm afraid she's not pregnant, Gus. See here on the screen. This is the uterus, and there's nothing here to indicate a pregnancy."

Gus stared at the screen and crossed his arms, noncommittal.

Cole finished up the procedure, taking a couple screen shots and printing them out, one for his records and one to send home with Gus.

He removed the transmitter, cleaned it, and then stripped off the soiled sleeve, throwing it into the trash. "How long ago was this mare bred, Gus?"

"I don't know."

"A week, two weeks, a month?"

"I don't reckon I know when she was bred."

That was a strange answer. "We can see a pregnancy at about twelve to fifteen days on an ultrasound. Was she with a stallion at least two weeks ago?"

Gus shook his head and looked down at the floor. "Not that I know of."

"More recent?"

"I don't think so."

Gus looked up at him briefly before sliding his gaze off sideways. In that second, Cole sensed confusion mixed with a hint of suspicion in his client's eyes. Did Gus think he was lying to him?

Cole handed him the ultrasound photo and pointed out landmarks while he explained. "Here's a picture of her uterus. When a mare is pregnant, we see a dark spot inside here where the embryo implants. There's nothing like that here. She's open."

Gus took the photo and stared at it.

Cole had another thought. "Did you have this mare artificially inseminated?"

"Nope. Not by my choice."

He waited, but Gus seemed to have no further explanation. "You can keep that," he said when Gus started to hand the picture back to him. "Why did you think the mare could be pregnant?"

Gus folded the picture slowly and put it in his shirt pocket. "The way she looks."

"How's that?"

"She's gettin' pretty big through the belly."

Cole studied the mare. The sorrel horse stood about fifteen hands, maybe less, built short and sturdy. Her stout neck and full hip, as well as her torso, showed that she'd packed on some extra pounds. "She's gained some weight over the winter. Have you been giving her grain?"

"Yeah."

"You might eliminate that and just stick to grass hay. Be careful if you turn her out to grass this spring. We don't want her to founder."

Gus couldn't have looked more alarmed if Cole had told him the mare had sprouted two heads. "Don't want that. I . . . I'll keep her in the corral."

Surprised at the man's reaction, Cole wondered if he'd been too blunt. Perhaps he should try harder to explain. "What I'm saying is, she's carrying some extra weight, so she might be at risk to founder if she goes out and eats all the lush green grass she can find. You can help her out by not feeding her grain now and sticking to grass hay, just a flake in the morning and evening. We can take some weight off her now so she's ready for pasture later. But when you turn her out onto grass, just let her out for an hour at first. Limit her time on pasture so she doesn't get an overload. That's what causes the founder."

Gus seemed to be paying strict attention, hanging onto Cole's every word and nodding. "Okay, Doc. I'll take care of her."

The discussion about foundering aside, Cole felt more confused by the minute. Surely Gus knew what caused an animal to get pregnant. And the man seemed overly sensitive to whatever he tried to tell him. He didn't know what else to say, and his next client would be waiting by now, so he decided to wrap things up.

"Let me know if you have any more concerns or questions, but I'm sure she'll be fine. She's a stout, healthy mare. An easy keeper, right?" He crossed over to the mare, flipped up the latch on the stocks, and started backing her out. The gentle mare moved slowly and steadily backward and out the door.

Cole handed the lead rope to Gus, their earlier conversation about the disconnected phone line on his mind. "Do you want to pay for this next month, Gus? We can run an account and bill you if you want."

Gus looked offended. "I can pay my bill today."

"All right. Just wondered, with the charges last night for Dodger and all." Cole offered a handshake to say good-bye. "Call me if you need me. Once you get her loaded, come back inside and settle up with Tess."

At hearing Tess's name, Cole noticed the man's face flush before he turned to lead the horse away and then hurried to pack up the ultrasound machine so he could get to his next appointment. He didn't know much about Gus. He looked to be about fifty-something. Didn't know if he'd once been married or if he'd always been single. He seemed uncomfortable around others, but more so now than in the past.

For some reason, Gus had changed.

Chapter 8

Mattie's radio crackled before the dispatcher, Rainbow Sanderson, spoke. "K-9 One, copy?"

Mattie keyed on the transmitter and responded with her location. "Timber Creek High. Go ahead."

"Return to the station at your earliest convenience."

"Copy that."

She placed the transmitter back in its cradle and turned the key to start the Explorer, bringing the engine to life. She and Robo had completed a thorough search of Smoker's Hill, but all they found was trash. No backpack. She believed whoever had been with Candace at the time of her death must have taken it. Still, she had lots to show for their efforts—she'd bagged everything outside the environmental norm that Robo indicated. Even if there was nothing inside the bag that was useful as evidence, she and Robo had at least done a thorough cleaning of the area.

A squeak came from Robo in his compartment, and she glanced at the rearview mirror to check on him. His pink tongue curled while he finished his yawn, making her fight one of her own. But then she decided, *What the heck?* Her ears popped while she allowed herself the widest yawn possible.

After spending time with Cole and Angela, it had been a short night. She hated to admit it, but having something to concentrate on at work helped keep her head straight, and she'd slept better the few hours she spent in bed than she had in days. She'd taken Robo out for his morning run, and they'd both seemed sharp and at the top of their game during their search, though perhaps a little sleepy now that the job was finished.

The call to come back to the station meant that Stella had arrived and would have news about the autopsy. Mattie turned onto Main and cruised slowly to the station, noting that all was quiet in town with the kids in school and very few patrons at the scattered shops.

Several cars and pickups were parked at the Watering Hole, representing the early lunch crowd at the local bar and grill. She studied the vehicles, looking for anything different that caught her eye, anything off. After Candace's death, she needed to be hypervigilant.

As she drove past, she noticed four men who were opening doors to a silver SUV parked diagonally at the curb. They were all dressed in neutral-colored outdoor gear, khakis and greens, with warm caps pulled low on their heads. They looked like hunters—only it wasn't hunting season. And another thing caught her attention. As if choreographed, they all averted their faces and hurried to enter their vehicle as she drove by. Taking shelter? It was enough to make Mattie take a mental note of the license plate number, a reflexive response.

If she hadn't been headed to a meet at the station, she might have turned around and followed them out of town, just to see which way they were headed. But under the circumstances, she jotted down the license plate number on a pad she kept affixed to her dashboard, tore off the page, and stuffed it into her shirt pocket. She'd ask Rainbow to look up the plate and make sure the vehicle wasn't listed as stolen.

She parked beside Stella's silver Honda and unloaded Robo. He walked sedately beside her at heel, evidently having had enough exercise this morning to make him well behaved for the rest of the day. When she entered the building, Rainbow lifted a hand in a gesture to wait while she finished up a phone call.

The dispatcher looked resplendent in a gauzy lined tunic of tie-dyed design, featuring all the colors in her namesake, worn over black leggings. She'd gathered her blond hair up onto the crown of her head and secured the tresses with what looked like a pair of chopsticks.

"How are you doing?" Rainbow asked as she disconnected her caller.

"Okay. You?"

Rainbow wore a concerned expression. "That's awful about Candace Banks. Thank goodness Robo found her, or she might still be up on the hill. Or worse yet, one of the kids from school would have stumbled across her." At the sound of his name, Robo pushed forward to fawn against her while she patted and stroked him, and she continued talking in sweet baby talk. "You're such a good boy, aren't you, Robo? Such a good boy."

Mattie could tell the baby talk was getting him too excited. *Worse than a kid.* "Okay, Robo, that's enough. You and Rainbow can play after hours. Right now, you're on duty."

She settled her dog at heel as she drew the scrap of paper from her pocket. "Could you look up this plate while I'm in the meeting and make sure this vehicle isn't stolen? Interrupt me if it is."

"Sure," Rainbow said as she took the note.

Mattie started to leave but then stopped for a moment. "Do you know the Banks family, Rainbow?"

"No, not really. But I've met the mom, Juanita, at Rancher's Supply Feeds, where I buy grain for Miss Nanny."

Her goat. Rainbow lived out west of town, where she rented a cabin beside the creek and kept a few animals for pets. "Met her how?"

"Oh, she works there."

"Has she worked there a while?"

"Yeah, I'd say a year or two."

"Did you ever get into a conversation with her about anything personal?"

Rainbow paused, a furrow on her brow. "Not really. Maybe she asked me about my animals, but I don't remember her saying anything about herself."

"So you never met Candace?"

Sadness crossed her face. "No, I didn't."

"Okay. Well, I better get into the meeting."

"Wait, I almost forgot." Rainbow ducked down to peer under her desk, drawing out a paper bag. "I made some zucchini bread last night, and it's absolutely divine. The best recipe I ever made. I brought this for you, and don't give it to any of the others, okay? Have some at lunch and let me know what you think?"

Rainbow had been trying to tempt her with all kinds of foods, brought to work or to her home. Mattie knew that her friend worried about her weight loss because they'd already tangled over it. She'd told Rainbow she didn't like people worrying about her and to quit asking her if anything was wrong. This had resulted in a long string of goodie gifts that Mattie ended up giving to Mama T, since for the most part, she didn't feel like eating.

"Thanks, but you shouldn't be bringing me food all the time."

"Never mind about that. Just tell me what you think of it. You can be my taste tester."

Mattie had to give her friend credit—she was getting very creative with her efforts to conceal her motives. She hurried into the staff office to leave the bag on her desk and then went to the briefing room. As she entered, she encountered a familiar sight. The dry-erase board had been wheeled to the center of the room, and Stella was writing on it while Brody and the sheriff sat at a table in front.

"Deputy," McCoy greeted her before turning his attention back to Stella.

Brody's back was toward her, his broad shoulders straining the fabric of his khaki shirt. She crossed between the Formica-topped tables and took a seat beside him. Robo circled and lay down at her feet.

Brody rolled his shoulders and leaned his head from side to side, stretching his neck and setting off muffled pops as his bones cracked, a familiar noise. Brody was wound pretty tight.

"We're setting up the grid, Mattie," Stella said while she continued to write. Fatigue showed in the detective's eyes, and Mattie wondered if she'd worked the case most of the night.

The name "Candace Banks" had been written at the top of the board, and an enlarged photo of the teen was taped next to her name. It looked like a recent school photo, and Mattie took in the happy brown eyes, walnut-colored curls, and confident grin. The child's happiness made her sad. Candace didn't look like a troubled child, at least not in this photo.

Starting on the left, Stella had written "Evidence" and listed several things: "Tire-tread print beside Highway 12—B. F. Goodrich/ TKO (common brand for trucks and SUVs)"; "Boot prints—around size ten/smooth sole"; "Photos with HS friends"; "Clothing from room"; "Magazines"; "Cell phone."

"We'll add in the cap you found on the escape route here too. Just in case it turns out to belong to our killer." Stella added it to the list. "We've discussed the things we found in Candace's room and your theory about them prior to your arrival, Mattie. The clothing and magazines might not be evidence. If we find that these items have nothing to do with our victim's death, I'll eliminate them for the sake of keeping the information confidential. For now though, everything should be considered."

Mattie nodded, turning over the information in her mind. She decided to tell the others what she'd learned from Angela. "I spoke to a high school student last night. Unfortunately, Candace had a bad reputation, and if rumors are true, boys from the high school have been taking advantage of her."

"I've found evidence on the cell phone to support that as well." Stella tipped her head at Mattie as if conceding the point. "Do you have anything to add from your search this morning?"

"Robo pointed out lots of stuff on the hill, but I think it's probably all litter. I've bagged it, if you want the CSU techs to go through it."

"Still no backpack?"

"Right."

"I'll add 'Missing backpack' here. It could be important if we find it. We'll talk about the autopsy and then go back to the cell phone." Stella wrote "Autopsy" to the right of "Evidence" and started a new list. "Cause of death: asphyxiation from a severe asthma attack. Doc McGinnis was right on the money with that theory last night. But there's enough evidence from the autopsy that we're classifying the manner of death as a homicide."

Stella finished writing "MOD: Homicide" on the board. She continued to list items as she spoke. "This evidence includes burlap fibers in the victim's airway and on her clothing. Brings to mind something like a burlap sack. The ME was leaning a bit toward classifying this as an accidental death, because he thought it might have just been some kids horsing around. You know . . . someone putting a bag over Candace's head in play. But combined with other things found, he decided to go with homicide."

"Other things?" McCoy asked.

"Bruising on her arms in a pattern that would suggest someone held onto them by gripping tightly. Bruising and contusions on her torso consistent with her falling onto the rocky ground. Broken fingernails suggesting she fought. Scrapings from under her fingernails that included skin cells that we'll send to the lab for DNA."

Stella paused while they took it all in. "Someone held that bag in place while she fought for her life."

Mattie conjured the scene in her mind. Candace, fighting someone bigger and more powerful until the results of the asthma attack overtook her and she collapsed, unable to breathe. Mattie suppressed a shiver.

"The feed store," she said.

Stella gave her a sharp look. "What about it?"

It surprised Mattie when Brody answered before she could.

"Juanita Banks works at Rancher's Supply Feeds, where they sell livestock feed and grain in burlap bags. She also cleans rooms at the Blue Sky Motel."

Brody was good at finding out things about people.

Stella turned to the board and wrote "Interview" on the far right. Skipping down a space, she wrote "Rancher's Supply Feeds/ Juanita Banks." She turned and scanned their faces. "What do you make of that?" she asked, inviting opinions.

"Could be purely coincidence, but it's a definite connection," McCoy said.

Brody shifted in his seat. "Can you imagine the number of people around here who buy feed at that store and have a stack of burlap bags in their sheds?"

Mattie thought the number would be in the high hundreds. Still, it might be worth looking at.

Stella nodded thoughtfully. "Mattie, could you go to the feed store and try to get a handle on that?"

"Yes."

"Okay. Now let's talk about the evidence from the cell phone. It leads us to some people of highest priority." She wrote "Cell Phone Leads" in the space she'd left at the top of the list. "I'm keeping names of the kids from the cell phone off the board, since we're dealing with minors here. Mattie already knows these kids, which is good, because we're going to have to interview several of them. I'd like you to do that with me." Stella looked at her.

"All right."

"I'll sum up the bulk of the text messages by telling you there was a lot of sexting going on with that phone. Naughty talk, pictures of body parts. Candace was evidently using the porn magazines as examples for creative posing. The boys used code names, but we've been able to match up phone numbers with real names. Actually, in all cases, the accounts were set up by their parents. They should be real happy to learn how their youngsters are using the cell phones they've been paying for."

"No different than the fancy cars they buy for them," Brody muttered, grumbling. Mattie had to agree with him; kids and their cars kept Garcia, the night deputy, hopping during his shift, especially on weekends.

"The best leads we found on the cell phone were the appointments that Candace scheduled with the boys," Stella continued, "which brings me to the best one of all. She had an appointment with one boy in particular at 3:30 yesterday, up on Smoker's Hill. You'd already given me his name, Mattie."

Stella placed the photo with the boy posing alone with Candace on the table. "Brooks Waverly. What can you tell us about him?"

"He's the football team quarterback," Mattie said. "High school senior, runs with the jocks. He's the son of a cattle rancher and lives west of town about ten miles."

"Any juvenile violations?" McCoy asked.

"None that I know of." Mattie looked at Brody for confirmation.

"Nope," he said. "He's golden."

Mattie knew Brody meant that the kid not only had a clean record but was a golden boy in the eyes of the school and probably in the eyes of his parents.

Stella evidently was thinking along the same lines. "Well, he won't be so golden later today. He's our top priority, but I want to bring in these other two boys as well." She placed the photo with Candace sandwiched between the two boys on the table. "Casey Rhodes and Joshua Barnaby. They were setting up appointments with her a few weeks ago. What about these guys, Mattie?"

"Both on the football team with Waverly. Rhodes lives here in town, but I'm not sure where Barnaby lives."

"He's here in town," Brody said.

Mattie nodded. "These kids do their share of roughhousing after school and driving around town, but as far as I know, none of them have ever been in any real trouble."

"There might be a speeding ticket on Barnaby," Brody said, "but I'd have to look it up."

Stella paused, lips pursed. Then she looked at McCoy. "I think it's best if we call the parents and have them bring these kids in to interview. Schedule them one by one. Would you agree?"

McCoy was already nodding. "Since they're minors, we have to question them with a parent present. If we do it that way, we accomplish two things—notify parents of this behavior and interview the young men at the same time."

"I'll get right on it; schedule the interviews for this afternoon. Let's take them out of school," Stella said. "Show them and their parents this is serious. We'll finish this up so I can get on it."

Stella turned and wrote "Burt Banks" on the board below the word "Interviews." "Since we've gained enough evidence to verify

Mattie's suspicions about promiscuity, I think we have to lean on the victim's father. Especially since we know he has access to burlap through his wife's employment."

"What would be his motive?" Brody asked.

"If he's been molesting his daughter, he wouldn't want her to talk. She's seeking new friends, becoming sexually active with others. Jealousy," Mattie said.

"He was dodging something when I questioned him about his alibi last night," Stella said. "Brody, could you check out his alibi for us? See if anyone can confirm his presence at the Hornet's Nest in Hightower, and if so, the time he arrived and departed?"

"Sure."

"Anything else for now?" Stella asked, waiting for a moment before continuing. "All right, let's get to work."

Chairs screeched as they pushed back and stood up from the table. The autopsy results made Mattie heartsick; here they were, dealing with another murdered child. Robo came with her as she strode to the door. They had an assignment to do, and it was time to get started.

Chapter 9

Mattie pulled up in front of the feed store, a small white clapboard building on the highway. Anchored to the roof was a hand-painted sign in yellow and black that read, "Rancher's Supply Feeds." The temperature was mild, so she rolled down her windows and left Robo in the back. This would take only a few minutes.

A bell over the door jingled as she stepped inside, and immediately the thick, sweet scent of grain mixed with sorghum assailed her. Right inside the door, baby chicks, peeping like mad and looking like tiny balls of yellow fluff, scurried around inside a large cardboard box with a heat lamp hanging over it. Mattie scanned the room quickly, taking in the colorful paper bags of livestock feed stacked at the front, the larger burlap bags of feed stashed at the back.

A young man wearing a dusty green canvas apron came from a back room. He stood about six foot three, as tall as the sheriff, but that's where the similarity ended. While the sheriff was built like a fullback, this kid—probably in his early twenties—was thin as a rail. It looked like a stiff wind could pick him up and blow him away. "Can I help you?" he asked.

"You can. I have some questions about your feed."

The kid had earnest brown eyes, longish dark hair, and had managed to grow a scruffy beard. "I'll try to answer them. The owner left for lunch, but he'll be back around one."

"And who's the owner?"

"Moses Randall."

"And your name is?"

"I'm Jed. Jed Franklin."

When Mattie shook the hand that he offered, she noticed he had a firm grip and his fingers were bony. "I see you have feed in both paper sacks and burlap bags. What's the difference?"

He led her down the aisle to show her the different types of feed. "The difference is mostly in whether you want to buy in bulk or not. Most of this stuff comes in the smaller paper bags, or you can buy the larger size that comes in burlap. We've got feed here for chickens and other fowl, pigs, goats, cattle, and horses." The paper bags rustled as he tapped them. "What are you looking for?"

"What kind of feed comes in the larger size?" Mattie moved toward the stacks of burlap bags, which looked full and heavy. When she ran her fingers over it, the burlap felt coarse and scratchy, bringing the abrasions on Candace's face to mind, and dust from the grain inside the bag filtered through the weave of the fabric. One of these dirty bags could definitely cause an allergy attack for someone as susceptible as Candace.

"Cattle and horse feed come in the larger size. Some of the pig feed too," Jed replied. "Is that what you're looking for?"

Mattie could tell he thought he was going to make a sale. "How many of these large sacks of feed do you sell each day?"

"Oh . . . it varies. Some days, none. Some days, a rancher comes in and we load up the bed in his pickup." The kid tried again. "What type of feed do you want? Horse?"

"That's what you said comes in the larger bags, right? Feed for horses, cattle, and pigs. So it's mostly ranchers and farmers that buy the large size?"

He seemed to finally get it that she wasn't here as a customer and it was information she was shopping for. "Pretty much. Town folks need the chicken feed, a few keep goats. The folks living outside of town are usually the ones that buy in bulk."

Outside of town, like Brooks Waverly's family.

"Tell me, does Mr. Waverly buy his feed here?"

"He does. He buys feed for both cattle and horses."

She realized it might have been fortuitous that the owner had left for lunch, because this kid didn't seem at all reticent to talk. "I suppose you keep records of who your customers are."

He paused, thinking. "Well, there are credit card slips. Some of the big customers keep an account, and Mr. Randall bills them once a month."

"Does Juanita or Burt Banks buy the feed in the large bags?"

Jed's face darkened. "Juanita isn't here today. I suppose you know about her daughter, you being a police officer."

Mattie nodded and waited for him to answer her question.

After a pause, during which she could literally see him thinking about his coworker and her daughter, he gave himself a slight shake and turned back to their previous conversation. "As far as I know, they don't have big animals. Juanita lives here in town."

"Did you know her daughter?"

He bowed his head. "I've seen her. She's come by the store a couple times. Can't believe she died. Poor Juanita."

When he raised his eyes and met Mattie's, she saw genuine sorrow and sympathy there. She nodded to indicate her agreement. Wondering which other ranchers and farmers bought feed in bulk, she decided to test her boundaries. "Could I see a list of people who keep accounts?"

A look of regret crossed his face. "Mr. Randall keeps the accounts in his office. We make a note of a sale on the day sheet and pass it on to him. I'd better not take you in his private office, but I'm sure he'd be glad to talk with you when he gets back around one o'clock."

"Do you know how many people around here buy the large bags? Just a guess."

He seemed puzzled but continued to try to be helpful. "Gosh, I don't know. Maybe fifty or so."

Not as bad as they thought, if they narrowed it down. "You've been a lot of help. Thank you for your time."

He smiled, sort of a boyish grin. "Sure. Do you want to buy some chicks?"

Mattie moved toward the door where the chicks were on display. They'd stopped cheeping earlier, but as she approached the box, they got with it again. "No, thanks," she said, smiling. "I have a German shepherd who might not take kindly to sharing his yard with chickens."

The kid grinned back at her. "I guess not."

Mattie said good-bye, and the bell over the door tinkled as she let herself out. It didn't matter that she hadn't been able to look at the customer list. It was enough to know it existed, and if they needed a copy of it, she was sure they could get a warrant. Judge Taylor wouldn't drag his feet this time, not with the death of another teenager under investigation. He'd learned that their team didn't ask for warrants without solid reason.

Robo greeted her with his sharp grin as she climbed into the Explorer. Around fifty customers that bought feed in bulk didn't seem too overwhelming. Of course, there might always be the customer that bought the odd bag here and there, but at least it was a place to start. And the most valuable nugget she'd gleaned was that burlap bags held cattle, horse, and pig feed.

The kids from farms and ranches would be the ones most likely to have access to the empty bags. Like the quarterback, Brooks Waverly.

★

By midafternoon, they'd interviewed the town kids, Casey Rhodes and Josh Barnaby. Their stories were close to identical, and the parents seemed as dismayed to hear about their offspring's wayward behavior as the law enforcement officers had been. Both boys confessed to sexting with the victim—there was no use denying it when Stella produced proof—as well as setting up appointments to "hook up" with the girl in a threesome.

Mattie's gut flinched when she heard it.

Both stated that they were innocent of any foul play centering around her death and, with parental permission, allowed Stella to swab the inside of their cheeks for DNA samples. Both denied ownership of the black cap Robo had found on the hillside.

The boys also insisted that their fling with Candace had ended, and they had no qualms about throwing Brooks Waverly under the bus. Both indicated that Brooks was the one currently involved with Candace.

When the parents escorted their sons from the interview room, Mattie had the distinct feeling that the boys might be grounded for life, or at least she hoped they would be. Rhodes's father actually smashed his son's cell phone under his boot right outside the station door in the parking lot.

Mattie stood by Rainbow's desk in the lobby waiting for Brooks Waverly and parents to arrive, so she was first to notice the long, sleek Cadillac glide into the parking lot. It bore license plates that proclaimed, "HOTSHOT," and she knew that Justin McClelland, Timber Creek's sole attorney, owned that car.

When McClelland didn't get out of his car to come inside, she decided he was waiting for someone, and she had a suspicion she knew whom that someone might be. She excused herself from her conversation with Rainbow and went to Stella's office.

She tapped on the door and stuck her head inside. "Justin McClelland is waiting out in the parking lot. Probably for our next appointment to arrive."

Stella pushed her reading glasses up to the top of her head and gave Mattie a pained look. "Okay. Thanks for the heads-up. Let them wait in the interview room for a while."

By the time Mattie returned to the lobby, McClelland was leading the way into the station with Brooks Waverly and a man who had to be Brooks's father. Brooks was a tall, muscular kid with auburn hair, handsome features, and dark-brown eyes surrounded by thick lashes that any girl would love to have. When Mattie saw him at school, he was typically polite, well liked by teachers as well as students, but today, his handsome face appeared tight with stress, and his friendly smile was absent. His father was an older version of Brooks—a little thicker around the waist, a few gray hairs at the temples—and he also wore a grim expression.

Mattie decided to treat the teen like an adult and met him half-way across the room with her hand outstretched. "Hello, Brooks. Thank you for coming in."

"Deputy Cobb." The kid's familiar smile flashed briefly while he shook her hand. "This is my dad, Jack Waverly."

When they shook hands, Jack took hers in a strong, callused paw. She wondered if his grip reflected the strength within him.

"Mr. McClelland," she said, showing that she didn't need an intro-duction to the attorney as she offered a handshake. His dark, bushy eyebrows made a solid slash over his eyes and were his most outstanding feature. McClelland had on his signature Stetson hat and Western suit that he wore during all seasons of the year, including summer. He stared at her nametag and repeated her name aloud while he shook her hand.

"Let me show you to the room where we'll conduct the inter-view, and I'll let Detective LoSasso know you're here," Mattie said.

"Thank you," McClelland said, taking the lead.

Mattie ushered them into the interview room, where four hard-plastic chairs sat around a utilitarian stainless-steel-topped table. There were no other furnishings, and Mattie had always considered the place cold and bare.

"I'll get us another chair," she said, leaving to go to the staff office, where Robo was having a midday nap on his cushion. When she returned with a plastic chair she'd found beside one of the staff desks, McClelland had arranged three of the others on the far side of the table. She placed the one she had in hand next to the chair in front before leaving them alone again.

She found Stella in Sheriff McCoy's office, evidently talking strategy. "They're waiting. McClelland's got them all sitting on one side of the table. A united front."

"That's fine," Stella said. "We'll see how cooperative they plan to be and take it from there. I know I'm going to want this kid's DNA, and Sheriff McCoy can get us a warrant if we have to go that way."

Mattie nodded and then followed Stella to the interview room, where all was silent. She wondered if even a word had been said in her absence. The three men stood when she and Stella entered the room, shaking hands with Stella as she introduced herself.

McClelland smiled warmly at the detective while he assured her he remembered her well. Stella had once interviewed him as a person of interest during the Grace Hartman investigation, and he'd ended up asking her to dinner, which the detective had declined.

"Let's all have a seat," Stella said, taking direction of the interview, and the three settled back into their chairs, with Brooks seated between the two men. "Thank you for coming in with Brooks today, Mr. Waverly. Your son has come to our attention as someone who can provide us with information regarding the death of one of our local students, Candace Banks."

Jack inclined his head slightly, but it was McClelland who spoke. "I want it made clear for the record that Brooks Waverly and his father are here today of their own free will and plan to provide whatever information they can for the purpose of assisting you with your investigation. As long as said information is for said purpose and not aimed at an attempt to deceive or maneuver culpability on the part of my client in the aforementioned young lady's death."

Stella sat back in her chair and aimed her too-sweet smile directly at the attorney. Mattie knew the detective well enough to tell that she was suppressing laughter. "Mr. McClelland, believe me when I say that I would never attempt to deceive or maneuver. You'll know what information I need and why I need it when we get there."

And with that, Stella turned her full attention to the teen. "Do you know Candace Banks, Brooks?"

"Yes, ma'am."

"Have you called her on her cell phone and texted her?"

"Yes, ma'am."

"Is she one of your friends?"

Brooks squirmed slightly. "You might say so."

"How did a girl from the junior high get to be one of your friends?"

"She's friends with a lot of us older kids."

"Is that unusual, older kids befriending someone that much younger?"

Brooks looked down at the table. "Not really."

"I have her cell phone, Brooks. I've read the texts, seen the pictures."

Brooks blanched.

"I need to see that cell phone," McClelland interjected.

Stella gave him a withering look. "You're way ahead of yourself, Counselor. It's not available, nor is it appropriate, for you to see it at this point." She shifted her attention back to Brooks. "Please explain your relationship with Candace, Brooks."

Jack Waverly turned sideways in his chair so he could look at his son, but Brooks kept his face tilted downward toward the table. "I . . . I was having sex with her," he muttered, barely audible.

Jack's eyes narrowed, and he shifted slightly away from his son, but he didn't say a word. *Well coached by his attorney*, Mattie thought.

"Let me clarify. You were having sex with a thirteen-year-old girl. Were other boys at the high school having sex with Candace?" Stella asked, evidently wanting to see how much Brooks would say.

"Yes." Brooks looked up at Stella, possibly seeing a way to avoid being singled out. "A bunch of guys have had sex with her. She's willing to put out for anyone. She . . ." His words trailed off as he apparently realized he wasn't making himself look any better.

Stella prompted him. "She what?"

Brooks shook his head, looking down at the table. "I was going to say she was the town tramp, but that's not a very nice thing to say about her."

"Especially now that she's dead, right?" Stella tapped a nail on the table. "Tell me about the last appointment you had scheduled with her."

Brooks swallowed. "The one yesterday?"

"Wait, Brooks," McClelland said. "What appointment are we talking about, Detective?"

"Brooks had an appointment scheduled with Candace Banks at three thirty yesterday afternoon. It's documented in the cell phone texts."

"I never saw her," Brooks said to McClelland. "She wasn't there."

McClelland seemed to be considering the information and then nodded. "Go ahead."

"I was supposed to meet Candace on Smoker's Hill . . . yeah, at the time you said. But I got hung up in a meeting with the coach about baseball practice, and by the time I got up there, she'd left. She wasn't where we were supposed to meet. I figured she'd gone home, so I left too."

Brooks fanned his hands, palms down, on the table, and Mattie noticed scabs on most of his knuckles. He'd worn a long-sleeve T-shirt, so she couldn't see if he had scratches on his forearms. She'd already looked at his feet to see what type of shoes he wore—tennis shoes, like the other boys had worn, not smooth-soled boots. But that didn't mean he hadn't been wearing boots yesterday.

"What time did you go up the hill?" Stella asked.

"I left the gym about four o'clock. I remember checking the time on my way out."

"We'll be confirming your story with the coach, Brooks," Stella warned.

"It's the truth."

"Who else has been with Candace?" Stella asked.

Brooks studied the detective's face. "I'd rather not rat out anyone. Besides, if you have the cell phone, then you already know."

Stella smiled at him, but somehow, there was no humor in it. "You might reconsider your position on that. This is a homicide investigation. Homicide. That means someone killed Candace. Withholding information is a crime."

McClelland raised his bushy unibrow and turned to his client. "It's not ratting out your friends, Brooks, it's cooperating. Go ahead and say what you know about the others."

Brooks wore a strained look on his face, but he gave up the names of the two boys who'd already been interviewed as well as two others.

"Were any of these boys jealous when you started seeing Candace?" Stella asked.

"Nah. It was my turn."

Mattie's stomach lurched. Stella kept a calm demeanor while she took her time, slowly looking back and forth between Brooks and his father, searching their faces. Crimson leached into the son's pale complexion and he hung his head, while the father's expression grew stony.

McClelland broke the prolonged silence by clearing his throat. "Is that all, Detective?"

Stella threw him a look that could kill. "No, Mr. McClelland, that is not all." She leaned toward Brooks. "It appears you have no respect for this young girl, Brooks, even now, after her death. Did she mean so little to you that you might have hurt her?"

Brooks looked into Stella's eyes. "No, ma'am. I did nothing to hurt her."

"That's debatable. I could argue that you and the others hurt her a lot by the way you treated her. Did something happen between you and Candace yesterday afternoon, Brooks?"

"I told you, I never even saw her yesterday."

"Did something get out of hand?"

"I don't know what you're talking about."

"Did you kill her, Brooks?"

"That's enough," McClelland said.

"No, I did not," Brooks said, leaning forward and clutching the edge of the table. "I didn't kill Candace."

Stella persisted. "Was there an accident? Were you playing around, and she died by accident?"

"No! I didn't even see her. She wasn't there when I got to our meeting place."

Jack Waverly pushed back his chair, looking like he wanted to lunge up out of it.

"That's enough, Detective," McClelland said. "You must stop badgering the boy."

Stella sat back in her chair. "The boy," she repeated. She appeared to be weighing the words, and in her mind, they'd fallen short. "A boy. I guess that's what you are, Brooks. Even though you thought you were man enough to have sex with a girl who was little more than a child."

Mattie keenly observed Jack Waverly. *He must be a good poker player; that wince was barely detectable.*

"It's time to wrap this up, Detective," McClelland said.

Stella relaxed back into her seat and placed her hands on the table as if she had all the time in the world. She adopted a pleasant attitude as she readdressed the teen. "All right, so you didn't see Candace yesterday. Do you know who did?"

"No one that I know of."

"Someone was up on that hill with her," Stella said with an edge of impatience. "Brooks, do you know who killed Candace?"

"No, ma'am," Brooks said, giving Stella eye contact, acting sincere. "I don't know anything about how she died. I didn't know she was dead until I got to school this morning."

"Could you roll up your sleeves and show me your arms, Brooks?" Stella asked. Like Mattie, she'd evidently noticed the scabs on the teen's hands.

Even while McClelland protested, Brooks pushed up the sleeves of his tee, revealing scabbed-over patches that looked like partially healed road rash and a few slashes that appeared more recent.

"How did you get so bunged up?" Stella asked.

"Baseball." He fingered a long scab on his forearm. "Sliding practice."

"Even these?" Stella waved a finger over the fresh scratches.

"I got those trimming my mom's rose bushes last night."

Stella looked at the father. "Is that true?"

He nodded, his lips tight, his face red. He looked like a volcano about to erupt. Mattie couldn't tell if he was mad at Stella, his son, or the entire situation. Possibly all three.

Stella reached inside a manila envelope she'd laid on the table and extracted the evidence bag containing the black cap. "Brooks, do you recognize this?"

Brooks glanced at his father, so Mattie did too. While Brooks examined the cap, she continued to watch Jack, and she noticed his eyes narrow.

"No, ma'am," Brooks said. "I mean, lots of us guys wear these when we train, but I don't recognize this one specifically."

Stella tapped a pink-painted nail on the bag. "It doesn't belong to you?"

Brooks squinted at it. "No. I have one that looks sort of like it, but that one's not mine."

"Lots of you guys wear them?"

"Yes, ma'am."

"And you don't know whose it is?"

"No, ma'am."

"But you're sure this one doesn't belong to you?"

Brooks shook his head. "It's not mine."

A muscle in Jack's jaw contracted as he gazed at his son. After observing his father's body language, Mattie wished she had a way to prove that Brooks was lying.

"Mr. Waverly," Stella said, shifting her attention to the father. "What do you do with your old feed bags?"

"My feed bags?" Jack asked, his voice gruff.

"Yes, sir. The bags that your cattle feed comes in, once they're empty."

"What does that have to do with anything?" McClelland asked, his tone harsh.

Jack crossed his arms over his chest and leaned back in his chair. "It's no secret. I store them in the feed room, and then I take them back to the feed store so they can be used again. We get a discount for returned bags, and that's what most ranchers do."

Stella nodded. "Thank you, Mr. Waverly. I only need one more thing, and then I'll let you go. I'd like your permission to swab your son's cheek for a DNA sample."

"I recommend against that, Jack," McClelland said.

Stella kept her attention focused on Jack. "If he's innocent, there's no reason he shouldn't cooperate now."

"I'm innocent, Dad," Brooks said, and for the first time, his eyes brimmed and his chin wobbled before he reset his face.

Jack looked at Brooks and then indicated his permission by giving a brief nod. "Go ahead. What's most important here is that a young girl is dead." His eyes grew fierce as he held his son's gaze. "A man would step up and help the police, even if it's only to eliminate himself so they can move on to the next guy."

Brooks nodded. *Message received*, Mattie thought. She respected this father's integrity.

"Thank you, Mr. Waverly. I couldn't have said that better myself." Stella withdrew a DNA kit from the pocket of her suit jacket. It took mere seconds for her to swab the teen's open mouth.

Handshakes were exchanged, and Mattie escorted the three from the interview room and back through the lobby, her purpose to observe them in the parking lot. But McClelland was too experienced to allow her to see nonchoreographed movement. With a glance her way, she heard him say, "Let's go back to my office."

"That won't be necessary," Jack said, heading out the door toward his car, a silver Toyota 4Runner. "We can talk over the phone."

The two cars pulled out of the lot as Stella walked up behind her.

"What do you think?" Stella murmured.

Mattie shook her head, sadness washing through her. "I'd hate like anything to find out that our killer is that kid. But after what we learned at the feed store, those marks on his arms, and the evidence you found on the phone, we've got to consider him a suspect. Besides, I think he was lying about that cap not being his."

Stella nodded, crossing her arms over her chest. "I'll call the parents of those two new boys and set up interviews."

As Mattie and Stella started back toward their offices, Brody came out of his.

"I got ahold of the bartender from the Hornet's Nest," he said. "She says she knows exactly who Burt Banks is, and he didn't stop by the bar at all yesterday. He lied about his alibi."

Chapter 10

"How do you want to do this?" Mattie asked Stella as she drove toward the Banks' house.

"Let's confront Burt and Juanita with his lack of an alibi together if we can. Then see how things shake out."

Mattie parked behind Juanita's car, but Burt's truck wasn't anywhere nearby. "Looks like he might not be here."

She checked Robo in the rearview mirror, and he met her gaze, looking expectantly back at her. He seemed to have mastered the art of watching her with the mirror. "You're going to stay here," she told him, speaking to his reflection.

They exited the car, went to the front door, and knocked. Eyes bloodshot, Juanita answered within a few moments.

"Oh, come in," she said in a weak voice. Her shoulders rounded, she led them through the kitchen toward the living room. "I was cleaning Candace's room."

The scene had been released that morning. "That must be hard," Stella said. "Is there anyone who could help you?"

"No, I want to do it myself."

"Is Mr. Banks here?"

Juanita shook her head, settling onto the sofa and staring at the coffee table. "He left."

"Where did he go?" Stella asked.

"Who knows? Probably headed to the Hornet's Nest in Hightower. He's never here when I need him."

Stella sent Mattie a quick glance as they each took a seat. "I'd like to speak with you for a few minutes. Are your boys here at the house?"

"They're next door at Rosie's."

"I imagine this has been a rough day for you all."

With a heavily lined face and downturned mouth, Juanita showed the ravages of her grief. "Yes. The boys wanted to go to school, but both of them had to come home by noon."

"And you say Mr. Banks isn't around to help much," Stella said.

"Since he took the job in Rigby, it's like an excuse to never come home."

"It's hard to commute that far."

"Others do it, and they make it work."

Stella nodded, leaning forward. "Is Mr. Banks involved with the children?"

Fresh tears came to Juanita's eyes. "No. I told him this morning that I didn't buy his act that he's lost his baby girl. He's never had anything to do with Candace."

Probably left right after that discussion, Mattie thought.

"Why is that?" Stella asked.

"It's just the way he is. He doesn't care."

"Did he at one time?"

Juanita shrugged. "Not really."

"Last night you indicated that he has a problem with alcohol," Mattie said.

Juanita nodded.

"How long has this been going on?"

"Years. Since before the boys were born."

"Is he violent when he drinks?" Stella asked.

"No, he's even more withdrawn if anything. He usually stays away until late, and when he comes home, he falls into bed and goes to sleep."

"Have you ever noticed him being abusive to the kids?"

Though Mattie tried to sit still, Stella's question made her cringe. Even mention of the possibility of Burt abusing Candace sent her back to her own tiny bedroom, its walls closing in on her when she heard the door squeak, a signal heralding her father's nighttime visits.

"If you count neglect as abuse, I would say so," Juanita answered.

"How about physical abuse?" Stella asked.

Juanita shook her head, her eyes sad. "No, that's one thing I've never been concerned about. That would've made a huge difference, and I would have left him years ago. But until recently, I needed his paycheck to make ends meet. Now he doesn't even bring home much of that."

"Because of the drinking?" Mattie asked.

Juanita nodded. "He says he stops at the bar to unwind. He's spending his paycheck somewhere."

Workers made pretty good wages at the mine in Rigby. Burt would need a huge bar tab to spend it all. "Where else might he spend his money?"

Juanita shook her head, avoiding eye contact. "I have no idea."

Both Mattie and Stella waited, but Juanita didn't jump in to fill the gap with speculation.

"Have you ever seen any sign that Candace might have been molested?" Stella asked.

Juanita's eyes widened. "No! Why would you ask such a thing?"

"Not by your husband?"

"Absolutely not. I would know about it. I wouldn't allow it."

Mattie felt ill. What role had *her* mother played? Had she known what was going on behind closed doors?

"Are you sure, Mrs. Banks? Take a moment and think back over the years. Is it possible?" Stella asked.

Juanita appeared to be examining her memory. She sat very still, her eyes moving slightly side to side. "No. I'm telling you. I can't imagine him molesting a child, even when he's been drinking. Why are you asking me this?"

"We've uncovered evidence that Candace was sexually active," Stella said. "Were you aware of it?"

Surprise filled Juanita's face. "She's only thirteen."

Stella nodded but remained silent.

Juanita put her hand to her mouth. "And you think that Burt . . . No. I still say he'd never molest a child. He might be a poor father and a worse husband, but he's not a child molester." She looked from Stella to Mattie. "Who? Who was Candace involved with?"

"Local boys, Mrs. Banks," Stella said. "More than one. I can't release their names."

Juanita rocked forward, collapsing upon herself. "How could this be true? What kind of a mother am I that I didn't know?"

Her shock appeared genuine. Mattie knew that Juanita worked two jobs, and she could only guess how hard it would be to raise children under those circumstances, especially when you had no help from your partner. "You work at two different places in town, Mrs. Banks, and your husband works out of town. I suppose your children are here alone after school?" She turned it into a question so that it wouldn't sound like an accusation.

"When Candace turned twelve, I started giving her an allowance to watch the boys and give them a snack. She seemed responsible enough . . ." Her voice trailed off, unsure.

"Had you noticed changes in Candace's behavior?" Stella asked.

Stress filled Juanita's face, and she covered it with her hands. "It didn't start at home, her sleeping around. It didn't start here."

"That's possible, but we need to know," Stella said.

"Oh, my God," Juanita groaned, and she covered her mouth as sobs shook her body.

Mattie felt herself detach. She couldn't handle this kind of pain. This mother's view of her daughter had been shattered, but was Juanita also partially responsible? Mattie had been too young when her own family split to remember the dynamics between her mother and father. Had her mother tried to put a stop to the abuse? Had she tried to protect her? Or had she been blind to the signs, as Juanita seemed to have been?

With a jolt, Mattie realized that maybe her mother *had* tried to protect her. Maybe that's what had caused the escalation in that final argument the night her father tried to kill her mother. Maybe her mother loved her after all. But then, why had she disappeared?

Catching herself, she fell back on a familiar mechanism and shut down her feelings so that she could regain her focus. *This investigation isn't about me.*

Juanita brought herself back under control. "I'm sorry. I can't talk about this anymore."

"All right," Stella said. "Think about what we've said, and let me know if you come up with further thoughts. We also need to speak with Mr. Banks again. Would you call me and let me know when he comes home?"

Juanita nodded, her face taking on a fierce look. "If you find out he's hurt my children in any way, will you tell me?"

Stella seemed to be observing the mother closely as she stood. "We'll be discussing these things together."

Like Stella, Mattie rose from her seat, but Juanita remained huddled on the couch.

"Can I call someone to come be with you?" Stella asked.

"No. No, I need to just sit here a moment." Juanita stared out the window.

"We'll let ourselves out."

When they stepped onto the porch, the Banks brothers were coming out of the neighbor's house and heading toward home. Mattie slowed to say hello, but both boys gave her a shy look as they passed, saying nothing.

Before climbing inside her Explorer, Mattie had a thought. "Let's go talk with Rosie Gonzales."

Stella pursed her lips, looking out the windshield at the neighbor's house. "Okay. Do you want to take lead on this one?"

"Sure."

Together they walked next door, crossed the sidewalk that split a tidy yard filled with flower beds, and went up the steps onto the porch of a small clapboard house with dark-green siding and newly painted white shutters. Mattie knocked on the door.

Rosie Gonzales looked surprised to see them standing on her doorstep. "Yes?"

"Could we come inside and speak with you for just a few minutes, Mrs. Gonzales?" Mattie asked.

Rosie glanced toward the Banks house but then opened the door wide. "Of course."

The house opened directly into a living room, where a boy and girl about the same age as the Banks brothers sat watching an episode of a game show. The room seemed cozy, well lit with floor and table lamps, and a bowl containing a handful of leftover popcorn sat on the coffee table in front of the children.

"Turn off the television and go to your rooms to finish your homework," Rosie said. Perhaps it was Mattie's uniform, but both children took one look at her and did as they were asked without protest.

"Please, sit," Rosie said, taking a seat in a deep armchair with mauve cushions, while Mattie and Stella sat on the matching sofa. "How can I help?"

"First let me say I'm sorry for your loss. I'm sure Candace's death came as a huge shock," Mattie said. "Did you know her well?"

Tears brimmed Rosie's eyes, but she held them in check. "I've known all those kids since they moved in next door."

"And when was that?"

Rosie appeared to think. "About three years now. My kids were just starting school. Candace was a little older than the others, and she didn't come to play like the boys did. But she was always sweet to my kids."

"Did Candace have friends over while her parents were at work?"

"No, not really. Not that I noticed. Sometimes the older kids drive their cars up and down the street, but I just step outside and work in my yard. They drive away."

Mattie liked the woman's version of neighborhood watch. "Do you know anything about Mr. Banks having a drinking problem?"

Tightening her lips, Rosie nodded slowly. She looked down at the arm of the chair she was sitting in and brushed at the nap on its upholstery. Mattie was afraid she wasn't going to say anything more, but then she spoke. "Burt spends most of his paycheck on booze and other women. It's a sad situation."

Other women?

Mattie nodded as if she already knew. "Can you give us the names of any of these women?"

"Nah. Juanita, she doesn't even know. She just suspects. But he's never home, never around. He's tomcattin' around somewhere."

"Have the kids ever said anything to you about him being abusive toward them?"

Rosie shook her head. "No, there've been no complaints. Really, he's rarely home. Never spends time with the kids that I know of."

"Juanita hasn't shared any suspicions about abuse with you?"

"No."

There seemed to be no waffling regarding her answers, so Mattie had to take them at face value. "Do you have any idea who might have hurt Candace?"

Rosie's eyes filled, and this time, tears spilled over. She let them fall. "No, I wish to heaven that I did. I would like to see the person who killed that sweet child suffer."

Mattie looked at Stella to see if she had any more questions. The detective withdrew a business card from her pocket and handed it to Rosie, thanking her for her time and giving the standard instruction to call if she thought of anything that might help them with the case. Mattie thanked her as well, and they took their leave.

After entering the SUV, Mattie and Stella looked at each other. "Neither of these women suspects that Candace has been abused by her father," Stella said. "And if he's got another woman, that could explain where Burt was yesterday afternoon."

Mattie started the engine and set off toward the station. "He could've been up on that hill with Candace."

"When we talk to him, we'll pin him down on exactly where he was."

The knots in Mattie's shoulders were so tight they hurt. "And I think we should confront him about his relationship with his daughter."

"Question, Mattie, not confront. I don't have any preconceived notions about it. Don't let your past color your judgment on the case."

Mattie shrugged.

"Your instincts are usually good, but I'm not sure this time. Right now, I like Brooks Waverly the most for this one."

Mattie pulled into the station's parking lot and steered the Explorer into a space. She sat for a few moments, thinking about it. "Maybe so, but I'm not ready to lock in on him yet."

"I agree. We still have a lot of work to do."

Mattie let Robo out the back, and he ran to sniff the lot before coming back to join her at the station door. Once inside, she and Robo went to the staff office, while Stella went to hers. Mattie sat and turned on her computer.

She'd retrieved the slip of paper with the license plate number on it that Rainbow had checked out earlier. Although the vehicle had been clean, there was something about the men's furtive behavior that Mattie couldn't let go. After opening the DMV website, she plugged in the numbers and letters on the plate and waited for the registration to load. It took only a few seconds.

A silver Nissan Pathfinder registered to Merton Heath. City of residence: Denver.

She went into the Colorado Crime Information Center database, and after typing in the name Merton Heath, his name and record popped up on her screen. She scanned through it. Merton Heath—registered sex offender.

Having trouble taking a full breath, Mattie sat back in her chair and stared at her computer. She scrolled through the information. He had been convicted of molesting a minor.

A pedophile. In Timber Creek. The day after a child's death. What were the odds?

And she'd driven right past him.

Her body tight with anxiety, she strode from her office to tell Stella and the sheriff what she'd found. They needed to put a BOLO out on that vehicle ASAP. She wanted every cop in the state to be on the lookout for this guy.

Chapter 11

Cole sat in his truck, waiting at the end of their lane for the school bus. Angela was staying at school for a yearbook meeting, so Sophie was riding home on the bus alone. She was capable of walking down the lane by herself, but Cole liked to meet the girls when he could.

Brakes squeaked and pneumatics hissed as the driver stopped the bus and opened the door to let out Sophie. The girl grinned and waved while Cole hopped out of the truck and hurried around to the passenger side to let her in. He waved at the bus driver as she forced the bus in gear and rumbled off.

"Daddy!" Sophie said as she approached. "Wait'll I tell you what Cindy Martin got last night!"

"I can't wait," Cole said, boosting Sophie up into the passenger seat. "Tell me now."

"Baby chicks!"

"No!"

"Yes! She brought pictures of them to school and told us all about 'em. She got two, and they have yellow feathers, and she has to keep them under a heat lamp until they grow bigger, and she has to feed them in jar lids because they're so tiny, and she keeps their water in a special pan that automatically waters them—but only a little bit at a time so they don't fall in and drown." She paused for a breath. "And can I have one? Can I have a baby chick, Dad?"

He figured that was coming. "Let's talk about that. Baby chicks are a big responsibility, Sophie. I'm not sure you're ready for that."

"I'll be nine next week, and I'll take care of them. I feed Belle and Bruno most of the time."

True.

"We don't have a chicken coop, so where would we put them?" Cole asked.

"They live in a box at first. We could build them a coop behind the clinic. Out by Mountaineer's pen."

Mountaineer was Cole's horse, a roan gelding that could handle any mountain trail. He'd been invaluable last fall when Cole rode him up into the wilderness during the first snowstorm of the season to find Mattie.

"Build *them* a coop? I thought you were asking for just one chick."

Sophie looked down at her lap for a split second before looking up and grinning. She wasn't much of a fibber. "One chick would be lonely. We'd have to get at least two. Please, Daddy."

"Remember, no begging allowed, and no whining," Cole interjected. He knew Sophie could escalate quickly, and he wanted to nip it in the bud. "You've made your point. Let me think it over."

Sophie settled back in her seat, obviously trying to control herself. "Just one more thing, okay?"

"Okay . . ."

"The chicks are on sale at the feed store, so we wouldn't have to go anywhere far to get them, and they could be my birthday present, and I would take care of them and help you build their pen."

"That was several more things, not just one. But you've presented your case well, and now I'll think about it while we go have a snack."

"Okay, but we've got to decide soon, because they're on sale now, and we might miss out if we wait too long."

"Enough," Cole said, ending the discussion. "Now, tell me what else happened today?"

Sophie's face fell as she told him about how her teacher had broken the news about Candace's death at school. "Robby Banks came to school today, but he started crying and had to go home."

Cole slid Sophie a sideways glance as he drove slowly down the lane toward home. "Maybe that was better for him anyway. To be home."

"Yeah, but Robby likes school. He's real smart too."

"Maybe that's why he decided to come to school this morning. You know, because he likes it there. Then it got to be too much for him."

"Yeah, maybe." She leaned back against her backpack, a frown on her face as she considered it.

Cole was sorry to see her mood had shifted. He decided to go get the chicks as soon as she'd had her snack. He would let her pick out three, just in case one didn't make it, and he would set them up at the clinic until the chicks grew large enough to be transferred outside. But he'd tell her later, after she'd eaten a snack and cheered up. He didn't want to reinforce her melancholy by giving in now.

★

The chicks peeped and cheeped while Moses Randall, the feed store owner, rang up the sale of three of them, a sack of chicken feed, a heat lamp, and a water dispenser, the supplies costing quite a bit more than the chickens.

"So this is your birthday present, huh?" he said to Sophie, raising his silver eyebrows. An elderly man, Moses had kept the feed store going for over a decade and catered primarily to ranchers and farmers.

"Yes, I'm going to be nine," Sophie said, looking up at him and hopping on one foot in her excitement.

"Well, I'll throw in the cardboard box for free then."

Big of him, Cole thought as he paid the bill. But the price to pay for Sophie's joy over these chickens was more than worth it.

A kid with a scruffy beard helped carry out their purchases while Sophie twirled and danced on the way to the truck.

"Careful now, Sophie. Don't run into anything," Cole said as he followed her. He opened the truck door and shoved up the seat so the kid could deposit the cardboard box containing the chicks in the back. Cole thanked him while he helped Sophie get in.

"I'll sit in the back with the chicks," Sophie said.

"You take care of those little birds now, you hear," the kid said to Sophie with a teasing smile.

Sophie grinned back at him, her freckled cheeks bunched. "I will."

The kid waved as he turned to go back inside the store.

"Don't forget your seat belt," Cole said as he turned on the engine.

"Be careful, Daddy. The chicks aren't buckled in. Drive slow."

Cole did as he was told, driving one mile out of town to their lane and then going past the house to the clinic. His cell phone rang as he pulled up in front of the building. He took it from his pocket and answered: "Timber Creek Veterinary Clinic."

"Hey, doc. This is Gus Tilley."

This was the fourth time Gus had called him since bringing Lucy in this morning. "What can I do for you, Gus?"

"Something happened to Lucy's eye. Can you take a look at it?"

"What happened?"

"I'm not sure. Looks like she got hit. Or something."

Unbidden, Cole's mind conjured a memory of a horse he'd seen when he was in vet school. The horse had been hit in the face, and the blow had popped its eye out. Although the owner swore the horse must have hit its head against something, the faculty vet had shared with the students his suspicion that the owner might have actually hit the horse with a rope or a whip himself, although it couldn't be proven. The sight of the injury to the poor horse had been unforgettable, but in all his years of practice, Cole had never found cause for an eye injury to be anything other than accidental.

"How bad is it?" Cole asked.

"It's swollen. Tears coming out of it. She keeps it shut."

It was almost four o'clock, and Cole still had a couple hours of patients scheduled. Besides, if true to form, Gus was probably calling from a phone at the edge of town. "Can you bring her in?"

"Yeah. I can get there in about forty minutes."

"I have other clients scheduled, but come on down. I'll work you in."

After disconnecting the call, Cole realized that Gus must have straightened out the phone situation at his house. Earlier, he'd expressed concerns about pretty much everything, from wanting to know if he should still be treating Dodger's ear to wondering how a person could impregnate a horse. Cole had found himself delivering a talk on Artificial Insemination 101 between seeing other clients. It seemed odd that Gus was still fixated on Lucy being pregnant, despite the fact that she wasn't.

He helped Sophie carry in chicks and supplies, and they set up the cheeping babies in the kennel room.

"I'm going to name this one Chicken Little," Sophie said, cradling the smallest chick in her hands. Although Cole had warned her that the smallest chick in the group might not be the healthiest, she'd insisted they get it anyway.

"Hi, hi," Tess called from the front of the clinic. She'd come back to help with the late afternoon schedule.

"We're back here," Sophie called to her. "Come see."

Cole left the two of them to marvel over the chickens while he prepared for his first client. His appointments went smoothly, and within a half hour, Tess told him that Gus Tilley had arrived. He finished up with the dog he had on the exam table and went to the equine treatment area, noticing that Sophie was still in the kennel room with the chicks as he went through. He experienced a feeling of déjà vu as he rolled back the double door and revealed Gus and Lucy waiting on the other side, like they had been this morning.

But this time Lucy didn't look so good. Her left eye was swollen shut, the hair and skin under it wet with tears.

"Bring her on in, Gus."

They secured Lucy inside the stocks, and Cole snugged her lead rope down tight to the front, so she couldn't move her head freely. He examined the external part of the eyelid, noticing an abrasion above the top of it.

"There's an abrasion here," he told Gus, showing him the spot.

"I saw that too."

"She probably bumped her head against a post or something. I'll get some things and take a peek under the eyelid." Cole went into the clinic to retrieve an ophthalmoscope, a bottle of fluorescein dye, suture, and a surgical pack. As he went by the pass-through, he called to Tess. "I might need your help."

She was finishing up with his last client. "I'll be right there."

"Daddy, come look at my chicks," Sophie said as he traveled through the kennel room with his hands full.

"Can't now, Sophie-bug. Later."

She hopped up, hurrying to open the door for him. She followed him into the equine treatment area, moving slowly and quietly as she'd been taught. Cole was impressed, knowing what kind of energy the child needed to harness.

"You know Mr. Tilley, Sophie," Cole said, more as a reintroduction for Gus than Sophie. He felt certain that Sophie hadn't forgotten the man's name since meeting him last night. He placed his supplies on the stainless-steel exam table beside the stocks.

Gus tugged his cap and gave Sophie a shy glance.

"Come see my new baby chicks, Mr. Tilley," she said.

Immediate distress filled the man's face, and Cole could tell that he'd been thrown a hardball by the invitation. "Gus is busy right now, Sophie. We've got to examine Lucy's eye. You can stand over there and watch if you're quiet," he said, gesturing toward the front of the room in an area where she would be out of the way.

"I'll go outside and play with my ball," Sophie said, choosing that over standing still and being quiet. "If you want to, I can show you the chicks when you're done, Mr. Tilley."

"She's a nice kid," Gus murmured after Sophie went outside.

"Thanks. I kinda like her. Do you have kids, Gus?"

"Me? Oh, no. Never been married." Gus shuffled, kicking one boot against the other.

"Well," Cole said, turning back to business and picking up the ophthalmoscope, "let's see what we've got going on here."

Gently, he pried the swollen lid open and shone the light into the eye, peering through the ophthalmoscope. Lucy tried to toss her head, telling him the eye was sensitive to light, but the pupil constricted normally. The eye's sclera was reddened, looking like it had suffered a blow of some kind, but he couldn't detect any foreign bodies. The conjunctiva was also red and irritated. While he was looking at the eye, Tess came quietly into the room.

"I'm going to use a fluorescein dye, so I can see if there's any damage to the eyeball itself," Cole explained to Gus as Tess handed him the bottle. With her help, he pried the eyelid open again and delivered the drops. After Tess handed him the ophthalmoscope, he examined the eye. This time, the fluorescent-green stain allowed him to see if there might be an injury to the cornea, as well as any small amount of debris that might be irritating the eye.

While Cole was looking through the ophthalmoscope again and concentrating on what he was seeing there, Gus said, "What do you see, Doc?"

"There's a small abrasion here on the cornea. It's not too bad, but it's going to need treatment several times a day if we're going to get it to heal."

"What do you think caused that?"

"It's hard to say, but with the abrasion over her eye, I think she might have knocked her head against a fence or the side of her box stall."

"She's been in the corral today, like you said. It has a loafing shed at the end that she can go into." Gus took a few steps back and placed his hand on Lucy's neck, rubbing it fondly with a circular motion. "She's used to that corral. I don't think she'd bump into anything accidentally. Do you think someone could've gone in there and hurt her?"

What's with these assumptions that someone is hurting his animals?

"Do you think that's possible, Gus?" Now Cole studied the owner instead of the horse.

Gus hung his head, continuing to rub Lucy's neck. "Maybe."

"Do you have any idea who might have hurt her?"

He shifted his feet, looked distressed. "No. But somebody."

Cole had a niggling thought. Could that somebody be Gus himself? Was he projecting his own actions onto others? "Did you accidentally hit her when you were working with her, Gus?"

The man's head snapped up and he looked Cole in the eye. "Lord, no. I was inside the house, cleaning. When I came out to feed her, she was like this."

Gus looked sincere enough, and Cole didn't think he was lying. "Then maybe something spooked her. She swung her head and cracked it against a fence or a post. These things happen." Cole turned back to the horse's eye. "This should heal up without me having to sew it shut. You've caught it before it ulcerated. I'll clean it and put some ointment in. You'll have to put the medicine in twice a day."

"I can take care of it, Doc. Just show me what to do."

With Tess assisting, Cole used eyewash to flush the eye. Lucy squinted tightly, and Cole knew it was painful for her. He showed Gus how to apply the ointment. "She's not going to like this, Gus, so you'll probably need to tie her real snug in order to treat her. This eye is painful, and she'll be sensitive to light. Can she stay inside the barn in a box stall?"

"Yes, sir. She has a nice clean stall inside the barn."

"I'll put a patch over it. We need to keep it clean, apply the ointment twice a day, and give her an anti-inflammatory. That will also help her with the discomfort."

Tess left to get the other supplies Cole needed to finish the treatment.

"You've had a rough patch with your animals here the last couple days," Cole said.

"Yeah, but Dodger's doing fine now. Still scratches his ear once in a while though. Could there be something inserted under the skin of the flappy part?"

"You mean like a sticker or a grass seed? I didn't see anything like that when I examined him."

"I mean like . . . well, like an implant."

Frowning, Cole searched Gus's face. "An implant? What kind of an implant?"

Gus shook his head and avoided Cole's gaze. "I don't know. I . . . I don't know. Growth hormone? A tracker?"

Did Gus insert something into Dodger's ear? "Did you bring him with you?"

"He's in the truck."

"When we're finished here, let me take a look at him."

Tess returned with the medications and eye patch, and Cole finished up quickly, showing Gus how to dose with the anti-inflammatory paste. The gentle mare tolerated everything well, and he hoped Gus wouldn't have a problem treating her. "Let's have you bring her back for me to take a look in two days, but call me if you have concerns about it sooner," Cole said as he untied Lucy's head and opened the stocks. Lucy backed out slowly.

"Your next client is waiting," Tess said as she started cleaning up.

"I'll be right there. I need to take a quick look at Dodger."

Gus led Lucy to the trailer, and Cole watched as he carefully opened the end gate, making sure it didn't hit the horse. She stepped up into the trailer without hesitation. Gus's mannerisms were as gentle with Lucy as they had been with Dodger, and Cole began to feel foolish for suspecting he might have done anything to hurt one of his animals. He noticed Sophie out a ways, kicking her ball and running behind it.

After Gus tied Lucy inside, he closed and secured the trailer gate and went around to the passenger side of the truck. "Good boy, fella," he said to Dodger, using a voice pitched high enough to border on baby talk. "Come on. Jump down."

The dog jumped down from the seat and trotted around, looking up at Gus with nothing short of adoration. Gus squatted and Dodger wiggled into his arms, wagging his tail and his whole body. Gus held him gently while Cole bent over him to examine the ear. The pinna was soft, smooth, and showed no sign whatsoever of inflammation or a foreign object.

"There's nothing here, Gus." Cole peered inside the ear, and it looked squeaky clean. "Looks good inside too. Keep up the treatment for one more day and then stop. I'm sure he had an irritation of some kind, and he's getting over it. He's doing fine now."

Gus beamed and loaded Dodger back into the truck. Cole wanted to tell him not to worry so much but wasn't sure if that was what the man needed. Sometimes these problems came in clusters. He wouldn't see a client for months, and then he'd see the same client for different problems several days in a row.

He was about to say good-bye when Gus surprised him. Taking off his cap and fingering it, he looked up shyly. "Can I see your little girl's chicks?"

"Why . . . sure." He called out to Sophie, making her catch her ball and come running.

She was ecstatic to show Gus her chickens, and Cole left them in the back of the clinic, peering into the box. He asked Tess to check on them after a few minutes, and she returned from the kennel room shaking her head and chuckling. "They're talking about the best design for a chicken coop. Prepare yourself."

When Cole finished up twenty minutes later, he discovered Gus still there with Sophie. Gus sat cross-legged on the concrete floor, one elbow propped on his knee bracing his head on his hand, looking enthralled while Sophie told him the story of Chicken Little. Complete with dramatic flourishes, she was saying, "The sky is falling. The sky is falling."

Cole took a moment to lean against the doorframe and enjoy watching his daughter tell the story, too, understanding completely what his client found so fascinating.

Chapter 12

It was late afternoon, and Mattie sat at her desk, thinking.

She and Stella had finished interviewing the two high school kids named by Brooks Waverly. Their involvement mirrored that of the other boys, and Mattie felt sick at heart after talking to them. This case stirred up old feelings of fear and helplessness that she didn't quite know what to do with. Her therapist's assignment to think about trust and emotional resilience came to mind, but she shoved it away, wanting to stay focused on solving the murder of Candace Banks.

All the boys they'd interviewed denied knowing anything about the cap found along the killer's escape route. It was frustrating that she couldn't turn this item into evidence that could point to a suspect.

Sheriff McCoy had called a meeting in the briefing room, but she still had a few minutes before it started. She pulled out her cell phone and dialed Sergeant Jim Madsen, Robo's trainer.

He answered after the second ring, his drawl friendly and teasing. "How ya doin', Deputy Mattie Cobb?"

"Not so well at the moment, Sarge." She shared with him that Robo had found a girl's body. "We tracked an unknown suspect away from the gravesite, and Robo found a black thermal cap by the trail. I've also got a lineup of people it might belong to."

"And you want to do a scent identification lineup, right?"

"That's what I was thinking."

"Robo hasn't been trained for that. It's more popular in Europe. We don't use it much here in the US, and it wouldn't be admissible in court."

"I don't care about that. All I want is a lead," Mattie said. "What do you think? Could I train him to do it?"

"Given a little time, you could train that dog to do anything, Deputy. Hell, he'd drive your vehicle if you'd let him." Madsen paused for a few beats. "Do you still have that training clicker I gave you?"

"Of course."

"Here's what I think you should do."

★

The team sat around the table in the briefing room, all present except for Robo. Mattie had left him snoozing in her office on his dog bed. As tired as she felt, she wished she could join him.

Stella briefed the others on the results of the afternoon's interviews, ending with how the kids denied knowledge or ownership of the cap. "Both Mattie and I think Brooks Waverly was lying when he denied it. Whether or not he's our killer, I think that kid knows something about Candace's death."

Mattie took a breath before starting to speak. She felt like she was going out on a limb. "That cap has to be loaded with the scent of the person who wore it. I just got off the phone with Sergeant Madsen. We've come up with a way we could use it as a scent article, something quicker than DNA." She shared their plan.

McCoy frowned. "And this is something Robo hasn't been trained to do yet?"

"Right. But I'm sure he could learn it in a few lessons."

"I like to run these investigations by the book, and this sounds risky. We don't want to focus on someone without proper evidence."

"How do you plan to carry this off?" Brody asked.

"I'll get some volunteers and train him this evening. If he takes to it like Sergeant Madsen and I think he will, we'll be ready by morning. We can bring all those kids in before school."

Stella stared at her, lips pursed. Mattie looked to her for support, and the detective straightened. "Why not give it a try, Sheriff? If Robo isn't one hundred percent accurate with a volunteer lineup by tomorrow, we'll scrap the idea. But if he is, it would give us one more piece to look at. We can handle the information we get objectively, like any other piece of evidence."

Brody turned to McCoy. "I'll stay and help with the training. Cobb and I can decide together if he's ready or not in the morning."

"I'll stay too," Stella said.

McCoy took a moment to study the faces of each member of his team before focusing on Mattie. "All right," he said. "You're authorized to give it a try."

★

Mattie had bagged a scent article from each of her volunteers: a gauzy pink scarf from Rainbow, a rumpled sweat-stained handkerchief from Brody, and a pair of gloves from Stella's coat pocket. In addition, she scavenged a decoy from Garcia's desk, his baseball cap. The articles were set out in a row on a table in the briefing room.

She started with only one volunteer in the room—Rainbow, who now stood against the back wall.

"You have to stand still," Mattie said. "Don't speak to Robo and don't pet him, okay?"

"Got it."

Robo knew the first part of the drill. She offered him a sniff of Rainbow's scent article and told him, "Search," followed quickly by the command, "Show me."

He trotted across the room toward Rainbow, and when he got to her, Mattie told him to sit. As soon as he did, she used a metal clicker to tell him he'd done the right thing and then crossed the room to give him a treat.

Sergeant Madsen had reinforced Robo's new skills with clicker training, so her dog already knew what it was all about. The sergeant had given a clicker to each of the new handlers at academy when he demonstrated how to use it for training and reinforcement of new skills.

He'd told Mattie to teach Robo to sit beside the person who matched the scent article, since it was the way he already indicated a drug find.

The secret to dog training was to set up incremental steps ranging from easy to difficult, making sure the dog achieved success at each step. After a few repetitions, Robo sat in front of Rainbow without verbal prompting, and Mattie introduced Brody into the room. He took a spot beside Rainbow, standing about three feet away from her.

Still using Rainbow's scent article, Mattie asked Robo to identify her another time before switching to Brody's handkerchief. When she made the switch, Robo didn't miss a beat, and he went directly to Brody before sitting and looking at Mattie. She clicked and gave him a treat, grinning at him and telling the others, "Now I'll use Garcia's cap and teach him to come back to me." This had been Madsen's recommendation for Robo to indicate that the scent article matched no one in the lineup.

When she offered the article to Robo and gave him the "Show me" command, he wouldn't even leave her side. He looked up at her, grinning and waving his tail. She realized that, knowing the staff here at the station as well as he did, Robo was well aware that Garcia was absent. Why expend that wasted effort to go across the room to sniff?

Madsen hadn't told her what to do in this case. She decided to walk him over to the lineup and back and then told him to sit, giving him a treat for completing the sequence.

"I think he knows us all too well to make this challenging for him," she said. "We're going to need new subjects."

Rainbow held up her hand. "I'll call Anya and see if she can bring some of the gang in from the hot springs."

Mattie wasn't used to asking others for help. "Do you think they would come?"

"Of course. Anya thinks you're amazing. She'd love to help us with Robo."

It was hard for Mattie to know how to express her gratitude. "Thanks, Rainbow. Let me bring in Stella and add her to the lineup to complete this part of his training. Then we'll give him a break while we wait for reinforcements to get here."

Chapter 13

Thursday

Shirtless and toweling his wet hair, Cole strode from his bathroom to answer his cell phone as it jingled on his bedside table. He glanced at caller ID. No mistaking that number now; he'd seen it repeatedly. Gus Tilley.

He stifled his impatience. "What can I do for you, Gus?"

"I've got a problem, Doc. I can't get the medicine into Lucy's eye."

"Do you have her head snugged down tight enough?"

"I think so, I just can't get her eye open."

Cole realized his client had a legitimate concern. "It *is* tough. You have to use a firm touch, and it takes some practice. Make sure she's tied so her head can't move and you've got everything in hand before you start. The clinic opens at eight. If you haven't been able to get her done by then, call back and we'll work you in."

"Okay. I'll give 'er another try."

"If you want, you can leave her at my place until she doesn't need treatment anymore."

"I need to have her here where I can watch her," Gus said, his tone solemn.

"We'll work together until you can do it yourself then. It just takes practice. Call Tess after eight if you want to bring her in." Juggling the cell phone from hand to hand, Cole had tugged on a sage-colored Western shirt and snapped the buttons one handed. It was seven thirty in the morning, and he was already beginning to feel the pressure of running behind schedule. *Sheesh.*

After ending the call, he tucked his shirttail into his Levi's, swiped a comb through his damp hair, and put on his watch.

His thoughts went back to an article he read years ago on the topic of Munchausen syndrome by proxy with pets. It outlined experiences with clients who used their pets to get attention from their veterinarian. As he recalled, these clients might use naturally occurring illnesses but string out the treatment to seek attention, or they might even cause harm or injury to their animals themselves. Munchausen by proxy, whether with children or pets, was considered a serious mental illness, one that both doctors and veterinarians should be aware of. The typical client profile mentioned in the article was a woman with a small dog. Gus didn't come close to that description, and he'd never called attention to himself in such a way in the past, but even so, it was something that came to mind.

Cole snagged his cell phone from the dresser where he'd left it, tucking it into his shirt pocket and snapping the pocket flap closed as he ran down the stairs. Mrs. Gibbs and the kids were already in the kitchen.

Sophie was scooping dry kibble into Belle's and Bruno's bowls.

"Good morning, Sophie-bug. Thanks for taking care of the dogs this morning."

"You're late, sleepyhead," she said with a grin. "I wanna go to the clinic and see the chicks before school."

"We can manage that."

Mrs. Gibbs set a bowl of scrambled eggs on the table, and Angie was retrieving a pitcher of orange juice from the refrigerator.

"I've got a yearbook meeting again after school," Angie said as she carried the pitcher to the counter to pour juice into empty glasses.

"I need to go to Willow Springs this afternoon for groceries and supplies," Mrs. Gibbs said while she popped bread into the toaster. "Do I have time to get me hair permed, or shall I hurry home to meet the bus?"

Cole tried to recall his schedule while he poured coffee. "I can meet the bus. I have a couple stable calls this afternoon, but I can get home in time."

"Lovely," Mrs. Gibbs said, bringing a platter of toast to the table.

"And ye shall be lovely too," Sophie said, grinning at Mrs. Gibbs. Cole detected a trace of the lady's Irish accent sneaking into his daughter's speech.

Sophie pulled out her chair and was climbing up into it when suddenly she sneezed.

"Bless you," Mrs. Gibbs said.

Sophie sneezed again.

Mrs. Gibbs snatched a tissue from the box that sat on the cabinet by the phone and handed it to her. "You're not catching a cold now, are ye, girl?"

"Nope."

"You better not be. We have a party to plan for next week. We should write our invitations tonight," Mrs. Gibbs said.

Another sneeze interrupted Sophie's reply. Cole leaned over and put a hand on her forehead. It felt normal to him. "I don't think she has a fever, do you, Mrs. Gibbs?"

The housekeeper tested by putting her cheek against Sophie's forehead. "Feels normal to me. Perhaps you have a bit of fluff up your snoozle, Miss Sophie."

"Chicken fluff up my snoozle," Sophie said, evidently liking the sound of the words. She repeated it a couple times before starting to eat.

"Let's hurry, Sophie, so I can take you to the clinic to see the chicks, and then I'll drive you both up the lane to meet the bus. Will that work for you, Angel?" Cole asked.

"I'm ready to go. I want to see the chicks too."

They hurried to finish breakfast, threw on jackets and grabbed backpacks, and then spilled through the garage door to load into the truck. And with that, the Walker family launched the day. Cole felt like the race was on—he had a busy day ahead of him.

Another sneeze from Sophie resounded from the back seat, and his phone jangled in his pocket. Pulling it out, he checked to see who was calling. Gus Tilley. Again.

★

Before they'd called it quits the night before, Rainbow had rounded up a dozen volunteers, some from the hot springs, others her friends from around town. It surprised Mattie that so many were willing to help her train Robo. He'd responded like Sergeant Madsen thought he would, and he was matching scent articles to humans consistently by the time they'd gone home for the night. He'd also learned to come back and sit beside Mattie when he couldn't find a match. His new game made him wag his tail and grin every time he played it.

About half the volunteers had returned that morning so Stella and the sheriff could test Robo's accuracy. He performed at one hundred percent, and they decided to go ahead with the lineup.

Sheriff McCoy had called parents and asked them to bring their sons to the station. By midmorning, the five high school boys stood in a lineup against the back wall, each about three feet apart. Mattie had placed Brooks Waverly squarely in the middle, where he stood with a bit of a smirk on his face, showing some attitude for the benefit of his peers.

The others' expressions varied, from stony indifference to pasted-on smiles. Of the five, Casey Rhodes, whose father had seemed the strictest, appeared the most frightened. If they were looking for the one who acted guiltiest, he'd be it.

Mattie went to her office to get Robo. After sleeping through the night, he wasn't the least bit tired, so he'd been concerned when she told him to stay on his bed. He was waiting and watching for her to return.

He jumped to his feet when she entered the room, but stayed where she'd put him. She crossed over to reinforce the "stay" rather than calling him to her. After a treat and a pat, she told him they were going to go find someone. Familiar with the drill, he pranced beside her back to the briefing room, his eyes on her face.

Edgy with nerves, Mattie paused and took a breath before entering the room, letting it out slowly to center herself. Stella, Sheriff McCoy, and Brody watched from the near wall, while the lineup stood against the back.

Mattie picked up the cap, still in its plastic evidence bag, and offered it to Robo to sniff. "Search. Show me."

Robo trotted toward the lineup, tail waving, working right to left as he sniffed the air around each person. Brooks Waverly's eyes narrowed as her dog worked the line, but he continued to cooperate, standing in place without moving. Robo went up to him, sniffed his feet, and then sat and stared at Mattie.

Though the room remained silent, Mattie felt as if a bomb had exploded. As she patted and praised Robo for doing his job, she looked to see her colleagues' reactions. Their faces and body language were unreadable, but she would guess they felt as excited as she.

"Thank you for coming in today, gentlemen," McCoy said. "Brooks, I want to visit with you and your father, so come with me. The rest of you are free to go. We'll contact you if we want to interview you again."

Stella gave Mattie a slight smile and quirked one brow in recognition of Robo's prowess before following Brooks and the sheriff out of the room. Brody ushered the other boys out to the lobby, while Mattie took Robo to her office. Once within the privacy of the four walls, she grabbed Robo and hugged his neck, telling him what a good boy he was while he nibbled at her arm.

While she waited for Stella and the sheriff to interrogate Brooks, Mattie logged onto her computer and opened the detailed record from Merton Heath's conviction that Brody had retrieved. Despite the successful ID during the scent lineup, the information she found in the record made her uneasy. Convicted of molesting a twelve-year-old girl, he'd served five years before being released on parole. No other priors.

Even though things were pointing toward Brooks Waverly at the moment, she couldn't disregard the coincidence that she'd seen this pedophile in Timber Creek the day after Candace had been killed.

Soon after, Stella came into the room and leaned against the edge of Mattie's desk, arms crossed. "He confessed that the cap is his. Says he lost it sometime last week while running on the hill for cross country training."

"And he lied about it belonging to him because . . ."

"Says he was afraid we'd do exactly what we're doing—pin the blame for Candace's death on him. His words, not mine."

Mattie fiddled with a pen while she thought. "He could be our guy, but we haven't got a case against him yet. Did you take a look at Merton Heath's record?"

"I did. He's a strong person of interest, but so is our victim's father. I called Juanita Banks, and she says her husband is at home this morning, so we could interview the two of them together. Can you come along with me now?"

"Sure."

Mattie drove Stella to the Banks house. When they knocked on the door, Burt answered, a scowl on his face. "What do you want with me?"

"We want to talk to you about your daughter's case, Mr. Banks," Stella said, her voice mellow. "May we come in?"

"Fine." He held the door long enough for Stella to catch it and then stepped back into the kitchen, where he circled the table and sat, reaching for a mug of steaming coffee that sat in front of him.

Mattie followed Stella, and they stood for a moment until Stella spoke. "Is it all right if we sit here with you, Mr. Banks?"

"Suit yourself."

Juanita entered the kitchen through the door from the living room. "Please, sit."

They settled into chairs, Mattie purposely taking a chair across from Stella so they wouldn't be aligned on the same side.

After Juanita sat at the end of the table, Stella took the lead. "We're following up on every bit of information we get about Candace so that we can find out what happened. We want to keep you informed as we go. Some of it won't be pleasant to hear, but it's important we get your opinions about it."

"The wife already told me about Candace and the boys," Burt said with a growl. "I'd like to get my hands on the little bastards."

"Were you aware of her activity?" Stella asked.

He looked at her with disgust. "Hell, no! I would've put a stop to that in a New York minute."

Juanita sighed, raising her eyes to the kitchen window and staring at it.

"To your knowledge, had Candace engaged in this sort of behavior with anyone else in the past?" Stella asked.

"No way. Candace just hit thirteen this year. She must have been experimenting. You know, hormones pop up about then and all that stuff."

"Have you ever had any interactions of that nature with Candace, Mr. Banks?"

Burt stared at Stella for a beat before he unleashed a string of expletives. "What kind of a pervert would do a thing like that with his daughter?" he asked at the end of his rant. Mattie thought that Juanita was staring at her husband every bit as hard as Stella was.

"We're looking at every angle, Mr. Banks," Stella said. "I had to ask, and I have to talk to you about something else. We discovered that you weren't at the Hornet's Nest in Hightower on Tuesday afternoon . . . like you said you were."

Burt narrowed his eyes. "What's going on here? Am I a suspect? Trying to protect those little high school boys, are you?"

"We're looking at everything that comes to our attention. It seems strange that you gave us misinformation about your whereabouts during the time when Candace was killed. So where were you Tuesday afternoon?"

"I was in Hightower."

"But not at the Hornet's Nest?"

"I was there."

"We have a reliable witness who says you weren't."

Burt looked around the room as if looking for an escape route. "I can't say where I was."

"It's important that you do. We're investigating your daughter's homicide, Mr. Banks. I would be disappointed if I had to arrest you, her father, for obstruction of justice."

"Now you're threatening me?" he asked.

Stella gave a small shrug and turned her hands palms up. They all waited, the room silent enough to hear the clock on the wall tick.

"Oh, for God's sake, Burt. Tell us where you were," Juanita said through tight lips.

He glared at his wife and then turned his spite toward Stella. "I was in a poker game. Okay?"

Juanita's jaw dropped. "A poker game? Where?"

He looked at his wife. "In Hightower."

"At the Hornet's Nest?"

"No, you idiot. Poker's not allowed at the Hornet's Nest."

Now the grilling of the suspect seemed to have been picked up by his wife, and Stella and Mattie sat back, allowing her to take over.

"Of course not," Juanita said. "Gambling's illegal there. Where were you?"

"At a friend's house. It was just a friendly private game."

"What friend?"

He narrowed his eyes. "I can't say."

"Have you played poker there before?" she asked, her voice rising.

"Yes, if you must know."

"How long has this been going on?"

Burt cast a glance at Mattie and Stella and squirmed in his chair. "For a while."

Juanita's eyes sparked. "How long, Burt? How long have you been gambling away our money?"

"It's *my* money. I earned it."

"You're taking it away from *our* family."

Stella evidently decided it was time to step back in. "Mr. Banks, you need to talk to us. Tell us where you've been playing poker. There's nothing wrong with hosting a game among friends in the privacy of your own home, so there's no need for you to shield anyone."

"It's at Hank Wolford's house, all right?" He glared at his wife. "Are you happy now?"

"Oh, you want to protect your friend when you should have been home taking care of your kids." Juanita spat out the words. "You make me sick, Burt."

While Stella tried to calm the two, Mattie made a note of the name Hank Wolford. She'd never heard of him before. If Hank ran a friendly game with a buy-in, he'd have nothing to worry about. On the other hand, if this was a high-stakes game, and the house was taking a share of the proceeds, that was different, especially if drugs or prostitution were involved.

She and Robo would be headed for Hightower next, doing more than checking out Burt's alibi.

Chapter 14

It seemed like Cole had been playing catch up all day. After spending a long session with Gus Tilley, training him to dose Lucy's injured eye, he'd finally succeeded in getting the job done. Gus had left the clinic with Lucy in the trailer, looking satisfied to be taking her home, while Cole had loaded into his pickup almost an hour late to run his stable calls. Now he was still twenty minutes from Timber Creek and would be at least a half hour late to meet the bus.

He pulled out his cell phone and dialed home. When his call went to voice mail, he remembered that Mrs. Gibbs was in Willow Springs getting her hair done. And Angie had stayed at school for a yearbook meeting. He disconnected the call without leaving a message and put the phone back in his pocket.

Sophie would be all right; there was no reason to worry. It was a beautiful spring day, and she had come home alone several times before. She knew the drill and could let herself into the house. Still, Cole pressed down the gas pedal and edged up his speed.

He breathed a sigh of relief when he turned into the lane and headed toward his house. Sophie wasn't outside, but he didn't expect her to be. He parked out front under the cottonwood tree and strode up the sidewalk to the porch. Gripping the doorknob to open the front door, he found it locked.

Belle and Bruno kicked up a fuss on the other side of the door, their deep barks sounding a warning.

"It's okay you two, it's only me," Cole shouted to them as he pulled his key ring out of his pocket and sorted through to isolate his house key. When he opened the door and stepped inside, the two big dogs rushed at him in greeting, Belle wagging her tail and Bruno wagging his whole body. "Sophie," he called. "You here?"

No answer.

Bruno scratched at the door, his signal to be let outside. Cole opened it for him, and both dogs rushed through to the yard. It seemed odd that they were in such a hurry, because Sophie would have let them out when she came home.

He scanned the coat rack at the entryway. No jacket hanging on the peg. No backpack. Had she gone to the clinic first to see her chickens?

Cole took the stairs two at a time, calling her name. Still no answer, but he checked her bedroom to make sure she hadn't come home and gone to sleep. Empty. Going back downstairs, he checked the kitchen. No sign of her making a snack.

Heading out the front door, he noticed that both dogs had left the yard and were nowhere to be seen. Thinking the dogs must have run to the clinic to find Sophie, he went to his truck and drove the hundred yards farther up the lane. As he parked, he saw neither dogs nor child outside the building. With growing concern, he unlocked the door and went through the horse treatment area to the clinic kennel room.

The baby chicks cheeped, scurrying around inside the cardboard box. But Sophie wasn't there watching them.

"Sophie!" he called, hurrying through to the rest of the clinic. The place felt undisturbed, and he had a strong feeling that Sophie hadn't come in here after school. Where was she? Where were the dogs?

Going back outside, he hurried down the length of the shed row, checking box stalls, horse runs, and finally the corral where he kept Mountaineer. The sturdy roan gelding nickered and trotted up to the fence, expecting to be fed. Calling for Sophie, Cole paused long enough to throw Mountaineer some hay and glance at the automatic water tank to make sure it was full. Everything was as it should be, but no Sophie to be found.

He jogged back to his truck and climbed in. Driving past the house and back down the lane, he caught sight of Bruno and Belle, their large black shapes roaming the property at the edge of the road, noses to the ground. He wondered if the dogs were searching for his daughter too.

When he stopped the truck and got out, both dogs came running, Belle limping slightly—her hind leg still bothered her after the gunshot wound she'd suffered last summer. He moved to the front of the truck, and Belle came to him to press against his legs. Bruno ran back toward the highway with Cole calling to him to come back. A car zipped by, narrowly missing the Doberman as he jumped away from the asphalt. He started to head west, apparently following the car.

"Bruno, *komm!*" Cole shouted. Bruno turned and stared for a second, but then came to him. Cole opened the passenger side door, moved the seat forward, and gestured toward the back seat. "Belle, Bruno, load up."

The dogs jumped into the back. A feeling of urgency made Cole hurry around the vehicle, climb into the driver's seat, and take off for the school. He hoped Sophie had missed the bus, and he would find her there waiting for him.

★

With his jutting lower jaw, Hank Wolford reminded Mattie of a pug with a beard. He wore navy sweat pants and a gray sweat shirt dotted with stains, and he had a bushy head of graying brown hair and a full beard streaked with strands of silver. He'd opened his door when Brody knocked and stepped out onto the porch to speak with him.

Mattie and Robo waited in the yard, which was covered with closely cropped weeds that had barely started their spring growth. She stood below the porch and off to Brody's right where she could observe.

"And why are you here?" Wolford asked after Brody introduced himself.

Brody consulted a notebook he'd withdrawn from his pocket. "I'd like to talk to you about Tuesday afternoon, day before yesterday."

Wolford's dark eyes, deep in the sockets of his jowly face, moved slightly as he appeared to be thinking. Evidently he locked into the date and time, because he nodded as he crossed his arms over his chest. "All right."

"Burt Banks says that he was here at your house on Tuesday afternoon. Can you confirm that?"

Wolford raised his hand to his chin and stroked his beard. "I can. Burt Banks was here."

"And were there others who could also confirm this?"

"Yes, I had a few friends over for a game of cards."

"A game of cards?"

"Yes. A poker game. Just a game among friends. Small buy-in, and we play with chips. Top three split the pot."

His description sounded like a perfectly legal game. *Now*, Mattie wondered, *is he telling the truth?*

"Could we come inside and speak with you for a moment?" Brody asked.

"We're fine out here."

"I need the names of the people at the poker game." Brody removed a pen from his pocket.

Wolford gave him a list of four names, none of which Mattie recognized. She wondered how Burt Banks could've spent large sums of money on a small buy-in for a game. It didn't feel right. She moved closer to the porch, and Robo went with her at heel. Wolford eyed her dog and edged back a step.

Brody was still digging. "Can we get phone numbers from you?"

"They're in my cell phone . . . inside. I'll get it." Wolford opened the door wide enough to slip inside and then closed it right behind him.

Robo had sniffed the air when Wolford opened the door, his nose bobbing. As soon as the door closed, he ignored the steps and jumped onto the porch, sniffed the door jam, and then sat. He stared at Mattie, giving her a signal that she knew well.

"There's dope inside," Mattie muttered.

Brody glanced at Robo before looking at Mattie. "Probably weed."

"Might be, but we don't know that."

The door opened, and Robo stood. Wolford was looking at his cell phone as he started across the threshold but stopped dead when he noticed Robo looming on the porch. Wolford glanced at Brody in confusion.

Mattie peered beyond him, into the living room. There, a guy lay on the floor, his arms flung outward, and he looked unconscious. Or dead.

"Hey!" Stepping up beside Wolford, Mattie shouted to the guy inside. "Are you okay?"

Wolford tried to push her back. Robo growled, baring his teeth, and Wolford stepped away, his hands raised. The guy inside didn't move.

"Robo, guard! Keep your hands raised and stay away from me or this dog will attack," she said to Wolford. To Brody: "There's a guy inside there. Not moving. Medical emergency."

"He's just passed out on the floor," Wolford said. "Drunk."

After Robo had told her he smelled drugs, Mattie really wanted to get inside that house, and this guy was her ticket, drunk or not. "We don't know that. He looks unconscious."

"Mr. Wolford, step outside," Brody ordered. He tipped his head toward the doorway, throwing a glance at Mattie. "Go ahead and check on him."

Wolford moved out to the porch. Mattie brushed past him to enter the house, leaving him under Brody's watchful eye and taking Robo with her.

The guy on the floor looked to be twenty-something, thin to the point of emaciation, his long brown hair stringy and unclean. Sores festered on his face, more dense around his mouth. Even as she assessed him visually, she was pulling on latex gloves extracted from her utility belt. Robo started toward the guy, but Mattie stopped him and put him in a down-stay a few yards away.

The man's chest rose and fell, the sound of his breath loud enough to hear now that she was in the room. "Hey!" she shouted, stooping cautiously to give his shoulder a shake. "Are you awake?"

No response. She bent over and placed a finger on his neck. His pulse was rapid but strong. This guy was unconscious and under the influence of something stronger than alcohol. She rolled him to his side, leaving him there to protect his airway in case he should vomit. "We'd better get an ambulance," she called to Brody.

Taking a moment to scan the room, Mattie spotted the poker setup immediately. A poker table and chairs dominated the center of the living room, chips stacked neatly in a rack on the tabletop. She identified the thick, pungent odor of stale marijuana smoke mingled with cigarettes in the air. Even the walls were dingy and yellow from exposure. Rust-colored draperies sagged at the grungy windows.

Robo was getting a nose full, his head bobbing as he sampled the air. As soon as Mattie released him from his stay, he made a beeline for a scarred and battered old credenza that stood against the back wall, its top cluttered with bottles labeled with any type of hard liquor you could imagine. As he sniffed the doors in front, he jostled one of them, and it popped free from its magnetic catch and slowly drifted open. Robo sat and gave Mattie the look that said he'd found something.

Keeping one eye on the unconscious man, she moved to the credenza and peered inside without touching anything. There in plain sight she found a large bag of cannabis, its bits of green leaves and stems easily recognizable. She didn't need a scale to know that the stuff weighed well over the two-ounce limit allowed for an adult to possess at any one time. Beside the weed sat a baggie half full of white crystal shards—obviously meth. Mattie wouldn't be able to prove it yet, but she suspected Wolford not only provided a high-stakes poker game here at his house but also sold drugs and alcohol. One-stop shopping. Mattie felt a slow burn of anger start to flicker as she thought of Burt Banks and his involvement in this operation, spending his paycheck while his wife struggled to support their family. And was Banks really here Tuesday, or was this crook Wolford lying, just because he could?

Asking Robo to heel, she left the evidence he had found in the credenza and moved back to the porch, where Brody and Wolford were waiting. As soon as she stepped outside, she gave Robo another command. "Watch him!"

Robo went into guard-dog stance, an alert position with unblinking eyes fixed on Wolford. The man scowled.

"That guy's out on something more than alcohol," Mattie told Brody. "And Robo hit on a cabinet inside. We're going to need a warrant."

★

Cole drove to the elementary school and parked out front. No Sophie waiting on the steps. He found her teacher still in her classroom. Mrs. Stanford was a small woman with droopy eyes and cheeks, although he didn't think it nice to point that out, so he'd never mentioned it to Sophie.

Cole got right to the point. "Is Sophie still at school?"

The teacher looked startled. "Why, no. I put Sophie onto the bus myself. She wasn't feeling very well the last hour of school. Looks like she's got the sniffles. I was on bus duty, and she walked out there with me. I'm positive she got onto the bus."

Cole searched for possibilities. "She's not at home. Can we contact the bus driver? Make sure she didn't miss her stop. I don't know . . . if she didn't feel well, maybe she fell asleep in the back of the bus or something." Like that was going to happen. Theirs was the first stop.

"By all means." Mrs. Stanford went to her desk and opened a drawer. Taking out her cell phone, she swiped and tapped the screen and then held it to her ear. Impatient, Cole clenched his jaw.

"Hello, Clara? This is Mavis. Did Sophie Walker get off the bus at her house this afternoon? She did?" A pause while she listened. "Just a minute."

Taking the phone away from her ear, Mrs. Stanford spoke to Cole. "Sophie got off at the top of your lane and was walking home when the bus driver pulled away."

"Let me talk to her," Cole said, reaching for the phone.

Mrs. Stanford gave it to him.

"This is Sophie's dad," he said. "Was there anyone waiting in the lane for her? Maybe a white Honda sedan?" He'd described Mrs. Gibbs's car on the off chance that the housekeeper had returned home early and met Sophie's bus, although he believed that if Mrs. Gibbs had changed her plans, she would've called him.

"No one was waiting, Dr. Walker," the bus driver said. "Sophie waved to me and started off down the lane."

Fear circled Cole's heart and tightened his chest. "Did you see anyone at all turn into the lane?"

"No. What's going on?"

"You didn't see someone turn into the lane in your rearview mirror?"

"No. There was no one behind me when I stopped. I always check. There was a silver Jeep-like car coming down the highway in front of me, and the driver slowed down as it approached. I watched my rearview mirror and saw it keep going down the road toward Timber Creek after I pulled my stop sign back in."

"Did you recognize the Jeep?" Cole asked, his mind filing through his family's friends, trying to identify someone who might've picked up Sophie, taken her for an after-school ice cream or something. No one came to mind.

"No."

"Did you recognize the driver?"

"I'm not sure I even looked at the driver. I saw that the car was obeying bus safety law, and that's all I paid attention to," Clara said, concern evident. "What's going on, Dr. Walker? Is Sophie okay?"

"She's not at home, and I'm trying to find her." Cole noticed that his own voice sounded perfectly calm even as his thoughts jumped to Candace Banks and to his friend's daughter, Grace Hartman. Both girls now dead.

"Oh, dear. I can assure you that she was well on her way down the lane when I drove away, and I saw no other cars coming or going. I'm sure she's fine. She must be at your home someplace."

With a surge of irritation that the woman could sound so sure of something she knew nothing about, Cole ended the conversation and handed the phone back to Mrs. Stanford.

Worry consumed the teacher's face. "Do you need my help?"

"I'll go back home and look for her again," Cole said, not knowing what else to do.

"Call me when you find her," she said, writing down a number on a sticky note that had red apples stamped on it. "Here's my cell phone number."

Cole hurried from the building and got back into his truck. Belle had claimed the front passenger seat, and Bruno stood in the back seat with his paws braced on the forward console, ducking his head so that he could peer out the windshield.

"Get back, Bruno," Cole said, pushing him out of the way. Bruno settled into the back seat behind Belle and watched out the window while Cole drove the few minutes it took to get back to his turnoff.

He drove down the lane slowly, scanning the open grassy area. Cedars lined both sides of the lane closer to the house, and pine trees and lilac bushes surrounded the backyard. Cole rolled down his window and shouted Sophie's name, even though he didn't see any sign of her. After parking in front, he hastened out of the truck, leaving the door open so the dogs could bail out. He jogged to the backyard, Belle and Bruno trotting behind.

"Sophie!" Still no answer.

Taking his house key out of his pocket, he let himself in the back door, the dogs following. Calling Sophie's name, he searched through the house. His chest felt as hollow and empty as the house appeared to be.

Taking his cell phone from his pocket, he quick-dialed the first person who came to mind. One he knew would do anything she could to help him find Sophie as soon as possible. *Now* and with no questions asked.

Mattie.

Chapter 15

When Mattie's cell phone rang, she and Robo had finished searching the premises for more narcotics, and she was starting to bag the evidence. The drug stash had been limited to that inside the credenza, and the rest of the place was clean. Clean of drugs, that is; the house was actually filthy. So much so that she'd taken Robo out and secured him safely in his compartment when he'd finished his work. She didn't want him to have to lie on that floor in a downstay to wait for her.

Caller ID told her it was Cole calling, and she swiped the symbol to accept the call. "This is Mattie."

"Mattie, thank God you answered. I need your help."

She'd never heard such stress in Cole's voice. He was usually so calm and in control. "What is it, Cole?"

"Sophie's missing."

Her heart stuttered. "Tell me what you mean by missing."

"She's not here at the house. I . . . I was late to meet her bus, but I expected she'd be here or in the clinic. She's not. I can't find her anywhere."

"And Mrs. Gibbs? Angela?" While she spoke, Mattie hurried to bag the rest of the evidence. Brody came in from checking on Wolford, who was under arrest and waiting in the cruiser.

"Mrs. Gibbs is in Willow Springs. Angie stayed for a meeting at school."

The image of Candace Banks laid out peacefully with her hands folded across her chest flashed into Mattie's mind, and she fought back panic. "She didn't miss the bus?"

"No. I talked to the bus driver. She said Sophie was walking down the lane as she pulled away."

"I'm in Hightower. It'll take me about twenty minutes to get to your place. Hang on, and we'll see if Robo can follow her tracks."

"I'll take Bruno out and try."

"I don't want you to do that. It's important to keep the scent trail as clean as possible. Let me come into the area to search first." She thought of something else. "Have you called the parents of Sophie's friends yet?"

"No. I'll do that right now." The eagerness in his voice almost broke her heart. He was grasping the lifeline she'd thrown him. She imagined she could take her panicky feeling, multiply it by a hundred, and it wouldn't come close to what Cole Walker felt.

"Someone's mom might have come by and taken her home with her or something," Mattie said. The odds of that were slim, and she might be grasping too. Parents typically called other parents for permission, or at least to keep them informed. "Keep the dogs in the house and stay by the home phone in case someone calls. I'll be there soon. Call me if she turns up."

Brody raised an eyebrow as she disconnected the call.

"Dr. Walker," Mattie said, her words clipped as she marked the evidence bags with the date, time, and location. "His youngest, Sophie, is missing. Got off the bus, no one else at the property at the time, not there when Walker arrived. I need to go."

Brody's blue eyes became icy while she summed it up, telling her that he was thinking of Candace Banks too. "Right. I'll finish up here and take Wolford in and book him. You take Robo and go."

Mattie turned to leave, stripping off the latex gloves she'd worn to handle the bags of narcotics. "I'll call the sheriff and notify him."

"Ten-four. We'll be in touch."

Tucking her gloves into another bag, Mattie jogged to her SUV and climbed in. Robo stood to greet her, opening his mouth in a happy grin and waving his tail. His presence gave her comfort while she told herself to calm down.

Missing children are most often found safe and unharmed.

Soon enough, Mattie was on her way to Timber Creek. She drove through the outskirts of Hightower, and when she reached the highway, she accelerated well over the speed limit, lights flashing. She lifted her transmitter from its cradle and keyed on her radio to check in with Rainbow. "K-9 One to base, do you copy?"

Rainbow answered immediately. "Affirmative. Go ahead, K-9 One."

"I'm en route to Timber Creek Veterinary Clinic, ETA twenty minutes. Report of a missing child at that location."

"Oh, no!"

"Is the sheriff in?"

"Yes. He's on another line."

"Have him call me on my cell phone."

"Copy that. Drive safely, Mattie."

Rainbow . . . dependable despite her quirks.

While she waited for the call, she tried to compose herself and think of options. Children typically had special places to hide, often places their parents were completely unaware of. Sophie might be on the property. She could've come home from school tired, gone to her special place, and fallen asleep. In that case, Robo would find her.

And of course—whenever a child disappeared, it was usually because an estranged parent took them.

Why didn't I think of that sooner?

Cole's ex, Olivia. She could've happened to come back, found Sophie at home alone, and decided to give Cole a scare. And if that was the case, surely Sophie would be perfectly safe with her mother.

Her cell phone rang, announcing the sheriff's call. "What's this about Sophie Walker?"

Mattie relayed what she knew.

"I'll go there immediately," McCoy said.

Cole was part of the sheriff's posse in Timber Creek County, and he'd responded to the sheriff's request to help out many a time, so the fact that McCoy would drop everything and respond to Cole's need didn't surprise her.

"Could you make sure we don't let a lot of traffic in and out of that area until Robo and I get a chance to search?"

When he heard the word "search," Robo poked his nose through the heavy-gauge wire mesh that separated his compartment from the rest of the vehicle. Although tempted to put her hand through the screen to pet him, Mattie kept both hands on the wheel.

"We'll stay out of your scent trails as much as we can. I'll see you there."

After disconnecting the call, Mattie drove hard through the forest and over the pass that stood between her and Timber Creek. Most cars pulled over and let her pass as soon as the drivers noticed her flashing lights, but occasionally she hit the siren briefly when someone needed an extra nudge to move over. She was able to increase her speed as she drew near her destination, following the flat stretch of asphalt that ran between lush meadows.

As she drove through town, she whooped the siren once when she thought a pickup was going to pull out in front of her. The driver jammed to a stop and watched her roll by. A fast mile out the other side of town and she finally arrived at the lane that led to Cole's place. Since she needed a scent article, she drove on to the house, where Cole's truck and McCoy's Jeep were parked. Both men waited on the front porch.

She ratcheted on her parking brake, exited the vehicle, and strode up the sidewalk. As she approached, she could see the worry lines etched on Cole's brow. He held the scent article he'd sealed inside a gallon-size zip-lock bag—a small pink T-shirt, wrinkled and worn. With Cole, she didn't have to ask if it had been retrieved from the laundry basket rather than from a drawer, freshly laundered. He knew what she needed.

"Good," she said, taking the bag. She studied his intense brown eyes, dark with concern. She'd never felt more like reaching out to touch him. But she had to hold back. "Have you heard from anyone?"

"No. I tried getting hold of parents, but I couldn't get through to everyone. I left messages."

"I spoke with the bus driver," McCoy said. "She noticed only one vehicle that was nearby when she let Sophie off the bus. A silver Jeep-like SUV." He gave Mattie a knowing look, sending her a message.

Her heart sank as she received it. *The description matches the vehicle we've issued the BOLO on.* The Nissan Pathfinder registered to Merton Heath, the registered sex offender. The pedophile.

She looked at Cole. "You've searched the house thoroughly?"

"I have."

"How about the clinic and the outbuildings?"

"I've been out there twice."

She decided to express the thought that she'd had earlier. "Did you think of Olivia?"

Her meaning dawned in Cole's eyes. "You think she might have taken her?"

"I don't know, but it's common for an ex-spouse to be involved when a child goes missing." Mattie raised the bag to indicate the tee. "Let me and Robo search. Maybe he can find her."

She hurried back to her Explorer, where Robo stood, looking out the window. As she opened the back, she told him, "Wait."

He rocked back on his haunches momentarily but then pounced forward on his front paws, excited to get out. *He thinks it's time to play with the other dogs.* "You're going to work, Robo. Let's get ready to work."

Taking out his collapsible bowl, she filled it with a splash of fresh water from the jug she kept stored in his supplies. He slurped it up and allowed her to put on his tracking harness. From that point on, he was all business. No more play postures. Mattie invited him out of the car, keeping up a continuous line of encouragement to rev him up. With him dancing at her side in heel position while looking up into her eyes, she took him out into the lane.

Robo sniffed the scent article thoroughly. "Search," she told him, using a large sweeping gesture to indicate the area. He took off, nose to the ground, and she jogged after him.

At first he quartered the area in large sweeps, roaming back and forth, but then he moved into the lane. Mattie wondered if he'd found scent from Sophie catching the bus this morning or a trail she'd left this afternoon. She decided not to worry about it and stuck with him. He led her down the lane toward the highway.

Midway down, he stopped suddenly and sniffed an area carefully. He left the lane, moving off to the side into the grass, nose down. Mattie followed, searching the area, and spotted tire tracks left in the grass perpendicular to the lane, like a car had driven off it to turn around. With sinking heart, she thought of the silver Pathfinder driven by Merton Heath and wondered if the wheels were set at the same width.

Even as the thought came into her mind, Robo took off again and locked onto a scent trail, going back into the lane and heading for the highway. As they approached, she heard the hollow echo of a vehicle coming from the east. "Robo, wait!"

His training held, and he stopped, giving her a chance to catch up and grab his harness. Still worried about the tire tracks beside the lane, she took a thirty-foot leash from her utility belt and clipped it on Robo while the car sped past, moving toward Timber Creek. At the same time, a cruiser drove up with its lights flashing and pulled to a stop in the middle of the highway.

Brody. He'd come to back her up. What a relief to know he would handle traffic while she and Robo did their work. He must have really booked it to get here so fast.

Brody exited his vehicle and waved her on, giving her the right of way to enter the highway. Mattie left the leash clipped, but now felt free to let Robo go to the end of it out front.

He trotted on toward the highway while Mattie jogged behind, letting the leash play out about fifteen feet. A growing concern threatened her concentration. The last time she followed Robo on a scent trail, it had ended badly.

Mattie caught up to Robo and glanced in both directions as they stepped onto the asphalt. No cars, Brody on guard. Robo crossed the black width of asphalt and began sniffing the far side of the road.

Quartering back and forth, he swept out a few yards in every direction, coming back to the same spot.

He sat at the edge of the highway and stared up at Mattie. She thought she knew what he was telling her.

"Good boy, Robo," she said, stroking between his ears and putting one hand under his chin as he lifted his head to gaze into her eyes. She used the moment to try to calm herself.

"This is one end of the scent trail," she called to Brody. "This must be where Sophie got off the bus. I'm going to see if I can get him to go back now and show us where she went from here."

"I'll move behind you into the lane and block this end."

"Perfect. We've had enough traffic coming in." Cole, the sheriff, and her: enough to cover any other tire tracks.

"Okay, Robo, let's find Sophie. Search." Mattie indicated the scent trail by sweeping her hand along where she imagined it lay, in the direction toward the house.

Robo had become a pro at backtracking a scent trail, and he seemed to know exactly what she wanted. He moved off in the direction from which they'd come, keeping his nose down on a beeline that Sophie's footsteps must have created earlier. This time though, when they reached the midway point, Robo left the lane and quartered the area. He came back to the smashed grass and sat.

A black wave of fear made her breath quicken as he raised his eyes to stare into hers. He opened his mouth in a pant, pink tongue showing.
The scent trail ends here.

There was no scent trail between here and the house—Robo had picked up Sophie's scent right here when he'd searched for it earlier. One end of the trail was at the bus stop, the other here, where it looked like a vehicle pulled off the lane and turned around.

She cleared her throat to loosen the tightness. "Good boy, Robo." She took a breath and turned to find Brody. He'd left his cruiser at the end of the lane, lights flashing, and he'd walked partway down behind her. She waved him in to join up with them.

"Her scent trail ends here," she said.

A furrow of concern appeared between his brows as he scanned the area and noticed the flattened grass. "Vehicle turned around here."

"We need to look for tire prints."

"Be careful not to disturb this area." Eyes to the ground, Brody started to skirt around one side of the smashed grass.

After putting Robo into a down-stay, Mattie searched the other. She wanted desperately to find prints that might tell them if this vehicle's tires matched the ones found near Smoker's Hill. But if they did . . . Mattie knew what that would mean.

She read the story left by the indentations in the grass and choked out words. "I think someone came down the lane behind her, turned in here to switch directions, and then left the property."

"Agreed. There are some partial tire prints between the clumps of grass that we might be able to cast."

Mattie looked to where he was indicating and spotted a narrow strip of tread pattern that could possibly be a match for the one found along the highway at the Banks crime scene. She voiced her opinion to Brody.

He examined the print closely. "It's hard to say. This one's not as clear. But . . . maybe."

He straightened, looking up and down the lane, scanning the area. "I'm going to tape off this area so no one comes into it. You and Robo go ahead and search the rest of the property. Make sure she's not here somewhere."

Mattie had a feeling in her gut that no matter how hard they searched, they weren't going to find Sophie. She wasn't the type to play games. There was no way she was hiding. "All right. We've got to make sure, but Brody . . . I'm afraid someone might have taken her."

"What if her mom has her? Does she have custody?"

Mattie swallowed hard. "I don't know."

He gave her a curt nod. "Doesn't matter. We've got one child dead and now one missing. I'll talk to the sheriff about it. This is no time to wait to see if a parent is playing games."

"Agreed."

Mattie turned back to Robo. She needed to see if he could pick up a scent along the highway, then turn him loose to search the property—that would give her some time before having to go back to deliver this news to Cole.

Chapter 16

While Mattie and Robo were searching the property, Cole went back inside to search the house one more time, checking closets and the crawl space. He knew it was wasted effort, but he had to keep himself busy. The dogs followed him everywhere he went, hovering close. He didn't know if he was projecting his own fears onto them, but they seemed disturbed, and he wished he could determine what they knew. After turning up nothing, he decided there was no reason to wait to call Olivia. If she had Sophie with her, he needed to know, and he needed to know now.

His ex-wife had quit returning his calls sometime during their first few months of separation, so eventually he'd given up. They hadn't spoken to one another since last summer. This had caused pain for both him and his daughters, especially around Christmas time, but other than driving to Denver to track her down and force her to talk to her kids, he could think of nothing else to do about it.

He still had Olivia on his quick-dial list, so he swiped to it and dialed. As expected, there was no answer, and he left a message. "Olivia. This is Cole. I have an important question to ask you about Sophie. Do *not* ignore this message. This is an emergency. Call me back as soon as you get this."

He disconnected the call, swearing softly under his breath. After telling the dogs to wait inside, he stepped out onto the porch and rejoined the sheriff. McCoy was putting his cell phone back inside his pocket.

"That was Deputy Brody," McCoy said. "Tess Murphy is down at the end of the lane. Says she's here to work late-afternoon hours at your clinic."

Cole had forgotten all about that. "That's right. We have two hours of clients scheduled."

McCoy's phone rang again. He held up one finger as he answered it. "Yes . . . all right, just a moment." He turned to Cole. "Your clients are starting to arrive."

Cole looked in the direction of the highway, but shrubbery around his yard blocked his view. "Why are they not coming on down the lane?"

"Deputy Cobb and Robo have marked out a scent trail, and they're still working the area. We don't want anyone to come into it yet."

Cole nodded that he understood. Searching his memory, he tried to recall what he'd seen on his schedule from when he'd peeked at it earlier. "I think all we have is routine stuff this afternoon. I need to get down there and talk to those folks, reschedule." Intending to walk down the lane, he started to move off the porch.

McCoy restrained him with a firm grip on his arm. "Wait, Cole. Let's have Tess handle it. Can she call your other clients and tell them not to come?"

"She won't have their numbers with her, but I've got them on the schedule I have in the truck."

McCoy put his phone back to his ear. "Tell Ms. Murphy that we're going to reschedule clients. Have her wait there and explain it to the ones that arrive. Dr. Walker and I will call the ones we can reach to cancel them." McCoy disconnected the call. "Let's get your schedule out of your truck and start calling folks."

It was the last thing in the world that Cole wanted to do, but at least it would keep him busy, and he didn't want to have to deal with a pileup of clients at his doorstep right now. "I'll go get it," he said, setting off down the sidewalk toward his truck. McCoy went with him.

At his truck, Cole opened the door on the passenger side, spotted his book on the seat, and reached for it. As he raised his eyes, he was able to see out the driver's side window, and down the lane. Midway down, a rectangle of yellow crime scene tape fluttered lightly in the spring breeze. It snatched his breath away.

Finding his voice, he turned to McCoy. "What . . . what did they find?"

The serious look on the sheriff's face scared him almost as much as the yellow tape. "There's evidence of a vehicle turning there in the road that we want to preserve. We might be able to get some tire prints."

"I've got to see it," Cole said. Plucking his schedule book from the seat, he closed the door and headed around the end of the truck out into the lane.

"Wait, Cole," McCoy said. "Wait until Deputy Cobb is finished."

"My scent's all over this place. Robo knows the difference between Sophie and me." Cole kept walking.

McCoy matched his pace and went with him. "There's nothing to see but flattened grass and a few partial tire tracks."

Cole kept a grim silence, marching down the hard-packed lane until he arrived at the taped-off area. He stayed on the lane, where he knew he'd leave no prints and he wouldn't disturb the evidence they were trying to preserve. He scanned the ground, searching for dark spots—blood. Not finding any gave him little comfort.

McCoy stood firm and silent beside him. It was as if the sheriff had decided not to waste his breath on pointless reassurance. Cole met his gaze and connected with a fierce empathy in his eyes.

"We've got to keep our heads clear and find her, Cole."

Giving him a brief nod, Cole raised the schedule book slightly and continued down the lane. "I'll give this to Tess. She'll take care of the schedule. And then let's decide what to do."

★

Mattie pulled a pair of latex gloves from a pocket on her utility belt and tugged them on. Robo had found a small piece of white paper fluttering at the base of a clump of rabbit brush. It was a memo about a parent-teacher meeting being held on Wednesday evening in two weeks. Sophie must have been bringing it home.

Mattie closed her eyes and conjured an image of Sophie carrying the paper as she walked down the lane. A car pulled up beside her, and someone snatched her inside, kicking and fighting; this scrap of paper floated away on the breeze, scudding along the buffalo grass and finally lighting up against the rabbit brush, where it stayed until Robo found it. She opened her eyes, unable to bear following her imagination into the car or even to consider what might have happened next. Feeling light-headed, she put the paper inside an evidence bag.

Sophie was nowhere to be found. After Mattie cleared the property and gave up on trying to track the suspect car out on the highway, she led Robo over to where Cole stood, holding his cell phone to his ear, beside Sheriff McCoy.

Cole disconnected the call, shaking his head. "That's the last parent calling back after I left a message," he said to the sheriff. "She doesn't have Sophie either."

Cole's gaze connected with Mattie's, and she sensed a panic that was just below the surface. Or perhaps she sensed her own.

"I'll try Olivia again," he said, swiping and tapping his phone. With a grim expression, he held the phone to his ear.

"Olivia," he said after a moment, relief flooding his face. He took a few steps away from the group and turned his back. "Do you have Sophie with you?"

His shoulders slumped, and he turned to shake his head at McCoy. "You're in Denver?" He walked farther away, speaking quietly into the phone.

Sheriff McCoy beckoned to Mattie with his chin, taking a few steps in the opposite direction. She went with him. "I'll contact Deputy Brody," he said, "and we'll get the Amber Alert out. Detective LoSasso says she can cast the tire prints, and we'll courier them over to Byers County for comparison."

"What about calling out the volunteers to search the roads and area around town?"

McCoy gave her a sharp look. "You're thinking what?"

"I don't know." Her heart fluttered, making it hard to take a breath. "What if he released her outside of town? Maybe we could find her."

"I'll make the call. We'll focus on roadways and the county roads into the wilderness area."

A white sedan stopped at the end of the lane, and when a woman with curly gray hair exited the vehicle, accompanied by a slender girl with shoulder-length blond hair, Mattie recognized who it was. "That's Mrs. Gibbs and Angela, Dr. Walker's housekeeper and other daughter," she said to McCoy.

"Go ahead and explain to them why we have the road blocked. I'll make the call to activate the volunteers."

Telling Robo to heel, she struck off toward the newcomers, arriving just behind Cole, who'd ended his conversation with his ex.

"What's going on, Dad?" Angie was saying. "Why are the police here?"

Cole put his hand out to clasp Angie's arm, as if he needed to touch her. "When I got home, Sophie wasn't here," he said, not wasting time on preparatory comments. "The police are helping me look for her."

While Mrs. Gibbs put her hand to her throat, Angie scanned the property, her eyes landing on Mattie. "Maybe she's still at school?"

Mattie shook her head. "She got off the bus here." Unable to continue, she turned to Cole.

"When I got here," he said, "she was nowhere to be found."

"You weren't here to meet her?" Angela asked, frowning.

"I was running late," he said, his eyes downcast, and Mattie could tell that he felt terrible about it.

"Dad! I can't believe you weren't here to meet the bus."

"I should have been here," Mrs. Gibbs said, stress enhancing her accent, "instead of getting me hair done."

Cole raised his hands. "Passing the blame around won't change the situation, so let's skip that part. It looks like someone came into the lane and picked her up. That's why they have the area taped off."

Angie seemed to be searching for answers while her eyes swept the property, appearing to avoid the yellow crime scene tape midway down the lane. "Maybe a friend came by to get her."

"I've tried all the friends I know to call, and she's not with any of them," Cole said. "Who would you call? Maybe I missed someone."

The three collaborated on Sophie's friends and came up with the same group that Cole had already contacted.

"We can probably let you drive by to get to your house soon," Mattie said to Mrs. Gibbs. "Let me check with the sheriff."

"I need to search all of Sophie's favorite places," Angie said.

"Let's walk." Cole took Angela by the arm and led her down the lane, talking to her as they went.

Mattie knew he needed time alone with his older daughter. She and Robo waited beside the car with Mrs. Gibbs while she contacted Sheriff McCoy, who said to stay put until Detective LoSasso arrived. Mattie relayed the information to Mrs. Gibbs and directed her to move her car out of the way and park near the top of the lane.

Stella drove up in the county's plain car—a dark-navy Ford sedan—stopped at the top of the lane, and rolled down her window. Mattie joined her.

"I'll leave the vehicle here," Stella said. "Could you help me carry supplies?"

"Sure." Mattie heard the trunk pop open as Stella released it, and she went to the back of the vehicle, Robo staying close beside her. Inside were two large plastic tool kits and a jug of water. Stella and Mattie each picked up a case, Mattie grabbed the water, and they set off down the lane.

"I've upgraded that BOLO we have on the Heath Pathfinder to regional," Stella said while they walked. "Sandy Benson is spreading the word among the forest rangers and the wildlife department. I looked further into Merton Heath. He's no longer on parole."

Which meant he was free to travel about the country as long as he obeyed the law to register his place of residence, which apparently he'd done. They had every right to question him as a person of interest once they found him, but so far, they had nothing else on him.

All they had was a dead teenager, and now a missing child.

"The boys we interviewed have been at baseball practice since school let out, present and accounted for. All except Brooks Waverly. His father grounded him. Said he sent him to Hightower to pick up some parts for their tractor. He's going to call me when Brooks gets home," Stella said.

"What is Brooks driving?"

"The family's silver Toyota 4Runner."

Another silver Jeep-like car. "We can't wait. Let's call him on his cell phone."

"I thought of that. His dad took it away from him."

Mattie let out a breath of frustration along with a quiet curse.

"He expects him back soon. We'll go out there and search when he calls me. To add on more bad news, I couldn't locate Burt Banks, and Juanita doesn't know where he is."

"We know he's not playing poker," Mattie said.

"At least not at Hank Wolford's place."

They arrived at the area marked off with yellow tape, and Stella began searching through it. "This one will do right here."

Stella opened a case and took out a camera and tripod, which she set up directly over the print, and then rotated the camera so that the lens faced downward. Placing an L-shaped ruler beside the print, she snapped several photos of it. After removing her photography equipment, she opened the other case and took out a plastic gallon-sized bag holding a powdery substance. Sheriff McCoy strode up as she was laying plastic frames around the tire print.

"Dr. Walker and his daughter need some time alone," he said. "She's having a hard time of it."

Mattie closed her eyes for a brief moment, fighting the terror inside that she knew Angela and Cole were dealing with.

As if to keep her busy, Stella handed a cup to Mattie. "Could you pour this amount of water into this bag of dental stone and mix it together by squeezing the bag?"

While Mattie followed instruction, Stella updated the sheriff on the status of the suspects in the Banks homicide.

"We've got to pin down Burt Banks," he said, taking out his cell phone. "I'll get Deputy Brody started on that next. He sent the Amber Alert out through dispatch. We're classifying this as a suspected high-risk stranger abduction, and we're sending it out region wide."

Mattie knew that the region covered Colorado and the surrounding states. If they didn't find Sophie in the next few hours, he might broaden the alert to nationwide. She couldn't believe this was Sophie they were talking about.

She worked the mixture into pancake batter consistency while Stella sprayed the tire print with a fixative. She took the bag from Mattie and carefully poured the contents at the edge of the print, allowing it to flow into the print indirectly without disturbing any of the impressions. "We'll let that set for about a half hour," Stella said when she finished, sitting back on her heels.

Mattie knew she couldn't stand around and wait that long. Her nerves were beginning to get to her, and she wanted to stay moving. "I think it's best if Robo and I search with the volunteers," she said to McCoy.

"Agreed. But stay close to town. If we get a hit on that Heath BOLO, I want you able to respond immediately. I'll stay here with the Walkers."

"When Brooks Waverly gets home, Mattie and I need to go out to question him and search his vehicle," Stella said. "Maybe even their property."

McCoy looked at Mattie, obviously considering it.

"We'll have probable cause for the ranch if Robo hits on Sophie's scent inside the vehicle," Mattie said, "but we'll need permission first for the car itself. Or a warrant."

The sheriff nodded. "I'll get you that warrant. This is no time to delay and fiddle with permission."

It was a small thing, but it gave her a sense of relief. "I'll stay in contact."

With Robo at heel, she hastened to the house to get her vehicle, berating herself for letting Merton Heath drive away only so she wouldn't be late for a meeting. As she approached, Angela and Cole came out of the house onto the porch. They both hurried down the sidewalk to join her at her Explorer while Mattie loaded Robo into the back. She turned to face them, noticing Angela's reddened eyes and strained features. Cole didn't look much better.

"We're positive she's not anywhere on this property," Cole said. "What can we do next?"

"We've issued an Amber Alert, and we've called out volunteers to search. Since we can't identify a friend or family member who might have picked up Sophie, we have to treat this as if we're dealing with a stranger who's taken her." Mattie's eyes started to fill, and she blinked back the wetness. The last thing the Walkers needed was for her to break down, and she would never allow herself to cry in front of them. She looked away for a few moments while she stowed Robo's equipment, taking the time to regain control. "You need to stay here by the phone, just in case this is a kidnapping for ransom. Sheriff McCoy will stay here to wait with you."

"I can forward the home phone to my cell," Cole said. "No need to sit here and do nothing."

Mattie knew exactly how he felt. "I'll let you discuss that with the sheriff. I'm taking Robo out to search with the volunteers."

"We can use Bruno and Belle to search too," Angela said, her voice quivering with anxiety. "Mrs. Gibbs can stay here at the house."

This teen was no stranger to death. Mattie wanted to reach out to her, but she held herself in check. "Your dogs have both been trained to track, but apparently Sophie's scent trail starts where she got off the bus and ends where we've put up the yellow tape. I don't think Belle and Bruno would be able to find anything else."

"When I let the dogs out earlier, Bruno tried to head west on the highway," Cole said.

Both Timber Creek and the Waverly ranch lay toward the west. Mattie held his gaze while she considered it. "I'll call Jim Madsen, Robo's trainer, and see if he can bring in a bloodhound. That's the best breed I know that might follow scent coming from inside a car. I'll see what we can do."

Cole's face filled with hope. "That sounds good. Thank you, Mattie."

"Talk to Sheriff McCoy about what you can do next. It's best for him to advise you."

Cole nodded, and Mattie reached to open the car door. He stepped forward and got to the handle first, their hands brushing together as he opened the door for her. She pulled herself into the driver's seat, not knowing what to say—a promise to find Sophie would be useless. If a stranger had taken her, they both knew what they were up against.

Cole was the one who spoke. "I knew you were the first one I should call."

His words were almost her undoing. "I'll do my best to find her, Cole."

As she drove away, she slammed her fist on the steering wheel, wanting to feel anything but this empty helplessness. She vowed to find Sophie, and soon. She wouldn't be able to bear it if she couldn't return this child safely to the man and family she loved.

Chapter 17

Mattie fought to regain her professionalism; it was crucial to remain detached and focused. She shrugged her shoulders to try to relieve the knots that had invaded her muscles and touched the button on her steering wheel to activate her hands-free communication system.

She spoke into the receiver. "Call Jim Madsen."

He answered the phone with a question. "How did your scent lineup go, Deputy?"

The lineup seemed like years ago. "Robo did the job. But Sarge, now we have a missing child."

"How can I help?"

She explained what they'd found so far. "Is it possible for a bloodhound to follow a scent trail coming from inside a vehicle?"

"There are a few reports of it. I've known a bloodhound to be able to track for a while at least, and we can't afford to not give it a try."

"Do you have access to a dog that could help us?"

"I do. I can get to Timber Creek in about four hours."

"I'll meet you at the site. You'll pass it on your way into town. Just give me a call when you see the sign that says you're ten miles out."

"See ya soon."

She dialed Sheriff McCoy and gave him the update on Madsen. "It's best to tell Dr. Walker to keep his dogs out of the area, at least until Sergeant Madsen can get here."

"Will do. I'm glad you called."

She knew he was struggling to keep Cole from going off half-cocked, and as she disconnected the call, she'd never been so grateful for the sheriff's steady personality.

As she drove to the station, she checked the time. Almost six o'clock. Sophie had been missing for three hours, and there was only about an hour of full sunlight left. She found the station surrounded by cars, every space in the parking lot taken. She pulled up to the front door. The lobby was filled with people, so she decided to leave Robo in his compartment.

"You're staying here. I'll be right back."

He stared out the windshield, moving from side to side to get a better view. He knew something was up and seemed to be trying to figure out why so many people were inside his station. Mattie hurried to join the crowd.

Rainbow and Brody were in the middle of it. "Drive slowly and check the barrow ditches on both sides of the road," Brody was saying, his deep voice booming. "If the grass or weeds are high, get out of your vehicle and check the area more thoroughly. If necessary and if you're working in a group of three, one can drive while the other two walk along the ditch banks."

Then he began to call out names of people and names of roads, making assignments for search groups and areas. Mattie caught Brody's eye, and he acknowledged her with a nod. She'd made her own plans; all she needed was a moment to share them with him.

After receiving their assignments, people left the station in groups, and the crowd began to dwindle. Mattie recognized many individuals, including Garrett and Leslie Hartman, Cole's good friends whose daughter was murdered last summer. She swallowed the lump that formed in her throat. And there were Anya Yamamoto and Dean Hornsby from the hot springs resort, along with a blonde she hadn't met before, probably a new massage therapist to replace the one who had been murdered last fall.

Geez! What's happening to our community?

Eventually, Mattie spotted Juanita Banks standing across the room with her coworker, Jed, and an older man with gray hair. Juanita looked exhausted and drawn, and Mattie could only imagine the effort it must have taken for her to respond to this community emergency. She must have been motivated by the loss of her own daughter, and Mattie had to admire her for coming out to help search for someone else's missing child.

"Moses Randall, Juanita Banks, and Jed Franklin. You take County Road Six all the way to the intersection of Buckhorn Road," Brody said, cueing Mattie that the gray-haired man must be the feed store's owner. "Follow Buckhorn Road south back to County Road One and return to Timber Creek."

Randall nodded and gathered his troops. They passed by Mattie on their way out the building, and she followed them outside to the parking lot.

"Mrs. Banks," she called, catching Juanita's attention as she approached their group, "thank you for your help. Thank you all, actually, but I know this is hard on you, Mrs. Banks. We appreciate your help."

Juanita shifted, looking down at her clasped hands. "I can't sit at home anymore, so I went in to work. When Moses got the alert for volunteers, he closed the store, and we all decided to come."

"I'm Moses Randall," the storeowner said, extending his hand.

Mattie introduced herself as she accepted his handshake.

Randall glanced at Juanita. "The little Walker girl was in our store just yesterday, buying baby chickens. I hope we can find her," he said, giving the grieving mother's arm a sympathetic touch. "I hope we can make a difference this time."

Having given voice to everyone's fear, he scuffed a foot on the parking lot asphalt and looked everywhere but at the others.

Jed turned to inspect her Explorer and appeared to be studying Robo. "Did your dog turn up any clues as to where the little girl might be?"

Mattie wished she could give him an unequivocal yes. "Yes and no," she said. "When we can't define the exact area we need to search in, we depend on our volunteers. If you find any trace, we'll try to pick up a trail again."

"I hear your dog found Candace," he said.

Nodding to acknowledge the kid's statement, Mattie glanced at Juanita, who looked on, sadness sagging her features. She decided to put an end to their conversation. "I guess we'd better get started."

As the others walked away to load up into their vehicle—a white Toyota Tundra with an extended cab—Mattie headed toward her own, intending to take Robo inside with her. She paused, noticing that Moses Randall took the driver's seat. The truck was probably his.

Robo couldn't wait to get inside the building, and Mattie had to correct him, making him slow down and allow her to enter first. Once inside though, she released him to let him sniff the entire lobby, knowing he wouldn't be content until he'd swept the place thoroughly. He began to do his dog thing, nose to the floor, darting every which way.

The station had emptied out, Brody had gone into his office, and Mattie spent a moment to check in with Rainbow.

"How are you holding up?" Rainbow asked, her brow furrowed with worry.

"I'm hangin' in. You?"

Rainbow shook her head. "I'm so sad for Candace and so scared for Sophie."

Mattie swallowed hard and reached for Rainbow's hand. Her friend had taken the words right out of her mouth. "I need to check in with Brody."

She went to Brody's office and rapped on the door before peeking inside. When she saw he was on the phone, she started to withdraw, but he beckoned her to enter. She stood at the doorway until he waved toward one of the two hard-plastic chairs that sat in front of his desk, indicating that she should take a seat. As she listened, she gathered he was still trying to track down Burt Banks.

"Give me a call if he shows up, will you?" he said to the person on the other end of the line. His frustration was apparent when he ended his conversation. "I couldn't find Banks at the Hornet's Nest, so I've tried every other bar in Hightower and in town. He's not at any of them."

Mattie sat on the edge of her chair. "What do you make of that?"

The furrow in his brow grew deeper as he stared at her, evidently mulling her question. "It's suspicious as hell."

She nodded. "I'm going to comb the streets with Robo. Check around the Banks place, go up and down the alleys. We'll cover as much ground as we can before we head out to the Waverly ranch."

She told him about Jim Madsen bringing a bloodhound in to help.

"What are the chances of the dog being able to follow a scent trail down a highway like that?" Brody asked.

"Slim, but it's worth a try."

"It'll be dark when he gets here."

"There'll be less traffic on the highway then, and I'll have to light his way from behind. We can't afford to wait. The scent trail will decay more every hour."

"I'll plan to light up the road in front of him," Brody said. "If he works between us, we can keep him safe from oncoming traffic."

"Good plan. He's supposed to call when he's about ten miles out. I'll contact you then. Let me know if you locate Banks, okay?"

"Will do." Brody gave Mattie a hard look. "I know this kid means something to you. Stay strong."

His words surprised her. "Always." She added something that probably could go without saying: "We can't lose sight of finding Candace's killer, either."

Brody nodded. "I think we're dealing with the same person. Finding Sophie Walker could lead us to our killer. You know that, right?"

"I do." It was what she'd feared from the moment she heard Sophie was missing.

He gave her a brief nod of dismissal.

As she passed through the lobby, she called Robo to come, and he scurried toward the door to follow her outside. She loaded him up and then drove toward the west side of town. A headache had started at the base of her skull. She circled her head, making the bones in her neck pop.

After parking the car, she slipped from the driver's seat and went to the back to retrieve a pair of white cross-trainers from a bin that held her supplies. Robo hovered behind her, brushing against her as she braced herself on his compartment floor to change her shoes. She began to chat him up, letting him know there was more work to do, and he looked eager to go.

"Let's find Sophie." Taking out the bag that held the scent article, she lowered it to his nose. He barely took a whiff. She wondered if the word "Sophie" and the child's scent were locked together now in his memory. She wouldn't doubt it. Stuffing the plastic bag that held Sophie's T-shirt back inside the pocket on her belt, she hurried to direct him toward the Banks house, giving him the search command.

She led Robo in a sweep of the yard. Since there was no backyard fence, she circled the house, going back to the alley and around. Nothing. No hits. Disappointed, she let him go where he wanted as he continued to search, alternating nose to the ground and then to the air as he tried to catch the desired scent. He trotted down the street, and she played out the leash to the very end, giving him the freedom to move wherever he desired as she jogged behind.

We'll search this whole damn town if we have to.

★

Mrs. Gibbs set a plate of thick ham sandwiches on the kitchen table. "Would you like another cup of coffee, Sheriff?" she asked, waving the pot that she'd brought with her.

"I'd better cut myself off," he said.

"Dr. Walker?" Mrs. Gibbs offered the pot to him.

His stomach lurched. "No, thanks." He drew a breath and got up from the table. Although he typically loved the way Mrs. Gibbs fixed sandwiches, slathering plenty of mayonnaise on thick slices of meat, the smoky scent of the ham made him queasy.

At the sheriff's insistence, Cole had called his parents. Thankfully, he'd reached his dad and didn't have to talk to his mom. Although his dad offered to come over to sit with him—something he was certain the sheriff had hoped for—Cole had declined. His mother was difficult to be around in the best of times, and he didn't have it in him to endure her judgmental observations. He'd asked his parents to help with the volunteer search instead.

He'd also contacted his sister, Jessie, and when she insisted she was going to come from Denver, he didn't turn her down. He expected her to arrive sometime in the next few hours, and he hoped she could help him with Angela. His eldest was terrified that her sister had been killed, and his own terror—plus the fact that guilt was riding him hard—hampered his ability to reassure her. Mrs. Gibbs had ended up soothing her with a cup of chamomile tea and a suggestion for her to call a friend for support. She'd been upstairs in her room for a while now.

His cell phone rang, and he checked caller ID. It was Tess. Earlier, they'd forwarded the clinic line to her phone, and she was screening calls. He couldn't deal with talking to clients right now, and he was grateful for her help. He connected the call.

"Any word?" Tess asked.

"No."

"I've had two more calls from Gus Tilley. I've been able to answer his questions about his animals, but he seems anxious to talk directly to you. I've put him off but wanted to warn you that he might show up on your doorstep."

"Does he have an emergency?"

"No. Just follow-up questions about Dodger and his horse, Lucy. Actually, he's repeating the same questions over and over. Something's not right about him, Cole. He's acting odd."

Cole felt a wave of irritation; he didn't have the reserves to worry about a client. It was dark outside, and Sophie was still missing. His head felt like it was going to explode. He brushed his fingers through his hair and kneaded his scalp.

As if sensing that his silence meant he was at his wit's end, Tess went on. "I know you can't deal with him right now, so I'll try to keep him pacified. I just wanted you to know what was going on."

"Thanks, Tess. I appreciate that."

"Tom and I are finishing up our route in the search. We're heading back into Timber Creek to check in at the sheriff's station. Is there anything else I can do to help? Do you want me to come over?"

"No, but if you can keep screening calls, I'd be forever grateful."

"Of course. I plan to keep taking calls tonight. But will you contact me if you hear anything at all about Sophie?"

"You'll be first on my list."

"And call me anytime if there's something more I can do."

He sensed she was battling her own anxiety. She'd grown close to both of his kids since they'd been helping out at the clinic. Cole agreed that he would.

Detective Stella LoSasso had come in while he was on the phone, and after he disconnected, she ended her quiet conversation with the sheriff. "I need to speak with you, Dr. Walker," she said.

"Sure."

"Shall we sit?" She gestured toward the kitchen table and chairs.

"I need to stand."

"All right." She adopted a relaxed stance, leaning a hip against the cabinet facing him. "What do you know about Sophie's activities starting with yesterday? Tell me everything you can."

He forced his sluggish mind clear back to the day before. It seemed like a lifetime ago. Looking at Mrs. Gibbs for reinforcement, he began to outline what he could remember about the day. "We had breakfast as usual, then she went off to school."

"Did she ride the bus?"

"Yes."

"And the bus picks her up at the end of the lane, where it also drops her off?"

"Yes."

"Do you take her to the bus stop or does she walk?"

"She walks with her sister almost every morning. But I drove them both to the bus stop this morning, because they wanted to see the chicks at the clinic before they left."

"So it's routine for her to walk to and from the bus stop every day?"

Cole could see what she was getting at. "It's almost always routine for them to walk in the mornings, unless it's too cold or wet. But in the afternoons, I usually try to meet the bus."

"So it was unusual for you to miss meeting the bus today?"

Cole searched for judgment in her eyes, but all he saw there was a keen interest in obtaining information. "Yes. I've been meeting the bus almost every day for the last four or five months."

"But not every day. It's intermittent?"

"It's more likely that I'm there when the girls get home than not, if you're wanting to know our routine."

"I am. You said 'when the girls get home.' Is it typical that both girls come home on the bus together?"

"Yes, until lately. Angela has been staying at school to work on the yearbook. Do you think someone was waiting out there and planning to take Sophie?"

"That's what I'm trying to determine. If you're almost always there or she's almost always with her sister, a planned kidnapping seems unlikely. It makes more sense that it was an abduction of opportunity."

Her words touched him with an icy chill, and he suppressed a shudder.

"Getting back to yesterday," LoSasso said, "did you meet the bus yesterday afternoon?"

He looked at Mrs. Gibbs as he searched for the answer, and she nodded.

"Yes," he said. "I had to think for a moment, but I remember now."

"Any field trips or anything different about school yesterday?"

"No, none that I'm aware of."

"Okay, so you met the bus and then you drove her home?"

"Yes. After she ate a snack, I drove her to the feed store to buy baby chicks for her birthday."

LoSasso narrowed her eyes and glanced at the sheriff. "Who was at the store?"

"There were a few customers. There was a lady I didn't know and a young boy who left as we came in. I think the boy had been looking at the chicks. Moses Randall might be able to tell you who they are."

"So Mr. Randall was there also. Anyone else?"

Cole searched his memory. "Just one of his employees."

"Mrs. Banks?"

"No, a kid that helps him. Maybe twenty-something. I don't know his name."

"Did anyone seem to be watching Sophie or interacting with her in a way that caught your attention?"

Again, Cole tried to recall if anything had set off alarm bells, but he came up short. "No. Both Moses and his helper talked to Sophie, but it was just about the chickens and what we needed to buy."

"Then you came home? Any other stops?"

"We went directly to the clinic to get the chicks settled in."

"And where did Sophie go from there?"

Cole thought about it, and a concern began to gnaw at him. "She stayed at the clinic actually. There was one client she interacted with who seemed taken with a story she was telling him."

"Tell me about that."

He remembered Gus Tilley sitting cross-legged on the floor, hanging onto each of Sophie's words as she spun her tale. Although yesterday he'd thought nothing of it, the memory of his client's infatuation, coupled with Tess's statement that the man was acting odder than usual, caused a tremor to pass through him. Trying to stay calm, he began to relay the information to the detective in an objective manner, as much as was possible, wanting her to draw her own conclusions.

He'd never want to accuse an innocent man of anything. But his baby was missing, it was dark outside, and he'd never gone to bed before without knowing exactly where his children were and what they were doing.

"The client's name is Gus Tilley," he said. "I think we should go talk to him. He lives in the mountains west of town, and I can show you the way."

The detective's cell phone rang. She looked at her caller ID and answered it, listening for a moment, while Cole felt an urgency to get going.

"Please stay where you are and keep him there with you," she said. "I need to talk with him." She listened again before speaking. "That's your right if you want to, but I'll be there within twenty minutes."

After disconnecting the call, she turned to Cole. "This is a priority lead on Sophie that I need to follow. Get me Tilley's address, and we'll follow up there if nothing turns up on this one."

"Where are you going?"

"I can't say, Dr. Walker. But I promise that if we find Sophie, you'll be the first to know."

Cole felt like he was being left at the gate.

Chapter 18

It was dusk as Mattie and Stella drove through the wide wrought-iron arch that marked the entryway to the Waverly Ranch. As they pulled up to the ranch house, attorney Justin McClelland stepped out onto the well-lit porch, followed by Jack Waverly. Brooks was nowhere in sight.

"Waverly said he was going to call his attorney," Stella muttered. "Looks like he's as good as his word."

A frown punctuating his unibrow, McClelland met them as they exited the Explorer and moved to stand under the yard light. "Are you harassing this family, Detective?"

"No harassment, Counselor. I need to talk with Brooks is all."

"You got away with that lineup without me. I want you to know right now for the record that you're not to speak with Brooks again without me present."

"That's his right if that's what he and his parents want. Mr. Waverly was present at the lineup." Stella looked at Jack, and he stared back at her, his mouth set in a grim line and his hands in his pockets.

Using the too-sweet version of her smile, Stella looked back at McClelland. "Now that we have that settled, let me talk to Brooks."

Jack turned on his heel and retreated to the house. They waited in silence until he came back, this time accompanied by his son, his typically handsome face spoiled by a sullen expression.

Stella didn't bother with pleasantries. "Where were you this afternoon at three o'clock, Brooks?"

The kid threw a look at McClelland, who nodded at him. "I was on my way to Hightower on an errand for my dad."

"And you didn't get home until a half hour ago?"

"It took a while to find everything."

"Do you have a receipt?"

Brooks shrugged. "I think so. It's probably in the car with the supplies."

"I'd like to see it."

Brooks turned toward the silver 4Runner parked at the edge of the yard but hesitated when McClelland spoke.

"Wait, Brooks. What's your reason for seeing the receipt, Detective?"

Stella looked at McClelland and then Jack Waverly. "I'd like your permission to search the car Brooks was driving this afternoon, Mr. Waverly. I understand it was this Toyota right here."

McClelland answered for Jack. "No permission granted."

It gave Mattie intense satisfaction to see Stella pull the warrant out from the inside pocket of her jacket.

"All right. I'll execute this warrant then," Stella said, handing it to McClelland. "As you can see, it gives us the right to search the vehicle with our K-9, and it includes the vehicle's contents as well."

The attorney's frown darkened as he scanned the document. He nodded briefly at Jack and strode toward the Toyota.

"Wait right there, Justin," Stella said in a cutting tone. "Please step away and let Deputy Cobb work unimpeded."

He threw up his hands and went to stand beside Jack.

Mattie's anxiety had built while she'd watched the exchange, and she was relieved to be able to get back in action. She hurried to the Explorer's tailgate to get Robo. He'd been watching and seemed more than ready to go to work. It took her mere seconds to put on his equipment, and he jumped out, circling around her, looking up for his next instruction.

Her heart thudded as she prepped him and let him sniff the scent article. This was it. This would tell them what they were dealing with. Had Brooks Waverly taken Sophie, or had a stranger taken her? It was a toss-up as to which was worse.

"What is this, Detective?" Mattie heard McClelland say. "What's she looking for?"

She tuned him out and focused on Robo. Opening the 4Runner door on the passenger side, she asked him to search and directed him to sniff the interior of the door before gesturing him into the car. The car was immaculate and free of clutter. He jumped in and whiffed both front seats and the floor, then jumped to the back. Mattie opened the back door, keeping an eye on him as he sniffed the bench seat and then the floor. Then he clambered into the rear compartment and circled, giving a box filled with packaged automotive parts a cursory sniff before moving back through the car to check where he'd been.

Mattie's hopes fell as she realized he wasn't going to give her a hit. Without a hit, they'd have to stop. There'd be no searching the rest of the property.

After Robo came back to her to signal he was finished, she opened the SUV's tailgate and retrieved the receipt Stella wanted. She shook her head as Stella approached and handed it to her. The detective made eye contact and lifted one shoulder to acknowledge her disappointment. Feeling let down, Mattie hugged Robo to her knees and told him he'd done a good job.

Stella went back to the men with the receipt, holding it up so that she could read it under the bright light. "You were driving to Hightower at three o'clock this afternoon, but you didn't check out at the store until five twenty. It only takes a half hour to get to Hightower, Brooks. What were you doing all that time?"

Brooks flushed and shot a glance at his dad. "Like I said. It took a while to find everything."

"Two hours?"

"Don't answer that, Brooks," McClelland said. "I insist you tell me what's going on, Detective, or this interview is over."

"We have a missing child, Justin. One child dead two days ago and now another girl missing."

McClelland let his surprise show before he recovered. "My client has nothing to do with your first case, Detective, and I'm willing to go out on a limb here and say he has nothing to do with your second one either."

"I have a runner's cap that Brooks lost near the Banks crime scene, and now he has a huge chunk of unaccounted for time right when our second child goes missing. So, Justin, do you see why I'm not willing to take your word for it?"

"Who is the missing girl?" Jack asked.

"Sophie Walker."

Jack looked surprised. "Doc Walker's daughter?"

"The younger one."

"Did you find evidence of her being in that car?" Justin said, gesturing toward the 4Runner.

Stella shrugged.

"I guess not, or you would've made an arrest. Your work here is done. I'm ending this interview until I have a chance to speak with my clients."

Stella backed away, her disgust evident. "Then go to it, Counselor, but I'll tell you when our work is done. Deputy Cobb and I are going over this vehicle with a fine-tooth comb, and we won't be leaving until we're sure Sophie Walker hasn't been in it."

★

Mattie felt sick at heart as she drove Stella back to the station. They'd found nothing at the Waverly place that would lead them to Sophie.

"My gut tells me the person who took Sophie is also Candace's killer," Stella said.

"Brody and I think so too."

"And if Candace's death was accidental, we have hope that Sophie is still alive."

Mattie nodded, unable to speak, thinking of sweet Sophie with her big grin and boisterous spirit.

"We need to keep an eye on Brooks Waverly," Stella said. "I'm not sure how we're going to do it."

"Maybe Johnson?"

"I'll talk to the sheriff. I'm just not sure how we can stake out that place."

Even an unmarked car would be conspicuous parked on a highway with nothing but open meadowland on both sides.

"Might have to be satisfied with setting up a speed check between Timber Creek and watching for the Waverly vehicles that way," Mattie suggested.

"At least that would tell us if and when Brooks drives into town. I don't know what he was doing during that two-hour block of time, but I'll see if I can find out what time he actually arrived at that store."

"It's a concern," Mattie was saying when her cell phone rang. It was Jim Madsen, and she connected the call.

"I just passed the sign that said I'm ten miles from Timber Creek," he said.

She gave him directions to Cole's lane. "There's a sign out by the highway that says Timber Creek Veterinary Clinic. It'll be visible in your headlights."

"I'll be there soon."

"We'll meet you there." Mattie flipped on her overheads and picked up speed as she spoke to Stella. "Sergeant Madsen will arrive with a bloodhound within the next few minutes."

"Do you think this dog can come up with something when Robo couldn't?"

"I don't know, but bloodhounds have more scent cells than German shepherds. Let me call Brody and tell him Madsen's almost here."

Mattie hoped Jim's dog would be able to find Sophie's scent coming from the vehicle that had snatched her away. She knew that while most dogs had around 150 to 200 million olfactory receptors, some believed a bloodhound could have up to 300 million. The breed's large, wet flews and folds of skin around their nose and ears helped scoop up scent particles in the air or on the ground.

Bloodhounds could sometimes track a human scent trail that was over a week old.

By the time they arrived at the entry to Cole's lane, Brody was already parked there with his lights flashing. Even as Mattie pulled in to park, an unmarked SUV drove up beside her. The combined lights on top of her vehicle and Brody's created an eerie blue-and-red strobe that let her see Jim Madsen give her a brief salute as he parked.

"I'll tell the sheriff we're all here," Stella said, reaching for her phone.

Mattie nodded and left the car. Robo bounced from side to side in his compartment, checking out Jim's SUV. He'd evidently spotted the other dog. The bloodhound's nose pressed up against the side window of his own compartment as he sat calmly and stared at Robo, placid and apparently less excitable than her dog. His soulful eyes in his droopy face shifted to stare at her for a moment, and then moved back to watch Robo. She wondered what difference there would be in handling this calm, collected animal rather than the raw bundle of energy that made up her German shepherd.

She met Jim outside his car with her hand extended. "Thanks for coming, Sergeant."

A burly man with a shaved head that sported a police badge tattoo above his right ear, Jim Madsen reached to shake hands. Hers disappeared inside his big paw as he squeezed it. "I hope we can help," he said in his Southern drawl.

Mattie introduced Stella and Brody and then began to explain their plan. "Brody and I can light you up in front and back if that's the way you want to work this."

Brody joined in with more detail. "We'll also pull in a couple other vehicles to stop traffic and give you a buffer to work in. We can keep you inside a clear zone of about a mile."

"However you want to do this is fine by me," Jim said.

"I'll have a deputy stop traffic in town now," Brody said. "Sheriff McCoy will take care of it on this end."

Mattie oriented Jim to the layout of the scene, pointing out the taped area where the vehicle had turned, the place Sophie exited the school bus, and how Robo had tracked her scent between the two spots.

Headlights pierced the darkness as the sheriff drove from the house. A passenger exited the car with him. Cole. The stress on his face caused the pain she'd been suppressing to flare. He came to stand at her side, the warmth from his body contrasting with the coldness she felt in her chest, while the sheriff greeted the sergeant.

"This is Dr. Cole Walker," McCoy said, introducing Cole. "Sophie is his daughter."

Cole stepped forward to shake hands with Jim. "Thank you for coming and bringing your dog," he said, his voice low but solid, locking gazes with the rather intimidating sergeant. It was easy to see the strain he was under, and Mattie wondered how he was able to maintain his composure.

"We'll do the best we can to find your little girl," Jim said before turning away. "I'll go get Banjo ready."

Cole moved back to stand beside Mattie. Wanting to offer what little comfort she could, she did what she'd resisted earlier—she touched his forearm. Cole turned to her, his eyes haunted, and he shook his head slightly as if to say he couldn't believe he was trapped in this nightmare. They both turned their attention back to Jim as he asked his dog to jump down from the back of the vehicle.

Banjo stood quietly in the light from Jim's SUV, looking noble and ready to work in his red nylon tracking harness. He was a beautiful animal, with the black hair around his muzzle accenting his coppery-tan coat.

Jim patted him firmly on the side and then pulled him against his leg and rubbed him vigorously all over. That appeared to be Banjo's signal that it was time to work, and he wagged his tail as he gazed up at his handler. Jim clipped a long lead onto the dead ring of the harness and spoke to Mattie. "We're ready to rock and roll. You got a scent article for us?"

She took the bag from inside the pocket on her utility belt and handed it to him. Then she looked at Brody. "I'll follow if you'll take the lead."

Brody nodded agreement and headed toward his cruiser.

Cole touched Mattie's arm. "Can I ride with you?" he asked quietly.

His request surprised her. "Sure."

He headed for the passenger side of her vehicle while Mattie exchanged a glance with the sheriff. Evidently he thought the arrangement was okay, since he didn't protest.

"Detective LoSasso and I will set up the roadblock here. We'll all meet back together when Sergeant Madsen has some answers," McCoy said.

Cole waited beside her SUV until she got inside, and then he slid into the passenger seat. Robo turned away from watching Banjo to thrust his nose through the heavy-gauge mesh at the front of his cage to greet Cole. Putting his hand through the wire, Cole stroked Robo's head and then turned to put on his seat belt. Robo bounced back to the side window again to get a bead on the other dog, and as Mattie shifted into gear and started to move the SUV into position behind Banjo and his handler, he continued to bob around, keeping the other dog in sight.

Cole sighed. "I can't believe this is happening."

"I know. I can't either." Mattie touched the back of his hand, and he turned his palm up to grasp hers. They exchanged glances before he released her hand so she could return it to the steering wheel.

"I can't believe I wasn't there to meet her bus." Cole's voice sounded thick with emotion and self-blame.

"I know how your schedule can get. Things pile up during the day. Your kids should be safe on your property."

Cole shook his head, and Mattie didn't know what else to say.

The scene took on an eerie glow as the red-and-blue overheads lit dog and handler from front and behind. Brody drove out onto the highway and parked, while the sheriff headed east to set up a roadblock. Mattie waited, parking her vehicle where her headlights wouldn't blind Jim and Banjo while the handler oriented his dog to the search, offering him the scent article and using a sweeping gesture to indicate the area around the highway.

At first Banjo backtracked down the lane, where Sophie's scent was fresh, but Jim brought him back patiently, patted and praised him, and gestured toward the highway again. Banjo quartered the area in a methodical way, sniffing the ground.

Cole sat beside Mattie and watched in silence, tension radiating from him in waves. When Banjo moved into the ditch alongside the highway and started to go slowly toward the west, Mattie realized she'd been holding her breath. Exhaling, she watched Brody pull out ahead and then waited for dog and handler to get about thirty feet down the road. She pulled into the highway behind them, her headlights giving Jim the light he would need to navigate the ditch bank.

"Do you think he has a scent trail?" Cole murmured.

"We'll see."

Then Banjo surged forward, making Jim break into a jog to follow. Mattie's heart did a two-step. "Looks like he got a hit," she said. She continued to drive behind them, keeping about thirty feet away.

Silhouetted by their headlights, Banjo and Jim moved down the highway toward Timber Creek. A sideways glance at Cole told Mattie he was on the edge of his seat, his hands fisted on his door's armrest and on the console. After about a half mile, and as they neared the city limits, Banjo stopped his forward progress and began to quarter the area, moving from ditch to asphalt and back again. Jim swept the area with his flashlight for a minute, and then he set a wire spike with orange flagging tape into the ground beside the road before they moved on. But after about twenty feet, Banjo turned back and started searching the same area again.

Mattie's heart seized. She recognized the dog's behavior—he'd lost the trail he'd been following with such assurance. Something must have happened at this one spot to make him lose his confidence. Giving the bloodhound time to work, she waited until Jim waved her forward.

After cruising up to meet him, she stopped and rolled down her window.

"He's lost the trail, but I'm certain he was on it until we hit this spot," Jim said, his breath causing vaporous puffs in the cold night air.

"Yeah, he did look confident about it back there," she said.

"I marked the spot, because there's a tire track just off the shoulder, right beside the asphalt."

"The vehicle pulled off the road?"

"Some vehicle did. I don't know if it's the same one that was at the doc's place, but we need to find out." Jim gestured toward the spot he'd marked. "If the vehicle pulled over here, something changed to reduce the flow of air from it. Maybe a window was rolled down before, and he pulled over here to roll it up? Just a guess, but something decreased the ventilation enough to extinguish the scent trail outside the vehicle. I'll try a little farther down the road to see if Banjo can pick it up again."

"But we can be certain the vehicle headed west toward town?"

"That's what I'd say."

Mattie knew they were in territory outside of proven theory. But they were pinning their hopes on anything that would help them discover Sophie's location, and that was all that mattered right now.

"I'm gonna walk him farther down the highway," Jim said before leaving Mattie's car to do just that.

She rolled up the window.

"We need to head up to talk to Gus Tilley," Cole said. "He lives west of town."

"Gus Tilley?"

"I already told Detective LoSasso about how he interacted with Sophie yesterday." Cole described how Tilley seemed taken with Sophie's storytelling. "He's been acting strange lately, like he needs a lot of my time. Yesterday, I even wondered if he was hurting his own animals so he could get my attention."

"Like Munchausen by proxy? With animals?" Mattie had never heard of it.

"It exists. But I'm not convinced he would hurt one of his animals, and they don't seem to be afraid of him. Besides, he doesn't fit the typical profile."

"Which is?"

"A woman with a small pet, usually a dog." Cole shrugged. "I don't mean to stereotype, just quoting the literature."

"I understand." Mattie was thinking of what to do next. "Let's finish up here. Stella and I can drive up to Tilley's place, and I'll get his permission to look around with Robo. If Sophie's there, he'll find her."

"I'm going with you."

That would be going way against protocol. "I can't agree to let you do that. Let's see what the sheriff has to say."

"I'll drive my own truck, show you the way. I'm going with you." He'd obviously made up his mind.

"Let's talk to the sheriff."

Chapter 19

Sheriff McCoy told Cole that a civilian's presence at an interrogation was unacceptable, and he wouldn't allow it in his jurisdiction. Mattie understood Cole's position, but she was glad the sheriff remained steadfast. They had no idea what they would find at the Tilley place—could be anything from an innocent man to a deranged kidnapper and child killer. Although Cole had proven himself capable of handling a dangerous situation before, she'd never seen him this distressed, and she didn't want to worry about how he would react or how she would keep him safe.

Sergeant Madsen volunteered to take Banjo and continue the search for Sophie within the city limits. Sheriff McCoy stayed with Cole at his house and called in the crime scene unit from Byers County to photograph and cast the tire track that Jim had found. Mattie plugged Tilley's address into her GPS unit, and they decided Stella would ride with her while Brody followed in his cruiser as backup.

Once they were on the road toward Tilley's place, Stella broke the silence. "How are you holding up, Mattie?"

"Worried." She glanced at the clock on her dashboard: ten o'clock. "We're about seven hours into it now."

"This is a strong lead," Stella said, her syllables clipped. "In a perfect world, we'd find her at this guy's house, telling him stories."

The image made Mattie ache with longing. "Yeah."

"Sheriff McCoy says that Burt Banks is still missing, and he's going to put out a BOLO on him."

Now other jurisdictions would be on the lookout for both Merton Heath and Burt Banks. "Good."

"And the Heath vehicle should have been spotted by now if it's out on the highway. I've asked the sheriff to divert the volunteers toward searching every trailhead and jeep trail around here. Maybe we can find him off road."

"That's good thinking."

"We're telling the volunteers not to approach him, but to contact us if they find his vehicle. There's a large group starting tonight, and Rainbow is staying on duty to coordinate."

Mattie nodded, grateful for the teamwork. Candace might be lost to the community forever, but there was still hope that Sophie could be found alive.

"I was wrong about her," Stella said.

Mattie was thinking of the girls. "Who?"

"Rainbow."

"Oh. Yeah?"

"She's one tough cookie. She's better at her job than I thought she could be."

"She's great at her job," Mattie said. "Maybe a little unorthodox at times."

Stella stared out the window. "But, you know, the way she dresses."

"Hey, she's allowed to wear civilian clothing the same as you. If she chooses to wear frilly things, that's her prerogative. And that's between her and the sheriff, since he's the one who runs things. Rainbow grew up here; she knows this community, and most of them know her for who she is. She's a great person to have on our team."

"I suppose you're right."

Mattie didn't want to talk about Rainbow anymore, and she decided to end the exchange. The conversation lapsed, and she shivered, her tight muscles seeking release. She tried to relax but couldn't.

Tilley's place was located about ten miles outside of Timber Creek in an area bordering the national forest, where an old Spanish land grant had been subdivided and sold as private properties. A few of the original log buildings, tumbled down and decayed, dotted the development, but many new homes had been built on five- to ten-acre parcels filled with trees, primarily cottonwood, pine, aspen, and spruce. Most of the homes were nothing fancy. Small log cabins, prefab houses, trailers, and doublewides. Sheds and barns marked each household, and either barbed wire, sheep fencing, or wooden fences delineated each boundary.

Mattie turned off the highway onto Soldier Canyon Road, which wound upward into the foothills, and she knew she only had a couple miles to go. It would be slow going, following the hairpin curves that led through the forest. She passed a few houses, scattered here and there. Most had lights still on, but a few were dark for the night.

A mailbox with the address painted on the side marked Gus Tilley's place. He lived in a one-story log cabin that was still lit from the inside, although Mattie couldn't see into his home. The view was obscured by some kind of film or substance on the windows. A bright light on a tall pole lit his yard, which had been left natural, covered in short buffalo grass and dotted with evergreen trees. Wooden corrals and a barn sat a short distance from the house, also lit by a glowing light on a pole. Silvery moonlight bathed a small meadow beyond, dotted with shadows and surrounded by forest.

Mattie pulled her SUV into the driveway and parked beside the house. "How do you want to work this?"

Before Stella could answer, Gus Tilley stepped onto the porch, a baseball bat cradled in his arms. A medium-sized brown-and-white dog pushed open the screen door from inside the house and scooted around Tilley to run into the yard. It barked and barked, all the time grinning and wagging its tail.

"Weapon," Stella warned, though Mattie had already spotted the bat. "Wait 'til Brody parks."

Taking the radio transmitter from its cradle, Mattie keyed it on and sent a message to Brody. "K-9 One to Chief Unit. Our subject is on his porch, armed with a baseball bat."

Brody's headlights lit her SUV as he pulled in behind. "Copy that. I have a visual. I'll cover. Keep your distance."

The dog circled their vehicles, barking but looking more like a greeting party than a guard dog.

Brody parked and opened his car door, while the dog focused most of its attention on Robo. Brody would be armed with a Glock 17 pistol that he could handle like an expert.

"Brody's in place," she said to Stella. "Keep your distance from the subject."

"I'll start the talking. Jump in if you want," Stella said before opening the door and stepping out. When Mattie did the same, the dog ran up to her, wagging its tail and then flopping onto its back for a belly rub.

No resistance from this one, Mattie thought, noticing the dog was a male. She spoke to him in a friendly tone but didn't lean over to touch him, and she kept her eyes on Tilley.

"Dodger, come here," Tilley said, and the dog scrambled to his feet, trotting off to join Tilley on the porch. There he stood, now quiet, tail still wagging.

Mattie mirrored Stella, moving to the front of their car but staying well away from the porch. "Are you Mr. Gus Tilley?" Stella asked.

"Who are you?"

Stella introduced herself and then Mattie and Brody. "We'd like to talk with you for a few minutes."

"How do I know you're who you say you are?" Tilley asked.

Mattie thought it was a strange question. They'd arrived in vehicles clearly marked with Timber Creek County Sheriff's Department emblems. True, Stella was dressed in plain clothes, but Mattie and Brody wore uniforms.

"I'll show you my identification. I'm going to pull back my coat," Stella said as she slowly did so. "My badge is clipped to my belt."

Tilley narrowed his eyes and stared at it. "I can't see it from here."

"Put the bat down and we'll meet halfway. I can show it to you."

Looking at Mattie, Tilley gestured toward her SUV with the bat. "You got a police service dog in there?"

"I do," Mattie said, noting his use of the specific term. "Do you know something about police dogs?"

Tilley nodded.

"As you can see, my car has a Sheriff Department decal on it. Deputy Brody's car is clearly marked too. We're the real deal. And we came to talk with you about something."

"Go ahead and talk."

"Would you put the bat down, so we can all relax," Mattie said. "I'd like to show you my dog, but I can't take him out of the vehicle if you have something he might detect as a weapon in your hand. You know how these dogs are." Robo had a way of making inroads with resistant people, and Mattie intended to exploit it.

Tilley looked like he was considering her words. "I've been having trouble with someone hurting my animals lately. Can't be too careful."

So I've heard, Mattie thought. "I'm sorry to hear that. Tell us what's been going on."

"I think someone put a chip in Dodger's ear." The dog looked up at him, sweeping the porch as he wagged his tail. "And someone hurt my horse's eye."

"I could look into that if you want me to." Mattie hoped this would lead to his permission to search the barn and outbuildings. "I noticed that Dodger seemed to trust us when we arrived. He acts friendly."

Tilley looked down at Dodger, who grinned up at him in an open-mouthed pant, and she could tell that she'd made her point: if his dog trusted them, maybe he should too.

Tilley leaned the bat against the wall of the house and stepped off the porch. "I'll look at your identification now," he said to Stella.

Stella unclipped her badge from her belt and held it where he could see it. He examined it carefully, stepped back, and nodded. "Why are you here?"

"We're searching for a missing child—Sophie Walker," Stella said.

"The lady that works at the clinic told me the doc was busy looking for his daughter, and that's why he couldn't talk to me himself."

So much for the element of surprise, but it should be expected. By now, most of the townspeople knew Sophie was missing.

"Do you know Sophie?" Stella asked.

"I saw her a couple of times. She has some baby chicks. She showed them to me."

"We're talking with everyone who interacted with her yesterday. Do you have any idea where she might be?"

Surprise crossed Tilley's face. "Why would I know?"

"We're asking everyone, Mr. Tilley. We need to find this little girl as soon as possible," Stella said.

"Sure, that makes sense," he said, looking at Mattie. "Did she wander away from her house and get lost? The doc lives out there in the country by himself, you know. There's a lot of hills and scrub around that area. Can your dog track her?"

Mattie decided to divulge a bit of information to see his reaction. "We did try that. He tracked her for a ways, but it looks like someone might have picked her up in a vehicle."

"Who?"

"We don't know."

"Her mom?"

Mattie wondered if he knew that the mother wouldn't be on the property after school. "No, not her mom."

Tilley seemed to roll that information through his mind, and a horrified expression dawned on his face. "A stranger?"

"That's what we're afraid of."

"Oh, no," he said. "Oh, no . . . that's awful."

It was as if Mattie could see the man's mind working, and he seemed truly upset. Then again, he might be a great actor.

"Can I do anything to help?" he asked.

"You can help us a great deal by talking to us like you are now," Stella said. "You said you saw her at the vet clinic?"

"Yeah. She showed me her chicks and told me a story. She's a nice little kid."

"A story?" Stella said. "What about?"

"Chicken Little. You know it?"

"Sure do. What else did you talk about?"

"Just the chickens and how to take care of them. Doc came in, and he told her she needed to let me go home if I wanted to."

"And?"

"Lucy was waiting in the trailer, so I said good-bye and left."

"Lucy?"

"My horse."

"The one with the eye injury?"

"Right."

"Did you see Sophie again after that?"

"No." He looked like a thought came to him. "Do you think the person that's been hurting my animals could have taken her?"

Mattie didn't know what to think. On the surface, this guy seemed simple and open, but on another level, and especially if he was projecting his own actions onto others, his words could be construed as suspicious and guilty. "What do you think?" she interjected before Stella could answer.

"Maybe so," he said.

"Mr. Tilley," Mattie said. "On the chance that you're right, we need to look around."

"Look around for what?"

How could she say it so that he wouldn't decline permission? "We're looking for anything that might help us find Sophie. Any clues that might tell us where to search."

Interrupting her, headlights pierced the darkness out on the road and a vehicle turned in, pulling to a stop behind Brody's.

Cole's truck. What's he doing here?

Cole jumped out from the driver's side and barreled toward them, dodging around Brody as he tried to head him off. "Gus, do you know where Sophie is?" he called as he came.

Confusion filled Tilley's face. "Hi, Doc. I was just talking to these people about that."

Cole moved forward steadily despite Brody trying to edge him out. "What do you know, Gus?"

Mattie stepped between the two, blocking Cole.

Tilley showed no fear, only curiosity. "I don't know anything about her. I haven't seen her since I left your place yesterday. I was just saying that."

She grasped Cole's forearm to get his attention and locked eyes with him. "You need to let us do our job," she said, her tone quiet but firm.

He raised his hands and took a step back, lining up with Brody.

She turned back to Tilley. "You can see how important it is to help us get Dr. Walker's little girl back to him. In case we can find something that helps us, is it okay if my dog and I look around?"

"You won't find anything like that here."

"Maybe not, but if it's all right with you, I'd like to look."

"Your dog won't make a mess of my property, will he?"

"No, he doesn't dig or chew at things."

"Well, okay. I guess I can take your word for it."

"I need to get Robo out of the vehicle now, so could you put Dodger on a leash while my dog works?"

"I've got a chain right here." Tilley went to the porch and clipped a chain that was anchored at the bottom of one of the posts to Dodger's collar.

Turning to get Robo, Mattie signaled Cole to join her at the back of her vehicle. Brody came along with him. "What are you doing here, Cole? The sheriff told you to wait at home."

Illuminated by the yard light, Cole's eyes were dark wells in the rigid planes of his face. "I never agreed to that. I have to be here, in case you find her."

"Dr. Walker, we can't allow it. Your presence compromises our investigation," Brody said.

Cole stared at him, his jaw muscles working. "I have to be here."

Knowing she'd never be able to sit at home waiting either, Mattie grasped at a solution. "You can wait in Brody's cruiser. If we find Sophie, we'll notify you."

Cole studied her for a long moment, and she struggled to keep her cop face on. Finally, he nodded. "I'll wait here, but come get me right away if you find her." His gaze went to Brody. "Come get me." She could read the underlying desperation in his words.

"Come with me." Brody stepped back, and Mattie could tell he wasn't happy about letting Cole stay. He would need to keep an eye on him now, and that meant they were one man down for the search, keeping Brody from acting as backup. Not ideal.

Before Cole turned away, he reached out to Mattie, and they clasped hands for a moment. He squeezed hers hard and then walked away.

"I'll call the sheriff and find out what happened," Brody muttered before following Cole to his cruiser.

Her nerves taut, she focused on the job and opened Robo's compartment. He stood at the back waiting for her, and she buried her nose in the fur at his neck for a brief second before reaching for his tracking harness. As Tilley came toward the vehicle, Stella warned him to stay back, and they waited about ten feet away.

Mattie began the patter that signaled to Robo that it was time to work. When he jumped from the vehicle, he stayed close to her and ignored the others.

"Let's start out at the barn," she said, heading that way while Tilley and Stella followed. She had to depend on Stella keeping an eye on Tilley while she focused on Robo.

When they breached the double doorway, Tilley flipped a switch on the inside wall, and overhead spotlights lit the building. Movement caught Mattie's eye as several cats retreated into the haystack, their tails disappearing behind the bales.

The barn was immaculate, tools put away neatly in a rack or hung on pegs, an empty wheelbarrow tipped up against a wall, a few bales of hay stacked by a box stall with nary a stray wisp on the ground. Raking had left straight rows of indentations, and Mattie could imagine the meticulous work required to do such a thorough job.

She offered Sophie's scent article, unclipped Robo's leash, and asked him to search, following behind as he swept the alley. Mattie peeked into open box stalls as they went.

A horse with a patch over its eye stuck its head through the opening over a stall door. Tilley went to stand by it and stroked its muzzle while he observed. The horse rested its head against his shoulder, and he smoothed the hair on its cheek.

After a thorough search, Mattie decided that Sophie hadn't been anywhere inside the barn. Calling Robo, she turned to go outside, where two vehicles and a trailer were parked at the back: a white horse trailer, a brown pickup truck . . . and a gray Jeep Wrangler, an older model.

Taking Robo to the Jeep, Mattie led him to search the exterior. When he finished without detecting anything, she turned to Tilley, who, along with Stella, had followed her. "Can I search the inside of this vehicle?"

"Okay," he said, his agreement tentative, making her wonder if he had reason to hesitate.

Mattie opened the unlocked door and asked Robo to search. He jumped inside, but once again, he didn't hit on anything. Disappointed but wanting to be thorough, she directed him to the pickup truck, though she didn't expect to find anything.

Robo approached the passenger side and sniffed. His interest perked and he began to sniff in earnest, ears forward. He reared up and placed his paws on the open window, sniffing inside.

Mattie's heart rate kicked up a notch. "It's okay to search the inside of this one, too, right?"

"I guess so."

Mattie opened the door. Robo sniffed the door's interior, again focusing his attention up high near the window. He turned and sat, staring at Mattie.

He's got a hit!

Maybe the silver SUV the bus driver saw on the road had nothing to do with Sophie's disappearance. Because she knew one thing for a fact—Sophie had once been inside this truck.

Chapter 20

Mattie didn't need to say a word to Stella. The detective's gaze sharpened, and she stepped forward to visually inspect the inside of the truck, not touching a thing, while Mattie moved Robo back to keep an eye on Tilley. He stood watching, apparently unalarmed.

Brody strode into the light cast from atop the pole outside the barn. "Sheriff McCoy is here."

His statement confirmed her suspicion that Cole had somehow given the sheriff the slip earlier. Brody scanned the scene, his face registering recognition that they'd found something, and she nodded to answer his unspoken question.

"Mr. Tilley," Mattie said. "Robo and I need to search your house."

"Why?"

"I want to see if we can find something in there."

He raised his brows. "You're not gonna find anything in there."

Robo's hit on the vehicle combined with something as serious as a missing child gave her exigent circumstances to search the premises. She didn't need his permission. "We still need to look."

Tilley shifted his feet, his hands tightening into fists. Mattie glanced at Brody as he moved in closer.

"What are you trying to do here?" Tilley took on a frightened expression, his eyes moving back and forth between her and Brody.

"Robo smelled Sophie Walker's scent on the inside of your truck, Mr. Tilley," Stella said, coming from behind the truck to join them.

"That can't be. How do you know?"

"We can tell. How did her scent get there?"

He looked confused. "I don't know. I have no idea."

"Was she inside your truck yesterday?"

"No. She's never been inside my truck."

"Then how do you explain it?" Mattie asked.

"How should I know?" he said. "That little girl has never been inside my truck."

"Then how could her scent be there?" Brody asked, his deep voice a growl. He stepped in close.

"You're trying to set me up," Tilley said, holding up his hands, his gaze bouncing around.

"Mr. Tilley, when a K-9 hits on a scent that we're looking for, it gives us the right to search your property. I'd appreciate it if you would cooperate and come with us," Stella said.

His eyes darted from one of them to another, and fear consumed his face. "You've got me trapped. I'm outnumbered."

"What are you afraid of?" Stella asked in a soothing tone, evidently trying to de-escalate the situation.

Tilley's gaze raced around the light's perimeter, as if searching for a way to escape. "Stay away. Don't touch me."

Stella exchanged a look with Brody, shaking her head slightly and sending the message to back off. But Tilley's reaction led Mattie to believe he might be holding Sophie inside the house. All the more reason to get inside there and search.

"No one's going to touch you, Mr. Tilley. We're not here to hurt you or your animals. We're looking for a little girl. We need to find her, and we need to explore all the leads that come our way. Walk with me now. Let's go to your house," Stella said.

Pressed to move forward, Mattie couldn't understand why Stella was treating this suspect so gently. They had every right to search the premises, and if Tilley stood in the way, they could take him down and put him in cuffs.

Stella turned and began walking toward the house. Tilley watched her leave, swept Mattie and Brody with a frightened gaze, and evidently decided the detective represented the least threatening choice. He followed her. Brody, Mattie, and Robo fell in behind, staying close.

Sheriff McCoy's Jeep had parked behind Cole's truck, and Mattie could barely make out two silhouettes inside it. Not knowing what she'd find inside the house, her heart rose to her throat, and she wished Cole had stayed home, where he belonged.

"I want you to sit out here on the porch with Dodger," Stella said to Tilley when they reached the house. "Deputy Brody will wait with you."

"Don't tear up my things."

"We won't. Wait here." Stella gave Mattie a look as she opened the door, standing at the threshold.

Mattie moved forward, Robo at heel, and entered the house. The front door led into the kitchen, and she paused to take in her surroundings: slate-gray linoleum floor with a white fleck, aluminum table from a past decade with a Formica top and chairs upholstered in red plastic, immaculate light-gray laminate countertops, dishes drying in a rack.

She leaned over and patted Robo's side, ruffling up his fur and chattering about finding Sophie. Taking the scent article from a pouch on her belt, she gave him a whiff and then asked him to search. He rounded the kitchen and went through the door into the living room, another room filled with dated and worn furniture but clean and tidy.

She looked at the windows to determine what had caused the light to be filtered in such a weird way. Stella came up behind her, and Mattie waved her hand toward the large picture window. "Check this out."

The windows were painted black.

Stella nodded, and Mattie realized she'd already noticed the strange window dressing. She directed Robo to continue his search, moving from the living room toward the back of the house, where there were two more rooms, one set up as a bedroom with a double bed covered by a plain blue comforter that was pulled up and tucked neatly under two pillows.

The other room seemed to be a catchall for storage, boxes stacked neatly against one wall, several old pieces of furniture in the middle as well as some odds and ends that looked like antiques—an old butter churn, an icebox, a bank safe with the door hanging open. The windows in both rooms were painted black like the ones in the living room. Mattie told Robo to search closets, and she looked for cracks that could indicate a trapdoor.

Coming up with nothing, she went back to the hallway and spotted Stella in the bathroom, searching through the medicine cabinet above the sink. She held some prescription bottles in one hand, and she glanced at Mattie as she moved to the linen closet next to the tub. Stella opened its door and began searching inside.

"Have you noticed that our suspect demonstrates odd behavior, Mattie?" Stella continued rifling through the things in the linen closet.

"He acts like he's hiding something."

"He thinks someone's hurting his animals, he was afraid we weren't who we said we were, he thinks someone's out to get him. Paranoid behavior. And I might have found part of the reason." She'd finished her search of the linen closet and closed the door. She extended the hand that held the prescription bottles. "If I'm not mistaken, these medications are prescribed for a serious mental illness, and they're empty. I haven't been able to find bottles that have been refilled. It wouldn't be good to go off these meds cold turkey."

Impatience made Mattie edgy. "I don't care about that. I think this guy took Sophie."

"Maybe." Stella eyed her. "Stay objective, Deputy. Did Robo find scent here in the house?"

"No, but he did in the truck."

"The inside of the truck has dog hair consistent with Dodger's on the seat, but otherwise, it's clean. No sign of a struggle. The tires aren't even the same brand as those that laid the track at the Walker place, and the tread is very different."

Her words hit Mattie hard, and she searched for an explanation for the discrepancy. "Maybe we were wrong about the vehicle that turned around at the Walker property. Maybe it wasn't the vehicle used to take Sophie."

"That's possible, but I think Robo told us it was. And the bloodhound, Banjo, he seemed to indicate the same thing. That track beside the highway certainly looks like it matches the one on Walker's property. I think when we find the vehicle that has the tires that match those tracks, we'll have found our kidnapper. And Candace's killer."

Mattie still didn't believe the man was innocent. "How do you explain Sophie's scent being inside Tilley's truck?"

"I don't have an explanation for that, Mattie, but that truck was at Dr. Walker's clinic yesterday, and maybe Sophie decided to explore it while the adults were inside. Children do that kind of thing. I need to ask Dr. Walker about it. *And* Mr. Tilley." She paused, studying Mattie's face. "I'm not going to dismiss the possibility of Tilley's involvement yet, but I'm telling you, the evidence isn't stacking up the way we expected it would, and you need to not jump to conclusions."

"He acts suspicious as hell. Why would he have painted over his windows? Because he wants to hide something, that's why." Mattie paused and took a breath. "Robo and I are going to search this entire property."

Stella scrutinized her. "It's not a bad idea, and I wouldn't tell you not to. All I'm asking is for you to remain neutral. Be the savvy investigator I know you to be. Are you too close to this one, Mattie?"

"I can do the job."

"Good, because we need you." Stella headed for the kitchen, carrying the medicine bottles with her. "Let's talk to Tilley, and then you and Robo can finish your search."

Stella's inference that Mattie might not be able to do her work effectively irritated the hell out of her. Struggling to keep her temper under control, she followed Stella out to the porch. Tilley sat on its edge, his face tight with tension, cuddling Dodger and stroking his head. The image of man and dog reminded her so much of how she sought consolation from Robo during dark times that it threw her a curve ball. Stella's warning to keep an open mind sifted through her irritation, and she settled herself, ready to listen. Brody stood by about ten feet away, as if giving the man space.

Stella joined Tilley on the edge of the porch, sitting near him. "Mr. Tilley, we need to talk. Could I ask you a few questions?"

"It's getting late. I need to sleep." He hugged Dodger, putting his chin on the dog's head. Dodger swiped his cheek with his pink tongue.

"This won't take long. Are you willing to talk to me?"

"I guess so."

"I found these prescription bottles in your medicine chest, and I see they're empty. I didn't find any new refills, and I'm concerned about you. Have you been taking your medicine lately?"

"My pills didn't come."

"You mean they didn't come in the mail?"

"Right. My check didn't come either. I waited for a while, and then it did."

"So your check came, but not your pills," Stella said.

"Uh-huh. I think they'll come soon." Tilley rubbed the top of Dodger's head, his eyes downcast.

"The date on this empty bottle says it was refilled almost two months ago, and it was only a month's worth. So if I'm figuring it right, you've been without your pills for about a month. Is that possible?"

Tilley reached for the bottle and looked at the date. "Maybe. What is today, anyway?"

Stella told him, and he raised his brows as if astonished.

"Does that surprise you?" she asked.

"I didn't know it had been that long."

"Have you been in touch with your doctor?"

"I don't think so. It's been a while, I think."

"I think you need some help getting this straightened out. Do you have a family member I can call?"

He shook his head.

"A case manager then? Someone who helped you get your checks set up?"

"I can take care of myself."

Stella sat back and studied him—Mattie knew how it felt to be examined by those probing eyes.

"I'm going to have a person from the county contact you to help get things back on track," Stella said. He started to protest, but she raised her hand to stop him. "I know you can take care of yourself, but I'd feel better if someone helped you get your medicine started again. It's been too long since you've been without it."

Mattie had to concede the point about the man's illness to Stella. But that didn't mean he hadn't taken Sophie.

He was shaking his head, but Stella kept talking. "Now I need to switch back to our original concern. Finding Sophie Walker."

Tilley shot to his feet, paced a few steps away, and then turned to face Stella. Mattie tensed and felt Robo do the same beside her.

"I can't help you with that," Tilley shouted.

Stella stood facing him, her demeanor calm. "Do you have any idea how Sophie's scent got inside your truck?"

"No! I told you, she's never been in my truck."

"I'm sure you can understand how that dilemma still concerns us."

Mattie grew tired of listening, observing, and essentially doing nothing. "I still think you know something," she told Tilley.

His eyes darted to the sheriff's Jeep and then out toward the barn, refusing to meet hers. "I don't know anything."

Squaring her shoulders and hooking one thumb on her utility belt, Mattie stepped in close, staring up into his face. "Where is Sophie Walker? Is she somewhere on this property?"

Tilley backed up a few steps. "No!"

Frustration urged her forward. Could he be holding Sophie in a hidden structure in the woods at the edge of his meadow? Or, God forbid, could he have buried her someplace on this acreage? She stayed close, pressing him. "I'm going to search this property until I'm satisfied Sophie isn't anywhere on it."

Nodding, he gulped, anxiety consuming his face.

Stella intervened, blocking Mattie's advance. "You stay here with me, Mr. Tilley, while the others take another look around."

Mattie turned away, told Robo to heel, and headed back to the barn with Brody following. She planned to search through every structure on this place, around the perimeter, and through the meadow. Pressure built in her chest as she thought of how time was slipping away.

Sophie can't end up like Candace. She just can't.

She vowed not to leave this place until she was absolutely convinced Sophie was nowhere on it to be found.

★

Cole sat in the sheriff's Jeep, watching Mattie and the detective talk to Gus after they came out of the house. He knew if he dared try to get out of the vehicle, McCoy would force him to leave. His heart tripped when Mattie confronted Gus and then turned and strode back to the barn, Robo beside her and Brody following.

What's going on?

Soon, LoSasso came over, and the sheriff rolled down his window. She leaned in and spoke to both of them. "Mr. Tilley swears he didn't see Sophie after his time with her at the clinic yesterday. Dr. Walker, can you tell me what vehicle he drove to your clinic for the appointment?"

"His brown pickup truck and trailer. He brought his horse in."

"The tires on that vehicle don't match the prints we found at your property," LoSasso said. "Do you know if Sophie entered that truck?"

Cole searched his memory. "I'm sure she didn't."

"Was the truck parked where you could see it while you worked on the horse?"

"No, we were inside the treatment room. What's this about?"

"Was Sophie with you the entire time Mr. Tilley was at your clinic?"

"She was inside the clinic most of the time." Cole paused, trying to remember the sequence of events exactly. "I think she went outside to play with her ball at some point while he was there."

He saw LoSasso look at McCoy, and the penny dropped. He put one hand on the door handle, his muscles tightening, getting ready to spring. "Robo found Sophie's scent in the truck, didn't he?"

"Do you think Sophie could've gotten in the truck while you were inside the clinic, Cole?" McCoy asked.

"I've never seen her do anything like that. In fact, I've warned her against it. I don't think she'd get inside someone else's car."

"I don't know yet how to explain her scent being in the vehicle," Stella said. "Maybe Robo failed on this one. But his tires don't match the tracks on your property, and I think we'll find the person who took Sophie when we find the tires that match that print."

Cole stared at Gus, huddled on the porch holding Dodger. His hopes deflated, and he felt more helpless than ever before in his life. "So you're positive Gus didn't take her?"

"Mattie and Robo are doing a thorough search, and they'll make sure there's no scent trail outside the truck. But no, I don't think Mr. Tilley took Sophie."

McCoy looked at him. "You should go home now, Cole."

"Let me stay until Mattie finishes, and then I'll go." Cole gripped the door handle and stared out toward the barn, trying to spot Mattie through the darkness.

Chapter 21

Cole had come home after Mattie returned to the sheriff's Jeep. "We searched everywhere . . . everywhere," she'd said, her dark eyes burning. "But we didn't find a scent."

Now he leaned against the kitchen cabinets with his sister, Jessica Walker, who'd arrived shortly after his return. It had been such a relief to see Jessie. He even welcomed her take-charge manner, and as an attorney, she never lacked in that. A tall, athletic-looking brunette who worked out regularly, she was also not lacking in strength, and his ribs still smarted from the hug she'd given him. The pain had been worth it.

"There's fresh coffee in the pot, Miss Walker," Mrs. Gibbs said as she hovered near. As far as Cole could tell, she'd been cooking most of the night, although no one had been able to eat a thing.

"Call me Jessie. Everyone does."

"I have food warming in the oven if you're hungry."

"Maybe later. Thank you, Mrs. Gibbs."

Sheriff McCoy came in from the other room. "I need to get back to the office for a while. Cole, do you need anything from me before I go?"

Ever since Cole had gone up to the Tilley place, the sheriff had been by his side. In a way, it would be a relief to have him go, but in another way, it made Cole feel like the man was abandoning a sinking ship. "You'll call me immediately if you hear something?"

"Right. And you've got my cell phone number, so you do the same," McCoy said. "I'll check in with you in about an hour. Jessie, I'm pleased to see you again and relieved that you're here." The sheriff extended a hand.

Cole wondered how McCoy kept from wincing when Jessie shook it. "You couldn't keep me away," she said.

Mrs. Gibbs left to show the sheriff out, leaving Cole alone in the kitchen with his sister.

"You've talked to Mom and Dad?" Jessie asked.

"Dad. He's out with the volunteers."

"Does Sheriff McCoy think the kidnapper might call here?"

"If someone was going to call for a ransom, don't you think they would have done it by now?" His eyes stung, and he blinked hard.

"I don't know. I think that could come at any time. If that's what we're dealing with."

Cole didn't want to imagine what else they could be dealing with. "I can't stay and do nothing. I'm going to take Bruno out to search. Could you man the phone here at the house?"

"Okay. Where's Angela?"

"In her room. She blames me for not being here when Sophie got home from school." Cole shook his head and looked at the floor. "Which I wasn't."

"Geez, Cole. You're not Superman. You can't always be everywhere."

Mrs. Gibbs reentered the room. "That's the God's honest truth."

Jessie turned to Mrs. Gibbs. "Did Angela have any dinner?"

"Not unless she ate from the tray I took up to her."

"I'll go see." Jessie left the room and headed upstairs.

Cole hoped Angela's aunt could bring comfort to her, because he sure couldn't.

In the den, the dogs kicked up a fuss and rushed the entryway as the front door slammed shut. Having not heard a knock, Cole hurried to where Bruno and Belle stood, barking.

The doorbell rang.

Someone tried to enter, but the dogs stopped him. An intruder, his parents, Sophie's kidnapper? None seemed likely. He peered through the door's peephole.

Olivia?

"Bruno, Belle, quiet. Sit. Stay." Both dogs settled, obedient but watchful, and he opened the door.

Olivia stood on the step wrapped in a navy woolen pea coat, a chill breeze lifting her shoulder-length blond hair. Her blue eyes—which Cole had always thought matched the color of Colorado columbine—were reddened and showed her fatigue. Seeing the mother of his children standing on his porch as if she didn't belong almost shattered what little reserves he had left.

"Olivia," he breathed.

"What on earth are those dogs doing in the house?" she demanded.

Cole had always catered to her aversion to having pets in the house, even though some of his fondest memories growing up as a kid included his dogs.

"The kids have pets now, Liv." He opened the door wide. "Come in."

Olivia stepped across the threshold, eyeing the two large dogs, who in turn eyed her back. "Are they mean?"

"Just protective." No need to divulge the part about Bruno's attack training. "You surprised them."

"Where were these protective dogs when Sophie disappeared? And while we're on it, where were you, Cole?"

He had nothing he could say.

The anger in Olivia's eyes pierced him. "How could you lose my baby? Can't I trust you to take care of our kids?"

"Don't blame him." Angie's voice rang out from behind him. "It's not his fault."

Cole found it hard to believe his ears, but nevertheless, it came as a small bit of relief to hear Angie defend him.

Olivia's anger melted as she extended her hand toward their daughter. "Angela . . ."

Jessie came into the room from behind Angie. "Olivia," she said, surprise on her face. "We didn't know you were coming. Come in. Can I take your coat?"

As if unable to look away, Olivia stared at her daughter. Angie stood rooted in the archway between kitchen and den, and her mother gradually withdrew her outstretched hand. "How are you, sweetheart?" she said in a hushed voice.

Angie's face hardened. "What do you care?"

Cole felt trapped between mother and daughter. Considering Angie's current level of distress, this was a poor time for a reunion. But still, this was his child's mother, and she deserved her daughter's respect. He lifted his hand in restraint. "Angie, please."

Olivia sent him a hateful glance. "You've turned her against me."

"You're the one that did that! Dad does nothing but defend you. What are you doing here?"

Although he could have guessed at the answer himself—no mother who loved her children could stay away when one of them went missing—he thought it a fair question and decided to let Olivia field it.

"Your dad called to see if I had Sophie. I was so worried, I had to come."

"You never worried about Sophie before. You didn't care that she's just a little kid and she wants you and she cries herself to sleep and—"

"Angela, that's enough," Cole said, cutting off her tirade and going to her with his arms outstretched. "This isn't the time for this discussion."

Angie met his gaze and her eyes filled. "But Dad, she can't just walk in here and expect . . ."

"Shh." Cole drew her into a hug, and her last words were muffled against his chest. Her shoulders heaved as she began to sob. Fighting his own tears, he sensed that Olivia remained frozen by the front door.

He'd made such a mess of things. He tilted his head back as he held his child.

Where are you, Sophie? Where are you, baby girl?

Angie pushed away from his chest. Still sobbing, she ran up the stairway to her room, slamming the door behind her. Jessie gave him a fortifying look before turning to follow. "I'll go to her. You two need time to talk."

Talking was the right thing to do, and he didn't need his sister to say it, but what he wanted most right now was to go out and search for Sophie. He turned to his ex-wife, who looked wilted and broken as she leaned against the front door.

It surprised him to realize how much his feelings had changed. A year ago, he'd begged this woman to stay with him and ached to hold her in his arms. Back then, he would have done anything to soothe her, but tonight, he felt nothing—just a tired recognition that she was as stressed and worried as he was. If he felt anything at all, it was sympathy.

"She hates me," Olivia said, hugging her coat tightly closed.

"She doesn't hate you. She's mad because you've shut her out these past months."

Tears rolled down her cheeks, and she dashed them away. "Is it all right if I come in?"

"Of course." Feeling awkward, Cole gestured toward the den. "Come in and sit."

Together they walked into the den, and they stood beside the overstuffed leather sofa and armchairs, but neither of them sat.

"Why are you here, Liv?" he asked quietly.

Tears spilled from her eyes again. She let them fall, standing rigid with her hands thrust deep into her coat pockets. "Apparently I can't trust you to handle things. What's being done to find Sophie?"

Leaving out the part about Candace Banks, Cole summarized the search so far, knowing that it sounded like precious little had been done.

"Who's in charge?" Olivia asked.

"Sheriff McCoy."

"If they think a stranger took her, why hasn't he called in the FBI?"

"The Colorado Bureau of Investigation was notified this afternoon when they issued the Amber Alert. It's gone out region wide, and it might be expanded to a federal level if necessary. Evidently, it's somewhat related to time passing and need for resources. Right now, the local sheriff and county detective are handling things." Discussing it made Cole feel even more powerless.

"That's not enough."

Coldness washed through him. Things were never enough for Olivia. "It's the way it is. What are your plans?"

"I need to be here. To stay informed. To help if I can."

Cole searched for his own plan. He wouldn't leave Angela alone to fend for herself with her mother, and he knew she'd want to come with him to join the search.

"Come meet Mrs. Gibbs," he said, turning his back on his ex-wife and heading for the kitchen. She followed.

Their housekeeper was at the sink, wringing out a dishcloth.

"Mrs. Gibbs," Cole said as she turned to face him. "This is Olivia Walker, Angie and Sophie's mother." For some reason, he couldn't use the label "my ex-wife."

Mrs. Gibbs's eyebrows shot up. "Pleased to meet you, Mrs. Walker. My goodness, you must be exhausted, driving down from Denver so late. Could I get you something to eat? A cup of coffee?"

Cole had never been so grateful for this woman's stalwart nature. "Olivia, Mrs. Gibbs manages the house for us," he said, relieved to have a buffer between them. There was way too much to be said boiling up, and now was not the time to attend to it.

He spoke to Mrs. Gibbs, informing Olivia of his intentions at the same time. "I'm going to take Angela and the dogs out to join the search. We'll head to the sheriff's station first and check in there. You can reach me on my cell phone." Then he turned to Olivia. "I'm going to leave you and Jessie in charge of manning the phone here at the house. You can decide between the two of you how you want to handle it if a call comes in."

"What if I don't want to take orders from you, Cole?" Olivia said. She stood with her hands in her pockets, her shoulders hunched.

"Do what you want. I can count on Jessie to stay where she's needed."

Olivia winced.

"Thanks for your help, Mrs. Gibbs." Cole met her gaze and tried to impart his gratitude for what he was about to do—dump this angry and frightened mother who could also wield a sharp tongue in her lap. "I'm going upstairs to get Angela and tell Jessie what we're going to do."

And with that, he headed out of the room, eager to leave his ex-wife behind.

Chapter 22

Sheriff McCoy assigned Cole, Angela, and their dogs to Sergeant Madsen, who set them on a grid to do cleanup behind him. First, he and Banjo would work an area, and then Cole would follow up, bringing Angela along with him. He wouldn't allow her out of his sight, so the two stuck together—Cole leading Bruno, Angela leading Belle—letting their dogs range out front on retractable leashes, sniffing the area.

The dogs' previous owners had trained them for tracking, and Cole and the kids had reinforced those lessons by playing hide and seek with them. Sophie had thought it great fun. As Cole kept pace with Bruno, he imagined that one of the dogs would find her, and she'd clap her hands and squeal with joy like she always did.

Belle's limp slowed her down, so Bruno covered more territory. Cole felt grateful for the Bernese mountain dog's slower pace, since it eased the pressure on Angela to keep up. Cole had strict orders to call Madsen on his cell phone before following a lead if one of their dogs got a hit. But they'd been at it for a couple hours and there'd been nothing.

Cole paused at the top of an alleyway to wait for Angela. Her face was drawn and pale, and he realized it was time to give both her and Belle a break. He checked the time on his cell phone. Almost midnight.

"You look exhausted, Angie. It's time I take you home."

"I don't want to go home. I can't go there." Her voice sounded thick, and Cole knew she was fighting back tears.

"You need to go to bed."

"No, I'll stay with you."

He didn't want to go home either. "Let's take a break and go back to the station."

"All right."

They walked to his vet truck, the dogs staying close. Cole texted Sergeant Madsen an update and told him where they were going. Madsen replied, saying he'd keep searching.

The station was lit, and several vehicles were parked out front, including Mattie's. Cole was eager to see her. She would share news with him more readily than the sheriff. As they entered, the dispatcher named Rainbow arose from her desk and crossed the room to greet them. She reached out her hand to Angela, who took it.

"You're tired," Rainbow said, "and I bet you're hungry. We've got a table full of all kinds of food that people have brought in for volunteers. Let me get you something to drink. Do you like soda? How about you, Dr. Walker? Can I get you something? Coffee?"

Angie looked at him, and he nodded as they allowed themselves to be led over to the food table that had been set up against the wall at the back of the lobby. It was laden with sandwiches wrapped in plastic bags, chips, granola bars, a vegetable tray, and a variety of sweets. Volunteers rarely went hungry in Timber Creek.

"I'll take a cup of coffee," Cole said, and Angie asked for a Pepsi.

Rainbow bustled around getting drinks while Cole stuffed a granola bar into his pocket for later. "Is Mattie here?" he asked.

"She's in with the sheriff," Rainbow said.

"Do they have any news?"

Rainbow handed him his coffee. "Let me tell them you're here."

Cole watched her go to an unmarked door, tap on it, and enter. He clutched the coffee and took a gulp, feeling it scald his throat all the way down. A few seconds later, Rainbow came back out, the sheriff behind her.

"Cole, come in," McCoy said, holding the door open.

"Can I come too, Dad?" Angie asked, grasping his forearm.

"You're welcome to join us, Angela," McCoy said.

Detective LoSasso was turning a dry-erase board on wheels around, and she pushed it to the back of the room. Mattie came forward, extending her hand for Angie and ushering her toward a chair to sit.

Robo lay nearby, alert and watching the activity, his attention primarily riveted on Mattie, but he didn't bother to get up. He must've been as tired as Belle and Bruno. Mattie looked exhausted too, her face pinched with worry.

Deputy Brody greeted him as he passed by on his way out of the room. Stubble darkened the deputy's square jaw, and he seemed to be taking Cole's measure as he passed.

LoSasso sat down on the other side of the table. She reached out, squeezed and released Angie's hand in an awkward way before withdrawing hers to place both hands on the table. Fear fluttered his heart as Cole selected the chair beside Angie.

Do they have bad news?

"Have either of you thought of other people we should contact?"

Cole shook his head. "Do you have anything new?"

"I've extended the Amber Alert nationwide, Cole," McCoy said. "We've had an agent from the FBI assigned to us and have access to their databases. We're getting their input on both our cases, Sophie's and Candace's."

That sounded reassuring and should pacify Olivia. But the idea of any connection between Sophie and Candace made his stomach churn. Sophie couldn't end up like Candace. "Do you have any new leads?"

"We're following up on everything as it comes in. Nothing has developed yet."

"What's the status on Gus Tilley? Is he still a suspect?"

LoSasso shrugged slightly. "Our suspect list isn't exactly set in stone. People rotate on and off as more information comes in. We'll stay in close contact with Mr. Tilley."

The door behind him opened, and Deputy Brody spoke. "I need a word with you, Sheriff."

LoSasso looked at Brody sharply and left the room with the sheriff. They all stood, but Mattie stayed, her dark eyes searching his face before looking at Angie and touching her arm. "You're exhausted, Angie. Why don't you go home and get some rest? Even if you can't sleep, just lie down for a while."

Angie's eyes brimmed, and a tear trailed down her cheek. "I can't. I can't go home. Mom's there." She began to sob, her hands covering her face.

With a stricken look, Mattie took Angie into her arms and held her, burying her own face on the girl's shoulder.

"Mattie . . . please . . . find Sophie," Angela said between sobs.

Cole stood and wrapped the two in his arms, bending over them and fighting his own tears. He struggled to keep himself from begging Mattie too. He heard the door open and glanced up to see Deputy Brody peer in. The man withdrew, closing the door.

"I'll do everything in my power to bring her home, Angie," Mattie said, her voice thick and hoarse. "I promise you that."

★

Cole knew Mattie was right—he needed to take Angela home to rest. It was ridiculous to stay away because his ex-wife was there, and he needed to man up and take care of his daughter. After leaving the station, he led her to the passenger side of the truck and opened the door for her. "We're going home now, Angela."

She shrugged, looking resigned. "Okay, but I'm going to my room."

"That's fine. You need to get some rest, because if Sophie's not home by morning, we're going to go out again." He planned to go back at it tonight, but she didn't need to know that. She would insist on going with him.

She nodded.

"You'll need to talk to your mom sometime, Angel, but it doesn't have to be tonight."

"I have nothing more to say to her."

"Maybe not, but *she* might need to talk. Let's just take this as it comes, okay?"

Again, the shrug. Cole closed the door gently and went around to climb into the driver's seat. The one-mile drive home seemed to take forever, and Cole grew more and more tense as he neared the house. The crew who'd come to work the crime scene had come and gone, taking the yellow tape that had marked it with them. Everything looked back to normal.

But things were anything but normal. He hoped like crazy that Sophie was warm and asleep somewhere. She'd been sick at the end of the school day. How did she feel tonight? Was she awake and frightened? Awake and uncomfortable? In pain?

Oh, dear God, I hope not.

He pulled the truck into the garage so they could enter through the kitchen, where the lights were on. After unloading the dogs, he followed Angie into the house. Jessie came into the room, anxiety consuming her face, her movements stiff. She squeezed Angie's arm as the girl passed her to head up the stairs, Belle trailing close behind. Bruno went to his food dish.

"Do you have any news?" Jessie asked.

Cole summarized the updates. While he was speaking, Olivia entered the room, her eyes bleary. She'd thrown the chocolate-colored fleece blanket from the den over her shoulders like a cape, her slender hands holding it tightly bunched at her chest.

"What about bringing in outside help?" Olivia asked.

"They're coordinating now with the FBI. They're going to be working the cases too."

"Cases?" Olivia said. "What do you mean?"

He wished he'd phrased it differently. Now he needed to tell her what else was going on. "A girl was killed on the hill behind the high school earlier this week."

"You've got to be kidding me!"

"Bruno, come with me," Jessie said, leaving the room and heading upstairs. Bruno quickly dogged her tracks.

Cole leaned against the cabinet, needing support in the face of Olivia's rage.

"Who was killed?" Olivia asked, her face blanched, lips tight.

"A girl named Candace Banks, from the junior high."

She appeared to be searching her memory and then shook her head slightly as if coming up with nothing. "Do the kids know her?"

"They know who she is but weren't close. She was between them in age."

Cole could see her begin to shiver from across the room, and her fear struck a matching coldness inside him.

"I can't believe you continue to live in this town, Cole. First Grace Hartman, and now another child. It's too much."

He didn't know how to respond. "In light of school violence in the cities, Timber Creek seems like a safer option."

"Our child is missing!" Her eyes filled with tears. Clutching the fleece throw to her chest, she bowed her head and sobbed.

He felt his throat swell, and the tears he'd kept at bay came on hard. The one thing he could relate to with his ex-wife was the fear and helplessness she was feeling right now. He took a step toward her but stopped short, unable to cross that gap between them. "We'll find her, Liv," he said, choking on the words. "We've got to believe it."

She stifled her sobs, still holding a hand to her face. "How? How are we going to find her?"

"The Amber Alert has been expanded nationwide. People will be looking for her. We've got good people here working on it, and now they're bringing in the FBI."

She nodded, looking away to scan the countertops. Evidently spotting what she'd been searching for, she crossed over to the end of the counter and swiped a tissue from its box. Taking a second one, she handed it to Cole and then blew her nose daintily. Cole trumpeted into his tissue, balled it up, and threw it into the trash.

He touched her arm and she melted toward him. Before he knew it, she was in his arms, letting him hold her against him in that familiar way, his chin resting against her hair. He tried to take comfort in it, but there was none to be had.

When he'd been in vet school during the early years of their marriage, they were a team. It was the two of them plugging along through the system, and she'd worked a job in retail so he could be a full-time student while they planned their future. Her pregnancy with Angela had been a surprise, but they'd taken it in stride, rejoicing in the birth of their baby girl. Then Sophie came, planned seven years later, after he'd graduated and started his practice. One happy family—or so he'd believed.

Where had it all gone wrong? When had the feelings changed?

Perhaps feeling the same lack, Olivia pulled away and huddled inside her blanket, leaning against a countertop opposite Cole.

He couldn't help himself. He had to ask. "Why have you disappeared from our lives, Olivia?"

"Do we have to talk about this now?"

He shrugged. "I suppose not, but I can't help but want to know. I mean, I understand why you wanted to leave my sorry ass. You made that perfectly clear. But you're a good mom, Olivia. Why have you turned your back on the kids?"

Her eyes filled again, and she turned to snatch another tissue from the box, using it to wipe her eyes and dab at her nose. He strained to hear when she spoke. "Sometimes I don't understand it myself. I want to see the kids, I do." Her eyes were earnest when they met his. "But then I just can't seem to dredge up the energy for it."

"Are you ill? I mean physically ill? I haven't heard from you since last summer."

She shook her head, eyes downcast. "I'm still working through the depression. It takes time, you know."

She sounded defensive, and he didn't want this attempt at conversation to dissolve into mutual frustration. He tried to remember techniques for communicating with the kids that he'd learned from their family counselor, but he was so stressed that he pretty much had to fall back on just being himself. "I'm not implying it doesn't take time. I'm just trying to understand why you feel like you don't have the energy for seeing your kids."

"It saps your energy, trying to find the right medicine, the right dose, working in counseling."

"It's been a year."

"I know that." Anger flared, giving her voice some oomph. "For what it's worth, I've been making progress. I was making plans to contact you to try to arrange a visit with them. And then this."

And then this.

This was the unspeakable, the unthinkable—the police called it a stranger abduction. Their child, their Sophie. He couldn't let his mind explore it, much less put it into words. He felt his own rage against Olivia build. She was the one person Sophie longed to see, to be with, to touch; and yet as a mother, she'd let the time slip away. Because she didn't have the energy for it?

He fought to control his temper. "You're right, we shouldn't talk about this now."

She studied his face.

He figured she knew him well enough to read his feelings, and he'd had enough. "I need to go out again and join the search."

"Cole, what do you know about this Mrs. Gibbs? Could she have anything to do with Sophie's disappearance?"

He stiffened. "Trust me. Mrs. Gibbs has nothing to do with it."

He turned to head upstairs to check in with Jessie and Angela before he left.

"You're leaving now?"

He paused and turned back to her. "I'll be in town. You can reach me on my cell phone."

"Oh, yes. Nothing ever changes."

He turned and left her, not wanting to say something he'd regret.

Chapter 23

When Mattie had left the briefing room, Brody told her that a volunteer had spotted the Heath Nissan Pathfinder near Reynolds Pass, on a jeep trail west of town, high up in the national forest.

She drove her Explorer while Brody rode shotgun, following the volunteer's directions, counting miles and turnoffs after leaving the highway. The dirt roads climbed ever upward and finally, they'd reached the rough, two-track trail that should lead them to their destination.

Mattie slowed to a crawl, and her SUV jolted over stones and potholes. She focused on the precarious trail in the headlights, gripping the steering wheel as she angled between low-hanging pine boughs that scraped the sides of her car. Old snowdrifts, dirty and half melted from spring runoff, spattered the trail, creating slick spots.

She was amazed that anyone had located the Heath vehicle way back in here. It spoke to the dedication of the volunteers.

Brody had been an easy companion, quiet except to give navigational input and directions. Thank goodness for that—she was about tapped out and needed time to pull herself together so that she could focus on the task at hand. She didn't know why the news that Cole's ex-wife was in town had stunned her. It wasn't like she'd planned a future with Cole and his family. Nothing like that. In fact, she'd worked hard to keep dreams like that out of her mind.

She thought what bothered her most was Angie's aversion to going home because her mother was there. It shouldn't be like that.

Families should cling together and support each other in times like these.

Then she thought of the way she avoided her brother, Willie. But that was different. The Cobb family didn't know the meaning of family support. She couldn't dwell on that now, so she switched her thoughts to the road and how to keep from damaging a tire on the sharp edges of half-buried rocks.

After what seemed like forever, the red reflection of taillights winked in the beam of her headlights. Soon she caught sight of the silver Pathfinder she'd seen in town, bearing the license plate she now had memorized, parked by the side of the trail. She pulled in behind it. Robo popped up in back, yawning, having awoken when the movement ceased.

"Let's take a look," Brody said, opening his door.

The volunteer had reported that no one appeared to be in the immediate vicinity of the vehicle, and she and Brody didn't know how far away the men might be. Maybe they hiked from the vehicle to camp somewhere.

"Is a permit needed to camp here?" she asked.

"Nah. It's legal to camp in this area."

Cold air washed over her as she left the warmth of the Explorer. She thought the temperature must be in the midthirties at this altitude, and it seemed an unlikely time for camping up this high.

She and Brody walked around the vehicle, noting the B. F. Goodrich stamp on the tires. TKO. Using their flashlights, they squatted behind the rear tires to inspect the tread. Mattie pulled out her cell phone to compare the photo she'd taken of the tire tracks. "Looks like a match to me."

"Close enough. Gives us a reason to question 'em."

"When we find them." Her breath lingered in the air as she spoke.

She shone her flashlight around the area, taking in the dense forest of pine and spruce that surrounded them, along with boulders and half-melted snowdrifts. They'd parked on a ridge, and there was a sheer drop-off to her left where she could see the tops of aspen and spindly pine.

She strode to the back of the Explorer and opened the door to Robo's compartment. She took a few minutes to prepare him and then asked him to search for Sophie.

He swept the area, alternating nose to the ground and to the air. She directed him to focus on the exterior of the Pathfinder, and he sniffed everything she asked, but not once did he indicate a find. Her hopes plummeted.

Brody straightened, scanning the ground with his flashlight. "We'll never be able to track them in the dark. Let's hunker down inside your car while we wait for sunrise. They won't come back here tonight, but we'll keep an eye open just in case. I can take first watch."

"Robo can track them in the dark."

"Maybe so, but this terrain is rugged, and there's no trail. I'm not excited about breaking an ankle out here while we stumble around."

"What if they took Sophie Walker? We've got to find her!"

"Use common sense. We can't help her if one of us gets hurt. And Robo didn't find her scent anywhere."

"What if they carried her?" Mattie checked her service weapon, making sure it was loaded and ready. "I'm going."

She turned and led Robo back toward the driver's side of the Pathfinder, where he could pick up the driver's scent on the ground. As she started the chatter to rev up her dog, she could hear Brody cursing behind her.

"Here, Robo. Scent this," she said, combined with a gesture toward the ground by the Pathfinder.

Mattie ignored Brody while Robo sniffed toward the ledge, circled around to the back of the vehicle, and then headed to the ledge again. She could picture Merton Heath exiting the Pathfinder, going to the overlook to scout out a way to go down, and then going to the back of his vehicle to get something.

Sophie?

Her heart quickened as Robo went to the drop-off and disappeared over the edge. She hurried over and shone her light down the steep slope. Aspen, spindly evergreen, and scrub oak clung to the downslope where Robo slid, heading to the bottom. Brody drew up beside her, his Colt AR-15 slung over his shoulder.

"He's on it. And so am I." Grabbing onto the branch of a pine, she took the first step, sinking ankle deep into the loamy soil before sliding a couple feet. She wavered, trying to maintain her balance while still holding the flashlight.

"I'll be behind you," Brody said. "Wait for me at the bottom."

She glanced at the moon and decided to try to navigate by its light. Putting her flashlight back into the loop on her utility belt, she freed up both hands to hang onto the vegetation. Gradually her eyes adjusted and she could make out Robo's shadow ahead of her, weaving downhill.

Following him, she half-slid while sharp rocks cracked her shins and ankles. Shifting her grip from pine to scrub to thorny current bushes, she made her way down slowly, a little bit at a time, until she'd descended about fifty feet. There, Robo stood waiting for her, waving his tail. He turned to leave when she reached him.

"Robo, wait."

Stones cracked together in a rockslide as Brody came down, farther off to her left. "Are you all right?" she asked, shining her flashlight toward where she'd last heard him cursing.

He limped up to her. "Yeah, let's go."

Sweeping the area with her light, it appeared they were in a meadow, and Robo took the lead, nose down on a trail indicated by smashed grass. Within twenty minutes, they reached a beaver pond, surrounded by evergreens that sheltered a campsite. In the dim moonlight, she could barely see the two orange tents set up beside a fire pit that held smoldering embers.

She extended her hand to stop Brody. "Robo, wait," she whispered. And to Brody: "They're here."

Brody unslung his rifle and gripped it in two hands while Mattie unsnapped the flap on her holster.

"How do you want to do this?" she asked.

Brody scanned the area and then pointed. "I'll use those trees for cover and wake them. You stay off to the side behind that boulder and cover me if they come out shooting. Otherwise, we'll go into camp and talk."

"Got it. Robo, heel."

Staying low, Mattie crept the last one hundred yards toward her position, keeping an eye on the tents as she went. Off to her right, Brody made it to the pine trees at the edge of the campsite and disappeared into their shadows. When she reached the boulder, she slipped behind it, making sure Robo was secure and well covered.

"Hello," Brody shouted. "Merton Heath. Timber Creek County Sheriff's Department. We want to talk to you."

Murmuring came from inside one of the tents, which billowed with movement. Then came the sound of the flap being unzipped.

"Who are you?" someone called from the tent.

"Chief Deputy Ken Brody, Timber Creek County Sheriff's. We need to talk. Come out nice and slow with your hands where I can see them."

More murmuring. "I need to put on my shoes."

After a pause, a man crawled out of the tent and stood, hands raised slightly, and another man followed. In the moonlight, it appeared both wore jeans and flannel shirts. Without blinking, Mattie watched the men's hands.

"You men in the other tent. I need you to come out too," Brody called.

Now would be the time for them to make a move. Mattie's senses sharpened and time suspended while she waited. The second tent showed movement, and after several long seconds, the flap unzipped and two men came out. All four men that she'd seen in town were now accounted for.

Brody stepped from behind the trees, holding his rifle in front of him but down low. "Which one of you is Merton Heath?"

"That would be me," the first man said, raising one of his hands a bit higher.

"Do you have any weapons with you?"

"No guns. A couple filet knives for the fish. What's this about?"

Mattie stepped out from behind the boulder, bringing Robo with her. All eyes looked at her and then went back to Brody.

"This is Deputy Cobb. We've been looking for you so we can talk. We're coming in. Don't make any sudden moves."

While Mattie edged closer, Brody crossed the distance to enter the camp, keeping about twenty feet between him and the men. Robo hovered at her heel, alert and on guard.

"Mr. Heath, would you build up that fire to give us some light?" Brody used the broadside of his rifle to gesture toward the woodpile.

Keeping his hands in sight, Heath threw a couple logs on the smoldering fire. They crackled and snapped as they caught fire and flared. Brody nodded toward the others. "You men, gather round where I can see you."

Firelight revealed basic features. Two blond and clean shaven, and two dark and bearded. Mattie glanced at their faces, but her primary focus remained on their hands.

"I need your names," Brody said.

"This is Jace Gardner," Heath said, waving a hand toward the other dark-haired man who came from his same tent. "These two guys are Frank and Ted Robbins." These were the two who had blond hair and lighter-colored eyes.

"Brothers?" Brody asked.

"Cousins," the one named Frank said.

"What brings you guys out here?"

"Fishing," Heath said, gesturing toward poles leaning against the trunk of a towering lodge pole pine.

"Kind of cold for a fishing trip."

"We needed to get out of Denver for some fresh air," Heath said. His eyes were dark, and Mattie thought they were probably brown. She moved a bit closer so she could see more clearly.

"What do you want from us?" Gardner asked.

"How long have you been here?"

"We got up here Wednesday afternoon late. Set up camp right before dusk."

It had been around noon on Wednesday when Mattie spotted the group in town. It was possible they could've made it here before sundown.

"When did you drive here from Denver?"

"Wednesday morning. Had lunch in Timber Creek and then came up here," Heath said.

"How about Tuesday? Where were you then?"

Heath glanced at Gardner before replying. "In Denver."

"All of you?"

"Yes, we came down together."

"Do you have someone who can vouch for where you were on Tuesday afternoon?" Brody asked.

Again Heath looked at Gardner. "Let me think," he said as if buying time. "Why do you ask?"

Brody stared at Heath for a beat. "So where were you, Mr. Heath?"

Heath frowned. "I took off work to get ready for our trip."

"Can anyone vouch for that?"

Heath looked at Gardner. "My friend here. We were together."

Gardner nodded.

"How about you other two men?" Brody asked, looking at the Robbins cousins.

Frank shrugged. "I'm a student. Community college. I was at the library Tuesday afternoon."

"Can someone confirm that?"

"Probably not."

Brody looked at Ted. "You?"

"Just hanging out, getting ready for the trip."

Her impatience growing, Mattie grew tired of the exchange. No one had a verifiable alibi, and they all were acting guilty as hell. One or all of these men could have killed Candace and kidnapped Sophie.

"So none of you can give me specifics or prove where you were?"

Heath shoved his hands into his pockets.

Mattie's adrenaline surged, and Robo stiffened into protection mode. She pulled her Glock from its holster.

Brody raised his rifle. "Hands!"

Eyes opening wide, Heath raised his hands again, palms empty. "Geez," he muttered. "Chill."

"I told you," Brody said. "Keep your hands where I can see them."

"What's got you on edge, man? Why are you grilling us? We've got rights, you know," Gardner said, the firelight revealing a scowl on his face.

"We had an incident in Timber Creek Tuesday afternoon," Brody said. "A young girl died."

Heath's gaze jumped to Gardner and then to each of the others in the group. When he looked back at Brody, he seemed to have worked things out. "And your K-9 officer spotted my Pathfinder in town on Wednesday, and one thing led to another. You're up here looking for me."

His response confirmed that Mattie hadn't imagined their furtive reaction on Wednesday. They'd spotted her the same time she spotted them. They probably even discussed it as they drove out of town.

Brody gave him a nod of acknowledgment. "Do you know anything about the girl's death?"

"No, I don't."

"Well, yesterday, another young girl went missing," Brody said.

"Jesus," Gardner muttered under his breath, shuffling his feet, eyes downcast. He looked up and locked eyes with Mattie for a long moment before his slid away and he resumed his study of the ground.

"We had nothing to do with that either. We were in Denver on Tuesday and we left Timber Creek Wednesday after lunch." Heath looked at Mattie. "We drove out of town soon after you saw us."

Finally, Mattie could break her silence. "We need to find that missing girl. If you had nothing to do with her disappearance, you'll let me and my dog search your tents. Can I have your permission?"

Heath looked at the others. The Robbins cousins held out their hands, palms up, as if to say they had no choice.

"They have no right to search our things," Gardner said.

Frowning, Heath looked at him. "We have nothing to hide."

Gardner shook his head. "Even still."

Brody was frowning too. "Either you have this child or you don't. It's easy enough to prove you're innocent. Will you let us take a look inside your tents?"

Heath looked at Gardner as if in appeal for him to give permission.

"We don't have your missing child here," Frank Robbins said. "Go ahead and search our tent."

Gardner gave him the stink-eye.

Ted Robbins murmured his consent as well.

"Searching our tent is all right by me," Heath said.

Clearly outnumbered, Gardner caved, though he didn't look happy about it. "Go ahead. You won't find what you're looking for."

Mattie led Robo to the tent the Robbins cousins had occupied, unzipped the flap, and peered in, looking for anything that could be of danger to her dog. Sharp objects like unsheathed knives, fish-hooks, or needles. Instead, she saw rumpled sleeping bags, backpacks tossed toward the back of the tent, and clothing scattered all over. No Sophie.

After refreshing Robo's memory with the scent article, she directed him into the tent. It didn't take him long to search the small area, and he came right back to her. No hits. She backed out of the tent, zipped it closed, and led Robo to the second tent. Inside, she saw pretty much the same thing, although their stuff was better organized, the sleeping bags straightened, clothing tucked away in backpacks.

Robo zeroed in on one of the backpacks, touched it with his nose, and sat.

Her heart skipped a beat. Was this Sophie's backpack?

After sizing it up in her flashlight's beam, she decided it was too big. It probably wasn't Sophie's. But had Robo hit on her scent? Or drugs?

Mattie crawled inside on her knees. After pulling a pair of latex gloves from her pocket, she picked up the pack and took it with her outside the tent. As she approached the group at the campfire, she held it up for Brody to see. "He gave me a hit on this."

Brody arched one brow and looked at Heath. "Who does this backpack belong to?"

Heath threw a glance of apology at his tent-mate. "It's not mine, man."

"Is it yours, Mr. Gardner?"

Gardner shrugged. "What if it is?"

Brody looked back at Mattie. "Is it her scent?"

"Either that or drugs."

Against the background of general declarations of innocence from the men and their denials of having done anything wrong, Brody appeared to be pondering the situation. Finally, he spoke. "Okay, I want to treat you guys fairly, so I'm going to let you know that you have the right to remain silent." And with that, he went on to give the entire group the Miranda warning from memory, ending with: "Do you understand your rights? Can we talk about this and clear things up?"

At this point, Mattie knew that Brody wanted anything these guys said to be able to be used as future evidence, so she prepared to listen carefully.

"Mr. Gardner, in addition to search and rescue, our dog is trained to sniff out drugs. There must be meth or something like that in this backpack."

"There's no meth in there!"

"Then what is it?"

Gardner looked around at the others as if for help, but there was none forthcoming. "There's nothing in there but a little bit of weed."

Brody stared at him.

Heath spoke up. "It's legal to have personal use marijuana in Colorado."

Brody turned his piercing gaze toward Heath. "You can have two ounces and smoke it in the privacy of your own home, but it's illegal to possess or transport it inside the boundary of the national forest. Which is where we happen to be standing right now."

Heath's bit of defiance wilted. "You're screwed," he muttered to Gardner.

Brody scanned the group. "My priority here is our missing child. Will you guys take a little ride with us back to the sheriff's office, where we can sort these things out?"

"Oh, come on, man," Ted Robbins said, whining. "You can't arrest us for this."

"You're not under arrest. But I need you to work with me. I've got to be convinced that you had nothing to do with our missing child so I can move on to someone else."

"The pot isn't ours, sir," Frank said, waving a hand between him and his cousin.

"We didn't even smoke it. He did," Ted said, evidently having no qualms about pointing a finger at his friend.

"At the very least, you're a witness. We'll take you in and sort this out." Brody turned to Mattie. "We have a unique situation here. While you were searching the tents, I learned that all of these guys are registered sex offenders, except for Ted."

The words fanned the anxiety she'd felt for Sophie since reading Merton Heath's case file. She looked at Frank, who seemed to be willing to cooperate. "How come you're all here together?"

Frank looked her directly in the eye. "The three of us met in a halfway house in Denver. All of us were convicted of basically the same crime, sex with a minor, but for all of us, the relationship was consensual. We just had the bad judgment of picking girlfriends younger than us. Girls whose parents were out to get us."

The girl from the Heath case had been only twelve years old, so this explanation didn't ring true, and at the moment, Heath was examining his feet and refusing to meet her gaze. She decided not to confront him with this now so that Stella could get the first shot at him back at the station.

"You met in a halfway house and you're still friends?" she asked Frank, thinking this had to be a violation if any of them were still on parole.

"We belong to the same support group. We're trying to put our lives back together."

The need to continue to search for Sophie pressed at her, but the thought that one of these men could have killed Candace made her cautious. She couldn't take Robo into the forest and leave Brody outnumbered four to one. "I still need to search outside the camp perimeter," she told him.

He nodded. "All right, gentlemen. Deputy Cobb and I need to put you in cuffs for the time being. Hands behind your back."

Despite their protests, Mattie helped cuff the men while Brody patted them down. At last she was free to leave, with the four campers sitting on a log by the fire and Brody standing guard.

She took Robo into the forest at the edge of camp, gave him a sniff of the scent article, and told him to search for Sophie. He trotted out front while she trained the flashlight on him, struggling to keep up in the dark. Pine needles poked her face and a tree root snagged her shoe. Falling to one knee, her palms scraped against deadfall as she went down. The looming forest triggered her claustrophobia, and she froze, her heart racing.

Robo came back to her. She clasped his solid body close and took in huge gulps of air. Calm gradually seeped into her, allowing her brain to take over.

I'm safe. Now get back to work.

Murmuring praise to Robo, she gave him a squeeze. She clipped a leash onto his harness, wanting to keep him close, but then decided against it. She needed to cast him out away from her, let him search for Sophie freely so he could cover more ground.

She followed at a slower pace, fighting the rugged terrain while Robo worked in huge sweeps. Finally they came full circle, and still no sign of Sophie.

Fighting tears, she paused on top of a ridge for a moment to regain self-control before going down into the campsite. Sunlight touched off a fiery glow on the jagged horizon, and birds chirped as the forest awakened.

She still needed to search the Pathfinder's interior, but now that it was light, she and Brody would be able to see tracks if it had left the road between here and Timber Creek.

And Robo would be able to smell Sophie's scent if . . . if she'd been left someplace on the way up. She swallowed her tears and forced herself to move again, unable to bear thinking beyond that.

Chapter 24

Cole sat in his truck at a pullout alongside the highway, Bruno curled up beside him on the passenger seat, sleeping. He'd watched the sunrise with an ache that filled his chest and spilled into his throat, his palm resting on the Doberman's warm shoulder, occasionally stroking the top of his head. They'd searched everywhere he could think of to no avail.

Some monster had snatched the very essence of Sophie from him, including her scent, while his back was turned. What else could he do to find her? He'd never felt this powerless before in his life.

He'd spent the rest of the night searching the town with Sergeant Madsen. Right before dawn, they'd gone to the station to debrief before Madsen left to go back home. "It's not that we're giving up," Madsen said, "but Banjo and I have finished the part of the job that we came here to do. If any new leads come in, it'll be up to Deputy Cobb and Robo to follow up. They're more than capable."

Cole knew that, and he nodded. "It seems like the more dogs we have, the better off we'll be."

"Yes and no. Yes, if we have a definite area to search. No, if we've covered the ground we need to and have found nothing. If you've got a fresh track, one good dog is all you need."

He knew that Madsen had come to do a specific search, along the highway, and that he'd stayed longer than he'd planned to hunt through Timber Creek. Besides, he had his own job to get back to. Recognizing there was nothing more either of them could do for now, Cole extended his hand in gratitude. "I appreciate you coming to help."

Madsen gripped his hand hard. He was a big guy, and he'd covered a lot of territory working behind Banjo during the night. Face drawn and shiny with the oily residue from dried sweat, Madsen looked exhausted; yet he planned to drive the hours required to get back to his home. "No one's giving up," he repeated. "Chances are still good your daughter will be found."

The constant ache in Cole's chest had started then, at first just a twinge, now full blown. He leaned forward to turn the key in the ignition, and his truck's engine roared to life. Bruno raised his head before struggling up to sit and look out the window.

"We might as well go home, fella, and check in there. You'll have to make yourself scarce. Maybe you can sack out in Angie's room with her."

Dealing with Olivia seemed like a bizarre twist in this nightmare he was living. His breath hitched, and he realized it seemed more and more difficult to expand his lungs. Tension. He rolled his head on his neck while he drove down the deserted highway, keeping one eye on the road.

Olivia's presence made it harder on Angie—hell, it made it harder on him. He wondered how Mrs. Gibbs was holding up, having to deal with his ex-wife. And Jessie. Cole felt it was his duty to make sure everyone in his household was comfortable, well fed, and secure.

Well, I'm a failure at that, aren't I?

He parked his truck in the garage and paused at the door that led into the kitchen, smelling the scent of bacon. When he opened the door, he spotted Mrs. Gibbs standing by the stove. Bruno came in behind him, so Cole stopped to fill the dogs' bowls with kibble.

Mrs. Gibbs turned from her cooking as he entered the room. He could tell that she'd spent a long sleepless night, her face rather gray, the wrinkles around her eyes and mouth etched a bit deeper, her eyelids heavy and reddened. He answered the question he saw in her eyes with a slight shake of his head. Her eyes filled, and she swiped at them as she turned toward the coffeepot.

"Can I get you a cup of coffee, Dr. Walker?" she asked, her voice quivering.

The small kindness created a thickening in his throat that drove the ache deeper into his chest, and he bent over Bruno for a few seconds, stroking the dog's long body as he cracked a bite of kibble between his sharp teeth and smacked his lips. Cole blinked to clear his vision. "Yes, please."

He took the steaming cup she offered him, carried it to the table, and sat. "Where is everybody?"

Mrs. Gibbs adjusted the heat under the pan on the stove and brought her own cup over to join him at the table. "Your sister is in Angela's room. They might have fallen asleep up there, or at least I hope so. Jessie came and went for a while, but the last time she went, she stayed. She's been up there a few hours now."

Cole sipped, swallowing the hot black coffee without tasting it. "And Olivia?"

"After she and I had a long talk, I sent her up to my room to rest."

"What did you talk about?"

Mrs. Gibbs studied her coffee mug. "This and that. My job here. The children. Her treatment with her doctors."

Cole was surprised. "That's more than I've been able to discuss with her this past year."

"Ach, I suppose I seem like a mother figure to her. She wanted to talk, and there wasn't much else to do while we waited."

Their eyes met, and Cole found himself soothed by the staunch look on her face and the sturdiness of her manner. "You're a good person, Mrs. Gibbs. A kind lady. I don't know what we'd do without you."

The gray pallor from her fatigue took on a pink hue. "Oh! Come now. You make more of it than it is."

"What did she have to say about her treatment with the doctors?"

When she raised her eyes to meet his, there was a certain set to her jaw that told him she considered what she'd been told confidential. "She didn't tell me much more than I already knew from you and the girls. She's been very depressed, but she's feeling better now. She did say she's trying her best. And that she hopes to reestablish a relationship with her children."

A flicker of anger at the delay in Olivia coming to that conclusion made him not want to hear anything more. He paused to measure his words before responding. "I'd like that. I hope she's able to."

He meant what he said. He hoped both of her children would be here soon for her to reconnect with, and he hoped she was capable of establishing that connection. Right now, those two hopes seemed to be pinned on nothing but thin air. He felt deflated, drained of emotion and energy.

Mrs. Gibbs stood and went back to her stove. "I'm going to make you a hot breakfast, and then you should go stretch out on your bed for a wee bit. I'll make sure you know if the phone rings or if we hear from the sheriff."

"Thank you," he murmured, staring out the kitchen window into the middle distance, unable to focus on anything. He supposed she was right. He should take a break. His cell phone battery needed to be recharged.

And he did too.

★

With a hollow emptiness in her chest, Mattie sat at her desk trying to finish her report, though she was so tired, her brain could barely function. She'd fed Robo and he'd fallen asleep on his bed.

Robo had found no trace of Sophie's scent inside the Pathfinder. After they transported the Heath foursome to the station in the cage at the back of Mattie's vehicle—Brody driving and Robo and Mattie wedged together in the passenger seat—Stella grilled the men separately for a couple hours. To no avail. Even Ted Robbins, the one with no record and deemed most likely to break, continued to profess the group's innocence.

After sorting through what they each had to say and considering the hard evidence Robo found, Stella decided to call in a US Forest Service law enforcement officer to ticket Jace Gardner for possession of marijuana on federal land. Afterward, Merton Heath demanded they be taken back to their campsite, and Stella could find no reason to hold them. Using the sheriff's Jeep, Brody had left to drive the group back into the high country.

Once done with the interviews, Stella had left for the social services office, hoping to consult a caseworker about Gus Tilley. Mattie was worried it meant that Stella was writing him off as a suspect. Though she rarely found herself at odds with Stella's opinions, she didn't agree with this one. Sophie's scent in Tilley's truck still haunted her.

Mattie pounded out the last of her report, put the printed copy in the paperwork out tray, and then went to clock out. Sheriff McCoy had ordered the team to take at least a few hours off to sleep as soon as they wrapped up their duties.

After clocking out, she noticed the massage therapist, Anya Yamamoto, sitting next to Rainbow at the dispatcher's desk.

Rainbow waved her over. "Anya's helping coordinate volunteers. Now that we've found the Heath party, we've changed the search focus to out beyond the perimeter of Timber Creek, on the county roads leading up into the foothills."

A wave of gratitude almost bowled her over. She reached her hand out to the therapist. "Thank you for your help. Our volunteers make all the difference in this type of case."

Anya held her hand with a delicate grasp, her fingers gentle. "I hope so. I'm praying we find Dr. Walker's little girl alive and well." She held Mattie's gaze. "You're exhausted. Could I give you a neck and shoulder massage for a few minutes?"

"No, thanks." Mattie pulled her fingers free. "I appreciate the offer, but I've got to finish up and go home."

"Let me know if you change your mind."

Mattie nodded and headed toward the staff office. Her therapist's assignment to find a local massage therapist—could that discussion have been only a few days ago?—came back to her as she walked through the lobby.

Maybe Anya after all.

But such plans seemed inappropriate now, so she dismissed the thought. Beside her desk, Robo had curled up in the middle of his cushion, his tail draped over his feet like a feathery throw. She couldn't bear to disturb him to go back out again.

Growing sleepier by the minute, she eased herself down on his bed and wrapped herself around him. He opened one eye for a second and then sighed before going back to sleep. Her mind drifted, entering places she usually kept off limits. Dark places. A small bedroom in the tumbledown shack she'd lived in as a child. Trapped there by a father she feared, the walls closing in on her. She blinked open her eyes and looked around the office.

You're safe. Get some rest.

She dozed, the murmur of voices and activity from the outer office like white noise lulling her to sleep. This place was probably the most comfortable spot for her on earth, one where she felt completely safe. She needed to rest for only a few minutes and then she would drive up to search around the Tilley place on her own time.

Her cell phone woke her. She didn't know how long it had been ringing; she'd been sleeping hard, and it took an additional moment to orient to her surroundings. Rising up on one elbow, she scrambled to fish her phone out of her pocket. Robo lifted his head and leaned back against her to stare at her upside down.

Caller ID told her it was Cole's office number, and she answered the call. "This is Mattie."

"Mattie. This is Tess with Dr. Walker's office."

"How are things there, Tess?"

"Weird. I just took another call from Gus Tilley, this one even stranger than some of the others. I don't feel like I can bother Cole with it, but I can't ignore it either."

The cobwebs swept from her brain. "What is it?"

"He called and said terrorists are in the woods, and the deer are screaming." Tess paused while the cryptic words made the fine hair at the back of Mattie's neck tingle. "He said the deer need the doctor's help, and he wants him to come out right away. This is different from his usual call. Typically, he's calling about his own animals, and he has a specific concern."

"You did the right thing to call me, Tess. I'll follow up."

"Mattie, do you think Gus Tilley could have Sophie, and this is his way of turning her back over to us? Or am I just reaching for a bone here? Maybe my imagination's getting the best of me."

"I don't know. But it's worth checking out." Mattie stood, feeling a tremendous urge to get out there as soon as possible. Robo looked up at her and opened his mouth in a wide, toothy yawn, a squeak coming from the back of his throat. In a hurry to get started, Mattie patted her thigh. He scrambled to his feet and came close where she could hug him against her leg. "I'll get back to you, Tess. And thanks for calling."

With Robo at heel, she strode through the lobby to the sheriff's office and tapped on the door.

"Come in."

When Mattie opened the door, she saw Stella sitting in one of the two chairs in front of McCoy's desk while he was finishing up a phone call. Stella pushed the other chair, slanting it a few inches as if inviting her to sit.

McCoy waved her in as he hung up the phone. "Have a seat, Deputy. I've just arranged media coverage with all of the major networks. We'll be able to broadcast a story about Sophie that should get the general public in the entire region looking for her."

Mattie stood at the door, not wanting to waste time. She told them about Tess's phone call. "I need to go out there. Tilley continues to call into Dr. Walker's office several times a day trying to contact him. It seems suspicious."

Stella frowned. "Sit for a minute. Let me brief you on Tilley's status."

Mattie perched on the edge of a chair with Robo at her side.

"Gus Tilley was diagnosed with schizophrenia decades ago and has been more or less stable enough on medication to take care of himself," Stella said. "A relative that used to check in on him died a few years back, but she set up a trust that sends him a monthly check. Evidently there was a problem in the system, and those checks stopped for a time. Our county social worker has the information now, and she'll look into it. But as you already know, his medications have stopped coming too, and that's the most pressing problem she needs to straighten out first—she's probably working on it as we speak."

"So his condition isn't stable at this time," Mattie said.

"That's right, but I've researched his history and background. There's no record of previous violence, charges, or arrests. His primary symptom is paranoia, and he has delusions that someone is out to get him. When that happens, he withdraws and isolates himself. Evidently, the recent news reports on television about terrorism have fed into that problem."

"Is he safe living at home by himself?" McCoy asked.

"He's taking care of his home and his animals, and there's no reason to suspect he's a danger to himself or others. Taking him out of his environment for no reason would only make things worse for him."

Mattie couldn't believe he wasn't a danger to others. "He might have hurt his horse. He might have killed Candace Banks. He might have kidnapped Sophie Walker."

Stella studied Mattie for a long moment. "He might have done all that, but there's no evidence to support it. The evidence tells us he's a harmless man who's having a rough time because he's been without his medicine." She paused, staring at Mattie, as if to emphasize her point before turning back to McCoy. "That said, under the circumstances, we can't dismiss this call for help. Did he hear screams inside his own head, or did he really hear a scream in the forest? We have to go check it out."

If I have sit here any longer, I'll scream!

"Then let's go." Mattie stood, shifting her gaze between Stella and the sheriff. It had been twenty minutes since Tess called, and it would take a half hour to drive out to the Tilley place.

"I'll ride along with you," Stella said.

"Deputy Brody hasn't returned yet, and I expect the first news crew to arrive within a half hour," McCoy said. "I need to be here for that. Do you want Deputy Johnson to go with you as backup?"

Mattie didn't want to wait for him to be called in. "If Stella's right about Tilley, there's no danger from him."

Stella gave her a look. "I agree there's no danger. This is little more than a welfare check. We can handle it."

Chapter 25

Mattie loaded Robo and then jumped into the driver's seat, strapping on her seat belt while she fired up the engine. Flipping on the overhead emergency lights, she drove toward the highway. Thank goodness she knew exactly where she was going. Once she hit the highway, she quickly brought the Explorer up to ninety miles per hour. She hoped to cut the time required to get there by pouring on the speed now, since she couldn't on the dirt roads.

"Don't go all cowboy on me," Stella said.

Mattie caught Stella's warning look out the corner of her eye. "You know me better than that."

"That's just it. I know you very well. This case is pushing all your buttons, and you're not fooling anyone. Brody even asked me if there was something going on with you and Dr. Walker."

Mattie shrugged it off. "Geez. Brody?"

"He was concerned you were letting your emotions get in the way of your judgment."

"He's one to talk."

Stella made a sound of agreement before turning a serious face toward Mattie. "True. But I'm concerned too."

Mattie threw a sidelong glance at her. "I can handle this."

Stella pursed her lips, a furrow of worry on her brow. "You talk a good line, Mattie Cobb, but can you follow through? Innocent until proven guilty. This man deserves your respect."

Astonished, Mattie gave her head a slight shake. "I know that. I've treated him with respect, and I will. There's no need for the lecture on police sensitivity."

"Brody also said that lately he'd had his first experiences of playing good cop to your bad cop instead of vice versa. Surprised the hell out of him."

"Bet it did him some good to try out a new role for a change. When did you and Brody have this conversation?"

"Before he left with Heath and friends. Said as your supervisor, he needed to get my perspective and my opinion about you being on the case. It's a fair question."

"Nice to be included in the discussion."

"I'm including you now. It's not just this case, Mattie. I've been concerned about you for weeks. You're not yourself. You look exhausted, and you're irritable as hell. It feels like you've got rage simmering inside of you."

Not wanting to prove Stella's point, Mattie bit off an angry retort. "Look, can we not talk about this right now? I've got to pay attention to my driving."

Stella paused long enough that Mattie darted another glance at her, finding herself squarely the focus of the detective's probing gaze. Stella turned away and looked out the windshield. "You're right. Later."

Mattie sped down the highway, slowing to turn onto the dirt road that led to Tilley's place.

If Robo can pick up a trail, just a trace of scent that leads somewhere, that's all we need. Just a trace of scent.

"Cut the overheads when we turn into his place," Stella said.

"I was going to." They were about a quarter mile away, and Mattie flipped the switch that turned off the flashing lights. "I'll shut them down now."

"Good."

Mattie turned into the drive and parked beside the yard. Tilley was nowhere to be seen.

"I'll go up and knock. You wait back here," Stella said, stepping out of the Explorer. She strode up to the porch and rapped on the door. Mattie unsnapped the strap on her holster for easy access to her Glock, exited her vehicle, and stood beside it.

The door opened an inch, and Stella spoke to the man behind it. "It's me, Mr. Tilley. Stella LoSasso. We've had a report that you heard screams coming from the forest. I'm here to investigate it for you."

The door opened a bit more, and Gus hovered at the threshold, baseball bat in hand, his face pinched with fear. Dodger scrambled through the partially opened door and came forward with his tail wagging to greet Stella like an old friend.

"It's the deer," Gus said. "They're in trouble, I tell you. It's terrorists. They're coming for us."

"Not if we have anything to do with it. Where did you hear these screams, Gus? Where were they coming from?"

"Down the road."

"Were you inside your house when you heard it?" Stella asked, probably trying to determine if the screams were real or figments of the man's imagination.

"No. No. I was at the barn. Taking care of Lucy. They hurt her eye, you know. I need to go out there and watch over her. I need to go."

"Are you still hearing the screams or did they stop?"

"A deer screamed. Down there." He waved down the road, a twitch of tension at his left eye. "Two times, maybe three. Then it stopped. It might be dead."

Mattie couldn't stand it any longer. She needed to get to the bottom of this. If Tilley was using "deer" to refer to Sophie, and if he'd killed her, Mattie would . . . "I'll go down the road and check it out," she said. "How far away do you think the deer was?"

"Quarter of a mile. Maybe. First I heard a noisy car speed past. Jammed the gears. The brake screeched. Then the deer screamed." He put his hand to his face and rubbed his temple as if the memories brought pain to his head.

The details made Mattie take notice, and she felt a slight shift in her thinking. "Did you see the vehicle?"

"No. No. No. I was at the barn. But it made a big noise. Maybe it was truck."

His truck?

She didn't know what to think, but she had to get Robo out and see if she could find Sophie's scent down the road. Now!

She went to the back of her vehicle to get her dog.

Just a trace of scent, please, just a trace that leads somewhere.

Moving fast, she put on Robo's search harness and strapped on her utility belt before snapping the safety strap on her holster, securing it so that she could run. She gave Robo water and started chatting him up. After a few slurps, he focused that look on her that told her he was ready.

Stella joined her. "I'll back you up."

Mattie knew the detective couldn't keep up once she and Robo started tracking. "Stay here and guard Tilley. Don't let him leave the house."

"He's afraid to leave his house. He's not going to interfere." Stella called over to Tilley. "Please stay inside your home with Dodger until we come back, Mr. Tilley."

He called Dodger and went inside, closing the door behind him.

Mattie didn't have time to argue and resigned herself to doing things Stella's way. "There's hardly any traffic out here, but if you could keep watch and stop cars coming behind us, that would help." Using Robo's long leash, Mattie headed out to the road, pausing to offer Sophie's scent article. Robo knew the drill, and he knew exactly what she wanted. He started to quarter the road even before she told him to search. She repeated her silent mantra. *Just a trace of scent.*

Robo trotted ahead, black coat glistening in the afternoon sun, his nose to the ground with an occasional check in the air. He carried his tail low, his ears forward, flicking back toward her now and then. Her feet thudded against the hard-packed dirt road as she jogged, and she vaguely picked up the sound of Stella falling in behind, but her focus was solely on her dog. Watching his body language, hoping and hoping for a sign.

She'd followed Robo about two hundred yards down the road when he darted to the right edge, sniffing furiously along the side. Mattie's heart rate kicked up a notch. She held back and let him do his work unimpeded, not distracting him with unnecessary direction. He doubled back onto the road, sniffed, and then returned to the edge.

Oh, please . . . just a trace of scent that leads somewhere!

Robo crouched, lifting one front paw slowly and then the other as he inched his way into the ditch and then up onto the slope at the edge of the forest, nose to the ground. Stella caught up with them but held back several yards, remaining unobtrusive. Although not at all winded, Mattie's breath came in short gasps, her eyes riveted on her dog.

And then Robo stood at attention, turning his head so that he could look directly into her eyes. A full alert! Exhilaration flooded her and she wanted to shout. "He's got a hit," she murmured to Stella while holding Robo's gaze. "We're heading into the forest."

"I'll stay as close as I can."

"No. Stay here. Watch Tilley."

Mattie went to Robo and patted his side, offering him the scent article again while she unclipped the leash from his harness. "Good boy! Search!"

Robo sprang forward, heading upward on a steep slope, weaving around stunted pine and scrub oak to enter the forest. Mattie took off after him, scrambling up the hillside, where she could now see sign of earlier foot travel. Not footprints, but scuff marks in the soil. It was too rocky here to actually see a track, but Robo didn't seem to be having any trouble. It was all she could do to keep sight of him.

At the top of the verge, Robo paused, waiting for her to catch up, and then he took off, nose up with an occasional check against the ground.

The scent must be fresh! Please, please let Sophie be alive.

Dead branches crackled beneath her feet and live ones whipped her face as she ran, trying to keep Robo in sight. Heart pounding, not so much from exertion but from fear of the unknown, Mattie tried to catch her breath, find her stride. But lack of sleep and poor nutrition took its toll, and she felt like she was slogging through a nightmare, pushing herself, trying to keep up, not wanting to call Robo back but not wanting to lose sight of him.

He paused where the pine thinned, looking back over his shoulder as she caught up. "Good boy," she said, puffing hard. "Search."

Robo moved forward through a grove of aspen, their new leaves glistening like bright-green spades, shivering in the breeze. A branch behind her snapped, and Mattie whirled. Had Stella tried to follow her? Was it Gus Tilley? Someone else?

The pine closed around her, too dense to see anything. When she turned back around, she realized she'd lost sight of Robo. Fear gripped her, making her gasp. Sprinting toward the aspen grove, she entered, slowing to part the foliage around the slender white tree trunks slashed with gray. Brush slapped her legs, and twigs snapped as she pushed through.

After checking her back, she focused ahead and spied an opening through the trees where she could barely make out the remains of one of the land grant's original log cabins, tumbled down and abandoned. A black shadow that could only be Robo streaked into the clearing and dodged around the side of the old building, disappearing around the back.

He barked, not his usual mode of operation. Mattie sprinted around the cabin, searching for him, following his bark. A large raised mound covered with dried leaves and dead branches stood in her way.

A gravesite? Her heart pounded so hard, it almost exploded. Too big. *What is it?*

Robo barked again. Skirting the dirt mound, she found him, scratching and digging at a wooden door that led into it. *An old root cellar.* He was struggling to get in, but the door had been secured by a jerry-rigged system of logs and boulders wedged up against it.

She fell in beside him and started pulling away the barrier. "Sophie!" she shouted. "Are you in there?"

Silence.

"Sophie, it's Mattie. And Robo."

"Mattie!"

The word sounded more like a scream, but it was Sophie's voice. *She's alive!*

Mattie shoved the last of the boulders off to the side. A splinter bit into her palm as she yanked open the door. Robo rushed inside, into the small, dark space. Mattie bent forward, ducking her head to avoid the low doorframe.

It took a moment for her eyes to adjust to the darkness. She heard a chain rattle and Sophie's sobs. The earthy scent of the root cellar was tainted with the odor of urine and feces. She stumbled inside, gradually able to make out the shape of a cot against one wall. And on it, Sophie with her arms wrapped around Robo.

Mattie sank onto the cot beside Sophie, taking her into her arms. Sophie transferred her embrace from Robo to her, scraping her neck with the links of a chain attached to her wrist. Sobbing, the child clung to her, and Mattie felt she couldn't hold the little girl tight enough.

With chilling flashes of scent and sound, memories from her childhood exploded into her consciousness. Locked in her small bedroom. Pain. Terror. She tried to push them away as sobs wrenched her chest and tore from her throat. She stroked Sophie's tangled hair, hanging on and rocking while she held her. Robo licked their faces.

Feeling the heat radiate from Sophie's small body, Mattie fought to regain control. She brushed the child's hair from her face and pressed her lips to her forehead. "Sophie, are you all right, sweetheart?"

"I'm . . . sick," she said between sobs.

"It's okay," Mattie murmured, holding her close. "We've got you now. Here, let me see how we can get you out of here."

Continuing to clasp Sophie against her, Mattie dashed the tears from her eyes and took stock of her surroundings. Earthen walls, a couple of canvas camp chairs, a small portable table with a lantern and . . . board games? A small battery-powered heater glowed in one corner, taking some of the chill off the small space. There was a bucket with a plastic trash bag liner in another corner, the source of the stench. The cot they were sitting on resembled an army cot, iron framed with a thin mattress. A stout dog chain locked around Sophie's wrist anchored her to an old wooden shelf built into the opposite wall. The shelves held bottles of water, cans of soda, bags of various snack foods, and on the bottom shelf, two backpacks. One Sophie's. And the other?

Candace.

Sophie had settled and lay inert in Mattie's lap, slumped against her chest. "I got away this morning, but he caught me on the road. He was so mad."

Anger flared in her chest as Mattie examined the abrasions the chain had made on Sophie's narrow wrist. "Do you know who the guy is, Sophie?"

"No. He kept his face covered."

No matter what, she would find a way to catch this guy, starting with the closest suspect, Gus Tilley. Tipping up the child's face, she studied it, trying to assess the degree of damage inflicted on this small girl. "Did he hurt you, Sophie?"

Sophie squeezed her eyes shut as tears flowed down her wet cheeks. "He killed Candace."

"Did he tell you that?"

She nodded, her face tight. "He said it was an accident, but he killed her." Her eyes popped open and she straightened, fear giving her new energy. "He might come back. We've got to get out of here."

The thought of Gus Tilley within mere yards of this lair gave Mattie the chills. He could slip away from Stella and imprison all of them. She gave Sophie a quick squeeze and helped her move off her lap onto the cot, pushing Robo over to make room.

She had to put on a brave front for Sophie. "Robo will warn us if he comes back, but let's hurry and get you free."

She studied the padlock at Sophie's wrist. Grasping the steel lock, she knew it wouldn't give. "Does the man leave the key here?"

"It's in his pocket."

The heavy-gauge dog chain looked like it might be something she could cut. Taking the Leatherman that Cole had given her last Christmas from a pocket on her utility belt, she extended the plier tool. She opened the plier wide and clasped the wire cutter at the joint on a link below the lock. Her hand wasn't big enough to get a solid grip, so she used both hands, straining to snap the link.

While she struggled, the walls of the root cellar seemed to shrink closer, prompting a wave of claustrophobia so strong she wanted to scream. Breaking into a sweat, Mattie fought back, holding the feeling at bay and getting up on her knees to brace one hand on her leg while she bore down on the plier with the other.

"Can you cut it, Mattie?" Sophie's breath hitched as she strained alongside her, trying to help.

Mattie sat back on her heels, her hands throbbing. "It's too thick." She scanned the chain links, looking for a flaw, until her eyes traveled to where it was anchored around the post on the shelf. Rising to cross over to it, she tucked the plier tool back inside the Leatherman and extended the knife.

"I'll cut you loose," she said, beginning to hack at the narrow post. The wood was old enough that it splintered away beneath her blade.

Sophie got up from the cot and moved to the doorway of the cellar, taking Robo with her. "We'll watch out for that creep."

Mattie marveled at her resilience. "Okay, but you shout if you see him and then get back on the cot to stay out of the way. Robo can take him down."

Hacking with all her strength, and ignoring the hammer of her heartbeat at the base of her throat, she continued to whittle the post until it was thin enough that she could grip the chain and rip it loose. The shelf tipped at a crazy angle when the post broke but had enough additional support that it didn't come tumbling down. Flooded with relief, she gathered the chain in loops as she hurried toward Robo and Sophie at the door.

"Wait!" Sophie scurried over to the cot, threw the blankets back, and grabbed a small stuffed toy that looked like a Husky.

Clasping the gray dog with white markings against her chest, she said, "Let's go."

"Can you walk, sweetheart?" Mattie said, guiding the child out into the sunshine, holding onto the looped chain.

"Heck yeah," Sophie said. "I can run."

After leaving the dank cellar, Mattie felt like she could breathe again. She looked down at the spunky girl and trailed her finger along her cheek, dirt smudged and clammy with fever. Sophie's freckles stood out like copper flakes against the pallor of her skin. "Running won't be necessary. Let's get into the cover of those trees, and I'll see if I've got a cell phone signal."

Robo bounded about as if on a lark while Mattie and Sophie scooted into the grove of aspen. Still worried that the kidnapper could be nearby, she drew her cell phone from her pocket and heaved a sigh of relief when she saw she had two bars. Swiping to her quick dial list, she tapped the icon that would connect her to Stella.

"Yes, Mattie! Where are you?"

"I've got her! We're coming down."

"Hallelujah, and thank all those who look after small children!"

"You need to slap a pair of cuffs on Gus Tilley."

There was a pause before Stella spoke. "Based on what evidence?"

She thought of the two backpacks left in the cellar, Sophie's and Candace's. Frustration took over. "For being in the wrong place at the wrong time," she snapped.

"You gotta do better than that, Deputy," Stella said. "I'll meet you on the road."

Chapter 26

Cole stood at the kitchen cabinet pouring coffee into an insulated travel mug. Somehow he'd managed to sleep for twenty minutes, his dreams filled with nightmares about Sophie. She'd been running through a forest, Gus Tilley chasing her until he morphed into a monstrous wolf with enormous teeth. The wolf took her down and ripped a gash in her throat, her blood spilling while her face registered surprise and then shock. He'd finally awakened when the wolf picked up a scalpel and slit open her belly.

He couldn't shake the nightmare. There was something not right about Gus Tilley, and he planned to go to the sheriff's station and see where they stood on the man. It was time he demand some action.

His cell phone, plugged into its charger and lying on the counter, lit up and started ringing. He hurried to pick it up and saw it was Mattie calling. His heart lifted with hope. "Hi, Mattie."

"Cole, we've found her. She's not hurt, but she's sick. We're taking her straight to Dr. McGinnis's office. Can you meet us there?"

He leaned back on the cabinet for support and tipped his face toward the ceiling. Tears streamed down his face, and he was unable to speak.

Thank you, thank you!

"Cole? Are you there?"

He cleared his throat. "I am. Yes. We'll meet you at his office. Is she all right? She's not hurt?" He knew what she'd said, but he needed to hear it again.

"We haven't questioned her about details yet. We'll do that with you present. But yes, she appears to be physically unharmed for the most part."

"Does she know who took her?"

Mattie paused. "We'll fill you in on what we know when we're all together."

"Of course. Sure. I'll be there." Cole started to disconnect the call but caught himself. "And Mattie. Thank you!"

"It's Robo you can thank, Cole. We'll talk later."

As he tapped the disconnect button, an adrenaline rush like none he'd ever felt hit him. Everyone was upstairs, shut away in various bedrooms, except Mrs. Gibbs. She had finally taken a break and was resting on the couch. Shoving his phone into his pocket, he raced into the den. "Mrs. Gibbs!"

She startled and sat up, her newly permed hair mashed on one side. Cole grabbed her in a hug and lifted her from the couch. "They've found her. She's okay."

Holding onto his shoulders, Mrs. Gibbs pushed him away to tip her head back and look into his face. She broke into a grin and then hugged him hard. "Thank the good Lord."

Cole took her hand, twirled her into a dance step, and pulled her in for another hug. He broke away and headed upstairs, taking them two at a time, shouting, "Angie, Jessie, Olivia! They've found her. Get up! They've found her!"

Tears choked him, forcing him to quit shouting as he awakened his household. He knew everyone would want to go with him to see Sophie. No one would be left behind.

★

Stella had called into the station when Robo got the hit, so Brody was with her when Mattie and Sophie met them at the top of the verge. He picked up Sophie and carried her down to the road. With his strong hands, it took only a few seconds for him to cut the chain off Sophie's wrist. It was such a relief to free her of the cruel restraint, especially since Mattie didn't want Cole to have to see her that way.

Sheriff McCoy had also come. Deciding that Sophie held top priority, and since she wouldn't let go of Mattie, they left the crime scene in Stella's hands and Gus Tilley under Brody's watch. Mattie rode in the back seat of McCoy's Jeep, Sophie snuggled under her arm, clutching the toy dog to her chest and sucking her thumb, a habit Mattie hadn't seen for months. Robo lay on the other side of Sophie, occasionally nudging her with his nose, and she would stroke his head with her free hand, an absent gesture as she stared at the seat in front of her. When Mattie leaned to press her cheek against the top of the girl's head, it was hot with fever.

McCoy made quick time of the drive into Timber Creek and arrived at the doctor's office. A silver Volvo was parked in front with everyone from the Walker household standing beside it, including Mrs. Gibbs. As they pulled up, Cole's eyes connected with Mattie's while he mouthed "thank you" before looking beyond her to search out his daughter. Sophie stirred and rose to peer at her dad. He placed his palm on the window, and tears streamed down the little girl's face as she pulled her thumb from her mouth and reached across Mattie to put her palm against his.

When she heard the backdoor locks disengage, Mattie unbuckled their seat belts and opened the door, helping lift Sophie across her lap and into Cole's arms. The family pressed around her, touching and hugging, and it was at that moment that Sophie spotted her mother.

"Mommy!" She threw herself from her dad to her mom, and Olivia staggered under Sophie's weight as Cole passed her over. He hastened to assist, putting an arm around Olivia, and together the two of them held their child.

The sight of Cole's arm around his beautiful ex-wife drew a lump to Mattie's throat. As she swallowed hard, Robo nuzzled her arm, and she took comfort by hugging him against her. Vaguely, she remembered she still hadn't given him ball-play to reward him for his greatest find ever. She reached into a pocket in her belt and gave him a treat. It would have to do until later.

McCoy exited the vehicle and approached the family. Spreading his long arms wide, he gently pressed the clustered family toward the front door of the doctor's office. "Let's go inside now," he murmured. "Dr. McGinnis is expecting us."

Since Robo didn't have the security of his own compartment inside the sheriff's Jeep like he did in their K-9 unit, Mattie hurried to clip a short leash on his collar and took him with her, following the group inside the building.

The receptionist, a kindly looking Hispanic woman, came from behind the reception window and opened a door that led to the exam rooms. "Just Sophie and her parents back here, please," she said.

The sheriff moved forward, gesturing with his hand toward Mattie. "And Deputy Cobb. She needs to attend."

Olivia looked askance at Mattie. "Must she come?"

Cole spoke softly. "Mattie's our friend, Liv. Sophie loves her. She's completely comfortable with her."

"I'm required to stay with Sophie until we have a chance to interview her, Ms. Walker," Mattie said, her tone respectful but firm. She handed Robo's leash to the sheriff.

Cole took Sophie from Olivia. "Let me take you now, half pint. You're too big for your mom to carry."

Still clutching the toy dog, Sophie encircled Cole's neck with her free arm. From over her dad's shoulder, she looked at Mattie, her dirty face pale and exhausted, and gave her a sweet smile that melted her heart. As she followed the group from the lobby, Mattie glanced back at Robo, who'd moved toward her until he reached the end of his leash, anxiety showing on his face.

She tried to reassure him. "I'll be right back."

★

By the time Dr. McGinnis completed his exam, Stella had arrived at his office in the K-9 unit. She and the sheriff had decided it best to interview Sophie in her own home, and now the child sat on the couch in the den, nestled between her parents, leaning against her mother with the toy dog in her lap. She'd been sponged clean by the nurse, given acetaminophen for the fever, and her wrist wound had been treated and bandaged.

Dr. McGinnis had used a gentle and expert manner to determine that Sophie had not suffered sexual assault or molestation by her captor. Although her torso and arms bore bruises from rough handling, and she'd developed an upper respiratory infection, he found no major concerns. Physically. Before leaving, Mattie saw him take Cole aside and tell him to get psychological support if needed. Cole assured him they were already connected to a counselor they would consult.

Stella and Mattie sat in chairs pulled close to the couch. Earlier, Mattie had moved the coffee table away, so that it wouldn't be a barrier between them and Sophie. Mrs. Gibbs was in the kitchen making soup, and Jessie and Angela had left on a grocery run to buy some of Sophie's favorite foods. Mattie couldn't help but recall the good times she'd shared with Cole, his kids, and Mrs. Gibbs in this room. And now Olivia was here, and Mattie wasn't sure she belonged anymore. She pushed away the sadness that threatened to overwhelm her, focusing instead on the joy of having Sophie back in their midst.

Since she had the best rapport with the family, and probably since Stella wasn't that comfortable interviewing kids, the detective had asked Mattie to lead the interview.

It was time to begin, before the drowsy child fell asleep.

"Sophie, we want to catch this man," Mattie said, "and I need to ask you some questions. Would that be okay?"

Sucking her thumb, Sophie nodded. Cole touched her hand with his finger. "Take your thumb out of your mouth so you can talk," he murmured. She did as he asked, never taking her sincere brown eyes off Mattie.

"Can you tell us about how he took you, sweetheart?"

The memory made her eyes widen, and she looked more awake. "I got off the bus and was walking home. All of a sudden, he drove up behind me, jumped out, and grabbed me. He put a piece of tape on my mouth and I couldn't even scream."

"Did you see his face?"

"He was wearing a ski mask."

"Did you see his car?"

"No, I . . . I was fighting to get away. Then he put something over my head. A pillowcase or something. He said—" Her breath caught. "He told me later that he used a gunny sack with Candace, and it killed her."

Mattie nodded, reached out, and took her hand; it felt small and a bit sticky around the thumb. She gave it a squeeze. "You were afraid, I know. I would have been too. You're brave to tell us about it."

Sophie nodded, her eyes wide.

"Could you see anything inside the car that you were in?"

Sophie shook her head. "He put tape around my hands, but I still tried to open the door to get out. I pulled on the handle, but it wouldn't open, so I pushed the button to open the window." She turned her head to look up at Cole. "I wanted to jump out, Dad, but I was afraid to."

"I know you did your best to get away, honey. Don't worry," Cole murmured as he stroked the curly hair back from her face. His jaw muscle bulged from clenching his teeth.

The open window made it possible for Banjo to pick up her scent, Mattie was thinking. "What happened after you opened the window?"

In a breathless voice, Sophie continued. "He drove for a little bit, but then he stopped. I was kicking at him and trying to hit him and stuff, and he told me to stop or he'd hurt me. He used more tape on my legs and put me on the floor in the back. He rolled the window back up and started driving again."

"What else do you remember about the ride?"

"We were on the highway for a long time, then he turned left and it got bumpy, then he turned right and it got real bumpy and wound around. I could tell we were going uphill. I tried to pay attention so I could run away and get back home. Then he carried me into that cave place and took the tape and the pillowcase off. I was . . . I was crying pretty hard—" Tears spilled from her eyes and washed down her cheeks as a sob wrenched from her, cutting off her words.

Cole pulled a blue bandana from his back pocket and wiped her face while Olivia, looking devastated, hugged her more tightly. Sophie pressed her face against her mother.

Mattie waited for Sophie to calm. Although Robo had led Mattie through the forest, following the scent Sophie left when she'd tried to make her escape, there'd been a rugged, overgrown lane farther down the road from Gus Tilley's place that led to the abandoned cabin. Sophie had mapped the route in her mind perfectly.

After Sophie quieted, Mattie continued, using a conversational tone, gently guiding the interview back on track. "You did a good job paying attention to the roads you took. That place you were inside is called a root cellar, Sophie. The pioneers built them beside their cabins to keep their food cool. We can talk more about that later if you want. It's not as scary when you know what it is." This was stretching the truth; she'd felt terrified of that dank, dark space herself. "Now I want you to focus on what you remember about the man. He left the ski mask on while he was with you. Could you see anything through the holes for his eyes and mouth that you can tell us about?"

Sophie straightened. "He had brown eyes. Not dark chocolate like Dad's, more like mine."

Disappointment set Mattie back for a moment as she realized her primary suspect didn't match Sophie's description. Stella's instincts might have been right and hers wrong, because Gus Tilley's eyes were blue. But she put on a smile for Sophie.

"Good job. Anything about the shape of his eyes or his eyelids that stood out? Was he white skinned or dark? And would you guess he was young or old?"

"Young, I think, but I'm not sure. White skin around his eyes."

"What about his voice? Did you recognize it as anyone you know?"

Sophie shook her head. "It was deep, like a growly bear. I think he was disguising it."

If he tried so hard to disguise himself, it might be someone Sophie knows. Or he could have planned to let her go and didn't want her to identify him.

"He said he was gonna take me away tonight, and I wouldn't be able to get away ever again."

Mattie's throat swelled as she realized how close they'd come to losing her. She squeezed the girl's small hand. "Robo found you because you got away. You did the exact right thing."

Sophie nodded, her eyes sincere. "I watched a TV show about a girl that was kidnapped. She tricked the guy by acting like she was his friend. I decided to do that."

"You let her watch that stuff?" Olivia murmured, looking over Sophie's head at Cole.

He ignored her and continued to watch Mattie. Their eyes met briefly when she glanced at him before focusing back on Sophie. "That's a great strategy, Sophie, and it works sometimes. Is that what helped you get away this morning?"

"Well, maybe. But it was mostly because I was sick. I guess I sort of played that up a little, you know, like when I'm trying to stay home from school." The glance she gave her dad this time seemed playful, and it made Mattie's spirits lift to see the old Sophie shine through, but the girl's face became pinched as she went on. "I was lying in that bed, crying, and I told him I was so, so sick. He said he was going to get me some medicine, and he left the chain off. I pushed so hard against that door . . . it took a long time, and I got it open enough to squeeze through. But then he was coming back and he caught me on the road. I screamed and screamed." She looked like she was going to dissolve again, but she held it together.

"Good job, Sophie! You did such a brave thing. That's exactly how Robo found you. He followed your trail through the forest."

Sophie's eyes were brimming. "He's such a good dog."

Mattie had to blink away her tears as well. "We're lucky to have him. What about this time, Sophie? Did the bad guy already have the ski mask on?"

Sophie looked startled and then her focus went inward. "Not at first, but he had it on when he caught me. I remember I saw him down the road. He *does* have a white face."

"Did he have a beard?"

"Uh." Sophie paused to think. "I can't remember."

"How tall is he? Try to compare him to your dad."

"About as tall as Dad . . . strong, but not wide and muscle-y like Dad. Skinnier."

"And his car?"

Sophie shook her head. "Kinda like the sheriff's Jeep. Maybe silver. I'm sorry, Mattie. I didn't look at it very long. I ran away."

"No need to be sorry. Of course you needed to run, Sophie. You're doing great." Mattie smiled, trying to back off on the pressure. "Did he talk to you much? He told you about Candace. What else did he say?"

"While I was crying, he told me I reminded him of his sister. That me and Candace both look like his sister."

Mattie exchanged glances with Stella. She'd recognized the resemblance earlier, but this meant that the kidnapper had exposure to both girls prior to their abductions, indicating it was probably someone from the Timber Creek community. Her mind raced through their remaining suspects. Burt Banks: he had brown eyes. But then, so did Hank Wolford. Both Merton Heath and Jace Gardner matched the description. What time had Brody dropped them back off in the forest? She'd have to check on that. And Brooks Waverly? His eyes were dark too.

"What else did the guy say, Sophie?"

"He talked a lot about his sister. She died in an accident a long time ago, and he said it was his fault. That's when I decided to act like I was his friend. He cried when he told me he accidentally killed Candace too. Then he told me from now on, my name was going to be the same as his sister's. Georgiana. But I didn't like that name, because I'm Sophie. He gave me this dog."

That surprised her; Sophie was so attached to the toy that she'd thought it was one of her own that she'd taken to school in her backpack. Looking grim, Cole nodded slightly when she glanced at him. Mattie had seen him try to take it from Sophie prior to the interview, but she wouldn't let him have it.

"I was so afraid when he left me alone in there," Sophie said, gripping the dog with one hand and Mattie's hand with the other. "He left that light on, you know the one? Did you see it?"

"The one that looks like a little lantern, but it runs on a battery?"

"Yeah. But after I tried to run away, the battery ran out. I was in the dark, and I got so scared. I stared at the light around the door, and I guess I fell asleep. You and Robo woke me up."

"Hooray!" Mattie lifted Sophie's hand aloft in celebration, trying to restore some normalcy to the girl's life. "Robo to the rescue."

Sophie's grin flashed before she sobered. "He could've taken me away forever."

"But he didn't. And we're going to catch him. Can you think of anything else about him that you should tell us?"

Her eyes taking on a faraway look, Sophie shook her head, and she slumped back against her mother.

Mattie squeezed her hand one last time before she released it and turned to Stella. "Anything else, Detective?"

"Just one last thing," Stella said. "Sophie, have you ever been inside Gus Tilley's brown truck?"

Sophie put her thumb in her mouth for a second before taking it out and glancing at her dad. "No, ma'am. I've never been inside it."

Stella leaned forward and squeezed Sophie's hand. "Thank you, Sophie. You've done a great job, and I hope you feel better soon. We might need to talk to you again later, after you've had some rest, okay? And if you remember anything else you think we should know, tell your parents, and they can call. Will you do that for us?"

Stella was learning, and Mattie appreciated how she moderated her typical brash manner. Sophie nodded agreement.

They said their good-byes, and Cole escorted them to the front door. After they stepped outside onto the porch, he caught Mattie's hand, gripping it in both of his. She felt a tug inside her chest as she turned to face him.

His tired eyes filled. "I just want to say . . . you and Robo . . . well, words can't express my gratitude." He pulled her into a hug.

Emotions churned inside her—joy for finding Sophie, the melancholy of fatigue, and a tremendous sorrow for, well, she didn't know what exactly. She placed her hands lightly against his sides in an awkward attempt to break the hug, but instead she found herself closing her eyes and leaning against him for a long moment.

Tears filled her eyes as she stepped back, fighting for control. She nodded acknowledgment. She didn't want to dismiss Robo's feat of finding Sophie as "just doing their job," so she didn't say the words. They'd worked hard to make this miracle happen, especially her dog.

"I'll be in touch," she managed to say as she followed Stella out the door and into the yard.

After climbing into her SUV, Mattie turned to Robo, who'd been sleeping in the back but had risen to greet her. She grasped the ruff at his neck and gave it a shake, taking comfort, and then she turned to put her key in the ignition.

Stella was leaning against the passenger side door, watching her with pursed lips. "Your vet has feelings for you."

Mattie shook her head, fighting to keep a surge of melancholy at bay. "He's grateful that we found his child," she said, starting the engine. "Let's go to the station and see what we can do with the information we have."

"Sounds like plan. And by the way, Mattie, did I ever tell you how much I respect you?"

She shook her head and forced a smile. "If I remember right, last time we talked, you were lecturing me on how to do my job."

Stella snorted.

"Besides, turns out you were most likely right about Gus Tilley, and I was wrong."

"We'll get back to that later. But you need to know that I think you're one hell of an officer, and I couldn't be more proud to serve as a part of your team." Stella's smile faded. "Let's get back to the station and figure out how we're going to track down this child killer."

Chapter 27

Stella had written up notes from the interview and shared them with the team. They touched base in the briefing room, each of them standing because no one seemed calm enough to sit. Despite her exhaustion, Mattie could feel their energy from finding Sophie build as their focus on finding a killer narrowed.

"How certain can we be that a child Sophie's age is accurate with reporting eye color?" Sheriff McCoy asked.

"That could be a concern," Stella said. "What do you think, Mattie?"

"She compared them to her dad's eye color, and she seemed definite. I think we should take her word for it."

Stella looked at the list of suspects written on the board. "That leaves us Waverly, Banks, Heath, and Gardner. And Hank Wolford, but he's a long shot. With him, there's no motive."

"What time this morning did you leave Heath and Gardner up by their vehicle, Brody?" Mattie asked.

"About eight o'clock. I pulled off in some trees down below and watched for about an hour to see if they drove out of there. They didn't."

Mattie pulled her cell phone from her pocket and checked the call log. "Tilley heard Sophie screaming at around eleven AM. Even if Heath left his campsite after nine, I think it's possible for him to get to the root cellar by then."

"What about Brooks Waverly?" Stella said.

"I called Jack, and he thinks his son was in school this morning," McCoy said. "But the secretary at the school said Brooks didn't arrive until eleven thirty."

"Time to bring him in again," Stella said.

Mattie had been wondering if her partner might be able to find evidence that humans could overlook. "I think I should take Robo up to the site and do a thorough search in that root cellar."

"Sounds like a good idea," McCoy said. "Deputy Brody, you go too. I'll call Jack Waverly and have him bring Brooks into the station, Detective. We'll interrogate him together."

As they left the briefing room, Brody said, "I'll be ready in ten minutes," and headed toward his office.

Mattie went to her own office to awaken Robo and check supplies in her utility belt. On the way, she remembered an important call she needed to make. Using her cell phone, she touched the number on her call list.

Sounding guarded, Sergeant Madsen answered immediately. "Deputy Cobb? What's up?"

"Robo found her. Alive."

Madsen whooped, making her grin.

"I'll tell you about it when we have time," she said. "But now we've got a crime scene to go search."

"You can tell me over a beer next time you come for training. Did you catch the scumbag that took her?"

"Not yet. The guy wore a ski mask. All we have so far is a description of his eye color."

"Don't be discouraged, Mattie. You got your girl back. That's something you can be proud of."

"You're right. Nothing beats the feeling of finding a child and bringing her home."

"I want to put you and Robo on a list for state search and rescue consultants."

"That's not my call. Our county bought Robo for narcotics detection, so I'd have to talk it over with the sheriff."

"That dog shows a great talent for finding people, and I hate to waste it when we have a missing person. After you wrap up this case, I'll give the sheriff a call. You can think it over in the meantime."

Hoping they *could* wrap up the case, she said good-bye and focused on preparing to go back out to search with Brody. The adrenaline from finding Sophie had started to subside, and fatigue made the muscles in her shoulders and neck ache. But there was no time to worry about it.

Time to get back to work and catch this killer.

★

Sophie had slept most of the day, clutching that infernal toy some monster had given her. Somehow, Cole was going to have to lose that thing.

Olivia stayed with Sophie much of the time, reading her stories, watching her sleep. His parents came by the house and peeked in on the child, and to his relief, his mother was civil to his ex-wife. Jessie had decided to move to their parents' house for the night, leaving before dinner.

Angie drifted around the house like a ghost—not wanting to be in the same room with Olivia, but not wanting to be away from Sophie either—until he asked her to go with him to the clinic to feed Mountaineer and take care of the chickens. While they changed the newspaper in the bottom of the box and gave the chicks clean water and food, he tried to engage her in conversation, but she resisted. He opted not to pressure her; she'd talk to him when she felt like it.

Deciding to keep the clinic closed until after the weekend, he called Tess and told her to go ahead and schedule the routine stuff for next week but to call him if an emergency came in. She seemed more than happy to continue to handle incoming calls. Right now, he felt too exhausted to talk to anyone about anything.

They ate dinner in shifts, a delicious chicken soup with home-made noodles made by Mrs. Gibbs. Sophie, Olivia, and Mrs. Gibbs ate early, and he and Angela later when they got back from the clinic. Her fever broken, Sophie soaked in a warm tub before dressing in clean pajamas and settling into bed for the night, with Angela taking a turn at story time.

Cole grabbed a minute to shower, and then he dressed in a light pair of sweats. Padding down the stairway in bare feet to the kitchen, he realized Mrs. Gibbs had shut things down early for the night, leaving a dim night-light glowing above the countertop, as was her habit. He found the chocolate cake he meant to eat, left over from her day of cooking. Finding the semidarkness soothing, he decided against turning on the overheads and served himself a big chunk of cake and a large glass of milk before taking it to the table.

Olivia came into the room, heading for the refrigerator but startling when she caught sight of him. "Oh! I didn't know you were in here, sitting in the dark."

"You can turn on a light if you want. It's just so peaceful here without it."

"Yes, we need that. I'll leave it off." She glanced at what he was eating. "That looks good. I think I'll have some too."

"It's time for a little sweetness."

Olivia served herself cake and milk and brought it to the table. "Mind if I join you?"

"Of course not. You're welcome here, Liv."

"I wish Angie felt the same way."

"You have some fence-mending to do with her."

"And you didn't have anything to do with her being so angry with me?"

Cole shook his head. "You should know that I didn't. I've always considered you a great mother to the girls."

Olivia watched him over the top of her milk glass as she took a sip. When she lowered her glass, she had a slender milk mustache, and he smiled while he raised his napkin to wipe it off. She smiled back at him.

"You've found a wonderful cook and helper in Mrs. Gibbs," she said. "I'm sorry I suspected her at first. I was such a mess."

"We're lucky to have her. It was pretty grim around here before she came."

She looked downward, guilt crossing her face.

"I didn't say that to make you feel bad. It's just a statement of fact, but we managed all right. Both the girls helped out, and it didn't hurt them to take on more chores."

"I suppose not, but I do regret the way I left, Cole. I wasn't really thinking straight, and, well, you've always been able to manage taking care of anything you set your mind to. I believed you would take care of your children, and you did."

Cole resisted the twinge of anger her words triggered. She had no idea how much turmoil she'd caused, how she'd hurt her children. Hell—how she'd hurt him too. But it was water under the bridge, and he held his tongue.

"I lost myself in it all, Cole. Working to get you through vet school while taking care of a toddler. And then staying home to cook and clean and raise kids while you worked all day and into the night. This little town, there's nothing here for me. I want theaters, museums, and nice restaurants. I didn't even have any friends here."

"We have friends here."

"*You* have friends here. I've always felt like an outsider."

He found her words confusing; from his perspective, she'd been welcomed with open arms by everyone. Well, by everyone but his mother. He couldn't argue with her other complaints, and he paused while he chewed his cake and thought. "I guess we don't need to rehash where we've come from and what went wrong. What's important is how we move forward from here. And how are you feeling now? How much have you recovered from your depression?"

She gave him a thin smile, and in the dim light, he thought he could see sadness in her eyes. "I've spent a lot of gray days in bed with the shades pulled, but I'm getting back on track, getting some energy for something more than just pushing myself out of bed and getting dressed. Being with Marci has helped. She's a good friend and easy to talk to."

Cole fought to remain silent. Expressing his dislike for Marci wouldn't help, and he knew that the last time he and Olivia talked heart-to-heart had been years ago, long before she decided to leave. And that was his fault.

"I want to be in the girls' lives." Her breath caught, and she blinked back tears. "I hope I haven't ruined it with Angie."

"I think she'll come around. She loves you, you know, but she's hurt. You'll have to talk to her, tell her how you feel. We have a counselor we work with in Hightower. She can talk to her about it too."

Surprise touched her face.

He answered her unasked question. "The girls and I had some hard adjustments to make after you left."

She shook her head and examined the crumbs in her plate, using her fork to push them around. "I'm sorry I made it so hard on you all."

Cole felt his resistance crumble. "I'm sorry I wasn't there for you."

She looked up at him. "I still love you, Cole. I guess I always will. When I left here, I thought I didn't, but now . . . sometimes I wish we could give it another try."

His surprise must have registered on his face, because she flashed him a quick smile before sobering.

"But I could never move back here," she said. After a pause and looking down at the table, she added, "Would you consider moving to Denver?"

He gave her his kneejerk reaction. "I don't think so. This is my home, and it's where I built my practice."

She looked away. "If you loved me, those things wouldn't matter."

He thought for a long moment, giving careful consideration to his words. "I believe you when you say you still love me, because I feel the same way. A part of me will always love you, Olivia. But loving me wasn't enough to make you happy here in Timber Creek. I would hate living in Denver, and I know I wouldn't last very long there. Can you see it's the same thing?"

"Maybe we could try living somewhere else. Someplace that would give us both what we want."

Again, he weighed her words. He sifted through the changes he'd made since she left, small things she wouldn't approve of like dogs in the house, the girls working at the clinic, giving the kids more freedom and responsibility. Mattie came to mind along with feelings he didn't have time to sort, so he set them aside to save for a time when he did.

"It's something we both should consider," he said. "But right now, we're tired and probably more than a little euphoric from getting Sophie back. Not to mention the cake." It did his heart good to make her smile. "I think we should relax and get a good night's sleep. I can sack out on the couch if you want to sleep in my room."

"Sophie wants me to sleep with her."

"I'll go up and say good-night to the girls, and then I need to go to bed." He squeezed her hand as he arose from the table to carry his dishes to the sink. She remained sitting, possibly disappointed in him, but now was not the time for making decisions about renewing commitments.

★

Cole couldn't sleep, so he lay on top of the covers, his room lit by the silent television, which he continuously surfed using the remote, keeping the sound off so he could listen to the sounds of the house.

His child's kidnapper was still out there. For whatever reason, this monster wanted Sophie badly enough to steal her. Was he out there watching their house, waiting to break in after they'd all gone to bed? He'd left the downstairs lights on with Bruno on guard. That should deter an intruder. But still, Cole felt he couldn't relax until the man was behind bars.

He didn't want to revisit his conversation with Liv, but of course, he couldn't help but go back over it. After mulling it over, he continuously arrived at the same conclusion: he liked the life he and the kids were piecing together, and he was ready to move on. It wouldn't be easy, but he'd have to find a gentle way to tell Olivia, and he still planned to help her find a way to establish a new relationship with the girls.

And as for Mattie? He'd never met a woman he admired more. Not only had she saved his life, but she'd saved his daughter too. And, well, he needed to make sure his feelings for her weren't hero worship, because he thought he was falling in love.

A quiet tap sent his attention to his partially closed door, where Sophie peeked in. "Are you watching TV?"

"Kind of. Do you want to join me?"

"Yeah." She went to the other side of the bed and climbed on, still clutching that dratted toy dog. Belle and Bruno followed her into the room, gazing longingly at the bed. "Can these guys come, too? Belle's sad that she has to sleep downstairs."

He pulled the covers back on her side and then tucked her in. Unable to resist Bruno's begging eyes, he decided to give him a chance to be with Sophie before taking him back downstairs to his guard post.

Patting the blanket, he invited both dogs onto the foot of the king-size bed, where they plopped down near Sophie. "I guess it won't hurt to let them up here with you. How are you feeling, sweetheart?"

"Okay I guess." She sniffed. "But my nose is stuffy and I can't sleep. Mommy took a sleeping pill, and she's snoring."

"She's really tired. None of us slept last night."

"Uh-huh," she said as if she already knew. She tried to suck her thumb, but her nose was too stuffy, so she pulled it out of her mouth. Cole decided that maybe that was a good thing.

"I keep thinking about that place," she said.

Cole rolled to face her, putting his hand on her small shoulder. She stared at the ceiling, clutching the toy dog. Would she be traumatized for life?

"Do you want to talk about it?"

She shook her head in a small back and forth movement. "Mattie cried when she found me. I cried too."

"You were both relieved." Cole fought back his own tears. Relief probably didn't even come close to describing how overcome they'd been. And Mattie . . . she wasn't one to cry. His chest swelled as he thought of how much this woman seemed to love his kids. It touched him.

Another tap at the door made them both look, and the dogs raised their heads.

"Angie," Sophie said, the word laden with pleasure. She scooted over to the middle, closer to Cole. "Come get in bed with us." And then she pushed Belle. "Move over, Belle. Let Angie in."

"Join us, Angel," he said. "Can't sleep?"

Angela climbed into bed on the other side of Sophie, and the two snuggled against each other. "No. I must've slept too much today."

"Me too," Sophie said. "Can we watch a movie, Dad?"

"Let's see what we can find," he said, deep contentment filling him as he flipped through the channels. They finally agreed on *Sleepless in Seattle*, and Cole turned the volume on low so they wouldn't disturb the rest of the household. Yawning, he settled back on his pillow with his shoulder bumping against Sophie's.

He would savor this moment, but once the girls fell asleep, he and Bruno would go back on guard duty.

Chapter 28

Saturday

Mattie covered her wet hair with a towel, giving her scalp a brisk massage to try to wake up. She took a moment to examine the ashen circles under her eyes before squeezing toothpaste onto her toothbrush.

No way around it. I look like shit this morning.

The search for evidence at the root cellar had turned up nothing, the Waverly interrogation hadn't ended with satisfactory results, and Burt Banks was still missing when the sheriff had called it a day last night and told them all to go home and get some sleep. Instead of going home, Mattie had driven to Cole's place to stand guard for a while outside his house, just in case the killer came back for Sophie. She might as well die if she let anything else happen to that dear girl.

After getting dressed, she went to the kitchen in search of something to eat when her cell phone rang.

Cole.

She connected the call. "How is Sophie this morning?"

"Much better. We're at the clinic feeding her chicks, and she wanted to call to tell you good morning. Do you have time to talk to her?"

His words warmed her heart. "Sure. Put her on."

There was a pause and a clatter as Cole shifted the phone to Sophie. "Good morning, Mattie. What are you doing today?"

Mattie closed her eyes as she savored hearing the child's voice. "Good morning to you too, Sophie. I'm getting ready to go to work."

"But it's Saturday!"

Mattie smiled. "Police officers have to be on duty over the weekend too."

"Can you come by today and see my baby chicks?"

"I'll call later and see if we can work something out, okay?"

"Okay." There was a pause before Sophie spoke again. "I really missed my babies."

"I bet you did. You'd just brought them home, right?"

"Yeah. That guy said he was going to buy me some more chicks, but I wanted my own."

Mattie straightened, all of her attention focused on Sophie. "Had you already told him about your new chickens, sweetheart?"

"No, I didn't tell him anything about them. I didn't want him to kidnap them too."

"So did he use those words? Did he say, 'I'm going to buy you some *more* chicks?'"

Sophie paused as if thinking. "Yeah, that's what he said. I'm pretty sure."

"Did you talk about your chickens with him then?"

"No, first he said he was going to take me away that night. Then he said once we got where we were going to live, he was going to buy me some more chicks. I was scared and trying not to cry."

Adrenaline was pumping through Mattie. "Thanks for telling me about that, Sophie. It might help us find the guy. If you think of anything else, let me know. I'll talk to you later today, but for now, could I talk to your dad again?"

"Sure." There was a pause, and Mattie thought she'd hear Cole's voice next, but Sophie evidently wasn't through talking. "I love you, Mattie."

Her breath caught. "I love you too, sweetheart."

Now it was Cole's voice she heard. "Mattie?"

"Did you hear that about the chicks, Cole?"

"I did."

"Who knows? Who knows besides Gus Tilley?"

"He's the one I was thinking of."

"It's not him. I'm sure of it. Think. Let's make a list."

"The family, Tess, Gus, all the kids in her class and their parents."

"Do you know Brooks Waverly?"

"Sure."

"Was he at the feed store when you went?"

"No, I'm sure he wasn't."

Her mind conjured an image of a tall, lanky young man with a friendly grin and scruffy brown facial hair. "Who sold you the chicks at the feed store?"

"Moses checked us out. A kid carried the box to the truck." Cole paused, and when he spoke again, his voice was charged with intensity. "That's the guy."

"I'll go right now and talk to him."

"I'm coming too."

"Cole, stay put. You have to stay out of this. I'll call you back as soon as I know something."

He made a sound that could be taken as agreement, and they disconnected the call. Mattie headed to her closet to retrieve her service weapon, dialing Stella as she went.

When Stella didn't answer, Mattie left her a message summarizing Cole's information and their conclusion. "The feed store opens at six, and I think this kid works the morning shift. I'm going over there now. If he's there, I'll take him to the station for you to question."

Robo hopped into the back of the Explorer, and she drove across town. When she parked in front of the store, no other vehicles were around. Releasing the holster strap on her Glock, Mattie opened the cage door, and Robo followed her out of the car. The sweet scent of grain wafted out and around her when she stepped inside the feed store.

Moses Randall, looking like Santa with his white whiskers, sat on a stool behind the counter, and his eyes lit when they zeroed in on Mattie. "Our local hero! And Robo! To what do I owe the pleasure of this visit?"

Mattie leaned against the counter, turning to scan the store. "I want to talk to one of your employees. Not Juanita, but the young man. What's his name?"

"That's Jed. Jed Franklin. You're lucky to catch him. He's leaving me today." Randall smiled. "Came in for his last paycheck, but I needed his young back to unload and stack some feed out in the yard before I give it to him. I'll call him in."

"No, let me go out there to talk to him," Mattie said, heading toward the back room. "Is there a door that leads out to the yard here?"

"Yeah, just go through there and out the back."

She hastened down a narrow aisle in between stacks of feed and stepped out the door into a large area surrounded by solid board fencing. She scanned the space, taking in the packed dirt dotted with stacks of lumber, barrels, fence posts, and fencing. Her gaze paused on two vehicles—Randall's white Toyota, loaded with feedbags and parked by a shed, and across the way, a silver Jeep Liberty, an older model.

As she focused back on Randall's truck, Jed Franklin sauntered out of the shed, spotting her at the same time she did him. Without hesitation, he broke into a run, charging toward the Jeep.

Mattie sprinted toward him as she shouted, "Stop! Stop or I'll send the dog!"

He ran even faster.

"Robo! Take him!"

Robo streaked ahead, arriving at the Jeep as Franklin opened the door and jumped inside. Robo grabbed his pants leg and tugged. Franklin held onto the steering wheel as he started the engine, jerking his leg to free his pants, but succeeded only in hauling Robo partway into the vehicle.

He slammed the door on Robo's chest and tried to kick him off. Robo hung on, growling and shaking his head. Franklin pushed the door wide, getting ready to slam it on Robo again. But her dog wrenched hard and pulled the man's leg out of the Jeep at the exact moment the door swung in. There was a crack, and Franklin howled in pain.

As Mattie reached the Jeep, Franklin jammed it into reverse. He spun out backward, billowing a cloud of dust and dragging her dog. Still Robo wouldn't release his grip, and he skidded along, braced, his paws digging into the dirt. The front tire narrowly missed him as the Jeep yanked him along.

There was no way Robo could win this battle. She pulled her weapon, planning to call him off.

A pickup truck with a vet unit in back screeched to a stop across the open gate that led into the alleyway, blocking the exit.

Cole.

"Robo, out!" she shouted, training her weapon on the Jeep's windshield, even though she knew she couldn't risk a shot. Not with Cole parked behind.

Robo released Franklin's leg and ran back toward her. Franklin poured on the gas, revving the engine as he stared at Mattie, not turning to watch where he was going. Speeding backward, he was giving her a sardonic smile when the sound of metal crunching on metal resounded through the yard. The Jeep crashed into the passenger side of Cole's truck, snapping Franklin's head back before throwing him forward into the steering wheel. The vehicle stalled, and he rolled out the open front door, landing on his shoulder in the dirt. He lay there, stunned.

What about Cole?

Mattie couldn't check on him now. She raced forward, her weapon trained on Franklin, Robo forging ahead in attack mode. "Robo, guard! Don't move, Franklin! Do not move, or this dog will attack!"

Franklin groaned as he blinked at her and then stared at her Glock, four feet away from his face. His eyes widened when they went to Robo, crouched merely inches away, his sharp teeth glistening.

"Hands on your head," she told him. As he complied, she added, "Roll to your stomach. Move slowly."

Within seconds, she caught his hands behind his back and cuffed him. Robo waved his tail as she called him off, looking like he'd survived the ordeal without major injury. She glanced up to find Cole standing beside the wrecked Jeep, squinting in the sun.

"You got him!" Cole headed her way.

She narrowed her eyes at him. "I thought I told you to stay home."

Cole smiled. "And miss all the fun? I wouldn't have missed getting to see you and Robo take this guy down for anything." Then he sobered. "He's the one, Mattie."

"Are you all right?"

"I bailed out before he hit. I'm fine."

"But he wrecked your truck."

He shrugged. "That's what insurance is for."

Chapter 29

Stella and Sheriff McCoy shut themselves away in the interrogation room with Jed Franklin. Mattie finished writing her report and decided to check in with Brody. Followed by Robo, she tapped on Brody's office door, and he called to her to come in.

"Have a seat," he said when she entered.

His office could have been decorated by the government. Photos of the Colorado state governor and the United States president were mounted on the wall behind him, the room anchored by a utilitarian metal desk with two standard-issue plastic-covered chairs stationed in front. State and federal flags hung in each corner. There were no personal items on his desk, except for an attractive wooden pen and pencil holder. Otherwise, the desktop held a computer, in and out baskets, and a rack of file folders.

Mattie sat in one of the hard-backed chairs. "I want to thank you for helping me with Robo the last few days. I appreciate your support."

Brody waved away her words with his hand. "You work real hard with that dog, Cobb. And good job on the scent lineup. No telling how we can use that skill in the future."

"I know it. Scent identification is a huge step up in his training. I'm pretty proud of him."

"You should be." Brody cleared his throat and shifted in his chair. "But I need to tell you that I've been concerned about you lately."

"Oh, yeah?"

"You're looking pretty strung out, and you're not acting like yourself."

Once, Mattie could've described his own behavior that way; she avoided his gaze by looking at the desktop. "Are you concerned about my performance?"

He paused, and she raised her eyes to look into his intense blue stare. "You're doing okay. It's hard to pinpoint. Maybe you're not as tuned in as you once were."

Mattie nodded. "I understand. I'll remedy that."

"And you can take a lesson from LoSasso about weighing the evidence before jumping to a conclusion. We could all do that."

Brody used to be the worst offender, but she agreed that she'd been the one this time. "Noted."

He pushed back his chair and stood. Brody wasn't as polished as the sheriff, but Mattie took it as a sign of dismissal and rose from her chair as well.

"That said, I want to add that I think you and Robo are the best K-9 team I've ever come across, and I'm proud that you serve in this department." Not used to giving out compliments, he looked embarrassed as he extended his hand.

Mattie shook hands, squeezing hard to match his grip. "Thanks, Brody. It means a lot to have you say that."

"Don't let it go to your head." He frowned, looking more like the Brody she knew. "Now clock out and go home. Overtime is through the roof."

"All right, but can one of you call and update me when Stella and the sheriff are done with Franklin?"

"Sure thing."

Mattie left his office and went directly to the time clock. After punching out, she went back to say good-bye to Rainbow and ask her something she'd been too busy to address. "I'm getting ready to go home, but I have a question for you," she said.

"Shoot." Rainbow giggled. "I guess I shouldn't say that to an officer of the law."

Mattie smiled and then felt her cheeks warm. There was no reason to be embarrassed, but the topic she was about to bring up felt loaded. "I was wondering if you knew about any yoga classes nearby."

"Oh, my gosh! I can't believe you just asked me that!"

Mattie braced herself. "Oh?"

"Anya and I have been talking about this for weeks. They want to start community yoga with a night class and a weekend class at the hot springs, and guess who they're going to hire to teach it!"

"Who?"

"Me! Did you know I'm a certified yoga instructor?"

"I didn't know that."

"Do you want to join a class?"

This was going too fast. "I don't know, but I'll think about it."

Rainbow examined her with a steady gaze. "If you want, I'll give you some private lessons first. Then you can decide about joining a class."

Her friend seemed to know her so well. "I'd love that. I need to learn the breathing stuff."

Rainbow grinned. "I'll teach you that and some of the basic poses. Want to start tonight?"

She couldn't help but feel lighter as she returned Rainbow's smile. "I'm beat. I need to take a night off. But how about sometime tomorrow?"

"Done. We'll set something up."

They ended their conversation, and there was nothing more for Mattie to do but go home. After loading up Robo, she began to drive, her emotions turbulent. She'd like to go see Sophie's chicks as promised, but she couldn't. Not with Olivia still there. As long as she could stay at work, she could avoid getting caught up in her thoughts, but now that she was heading home, they started to siphon her into a downward spiral. She struggled to remain objective.

She strived for perfection in every undertaking, and it smarted to know that others had found her performance lacking. Brody typically threw out sarcastic comments or sardonic observations while coaching his subordinates, and his conversation with her had hit home as both concerned and considerate. Something she wasn't used to. It made her feel even worse, and it undermined his praise. She winced, knowing she needed to get back on track.

When she'd been in the cellar with Sophie, memories had surfaced. Solid memories from her childhood rather than the amorphous hints she'd remembered earlier. And the good news was—it hadn't killed her. She'd handled it, just as her therapist had suggested she would. She needed to discuss it with Lisa Callahan during their next session, but she could already feel her intense anxiety starting to dissipate.

It would take longer to deal with the anger, but at least she could set up the right targets to shoot at. And maybe Willie and her mother didn't belong among them. Maybe it was time to get back in touch with Willie. Mama T had been nagging her to do it. Maybe she should.

Once home, she fed Robo, took a shower, and dressed in sweats. She unwrapped a large pressed-rawhide bone and gave it to her dog. He tossed it and play posed around it, making her laugh, before he settled down with it for a chew. Realizing she felt hungry, she made a turkey sandwich from lunch meat she thawed in the microwave, grabbed an apple, and took her plate out to the porch to eat. Robo trotted outside to the yard, carrying his rawhide by one end, the other dangling downward from his mouth. He placed it in the weedy grass, putting a paw on it to hold it still while he gnawed. She watched him while she ate.

It grew chilly as the sun set behind the western mountains, so she went back into the house, calling Robo to come along with her. He held the rawhide high like a trophy as he came.

Someone knocked on the door. She opened it to find Stella on the front porch.

"Can I come in?"

"Of course." Mattie opened the door wide.

"I told the others I'd update you on the interviews." Stella came inside, stripping off her jacket and throwing it on a chair. She kicked off her loafers and collapsed onto the far end of the sofa. "You got a beer for me?"

"Sure. You want a sandwich?"

"Nah, I'll get something at home."

Mattie went to the kitchen and retrieved a beer from the six-pack in the refrigerator, a supply she kept mainly for Stella. "Here you go," she said, handing it to her before settling, one leg tucked under the other, on the opposite end of the couch.

Stella took a long drink, sighing her approval. "I'll start with Jed Franklin, because I'm sure he's the one you're most interested in. He seemed eager to sing. We got a full confession, written and signed."

Mattie released a breath she didn't know she'd been holding.

"It was like he told Sophie. Candace reminded him of his sister, so he used a burlap bag from the feed store to put over her head to capture her. He'd been watching her for a while and knew she went up the hill to meet others after school. He worked the early shift and got off work by then, so he'd go up there to stalk her. He took a chance, but when he spotted her alone with no one else up there waiting, he grabbed her. Didn't know she was allergic. She died within minutes. He said that when he realized what was happening, there was nothing he could do. Sobbed his little ole heart out." Stella's disgust was evident as she took another sip of her beer.

Sadness over the girl's death overrode Mattie's other emotions. "What a waste."

"I'll say. He confessed to Sophie's abduction too. Said he never would have hurt her. I pointed out that he already did. Said he wanted to take care of her, and he was afraid he would accidentally kill her too when she got sick. He says he planned to bring her back to her house and let her go, although as you know, she says he told her he planned to take her away, so I hesitate to believe him." Stella shook her head. "He saw how much she resembled his sister when she came to the store to buy chicks."

Mattie realized she was sitting all hunched up. She forced herself to straighten and tried to relax. "How did his sister die anyway?"

"Car accident with him driving. Got hit by a drunk driver, if what he says is true. She was in the passenger seat, and he didn't make her wear her seat belt. He was sixteen and she was twelve. He'd picked her up from her friend's house at his mother's request. Parents blamed him for her death. It's been eating at him all this time."

"Geez."

"Yeah. Sad deal, but it doesn't give him a license to abduct and kill other people."

No, it doesn't, Mattie thought.

But she couldn't help but relate to the fact that Franklin's motive and goal were similar to one she had for herself—to regain a semblance of family.

"Do you have him on suicide watch at the jail?"

"Yep." Stella leaned her head on the sofa's cushion at her back. "He'll be assigned a public defender, and I hope he goes ahead and pleads guilty. Get him into the system and maybe get him some help."

Mattie drew a breath and released it slowly. Getting him the help he needed through the system would be unlikely.

"Burt Banks showed up at home this morning. When I talked to him, I leaned on him as hard as I thought I could, but didn't get any confession about him mistreating Candace. Although I respect your opinion, Mattie, I think your instinct on that one might be off."

She shrugged. "You could be right about that."

"Anyway, in light of the fact that we have no suspicion or accusation from Juanita Banks or the neighbor, we have to let it go. He seems to be grieving his daughter's loss like any normal dysfunctional parent." Stella tossed her a sarcastic grin before sobering.

Mattie caught her drift. "Agreed."

"Merton Heath and company stopped by to check in with us on their way out of town. Heath told me he'll never come anywhere near Timber Creek again when he goes on vacation." Stella snickered as she enjoyed a moment of cop humor. "Hey, if you want to avoid being rounded up as a suspect, you'd better keep your nose clean. A criminal record can be a bitch."

Mattie nodded, wanting to share Stella's laughter, but she felt too tightly wound up inside to let go.

Stella took another pull on her beer. "And of course, Wolford's still facing drug charges, but he had nothing to do with Candace and Sophie."

"I guess Brooks Waverly doesn't either."

"Yeah. I found out it took him an extra hour to arrive to the store on that errand. Probably hanging out with some kid here in town. He's playing games with his parents, but that's their problem, not ours. Or I should say, not ours yet." Stella shot a knowing glance at her.

"When we arrested Wolford, I hoped we could get Banks to testify against him on the gaming charges," Mattie said.

"Oh, I think we still can. Juanita might help us with that."

"And what's the status on Gus Tilley?"

"Social Services got him hooked back into his support system. They got him medicine from the pharmacy in Hightower for this month, and he should start receiving it through the mail again next month. They'll follow up and make sure everything is working the way it should." Stella paused. "I need to finish talking to you about him."

"Brody already did. I agree that I should stay more objective in the future."

"That's good, but there's more I need to say. I received crisis intervention training when I was working in Byers County. It teaches law enforcement officers how to identify people with mental illness as well as ways to handle crisis situations that involve them. That's why I knew what to look for. I've asked Sheriff McCoy to set up a training session for us. It's more important than ever these days."

"That's a good idea."

Stella gave her a sharp look. "Which brings me to you. Are you still working with your therapist?"

Mattie nodded.

"Do Brody and Sheriff McCoy know about it?"

"Just you."

Stella watched Robo chew his rawhide for a moment. "You have the right to take care of yourself privately, as long as it doesn't affect your behavior on the job. I told you I'm concerned about your anger, but I've got to say, you handled yourself like a professional during this case. With a little bit of coaching."

Mattie held Stella's gaze. "I intend to do what I can to get well. I'm focused on following my therapist's recommendations and taking care of Robo. I can work through this."

Stella reached out and squeezed Mattie's hand before withdrawing hers and looking away. "I believe you can too. Just remember you're not alone." She finished the last of her beer. "By the way, Robo was pretty spectacular in that scent lineup."

Robo pricked his ears at Stella but didn't stop chewing. His teeth scraped against the hard edge of the pressed rawhide.

Mattie smiled at him and leaned back into the sofa cushions. She finally felt herself unwind while she watched him. "He was, wasn't he? He's a pretty spectacular dog."

"That he is."

A knock came at the door, and Mattie and Stella looked at each other. "You expecting someone?" Stella asked.

Mattie shook her head, rose from the couch, and headed for the door; Robo left his rawhide and went with her. She flipped on the porch light and looked through the peephole. Cole was standing there holding a cardboard box.

She turned to Stella in surprise. "It's Cole."

Stella jumped off the sofa, carrying her empty bottle to the kitchen as she hopped on one foot and then the other, tugging on her shoes. "I'll be on my way," she was saying.

Mattie opened the door. "Cole, this is a surprise. I didn't know you knew where I live."

"It's not hard to find out these things in Timber Creek." He raised the box slightly. "Mrs. Gibbs sent you a care package."

Mattie held the door wide while pushing Robo out of the way. "Robo, get back. He's happy to see you," she said to Cole. "Come in. I don't mean to make you stand out there in the cold."

Stella was pulling on her jacket. "I've got to go home, Mattie. It's nice to see you, Dr. Walker," she said as she tried to pass by.

Cole juggled the box, holding it with one hand. "Don't go before I have a chance to thank you for helping us find our Sophie."

Mattie took the box from him while he shook hands with Stella. Cole expressed his heartfelt gratitude, which the detective accepted with grace.

"I need to tell both of you that Sophie sort of fessed up this evening. She said she climbed up onto Gus Tilley's truck to pet Dodger through the window. She knows she's not supposed to do that kind of thing, so she didn't want to tell me about it." Cole shook his head, looking sheepish. "She says she didn't climb inside the truck, so she didn't fib when she said she'd never been inside. I'm sorry. If she'd told us the whole truth during your interview, we could have factored it in much sooner."

"Kids," Stella said. "It's always hard to take what they say at face value. But to tell you the truth, Dr. Walker, I sort of suspected as much. She gave you a little look before she answered, and I thought she might be bending the truth."

Cole frowned. "I would hope my kids know it's safe to talk to me."

Stella gave his arm a quick touch. "Just hearing you say that tells me you'll do a good job with those daughters of yours."

"I'll keep trying."

Mattie had been thinking about when Robo alerted at Tilley's truck. "Robo indicated Sophie's scent at the open door of the truck. He didn't jump inside. I assumed he'd caught her scent on the seat, but I guessed wrong. He'd found her scent on the inside door, where she'd gripped to hang on."

She'd taken him away from the truck to preserve the scene. She'd screwed up, another pitfall of jumping to conclusions.

Sergeant Madsen's words came back to her. *Always listen to your dog! If you don't, you'll only be as good a team as a human cop can be. If you do, the possibilities are endless.* This was her mission, her life's work. She couldn't make these kinds of mistakes in the future.

Cole was studying her, his dark eyes soft with concern. "Don't blame yourself, Mattie. I've got so much guilt about this whole deal that I've decided I need to let it go. Mrs. Gibbs and I will never let the girls come home unsupervised again. All we can do is learn from our mistakes, make corrections, and keep going."

"That sounds like a road map for life," Stella said. "I've got to get home now, so I'll say good-night." Before she closed the door behind her, she glanced back at Mattie and gave her a wink.

"Let me take this to the kitchen," Mattie said, turning to carry the savory-scented box through the living room. Robo trotted behind her, tail waving. Cole followed, and after she placed the box on the counter, he reached in to unpack.

"Here's a casserole, some cheesy broccoli, and rice. I hope you like that." He raised an eyebrow in question.

"I like just about anything I don't have to cook."

"My girl. I hear ya." He grinned as he continued to unpack. "Meatloaf, a couple of salads, and some famous Molly Gibbs choco-late cake. She said to tell you that she thinks you're getting too thin, so she wants you to eat everything."

Her eyes prickled with hot tears, and she couldn't speak for a moment.

Cole glanced at her, and his face fell. "I hope that didn't hurt your feelings. It wasn't meant to."

"No, no. It's just so nice of her."

He drew the last item from the box, a package wrapped in white butcher paper. "Here's a fresh knuckle bone for Robo from Crane's Market. I'll put it in the refrigerator."

"Let's put the food in there too. I already ate dinner."

"All right. It'll be even better tomorrow. No problem finding room for it. I see you don't like to invest in a lot of food." He threw her a look over his shoulder as he moved the beer aside and placed the dishes in her almost empty refrigerator. He closed the door. "Sophie wants to invite you to her birthday party next Friday. She was going to invite her friends and have her first sleepover, but now she wants only you and Robo to come. I hope you can make it."

It made her sad that Sophie had changed her plans with her friends, and she wouldn't disappoint her for the world. "We're happy to come. If she changes her mind and returns to her original party plans, just let me know."

"She won't change her mind about having you. If she wants to add her friends, I hope you can stand being with a bunch of giggling girls." He shook his head. "I never thought I'd see the day when I hoped for that. It would be nice for her to get back to normal."

"It will happen."

"Do you have a minute so we could talk?"

"Sure," she said, turning to go to the living room. "Robo has his rawhide in here."

Robo trotted ahead, pounced on his chew, and took it to his bed. He plopped down and got back to business, comfortable with having Cole in the room. Mattie and Cole took seats on opposite ends of the sofa.

"Sheriff McCoy called and told me Jed Franklin confessed," he said, his eyes earnest. "But I need to know what it was like for Sophie. The cave she talks about. Everything you can tell me."

Mattie forced herself to go back into the root cellar—the dark, closed-in space, the dank smell, and the chill. Bending both legs up so she could hug them against her body while she sat, she described it to Cole as objectively as possible. By the end, she had to clamp her jaw against a shiver.

Cole was sitting on the edge of his seat, leaning forward and bracing himself, elbows to knees. "And the abrasion on her wrist? It was from a chain?"

She'd reported this to Dr. McGinnis during his exam. "Yes."

"How did you get her free?"

Mattie told him how she'd hacked through the shelf to free the end and how Brody cut the chain off Sophie's wrist later.

Cole drew a breath and released it in a quivery exhalation. "I'm not sure how I can deal with this. I want to throttle the guy."

"He'll be convicted." She knew it wouldn't be enough even as she said it.

He gave her a look and shook his head before turning away to stare at the coffee table. "She still carries around that damn toy dog he gave her. Last night, before she went to sleep, I heard her whisper to it. She said, 'My name is Sophie.'"

The tears that were always so close to the surface sprang to her eyes. She bowed her head, leaning against her bent knees, hiding her tears from Cole. In the silence that followed while she presumed he wrestled with his own emotions, she thought of her therapist's words about emotional self-reliance.

She cleared her throat so she could speak. "I've been working through some things from my past with a therapist during the last few months. She talks about learning to take care of yourself emotionally. I think that's what Sophie's doing. If the toy gave her comfort in that cellar, Cole, let her have it. She'll work through it. She won't carry it around forever."

"I suppose you're right." He studied her as if trying to really see her. She realized she'd wound herself up into a tight little ball.

"I've missed you the past few months, Mattie. All of us have. Is that why you haven't been around lately?"

She couldn't tell him how much it hurt to know he still loved Olivia . . . and now to actually see him with her. "For the most part. I've been a mess lately, not good company for anyone, but I'm working on it."

He winced as if her pain were his and reached his hand across the space in the middle of the couch, holding it palm up. She released her arm from around her knees, freeing her hand to meet his. He clasped her hand, his feeling large and warm, and held it while they sat listening to the sound of Robo's teeth scraping against his rawhide. When the silence between them lengthened, Robo quit chewing and raised his head to stare at Cole, ears pricked and alert.

Cole chuckled, easing the tension as he squeezed her hand and released it. "Lord help the man who tries to make a move on you," he said, tipping his head toward Robo, "threatening or otherwise."

Mattie smiled, swallowing her pain. "He's my buddy."

"That he is." Cole sobered, looking thoughtful. "I can't believe how much power you have harnessed in that dog. He would do anything for you. It's amazing to watch."

Robo returned to his chewing.

"Not always. He was being a bad boy just the other day. It takes a lot of time and effort to keep that much power and will focused in the right direction."

"I guess that could be said about all of us." Cole looked down at the floor. "I feel bad about pointing a finger at Gus Tilley. And here he's the one that led us to Sophie."

"You're not the only one who feels bad about suspecting him. I do too." She sorted through what she could say. "He's going through a tough time, but he's getting back on track. He'll probably start acting more like himself again soon, though he might still require your attention over the next few days."

"He's got that, as much as he wants. I'm forever grateful that he made the call that got you headed in the right direction."

Mattie nodded, feeling like she'd said all that she could.

Cole faced her. "Mattie, life is going to be messy for us at our house too, but please don't pull away. We—the kids, me, even Mrs. Gibbs—we enjoy having you around. Even if all we do is sit and watch a movie together."

She had to ask. "Will Olivia return to your lives now?"

He seemed to be observing her closely. "I think so. I hope she and the girls can have a relationship, and I hope she's willing to let them visit her in Denver. But we've got a lot of work to do with Angie. She's not too keen on the idea."

"It's good for them to be with their mother." Again, she struggled to contain her tears.

"One would think so. We'll have to see if it turns out that way. I'm not willing to let her hurt them again."

She remained silent, forcing herself to not ask what Olivia's return meant for him.

"I've had an epiphany regarding the term 'irreconcilable differences,' and now I fully understand what it means," he said. "I think I can let go of some of the resentment I've been feeling toward Olivia and move on. I want her back in the girls' lives if it's good for them, but as for me? It's hard to put into words, but my feelings for her have changed. I guess I'm ready to bury the hatchet, but I don't want to tear down the fence. Does that make any sense?"

"It's most important that it makes sense to you."

His eyes searched her face. "I admire you, Mattie, and you're good for me and my girls. Would you be willing to spend more time with us?"

Tears streamed down her cheeks, and this time she didn't try to hide them from him. "I can do that."

He stood, took her hand, and pulled her into his arms. "Oh, Mattie. I hate to see you in pain. Let me know if there's anything I can do to help."

She pressed her face against his chest and savored how wonderful it felt to be held by him again. *This helps*, she thought, but she couldn't say it.

Robo growled.

"It's okay, Robo. Quiet," she said, her voice low and tremulous, as Cole leaned back slightly to check on him while he continued to hold her. Robo scrambled up from his bed, leaving his rawhide to come press his nose between them, following up by inserting his whole body and forcing Cole to take a step back.

Still, Cole kept her in a loose embrace, leaning forward to lower his face close to hers. "I don't intend to be aced out by your dog."

She realized he was going to kiss her, and she closed her eyes, fighting the panicky feeling that threatened. His warm lips pressed against hers, soft, undemanding. Nothing to fear. A warm feeling of joy blossomed inside her as she kissed him back, holding onto the moment for a few seconds until Robo pushed her with his nose and barked.

Cole leaned away so that he could look at her. His dark eyes twinkled. "I guess your dog's not going to give up that easily," he said, taking a step back.

"Giving up really isn't a part of his nature."

He smiled. "It's not in mine, either. But for now, I'd better go back home before the kids send the cops out after me."

He ruffled the fur on Robo's shoulders and turned to leave. "Good night, you two. Take care of your girl, Robo."

Mattie followed him to the door, closing it softly behind him and then turning to lean against it. She touched her fingers to her lips, confusion edging out the joy she'd felt when he kissed her. Did he feel the same way about her that she did about him? If she allowed herself to love him, would she be opening herself up for more loss and heartache?

You're thinking too much. You're okay right now.

She shook her head. If she was ever going to get a handle on this trust thing, she'd better get to work on it. She joined Robo on his dog bed, lay down next to him while he chewed his rawhide, and cuddled against his warm furry body.

She fell asleep within minutes.

Acknowledgments

I want to express my gratitude to the readers of the Timber Creek K-9 mysteries and to those who've spread the word about the series and encouraged me along the way. I appreciate your support tremendously.

My sincere appreciation goes to the professionals who've helped me with law enforcement and veterinary procedures: K-9 Officer/ Trainer Beth Gaede (Ret.), Lieutenant Glenn J. Wilson (Ret.), and Charles Mizushima, DVM. Misinterpretation or fictional enhancement of any information provided by these folks is mine alone.

Special thanks to my agent, Terrie Wolf, who assists me in so many ways; to my editor, Nike Power, for her editorial skill and storytelling talent; to my copyeditor, Danny Constantino, for his sharp attention to detail; and to publisher Matt Martz, editorial and publishing assistant Sarah Poppe, and everyone at Crooked Lane Books for believing in this series and bringing each episode to print. I consider myself lucky to team up with these special people.

Thank you to manuscript readers Nancy Coleman, Scott Graham, and Susan Hemphill for their input and suggestions and also to friends and family whose encouragement kept me going, even when the going got tough.

Special thanks and hugs to my husband, Charlie, for helping me plot and making sure I have time to write, and to my daughters, Sarah and Beth, and son-in-law, Adam, for their input, love, and support.

Because of its mental health theme, *Hunting Hour* is a book of my heart. Millions live with mental health conditions, and I want to acknowledge the work of two organizations that provide services, although I know that these are just two of many in the United States. The National Alliance on Mental Illness (NAMI) provides educational programs and support groups for individuals and families; you can find more information at their website www.nami.org or call the NAMI hotline at 800-950-6264 to find a local affiliate near you. Crisis Intervention Team (CIT) International is an organization that seeks to bridge the gap between law enforcement/first responders and the community mental health system through the implementation of CIT programs; learn more about the CIT program at www.citinternational.org. And by all means, if you have mental health concerns about yourself or a loved one, reach out to the NAMI hotline, your primary care physician, or your county public health department or mental health service to find local help. As Stella LoSasso would say, you're not in this alone.